LADY OF
MAZES

Tor Books by Karl Schroeder

Lady of Mazes

Permanence

Ventus

LADY OF MAZES

Karl Schroeder

TOR®

A TOM DOHERTY ASSOCIATES BOOK
NEW YORK

LADY OF MAZES

Copyright © 2005 by Karl Schroeder

This book is printed on acid-free paper.

Edited by David G. Hartwell

A Tor Book
Published by Tom Doherty Associates, LLC
175 Fifth Avenue
New York, NY 10010

www.tor.com

Tor® is a registered trademark of Tom Doherty Associates, LLC.

Library of Congress Cataloging-in-Publication Data

Schroeder, Karl, 1962–
  Lady of mazes / Karl Schroeder.—1st ed.
    p. cm.
  "A Tom Doherty Associates book."
  ISBN 0-765-31219-0 (acid-free paper)
  EAN 978-0-765-31219-8
  1. Life on other planets—Fiction. 2. Human-alien encounters—Fiction. I. Title.

  PR9199.3.S269L33 2005
  813'.6—dc22

                                                    2004065949

First Edition: July 2005

Printed in the United States of America

0 9 8 7 6 5 4 3 2 1

Acknowledgments

Thanks to David Hartwell and Moshe Feder at Tor, for their editorial expertise, and to Rebecca Maines, for correcting my rampant capitalizations. Thanks are also due my agent, Donald Maass, for his patience in shepherding this project to completion.

Most of all, though, my gratitude goes to my wife, Janice Beitel, for keeping faith with me through the many versions and revisions of this tale.

PART ONE

The Conquest of Abundance

*Different ideas of social and political life entail
different technologies for their realization.*

—Langdon Winner,
Autonomous Technology, 1977

1

LIVIA KODALY OPENED her eyes to gray predawn light. All was silence within the crumbling stone walls where she had slept.

Real sheets, not virtual, were bunched around her legs; she clutched a pillow and watched the faint radiance of dawn swing down from the eastern sky. Around and about her, within the walls and ceiling and floating on every minuscule speck of dust, a thousand other eyes watched. To them she might seem like a figure of porcelain, her mop of fair hair touched only now and then by an errant breeze. So still was she that to those ubiquitous eyes and monitors, she might seem just another fixture of the room.

When the rectangle of black from the French doors turned gray, Livia sighed at the ceiling and untangled herself from rest. She walked through the French doors onto the broad stone balcony that encircled the estate's guest apartments. Curled up in one of the old crenels, she looked out over the manicured grounds with their posing topiary and past the indistinct forest tops. Stars still shone, Jupiter on her right, the pastel curves of the Lethe Nebula to her left. It was that time of day when the world seems to pause between breaths—the towering redwood trees that carpeted the hillside were motionless, and all would be silent if not for the chattering of thousands of wakening birds.

When the solitude began reminding her of sadder times, she looked out one last time at the empty gardens and then summoned her Society. A hum of voices welled up around her and ghostly figures began appearing above, below, all about; some seemed to stand on the air above the gardens. Each luminous person acknowledged her with a wave, a smile, or a bow. Some were engaged in conversation, some stood alert but motionless. Livia didn't want to talk to any of the real inhabitants of the estate right now, so she excluded them from her sensorium. For now, she was alone with her phantoms.

Mother's anima waved from an unlikely perch on one of the window lintels. "Up with the dawn today, Liv?" She laughed. "We have to drag you out of bed back home!"

She shrugged. "I need time to review my animas, that's all."

Livia strolled back to her bedchamber, hesitating by the dresser. She slept in the nude, and could easily eschew clothing for the day if it proved to be as hot as it was threatening; by default, she would appear dressed to anyone she met. Such informality didn't feel quite right when she was a guest in this house. Livia donned her shift and tuned it to resemble a Tharsis corset and voluminous silk pantaloons as she walked to the bathroom.

Conversations bubbled around her as she scowled at the mirror. Some dialogues were happening now in the manor, but most were the peers, laughing and chattering in diverse places back home. Some voices were real people's; some were imitations performed by AIs. They were filtered for relevance by Livia's agents so that she only got the gist of what was happening today: *"Devari has a new opera, but he won't show it to anyone. Claims he'll fall out of the manifold if he does!"* (Laughter.) *"We went flying yesterday. You should have seen Jon! He was practically blue."* *"What, he'd never been before?"*

"Livia, we all heard about your performance last night. You've finally mastered that Mozart aria, congratulations!"

"Have you heard? Aaron Varese has vanished!"

Livia had been crossing the room to her door. She stopped, looking for whoever had just spoken. It was raven-haired Esther Mannus, one of the most active peers; not the real woman, for she was back home in Barrastea, but rather her anima, which she regularly updated. She was laughing with an indistinct friend—someone not of Livia's Society, but not hostile to it either.

"Excuse me." The two phantoms swooped into tighter focus, almost becoming real enough to be opaque. Esther covered her smiling mouth with one hand. "Ah, Livia," said the anima. "We thought you'd heard already."

"Heard what?"

"Why, that Aaron has left the city and won't speak to anyone."

Livia had worried that something like this would happen. She said, "I'd wondered why he wasn't with me this morning. What's he working on this time?"

Esther glanced around, then said quietly, "Something to do with 'science,' whatever that is. He was babbling on about traveling through space last time we spoke." She sighed. "We're used to his provocations. But we also know that whatever he's up to, you're involved."

Livia shook her head. "Not this time." She didn't add that she and Aaron had been drifting apart lately. Anyway, it wasn't unheard-of for someone to isolate himself; everybody did now and then, just for sanity's sake. Still, no animas of Aaron had appeared in her Society this morning. Not to leave one behind was definitely an affront and maybe a deliberate insult. It was disturbing.

A tiny whistle sounded from the doorway. She saw a flicker of light there, whirling in circles near the latch.

"Coming," she said. As she went to the door, Livia kept Esther's anima beside her. "I'll go speak to him," she said. "In person. Maybe he has a good explanation for this."

Esther nodded. "I won't downgrade his anima until I hear from you, then," she said tartly. Livia nodded and dismissed the phantom.

Her two favorite agents were waiting at the door. Since they were not physically real, but rather images painted on her senses by her neural implants, she could make them look like anything she wanted. She'd always had them appear as tiny faeries. The first one, Peaseblossom, said, "You were very busy last night!" in a pipsqueak voice. Cicada muscled Peaseblossom out of the way and proclaimed, "You were all over the place!" And in unison: "We think you're in trouble!"

"Oh, great," she said. "What did I do?"

"Jachman and his friends were scheming against Rene," said Peaseblossom, its wings a blur. "They didn't know you have the hots for him."

"I do not!"

"You do. Jachman had your anima open while he was talking to the others, and you challenged him."

"To a *duel!*"

Livia groaned and put her hand to her forehead. "I did what?"

"That's not all!" Cicada puffed out his little chest in pride. "At the self-same time, you were defending Aaron's honor at a party across town!"

"The duel," she pressed. "What happened with the duel?" She strolled down the manor's marble steps, following the scent of fresh bacon that was drifting toward her.

"You fought Jachman, and he killed you," said Peaseblossom. "It's gonna cost you."

It certainly would. She was bound to lose some authority over this spat. If she'd been there in person . . .

She dismissed the idea as wishful thinking. If her anima had fought a duel, then Livia herself almost certainly would have done so had she been there in its place. Animas might only be imitations of people, but they were very accurate imitations.

"Okay," she said. "I'm going to have to visit that incident. You've got it ready for me?"

"Any time you say."

"After breakfast, then."

Cicada made an exaggerated gesture of toeing the ground (he was a meter in the air). "Well, I'm not sure you'll have the time," he said reluctantly.

"What do you mean?" She stopped and glared at the little man. "What else did I do last night?"

"You made a date with Lucius Xavier," said Cicada.

She gaped at him.

Peaseblossom elbowed his companion fiercely. "Not a *date*," he hissed. "Xavier's not that kind of friend." He cleared his throat and smiled up at Livia. "You agreed to meet him here this morning. In person, that is. You're going hunting Impossibles, remember?"

"No, I . . ." Oh. Was that what his visit had been about?

To be strictly polite, Livia should not have had her Society up during last night's soiree. After all, she was a physical guest of the Romanal estate, not just a virtual visitor. She owed her host and hostess her undivided attention at least during supper. Their daughter's confirmation as a true citizen of Westerhaven was important to them and Livia's own family had ties with theirs going back generations.

So she had gone through supper and cocktails completely present, and sung her set with her Society absent. Only afterward had she answered the urgent summons of an old family friend, to take a walk in the estate's garden with his virtual self.

Now she made herself visible and entered the guest house's kitchens. Here was Lady Romanal, her host, cheerfully flipping eggs on the giant gas stove in the corner. This, the real Lady Romanal, was talking to an anima of Livia herself, while her own anima chatted with another of the guests, Livia's violin player. The violin player was a taciturn man who looked uneasy under the lady's microscope. Livia had never really gotten along with him outside of a professional capacity. She split off an anima to join his side of the conversation and walked to the stove, quickly back-stepping through her other anima's conversation with the lady until she felt prepared.

Then she replaced her own image at the lady's side. "Our politics aren't that radical," she said. "Aaron and I simply think Westerhaven's become too complacent. Too . . . calm."

Lady Romanal sighed. "But is that a real criticism, or just youth speaking? Bacon?"

"Yes, thank you."

"You know what kind of reputation you'll get if you continue this pointless agitation," continued Lady Romanal. She was sweating from the heat, but seemed to enjoy cooking for these, her least important guests. "Your mother is quite concerned."

"Concern is Mother's chief talent," said Livia as she held out a plate.

"Oh, you are a handful!" complained the lady cheerfully. "Is it true you've been advocating that we should all abandon our manifolds and live together?"

"That was Aaron, not me. He doesn't see why we should deliberately limit our realities."

"Delightful!"

Livia glowered at her. "He takes his politics very seriously. So do I."

Lady Romanal smiled as she piled food on Livia's plate. "Maybe that's your problem. Too serious to be serious, if you catch my meaning." When Livia didn't answer she said, "Perhaps it's time to put the past behind you, Livia."

Livia left her anima to continue the conversation and went to sit down. That was a bit rude, but only a bit. Lady Romanal should know what subjects were sensitive to her.

As the kitchen filled up with other performers and incidental guests, Livia turned her attention to last night's adventures. She should review that duel, but didn't relish the prospect of watching herself lose. She should also loose some agents to hunt for Aaron. Instead, she backstepped into her conversation with Lucius.

"No, there's no emergency," he'd said as she sat down on a bench in the garden next to his virtual self. "But I'd like you here, if you can oblige me."

Livia had glanced at the party, decided she was safely alone for the moment, and replaced her own sensorium with the one at Lucius's locale. He too stood outside, but on a wide balcony a hundred meters above the city of Barrastea. The buzz of night bugs was replaced here by the incessant murmur of the city, whose glittering lights spread away to the horizon and reared here and there halfway to the zenith. Livia made the anima she now inhabited move to peck him on the cheek.

"How are you, Lucius?" she began.

He smiled at her in a distracted way. In this light he looked like a slightly shabby, careworn Poseidon, his hair and beard all atangle. "It's been too long since we talked," he said at last.

"That wouldn't happen if you didn't travel so much." She sat her virtual self down on a stone seat near him.

"It's my responsibility," he said, frowning into the night. "I sometimes don't like it much. But we're diplomats and ambassadors in Westerhaven, Livia—all of us, whether or not we want to simply stay at home and tend our gardens."

"Is that what you want to do?"

"Sometimes." He brightened a bit. "But not always. Sometimes an adventure beckons. Like tonight. That's why I called you—I wanted a traveling companion for a day-trip, and couldn't think of anybody else who might want to go with me on it."

"No? That seems unlikely."

At about this point Livia had been interrupted by some members of Romanal's party spilling out into the gardens. She had severed her connection to Lucius, leaving an anima behind, so she didn't know what had happened next.

She watched now as Lucius laughed. "You know perfectly well that most people run in tracks. We may be a manifold dedicated to bridging the gaps between other manifolds, but when push comes to shove, nobody you or I know has the courage to travel anywhere really exotic. Not across a real horizon, that's for sure."

Livia's anima (which she now observed from outside) looked intrigued, but a little disturbed. "You want to cross a horizon? To where?"

"I'm not sure. But I'd like you to come with me, if you would."

There was a pause. Livia's anima appeared surprised and confused. After a moment it said, "Please tell me that you thought of me because wherever you're going is a musical manifold."

"No," he said, looking momentarily guilty. "I know you don't like to be reminded of the accident, Livia, but it did give you a unique perspective that—"

Her anima stood up angrily. "Lucius, how could you? I will not travel outside of inscape again for you, or anybody else! Or to any manifold that doesn't use it. You of all people should know . . ." She turned away.

Lucius reached out to touch her virtual shoulder. "This won't be like that, I swear. I'm not proposing we leave inscape, or any of the manifolds you know. I just want to take a walk along the border of Westerhaven. Tomorrow. And I think you should come."

She turned, suspicious. "Why?"

He shrugged. "It might improve your authority. Won't hurt mine either. You see, people have been sighting Impossibles near the Romanal estate. It's been going on for several weeks now. So far it's all anecdotal; nobody's inscape has preserved a record. It's as if they're being seen by the eyes only, without the inscape system being aware of them at all."

Livia's anima shuddered. The mere idea of inscape having problems made her nervous—would make anyone raised in Westerhaven squirm. No wonder Lucius couldn't find anyone to join him on his little expedition.

"What are they seeing?" her anima asked, turning back to face him. Livia was a bit surprised that she hadn't turned him down outright; she might have if she'd been there in person. Then again, she might not. Animas tended to know the personalities of those they modeled better than the people themselves.

"Mythical creatures," said Lucius. "Bears and wolves that walk like men. Giant birds with masklike faces. They sound like Raven's people. All I want to do is verify that the sightings are genuine and not some kind of hysterical meme. I have no intention of going anywhere near one of the things, believe me."

"And you want me along because . . ."

"After the things you've seen, Livia, I think you're not too likely to piss yourself and run at seeing an Impossible."

Her anima smiled momentarily. "But I still don't *want* to."

"If we verify that there's a problem with local inscape, our authority goes up. Not much for me—but the boost could do you good right about now."

Damn him, he knew she was in trouble with the peers. Maybe he'd even set up her encounter with Jachman, knowing she might duel him and lose later that evening. It would be just like Lucius Xavier, who while he might be a friend, was also as sly a political player as Westerhaven had ever produced.

She smiled. "I'll think about it. Why don't you drop by tomorrow morning and we'll talk it over."

Livia skipped through the rest of the conversation, which was brief. Then, back in the breakfast room, she scowled at the slanting morning light. Inscape showed Lucius's aircar circling the estate already. So much for the quiet morning she had been planning. She quickly finished her breakfast and walked outside.

The gleaming, lozenge-shaped aircar touched down gracefully near a checkerboard of tennis courts. Lucius climbed out of it and waved brightly at Livia, kissing her lightly on the forehead when she reached him. "Glad you decided to join me," he said with a grin. "This should be fun."

He was dressed for a hike in stout canvas safari gear and solid boots. She was glad she'd worn her shift today; it was the work of a moment to adjust it to something rugged. Lucius was already striding toward the distant line of trees that signaled the end of the estate's manicured grounds. She hurried to join him.

"You really think there's Impossibles here?" she asked as she caught up.

"Six people from the surrounding area have seen them," he said. "The sightings were scattered all over, but the epicenter was near here. There, in fact." He pointed down the gently sloping hillside, bathed in forest, that led to a glistening blue lake.

Past the forest and meandering river the land rolled on in waves of wilderness into hazy vagueness. What looked like towering, half-visible clouds floated above the haze. These were the familiar Southwall mountains, blued to near-invisibility by a distance of over two hundred kilometers. Livia could see the white caps of glaciers atop some of the shortest peaks; snow never fell at the higher altitudes. Above them the sky was a uniform indigo.

Livia knew the lake Lucius was pointing to. There was a boathouse down there, a distant outpost of the Romanal estate. So she took the lead when they reached the trees. "There's the path."

They entered the hushed realm of the trees. Now that the estate was out of sight, Livia began to feel a bit nervous. That was irrational by any ordinary standard: she had her angels to protect her, and her presence in the heart of Westerhaven did not have anything to do with whether she was near some building.

Even so, she awoke her Society and let them walk alongside her as a reassuring crowd. For a while Lucius was silent, and Livia thought about how similar this walk was to her first official journey to a neighboring manifold, which had happened several months before.

It had been an occasion of sorrow. Shortly after her confirmation, the Westerhaven diplomatic corps had contacted Livia asking whether she would agree to help close out the estate of the Drummers. She had studied to be a diplomat like her parents before her, and she was a musician. So the request might seem natural; but she had given up on diplomacy when she realized she had no desire to travel to other manifolds. She suspected the hand of Lucius Xavier in her selection, if not of Mother herself. But she agreed to go, more from curiosity than any desire to improve her authority.

Livia joined the expedition on an empty road outside the city of Barrastea. There were representatives from a number of other manifolds as well as Westerhaven. Jachman was one of the other junior members of the Westerhaven contingent, and it was on this occasion that Livia first met Rene Caiser. He was acting as groomsman, caring for the stamping and proud horses that were to lead their carriages.

Trees towered beyond the carriages, but the slope here was steep enough that Livia could see past them into the deep valley below. Amid the dark, nearly black treetops lay the city of the drummers. To anyone within Westerhaven, it was invisible.

Serena Elesz, the expedition's leader, briefed them before they set out.

"The last drummer died a week ago," she said from her perch on the step of the lead carriage. "Officially, their consensual reality ends with that death. In fact, everyone who shared some of their values carries a template of the drummers' manifold with them, and these templates still have some authority over inscape and the tech locks. It is up to living representatives of those values to decide the fate of this manifold and its physical manifestations." She meant the land and those aspects of the city that were physically real.

Livia had put up her hand; she was never one to stay on the sidelines. "I was always told that Westerhaven gathers and preserves the cultures of other manifolds."

Serena nodded. "Yes, of course; and we'll try to do that here. We are the great integrators of the many threads of culture in Teven Coronal."

Livia put up her hand again. "I've had six people come up to me and tell me that what I need to do is make sure the drummers are shut down, so Westerhaven can recover their resources."

An awkward silence followed. Serena's take on Westerhaven had sounded like a quote straight out of the Fictional History. Livia had been raised to follow those values, but she was learning that the truth was always more complicated.

Finally Serena shrugged. "You need to vote with your heart, Livia—but remember that everything in Westerhaven is political."

Still chewing on this thought, Livia entered the carriage behind Serena's just as it began to move. They jolted down the dirt track that led off from the main road. Livia reached out with her senses and will, determined not to notice anything of Westerhaven: no buildings, no contrails. Her change of attitude and attention was noted by her neural implants and the mechology known as the *tech locks;* where there had been impenetrable underbrush, a pathway appeared leading into the woods. The horses joined this road without breaking stride.

She listened for rhythms in the sighing of the breeze, and soon she began to hear them. She listened for patterns in the chirping of the birds, and eventually, she heard music there. Even the clip-clop of the horses' hooves took on a complicated order, as Livia had been told it would. A sense of palpable presence began to build around the carriages, a subliminal excitement. "We're close," Jachman murmured beside her.

Rene was having difficulty making the transition. He began to fade even as the drummers' city appeared around the trunks of the redwoods that walled the road. He tried to speak but no sound reached Livia's ears. The last thing she saw before he vanished was his frustrated, embarrassed frown. She couldn't help but smile at the boyishness of it.

He would be back, as soon as he'd managed to properly purge Wester-haven from his system of habits and responses. Meanwhile, they were at the drummers' ruins.

Once a thriving community had come together here to worship in ways that were difficult or impossible in other manifolds. In some places, such as Westerhaven, the pace of life was wrong for the drum-mers' style of contemplation; or the attitude to music interfered with what they were attempting. The ancient and powerful religions of Earth still held sway in other manifolds and would not permit any iconoclasts or experimenters. So they had made their own reality, one in keeping with their ideals. And for several generations, it had held strong.

For some reason, they had built on low swampy ground. Water had reclaimed most of the tall brick structures. Marsh grass grew between the houses and waved on their roofs. This place had been in decline for a long time. It was more of a village, anyway, thought Livia; the houses ended not more than two hundred meters away. Once there had been frescoes on the sides of the buildings, and statues, but they had been weathered away long ago.

The drummers' microcivilization had run its natural course, and now uncomprehending outsiders had come to lay it to rest.

The expedition left the carriages and walked, sometimes wading, out into the city. They split up and began to poke about. The place was des-olate, like something out of a historical sim. Livia's feet were soon wet and she found herself shivering. When she met Rene coming around the side of a large (and empty) public building, she said, "Why would any-one stay here?"

He shrugged. "There were never many of them. But apparently it was quite the religious center once. Reaching the divine through music. You're a musician, you'd have loved it here."

"But they never wrote any of it down. And they didn't perform for pleasure."

They walked on for a while, but whatever possessions the drummers had once had, they were gone, toppled into the swampy water or taken away by those who had abandoned this place's values. Rene shook his head at last. "They're dead. I dunno about you, but I agree with the oth-ers. We should shut it down and reclaim the land."

Livia shook her head. "And just replace their reality with ours? Bet-ter if we could all learn to travel here. *That* would be diplomacy."

"But they're all dead. So what's to stop us?"

Livia opened her mouth to reply, then stopped. She couldn't explain why, but she felt there was still a presence here, however tenuous. It felt wrong to simply wipe the place away—but it was hard to justify preserving it; doing so would go against her very public political stance.

She decided to change the subject. "We lost you for a while back there," she said at last. "You're not very musical?"

He grinned. "Maybe I'm not. And you are not nearly as scary up close as I was told you'd be."

Her heart sank. "Who told you I was scary?"

He waggled his fingers in horror-show fashion. "You and Aaron Varese are the biggest political critics of the generation. You fight duels over *ideas*, for God's sake! And you . . . they say you blink out during parties, come out with odd pronouncements at odd times, have strange notions . . . You've Seen Things We Were Not Meant To Know. You're the one who led the survivors out of the crash zone, right? They say it changed you."

"But I don't remember doing it," she said seriously. "How can I be a hero if I—" At that moment they both heard the drumming.

It came from somewhere ahead: a single, steady beat, deep and confident. Livia and Rene looked at one another.

"Not dead after all!" Rene sprinted in the direction of the sound; more cautiously, Livia followed.

She found him staring up the side of a ten-meter mud-brick tower. The steady drumbeat sounded from somewhere overhead. He looked at her uncertainly. "Do we go in?"

She looked around for footprints on the muddy ground; there were none, not even at the shadowed entrance to the tower. But she would not look weak in front of this young man. "Of course," she said.

Inside, the tower was divided into three levels with ladderlike stairways leading between them. They found large clay pots filled with grain and dried fish; firewood and the hardened, cold remains of a fire; blankets and a crude pillow. But there was no other sign of life. The sound obstinately continued above. "A recording?" Rene whispered. She shook her head: recording equipment of any kind was forbidden by the locks in this place.

Cautiously, they climbed the creaking steps to the top level.

Someone had rigged a barrel on a tripod here to catch rainwater. From the base of the barrel, a spigot dripped steadily onto the taut skin of a large bass drum. The skin was discolored and worn where the water had been hitting it for days—weeks, probably. But the sound was steady, and impressively loud.

Huddled beside the drum was a half-skeletal body: the last inhabitant of the drummers' manifold. Livia couldn't be sure whether this had been a man or a woman. But it was clear he or she had died alone.

It stank up here so they retreated down the ladder almost immediately. Neither spoke until they were outside again. Rene waved to Serena and some others who were walking nearby. As they came over, Livia stood looking up—and listening.

"Why didn't he leave?" Rene asked after a while.

And of course, that was it: to leave this place, all you had to do was wish to be somewhere else. With a little concentration Livia could return to Westerhaven, and these towers would turn into trees, or rocks, or otherwise leave her sensorium. Barrastea's skyscrapers would appear over the crest of the hill. Inscape reticles and Societies would blossom all around her. This person, this last drummer, did not have to die alone. He or she could have chosen, right up until the last second, to abandon the Drummers' ideals—to join another manifold.

Yet the drum still sounded above, slow and steady, like the heartbeat of the world. Livia could not have answered Rene's question; she did not have the words. But, for a moment or two, as she stood within the realm of that beating heart, she thought she understood.

When Serena and the others came running up, Livia announced, "The last drummer may be dead, but the Drummers are still alive. We can't shut down this manifold while the drum still beats."

Unanimity was required for the manifold to be closed. And so the absorption of the drummers' resources into Westerhaven had been postponed—and while Livia's reputation had grown, her authority had begun to deteriorate.

"I DON'T KNOW why I did it," she said to Lucius as they walked. They'd seen nothing impossible in the past hour and she was getting tired. She had dismissed her Society, however, and was enjoying this rare chance for a solitary talk with an older male friend. "I think it was just to spite Serena."

He laughed. "A fine reason by itself. But is that all?"

"I don't know. For years now I've felt like an outsider. Ever since the accident. People look at me differently, you know. Since only Aaron and I survived . . ." She kicked at a fern. "It's like it was our fault, somehow."

She was used to people trying to reassure her on this point, but Lucius nodded. "It's hypocritical," he said. "People here talk about valuing other manifolds, but really Westerhaven is a culture of butterfly collectors."

"How do you mean?"

"You catch the butterfly alive, then you stick a pin through it and mount it on the wall. That's what we do with other cultures. Like your drummers. You were right to leave their world alone, Liv."

"Well, thank you! Practically nobody else has said that."

"We outsiders have to stick together," he said. "That's why I invited you along today." He hesitated. "Livia. There's something I have to tell you. It's about—"

She threw out her hand to stop him, practically falling herself. Raising a finger to her lips, she pointed ahead along the path.

He scowled, then turned to follow her gaze.

"Lucius, I think something impossible might just be happening."

Standing nonchalantly about ten meters ahead was a tall, bronze-skinned man dressed in tanned hides. A dozen beaded necklaces hung around his neck.

He was carrying a spear.

2

IT WAS HARD to tell the man's age; his face was lined and weatherbeaten, his brow sunburnt and his eyes narrowed to a perpetual squint. But he was fit and strong-looking, and Livia had no doubt he could throw that spear with great accuracy and force.

But he hadn't spotted them. He was staring up into the trees with a puzzled expression on his face. Livia took the opportunity to start backing away.

"What is he?" she whispered.

"Not an Impossible," said Lucius. "More likely a warrior of Raven. Their manifold overlaps ours in most places. They can visit us, but they rarely do."

Livia had known that for years, of course, but somehow, despite her experience with manifolds, seeing this man was a shock. She thought of invisible warriors ranging through the Romanal gardens, firing arrows at deer on the tennis courts.

"Aren't we . . . well, sort of at war with Raven?"

Lucius shook his head. "Only in the gamers' submanifold. It's purely voluntary—" He froze, because the man had spotted them.

For a while neither he nor they moved a muscle. Livia's heart was pounding, but her mind was clear. What was he doing here? Had he stepped out of Raven's people into Westerhaven? Or had she and Lucius strayed the other way?

Finally the man snapped out of his trance. Carefully, he leaned his spear against a tree, then walked toward them. Stopping four meters away, he cleared his throat.

"You have come to celebrate with us," he said.

"Yes," replied Lucius.

"What?" said Livia.

The warrior strode forward, extending his hand. "I am King Ghee," he said. "Do not be afraid, I was sent to find you. I am . . . you would call me a *diplomat*, I believe." He smiled at Livia, showing white, perfect teeth.

"I am Lucius Xavier, and this is my friend, Livia Kodaly," said Lucius. "So we are not too late?" Lucius seemed anxious.

King Ghee glanced up at the sky. "No. But we must hurry." The warrior set off up the path, snatching up his spear on the way.

"Lucius? What's going on?" Livia tried to keep her voice controlled, with some success, but anger and fear made her hesitate as the other two walked ahead.

"Come, Livia." Lucius waved to her. "This is important. You'll see why."

"But why didn't you tell me that you were meeting someone?" She verified that her angels were still around her, then reluctantly stepped after him. He had not replied.

"I am pleased to meet you," Raven's warrior said to her as she caught up. "You must be highly prized by your own people to be given this opportunity." Livia opened her mouth to ask him what he meant by that, then noticed Lucius making a warning gesture behind him. She smiled.

"Thank you," she said. "I am honored, yes." She needed to know what was happening, so she summoned an anima to replace her in this dialog, intending to split off and ask Lucius just what he was playing at. But inscape signaled an error: this warrior of Raven could not perceive animas. They walked now, it seemed, on the very edge of Westerhaven.

"So you will come with me to the city of Skaalitch?" asked the warrior. "It is not far, but it is under Raven's wing; your people would not normally see it."

Lucius grinned. "I'd be honored, Kingy." He said the name as if it were one word. Livia did still have access to her internal inscape systems, so she called up a database of Raven names. Qiingi—that was it. And *Skaalitch*? The database had a listing, but she had no time to examine it as the warrior spoke again.

"To come to us, you must open yourself to the sacredness of living things. Walk with me, under Raven's wing." He stepped off the path.

"So the real adventure begins," said Lucius. "Sorry I kept you in the dark, but you might not have come otherwise. Well, Liv? Are you up for it?"

She opened her mouth to chastise him, but somehow his enthusiasm was infectious. And, she realized, she was enjoying her surprise. "All right," she said with a laugh. "But there had better not be any more tricks. I need to be back by lunchtime."

Qiingi wavered in and out of existence ahead of them. He often paused, instructing Livia and Lucius in what they should look for. Livia tried to forget about Westerhaven—her Societies' intrigues, the arcing aircars and glittering cities—and instead focus on spotting the creatures of the forest. With Qiingi, she paused to gaze at tracks on the damp ground, and consciously drew in the scents of pine and moss. It was a game she'd learned as a child, not knowing its significance at the time; only later, when her ability to shift manifolds was unlocked at puberty, did Livia understand. Now, she stopped, staring at an owl she'd spotted on a branch. She concentrated, frowning, and the bird suddenly changed, its face momentarily becoming a shaman's mask. Livia laughed out loud. *Follow, follow the warrior of Raven,* she told herself, as she dashed after him. As she went, the bark of the trees shifted from randomness to patterned design. The birdsong ceased to be incoherent twitters, and became tiny, piping voices whose words she could understand if she concentrated.

So, by degrees of wonder, Livia left the world of Westerhaven behind, and came within the realm of Raven.

"THEY ARE HERALDS of the ancestors," Qiingi said. Livia had asked him about the Impossibles. "The ancestors are returning to us, so all things change. You should not be surprised if the walls of your world are beginning to crumble. The elders told us to expect it."

"Who are these ancestors?" she asked. She really wanted to grill Lucius about what he was up to, but the man kept cagily near Qiingi, and as they crossed the border into Raven's country, her normal inscape resources had shut down. She couldn't call upon Peaseblossom and Cicada to run sims of Lucius, nor could she ask her Society what he might be doing.

The term for this, she mused, was *working without a safety net*. Most of her peers prized the stability of their reality above all else, and she had no doubt they would have run screaming back to Westerhaven long before now. In that, at least, Lucius had judged right: Livia was unfazed by this journey. Or so she kept telling herself, while her pulse pounded and she jumped at every strange sound coming through the forest.

Qiingi smiled at her; he had been very impressed to learn she was a singer. He had taken to calling her Wordweaver Kodaly. "A time is coming when what you call the horizons of the world crack and fall," he said. "The ancestors wait beyond the horizons. They are returning to us to bring us the wisdom of centuries that they have gathered during our long isolation in this place. Our best have come to Skaalitch because this is the first place where the walls of the world will crack."

"Oh." She didn't know what to say to that. But it sounded like some new myth was being born in this place. Myths and stories were a common spark for birthing new manifolds. Was a new reality being born within Raven's people? Was that what Lucius had brought her to witness? If so, it was a momentous occasion, and a tremendous coup for both of them.

"You have followed me well," Qiingi said. "Behold the city of Skaal-itch."

Livia knew where they were. They had come to the shoreline of the lake that spread sinuously through the valley below the Romanal estate. The air here was cold and damp, full of the mist that hung around the redwoods. Livia drank in the sound of waves lapping on the shore of the dark water. She had been here many times; the Romanal boat-house should be right over . . . there . . . Where the boathouse should be, a jagged mound of boulders thrust up out of the ground.

Of course, that *was* the boathouse—or how it appeared from within Raven's country. She looked the other way, and gasped.

The lake was ringed by gigantic trees and backed by low mountains. For hundreds of meters along the shore, long canoes lay upended on wooden frames and tall totem poles presided magisterially over scores of men and women who were working near the water. Behind them, receding half-seen into the maze of trees, were dozens of log longhouses, their roofs adrift with woodsmoke. Bright things like flying banners flitted half-seen in the deepening green of the forest; birds and animals laughed, and out in the lake, something huge and dark breached the surface momentarily, then sank away.

Livia had sunbathed on these sands many times, and canoed with friends on those net-strewn waters. She had never imagined this place existed parallel to the lake she knew.

Drumbeats started up somewhere among the longhouses. "We must hurry now," said Qiingi. "The potlatch of the ancestors is about to begin." He hurried into the city, greeting people left and right as he went.

Lucius and Livia smiled and nodded at Raven's people, who grinned and talked about them as they passed. Children raced alongside them, laughing and screaming in mock fear. Ahead, a crowd was growing.

"You're a very bad man," Livia said. "Bringing me out here on a pretext, then kidnapping me!" *But I am having fun,* she was about to add, when she saw that he wasn't laughing. Indeed, he looked tired, and maybe even a bit frightened.

"Lucius, what's wrong?"

People were now appearing from all over—some blinking into view from whatever submanifold they had been inhabiting. All were converging on the great open circle that lay ahead. Lucius shook his head, and looked away from Livia.

"I had no one else I could trust with this," he said. "Nobody I knew who might understand. Except you."

"What do you mean?"

"Look at this!" He waved at the fabulous totems and rearing longhouses that surrounded them. "It's wondrous, isn't it—and you never knew it was here! Livia, don't you feel even the slightest bit claustrophobic living in just one manifold?"

She nodded, eager to have someone agreeing with her for a change. "Everyone says that Westerhaven is the most cosmopolitan place in Teven. We visit other manifolds, sure—but how many of them? What you were saying earlier about us being butterfly collectors . . . I know what you mean. We see the world only from our own narrow perspective. We're tourists in other people's realities."

He nodded enthusiastically. "I heard your friend Aaron Varese speaking in Barrastea last week. He was proposing that we eliminate manifolds altogether."

She laughed, a bit uncertainly. "He's just trying to stir things up. It's just not possible. Worldviews don't mix."

"Don't they?" He stared at her with an intensity she had never seen before, as if he were about to start yelling—or running. "Are you sure about that?"

"Lucius . . . I don't . . ."

Livia heard pounding feet, shouts. The noises came from the plaza they were approaching. People were crowded around its outskirts, all talking at once, some hopping up and down to see over others. The drumbeat was seductive; the musician in her responded, analyzing its meter even as her imagination half consciously wove melodies and patterns around it.

Qiingi waved to them. "The potlatch begins!" He was obviously excited, but from the way he kept looking about himself it was clear he was a bit nervous, too. By now the crowd was pressing in on all sides. Lucius grabbed Livia's arm.

"Stay close," he said. "I don't know how far this will go."

"What—" But he pressed on ahead through the crowd, and she followed. Livia had never been in such a strange situation, surrounded by people in buckskins and beads, permeated with the smells of woodsmoke, chicken fat, and tanned leather.

Silence fell suddenly; then a collective gasp rose from the crowd. Lucius let go of Livia's arm and she staggered to a halt. She was close to the front of the circle, and peered past a tanned shoulder to see what was happening.

All across the earthen plaza, ghostly figures wavered into existence. At first there were only a handful, but in seconds there were dozens, then scores of them.

The ancestors filled up the plaza, and they came bearing Impossible gifts.

THEY WERE TOO perfect to be human. Of course, in her lifetime Livia had seen people wrapped in many guises—as idealized sexual objects, as animals, as fabulous mythical beasts. She had seen people pretend to be angels. These ancestors didn't seem to be pretending.

She could see a kind of shimmering arch above and around the plaza; outside it, the world looked ordinary—that is, it was filled with wise trees, hollow-eyed birds that might in the blink of an eye transform into lynxes and bound away into the underbrush. Raven's world. Within the arch the plaza was still there, and in it stood beautiful, smiling men and women. That was fine; people could appear in mid-manifold like that. But in their hands, and around and above them, were things that could not exist here.

One woman stood next to a man-sized, chrome robot that looked around itself curiously with big lens-eyes. Substitutes for human labor were limited even in technophilic Westerhaven, yet here a robot stood where properly it could not be. Another of the strangers held up a big device Livia recognized as a laser saw; at least, she hoped that was all it was. Piled around the strangers' feet were all manner of machines, livedevices, and mobile bots.

The tech locks should be disabling, removing, or hiding all these things. Livia kept waiting for the gifts—for if this was a potlatch, then that was what these things were—to flicker and go out, the way that Rene had on the road to the drummers' city. It didn't happen.

She found herself blinking again and again, and backing away. Around the edge of the circle other people were doing the same. It was like looking at an object and it refusing to come into focus, even while everything around it became sharp. Control of reality should be as automatic as sight; it had been that way for Livia all her life.

Except once.

She found she had turned and was trying to run. *Stop!* she commanded herself. *You mastered this fear!* Or she'd thought she had. With an effort she turned back to look at the circle.

The closer she looked the worse it was. Some of the strangers were suffused in a golden glow that came from the clouds of programmable matter that suspended them as if they were weightless, ten or fifteen centimeters above the ground. The quantum dots composing the virtual matter swirled and glowed, making them appear like pillars made of countless infinitesimal stars—ostentatious, that, even gauche, given that the ordinary angels of Westerhaven were composed of just such fogs, but were careful to remain invisible. Embedded in the fogs were many strange objects: globes and rods of crystal and metal, things with handgrips that might be weapons; and humming, flittering things that could be alive but for the fact that they gleamed like bronze.

At an unspoken signal the strangers began to walk toward the crowd.

She became aware that Qiingi was standing next to her. "I didn't really believe it would happen," he said softly. "They have broken the walls of the world." He didn't sound happy.

It's not like after the accident, Livia was telling herself. *This isn't a crash. It's controlled, somehow.*

As the first of the "ancestors" stepped outside the earthen circle the crowd came to life. A sudden madness seemed to sweep them and Livia found herself getting caught up in it. Some people were shouting, shaking their fists. Others were laughing and crying. Was this a miracle or a nightmare? No one seemed to know.

As she edged back through the crowd, Livia realized that Lucius was missing. He was taller than most of these people. He should be visible.

Someone jostled her; she grabbed Qiingi's arm so as not to lose him, too. "But what are they? What are they doing here?"

He shrugged uncertainly. "Our founders have blessed their presence. They call them ancestors; so I must accept that this is what they are."

"But where did they come from?"

He looked at her and for a moment his composure almost broke. He was frightened, she realized with a chill. "Wordweaver Kodaly," he said stiffly, "if they are our ancestors, then they have always been here."

More of the strange people were appearing by the moment; as each waded into the crowd, he or she would stop to speak to people. As the ancestors spoke, they reached about in a leisurely way, picking now this, now that item from their belts or materializing it out of the fog of virtual matter, and handing it to the person they were talking to. The one closest to Livia was male, and had a sonorous voice; and it was a real voice, not processed by inscape. He turned his head and his eyes met Livia's. She felt the gaze as a shock.

"Livia Kodaly," he said. "This is a day of gifts. What would you like to receive from us?"

She backed away, suddenly aware that her only countryman had vanished and her Society was inaccessible. "I don't want anything," she said.

"Perhaps that is your problem," he said. "You want to want something. We can help you with that."

"W-what?"

The ancestor laughed, a rich and reverberant sound. "There is something new under the sun," it said. "There has never been anything like us before. We extend a hand of friendship to all in Westerhaven, through you." He did extend his hand, and she found herself staring at it as though it were a snake.

"Come with us," he said. "We have much we could show you."

"How do you know my name?" she asked.

"You wear it in your aura," he said.

"But that shouldn't be visible here," she objected. "We're in Raven's manifold."

He shrugged. "There are no more distinctions here. Come, I'll show you."

"No, please." She stepped outside of his reach.

The ancestor nodded, as if he'd expected this reaction. "You do not wish to see how other people live, because it might pollute your culture."

She bristled. "I don't know what you—"

"You have chosen not to see rather than to see wrongly," said the ancestor. "I understand. But there is another way of seeing. We have come to show it to you. Raven's people understand; I hope you will, too, soon."

The ancestor turned and spoke to someone else while Livia was trying to think of some reply. Livia turned to talk to Qiingi, but Raven's warrior had vanished in the throng. Without pausing to look for him she made a break for the edge of the crowd. Everything felt unreal; she was dizzy.

And where was Lucius? He should be visible even if her Society was quiescent; in Westerhaven his authority would make him a magnet for her sight. The sudden sense of aloneness was frightening—anything could happen to her here, and her audience and supporters wouldn't see it. It was like that other time, years ago, when reality had torn and Livia found herself with only the dead for company. Outside of inscape, she knew, was a world that would not talk to her or hide its ugliness under a veil of Society. She would not go back there again.

Fleeing blindly, she ricocheted from person to person until she reached the redwoods and then she kept running through them, enduring scratches and twisting her ankle.

She stopped when she came to the shore of the lake, and knelt panting in the shadow of a giant grinning totem pole. The beach was nearly deserted. Sounds of the potlatch echoed weirdly through the brown pillared ways of the city, but there was no one nearby to speak to and none of the spirits of the woods approached. Maybe she should go back and look for Lucius.

The sound stopped her. The murmur of the crowd seemed to be building in intensity, as if the mob were changing somehow, losing its human mind. Even with the distance and the renewed presence of her angels, Livia began to feel really afraid, not just spooked as she was a few minutes before. She had to get out of Raven's country, get back to the Romanal estate.

An angel—a physically manifest inscape agent—alighted next to her. "Let me treat your ankle," it said. With a wary look in the direction of the potlatch, she sat on the feet of the totem pole and let it wrap her foot. The physical form of this winged entity was actually her shift changing shape to brace the ankle, but inscape gave it a soothing human appearance.

She felt a bit calmer as she set out again; her angels were with her after all. She was ashamed of herself. Livia had thought herself healed of those old wounds. She was an independent woman; of all her generation in Westerhaven, only she and her friend Aaron had ever lived for months outside of the protection of inscape and the tech locks. That was years ago, though—back in a blurred time between luminous childhood and painful rehabilitation. There was a small seed in her that treasured the fact of having once been beyond all horizons, however traumatic the experience might have been at the time. Today's panic had been . . . unexpected.

Grimly, she found her way to the pile of boulders along the shore. There she planted her feet and willed the stones to become wood. Gradually, the rocks faded and the boathouse of the Romanals became visible.

Behind her, Skaalitch dissolved in the mist like a dream. And when Livia was once more alone on the lakeshore, with only gulls crying overhead and her heart slowed to a sane pace, she turned and walked up the path she'd known her whole life, back to the courts and libraries of Westerhaven.

3

THE TWO PEOPLE Livia most wanted to talk to were missing: Lucius was gone, and Aaron Varese was nowhere to be found when she returned to Barrastea, the city of her birth.

Late in the afternoon of the day following her strange adventure in Raven's country, she walked toward the ballroom where her parents were throwing a party. The towers and gardens of the city lay in tumbled glory about her and her laughing, bickering Society. The Kodaly family had their estate here in an amorphous set of submanifolds that overlapped numerous other Great Family lands.

The ballroom abutted one of Livia's bedrooms; the whole complex lay just ahead where several crumbling, ivied walls nearly intersected, leaving a gap where one could walk. Sunlight dappled through leaves and warmed the stones. Livia wore her shift today, but hardly needed it in the warmth.

Barrastea was the physical home of the diplomatic corps, who had a keen interest in Lucius Xavier's disappearance. The grilling Livia had been put through today by the senior members had been long and intense; it had started before her actual arrival there, as the members appeared in her Society and began demanding to know what had happened at Skaalitch. She could not explain it to them, beyond the obvious: the tech locks had failed somehow. Livia was tired, angry, and frustrated, unable to quite get over what she'd seen. She had even dismissed her Society for a while, since without Aaron in it, it seemed empty anyway. Now the sweet air and sunlight were beginning to revive her.

The towers that shimmered in the heat-haze were two hundred years old. Here at least was stability; here was the tangible proof of Westerhaven's faith in cross-cultural mixing, a riot of styles and traditions that made it the most vibrant city in Teven Coronal.

She strolled down familiar avenues of soaring stone and stretched tenting. The high pillars and curving walls served as attachment points for the sweeping wings of translucent tenting that roughly divided "inside" from "outside" throughout the parks and avenues. They also held up the various polygonal platforms that made up the floors of buildings implied, but not fully described, by the tenting. Vines, trees, and liana sketched processional ways and plazas throughout this riot of color and shape; even private spaces often had walls made up only of foliage. It was always warm here where no mountains moderated the gaze of the suns; and one's angels could be relied upon to provide personal shelter from any truly inclement weather.

Livia's two faeries suddenly dive-bombed her from somewhere above. "Danger, danger, Livia Kodaly!" piped Cicada, waving its arms to get her attention.

"Hang on, Mom," she said to the anima that had been speaking to her. She scowled at the little glowing figure. "What's the matter with you?"

"It's the peers! They're setting you up—"

"—for a fall," finished Peaseblossom. "Somebody snuck into the drummers' city and replaced the drum with a fresh one! While the drum beats the manifold still exists—"

"And nobody else can move in," said Cicada. "Jachman's blaming you and Aaron. After all, you stopped them from shutting it down in the first place. And Aaron's snubbing everybody—"

Livia groaned. "That's all I need. Okay, thanks, I'll deal with it on my own."

"But it's an attack on your authority!"

Livia half smiled. "And what's new about that?"

"Well, firstly—"

"Go away!"

They spiraled up and away, muttering in bell-like tones.

She rounded the stone and green intersection, and entered the Kodaly ballroom. This presented itself as a public park, open to the sky, surrounded by hedges and dotted with trees and ivied walls that stood in isolation like planned ruins. The place appeared completely empty and peaceful, save for several couples strolling enwrapped in the scent of grass and sound of buzzing cicadas. On the far side was a giant crumbling stone archway, its far end walled up except for a small door at the bottom. Invisible to everyone but Livia were several platforms attached under the top of the arch. For years chests of real cloth apparel, dolls, and books had sat on these platforms; various paintings and ceramics she had made as a child adorned the curving stone of the arch; and there sat her bed. That place was where she often lounged and usually slept—directly above the heads of public traffic through the park. She could lie on her stomach and kick her bare feet in the air while staring straight down at strangers strolling through the archway. This was how the Kodalys liked to live—in the interstices of the public world.

As she stepped onto the lawn the park was suddenly full of people.

She sauntered now between hedgerows festooned with centuries' worth of portraits and statues, and under long crimson and gold banners displaying the Kodaly crest. Knots of revelers were scattered across the grass, with children running back and forth between them and tables piled high with food. The strolling couples, having not been invited to this party, were invisible now.

This place was familiar and comforting to Livia. She had played here as a child, as her mother had before her. High overhead, giant parasols of tenting cunningly filtered sun and rain to indirection; the luminous light, the fine geometry of the distant parasols, the paintings—they were not furnished with alternatives, but were pleasant constants in an otherwise turbulent world. Westerhaven knew time intimately, after all, both in its fluidity and its fixedness. It was the Westerhaven Great Families' ability to live simultaneously in chaotic inscape and changeless tradition that attracted so many other manifolds as supporters and clients.

"Aren't you going to announce yourself, Livia?" asked Mother. She stood on the other side of the field, under a grotesque bronze statue of Shakespeare's Feste. Livia had once kissed Jachman's older brother behind that statue.

"I'll join in when I'm ready," said Livia. She draped herself across a comfortable leather armchair that she remembered playing hide-and-seek behind as a girl; this was a Kodaly chair, impervious to weather and imperceptible to any public visitors to the park. For a while she watched through a filigree of leaves as the peers danced, but she didn't yet want to merge them with her Society.

"Why isn't he here to support me?" she asked her Society.

"Is that who you're moping about?" Natalia, an old friend and former rival, came to perch on the arm of the chair. "Aaron's not your lover, he's just your friend. Livia, how you cling!"

The rest of the Society all made various pooh-poohing noises. "Why worry about such things?" asked Sebastian, who stood next to her as well as fifteen meters away in the heart of the party. "He'll turn up. And this authority thing will sort itself out."

"It's not even proper to talk about," said Natalia. "But you're a strange one, Livia, so we indulge you." They all laughed.

They were probably right. Even if she and Aaron had been an inseparable pair for years, working parties like this one as a team . . . They could exchange a nod from across a crowded room and know whom to talk to next, whom to convince or cajole to support or censure some mad plan of the peers. Until recently, they had shared a silent understanding of how the world worked, and more important, how it should work. Until the most ridiculous arguments, over abstracts and impossible dreams, had begun to separate them.

It did no good to think about it now. She stretched and stood up. "All right," she said. "Let's enter the lion's jaws." She changed her shift into a ball gown and with a single gesture entered the party at its center.

LIVIA'S TWO PIPSQUEAK agents watched her join the submanifold from a vantage point high above the city. Insofar as they had any consciousness at all, it was an imitation of Livia's own; they soared the virtual thermals and vortexes of the city with delight and abandon, because they thought that she would have in their place.

Spread below them they saw the whole panoply of Westerhaven life, a mazelike throng of people walking, gathering, talking, and working together—single-minded in the results of their labor, though all of them might be seeing a different city. Some would be cruising sexual submanifolds invisible to the majority; others would be meditating in plazas empty of all people. Some had only their own self-made phantasms for company; these mediated between them and the real people in their lives, who had forever gone beyond their horizons. And then, interpenetrating all of this, thousands of visitors from other manifolds walked in half or full immersion in their own realities. Some could be seen, some could not. Who knew what they were experiencing?

Yet all of this was merely the tacit, superficial reality of Barrastea. Cicada and Peaseblossom saw something few others bothered to see. Overlaying the city within inscape were hundreds of other Barrasteas, most containing the same citizens going about very similar activities. These were sims; and in any given sim, some citizens were making sims of each other too, until the ghosts and might-have-beens redoubled and recomplicated in an explosion of possibilities.

While this went on, Livia danced with an old friend; Livia hesitated at a drinks table, scanning the crowd for evidence of cliques forming and alliances shifting; Livia scowled in anger at a delegation of the peers who had come to confront her.

Her physical self—her Subject, as it was called—was talking to the stars of the party, six visitors from a distant manifold that had recently opened its doors to Westerhaven. Mother introduced them, saying, "Livia is continuing the family tradition of seducing strangers into our ways."

"Mother!" She grinned at the visitors. "She makes it sound so . . . prurient."

"Our founders might agree," said one, a handsome youth who represented himself as older, with silvery hair. His accent was stilted; his manifold had successfully invented its own tongue and he was obviously unused to speaking in Westerhaven's Joyspric. "It is only with our generation that our people have stopped feeling threatened by . . . manifolds like yours." He gestured around. "Big, uh, big cultures that eat little ones . . . for lunch." They all laughed.

"Your mother said you have a good singing voice," said another man. "We like to sing in our—at our home."

"Really?" She called a quick anima to serve as her mask; scowled at her mother from behind it; then dismissed it. "Would you like to hear something?"

"We would be delighted."

She considered, then smiled wickedly at her mother. "All right, since we're talking about how we lure people away from their realities . . . You may know this one, because it's a traditional, older than Teven: it's called 'The Stolen Child.'"

She sang for a while, only the song was real.

Under the shadow of the great stone arch, another version of Livia had been cornered by some friends. "Westerhaven has no existence unless we continue to create it, every day," one peer said as he hooked his thumbs in his ornamental belt and glared at her. He was one of the Golden Boys, a mover and shaker in the New City movement. "I think you've forgotten that. You think we can live with a foot in two worlds— be of more than one manifold at a time. But you know perfectly well that unless we all work together, all of this"—he gestured around himself— "will dissolve as if it never existed." He shook his head dismissively. "You've let down your generation, Livia Kodaly."

Livia's face went white with anger. "How dare you—"

Not that one. Peaseblossom pointed out another sim to Cicada. *This has more authority.*

Two young women sat with Livia. One held her hand. "We understand that you advised the committee according to what you thought the drummers would have wanted," she was saying. "But what makes you think that you knew them so well? You'd never visited their manifold while any of them were still alive. And yet you chose to speak for them in a situation of great ambiguity. That, I'm afraid, is what we can't forgive."

The real Livia Kodaly had finished her song and was laughing with both these women; their conversation had nothing to do with the drummers' land and their mutual affection was obvious. But as the agents watched, the authority given to this sim continued to grow. Cicada was trying to minimize it, but throughout inscape the animas of the other peers were rushing to the node. Any minute now this scenario would hit the tipping point, and what was now part of the artificial imagination would become reality. Livia would be chastised, and some of her authority revoked.

We must warn her!

She's blocking me. I can't get through to her.

Indeed, as the party wore on, Livia felt less and less connected to it. People began to vanish from her sensorium, starting with the ones she liked least. Eventually she put a stop to that, but at the same time she drifted into the shade of the stone arch. Climbing a ladder no one else could see, she sat on the lowest of her platforms to watch the party. Insects buzzed around her, and birds wheeled above the treetops. Music and pleasant voices came from the revelers, and it all would have been relaxing had she not been nagged by a sense of dissatisfaction.

She watched while the peers strutted and posed. The young men challenged one another constantly; their swords were not for show. For the peers, arguments about manners or fashion were far from academic: they were the building blocks of their own generation's civilized future. Westerhaven's existence and development depended on the excellence of this generation, and these youths knew it. They were all deeply passionate about such things and she loved them for that. But they felt it was gauche, at least, to express an interest in something outside their circle. Mysterious disappearances or upheavals in nearby manifolds were not the subject of polite conversation.

"You're not mingling," said Mother.

Livia shrugged, and leaned back so that an errant beam of sunlight could rest on her face. "It's just a party, Mother."

"You're worried about losing your authority? Well, don't be. It's a minor issue."

"Oh, Mother!" She scowled at the anima, tempted to dismiss it. "I just spent the past hour and a half engaging a dozen or more peers in idle chitchat to remind them of my position. I know what's going on here. I'm on trial for the drummers thing. Well, I've made my defense.

It's the prosecution's turn—let what happens, happens. Meanwhile, I'm going to enjoy this little sunbeam I've found."

A loss of authority wouldn't be the end of the world, she mused. She might not be able to requisition aircars quite so cavalierly, or count on the best guests for her soirees. Rene and Jachman might get diplomatic assignments instead of her for a while. Life would go on. She could always sing for her supper.

Livia was a bit surprised to realize that she wasn't just telling herself that—it was true. *I'm turning into Aaron.* Though he was as adept a political player as anyone in Westerhaven, he had contempt for the great game. They had argued about that recently, too.

What had he said at the time? "Nobody here has the balls to effect real change in the world." She smiled despite herself.

She knew why she was thinking about this now. Lucius's disappearance and the weird potlatch of the ancestors had served to remind her of a time of blood and pain and loneliness—a period when authority had been meaningless. She recalled the electric emotions of the crowd at the potlatch. That had been the moment when carefully suppressed memories had started to boil up in her again.

Like it or not, traumatic and ineradicable experience marked her as different from these careless people laughing and dancing a few meters below her. So maybe that was why she finally stood up and said, "Cicada, Peaseblossom, bring me an anima of Aaron—even a sim will do."

"We're going to find out where he's gone."

4

CICADA AND PEASEBLOSSOM were a bit distracted at that moment. Four people had entered the ballroom several minutes before. They did not appear at its center as Livia had, but popped into visibility on the periphery, as unobtrusively as possible. Still, heads turned throughout the park as the two couples strolled forward magisterially.

Founders! Cicada had clutched Peaseblossom and pointed. *Founders have come!*

Livia's friend Sylvie turned to the anima of Livia she'd been chatting with and said, "Oh, look! Isn't that Lady Ellis?" She pointed, hiding the gesture behind a mask. Livia's anima followed her gaze to look at the woman standing with her parents. It was indeed Ellis, one of the original creators of the Westerhaven manifold. Nearly mythological, Lady Ellis was seldom seen at this level. She and her own peers resided in mansions and realities of their own creation, rarely deigning to interfere with the affairs of their descendants. For her to be here was truly an honor for the Kodalys.

"Do you think we might be able to speak to her?" mused Sylvie.

Livia's anima laughed. "Try walking over there. You could vanish on the way!"

"Oh, wouldn't that be embarrassing!" Sylvie shook her head. "Better to wallow in real anonymity, I think."

Cicada glanced back to the authority sims he and Peaseblossom had been running, and gave the inscape equivalent of a shriek. *Look!* he said. *What are they doing?*

Agents of the founders were fanning out through the shifting clouds of simulations. Whenever they encountered a sim where Livia was being confronted over the drummers incident, they gestured imperiously and, using their unmatched authority, terminated it. The agencies of the peers fell back in confusion, and a few began trying to get the attention of their real counterparts, who naturally would not have been sullying their hands by participating directly in political scapegoating.

—*Why are they saving Livia?*

—*Let's sim them!*

—*Sim a founder? Impossible!*

—*Not impossible. Important! Come, let's try.*

Before they had the chance to try it, the founders' agents acted, generating animas that summoned corresponding ghosts of Livia herself.

—*What are they doing?*

—*I don't know. Let's tell Livia!*

The two faeries dove from the sky, ready to defend their mistress at the first hint of trouble, even if it came from the founders themselves. But just as they were about to manifest in front of Livia, another figure appeared before them. It stood on the air, beautiful and radiating authority, and put a finger to its faintly smiling lips.

"WHERE ARE THOSE guys?" Livia opened an inscape window herself and called up some generic agents. "I want to review my last conversation with Aaron Varese," she told one. "And find Cicada and Peaseblossom!"

The agent bowed and vanished in a puff of faux-smoke. At the same time, the sights, sounds, and scents of a different time descended around Livia: her last talk with Aaron.

It had only been a few days ago, so she remembered the occasion well even without artificial aids. Livia had been lounging on a couch in a gazebo on the grounds of Aaron's estate, while he paced the old wooden floorboards. It was evening and another party was winding down; the air was delicately scented and still warm from the day. The sky was clear, revealing thousands of stars, those to north and south wheeling slowly west, while those directly above turned grandly around the zenith. Aaron had sought her out to express his boredom with the other guests, then stayed for one of those half-drunken conversations that it was valuable but sometimes embarrassing to record.

"Everywhere I look I see limits," he was saying. "And I wonder why we tolerate them."

Livia had shrugged, languidly turning to look at the stars. "Limits are the fountain of creativity," she said. "Without them there is no novelty."

"So they say." Aaron crossed his arms and glared down at her. "*They* being inhuman powers that control our lives, and over which we have no control. Inscape; the demented AI of the tech locks; even the founders. They parcel out a tiny fraction of their power to us, just enough to allow us to live tiny, inconsequential lives. It's a tyranny. Something should be done."

She'd smiled ironically. "Like what? Should I gather the peers together and overthrow nature?"

He shook his head. "I've said it before, but the peers' plan to build a new city doesn't impress me. It's not ambitious enough by far. Westerhaven . . . we've deliberately limited ourselves like all the other manifolds. Discarded technologies that we could have used to increase our power and influence in the coronal. Nobody here has the balls to try to effect real change in the world. It's a mediocre manifold, Livy."

"Then change it," she asserted. "Or make a new one! You've got the charisma and the convictions to do it single-handedly. Lean on your Society, Aaron, and it will happen. That's how a manifold comes to be, after all."

"What, with fifty, a hundred years of wheedling and cajoling?" He shook his head. "In the old days they'd just blow up the capital and take over."

She laughed. "In many places, they still do. But that's not our reality, Aaron, you know that."

"Maybe it should be," he'd muttered. He rubbed at his eyes, making the gesture a bit too dramatic as with all he did. "Anyway, that's my point. We can only work within the system. Not jump out of it. And Livy, I do want to get out. And I think you do, too."

Stop, commanded Livia now. The conversation froze, a night moth paused mid-flap above Aaron's ear. The talk had deteriorated after this point anyway.

She scowled out at the green park with its dancing couples. What had she just learned? Nothing, really; only that Aaron had an ache he couldn't satisfy in Westerhaven. But would that be enough for him to abandon the manifold of his birth? She couldn't believe he'd move to another reality without discussing it with her first.

She had just raised her hand to invoke another inscape session, when Peaseblossom appeared in front of her, frantically waving. "Liv-Livia, you won't believe what's happening!"

Cicada popped into being next to him. "Hsst, you said you wouldn't tell."

"Yes, but—"

"Hallooo!" Someone was waving down on the ground, for all the world as if she could see Livia. Impossible, of course; this platform was a personal privacy zone.

"It's her!" Cicada pointed. Livia followed his eyeline and met the eyes of a woman whose face she knew, but whom she'd never met in person. She was staring up at Livia from the ground. She could see her.

"Sorry to barge in. Can I talk to you?" said Lady Maren Ellis.

Livia was too shocked to reply at first. Then she stalked over to the ladder and climbed down. How could anyone—even a founder—so easily penetrate a privacy zone?

The question—and indignation—went out of her head when the founder shook her hand and said, "You're the young lady of whom I've heard so many good things."

Livia smiled weakly back. Ellis knew of her? She would never have expected such a thing. The founders, after all, were impossibly remote from day-to-day life. No one saw them. No one knew them, anymore.

Ellis didn't seem so intimidating up close. She appeared younger than Livia herself; even her eyes gave nothing away, seemingly those of an ingenue. But she took Livia's arm without hesitation and created her own zone of privacy around them. "I've been hoping I could meet you," she said. "We need to talk."

"I'm . . . honored to meet you, Lady," said Livia, disengaging herself carefully so that she could curtsy. Warily, she said nothing more. Lady Ellis returned them to a bench directly below Livia's bed. With a wave she dismissed Livia's Society. The partygoers were still laughing and dancing only a few meters away, but Livia had no doubt that she and the founder were inaccessible to them now.

"We've been watching you," said the lady as she sat languidly on the bench. "Your veto over the annexing of the drummers' lands shows great promise; of all the youth of your generation, you and Aaron Varese have perhaps the most acute awareness of the world around you—the real world, I mean, not this paradise of phantasms we call home."

"I'm . . . not sure what you mean. In case you failed to notice, I'm actually in a state of disgrace right now."

"Oh, I'm well aware of that. You voted against the interests of Westerhaven. But I'm well aware that you did so because you had actively tried to put yourself in the drummers' place. However briefly, you let yourself see through the eyes of strangers. And that is the kind of human being we were aiming to raise when we came to Teven. The annoyance of your peers is of no account." She dismissed them with a wave.

"Oh. Well, to what do I owe this . . ."

The founder smiled dazzlingly. "I know, we've never approached you before. It's because we wondered . . . well, I wondered whether your particular character has not been shaped by a circumstance that my own peers would rather not believe could be so . . . fertile."

It took Livia a moment to see through the weave of words to Lady Ellis's meaning. "Character? The crash . . . you think Aaron and I are special because of the crash?"

"I?" Lady Ellis gently tapped her own breastbone, leaning in close. "Not I, Livia, but all of us. Whether secretly or openly; and therein has lain the problem, for some time now." She sighed heavily. "My own peers have conveniently forgotten the circumstances under which we created this place." She gestured broadly, indicating not just Westerhaven, Livia felt sure, but all of Teven Coronal. "We bought this place with tragic loss and personal discipline. We built a paradise, so that our children should not have to go through what we went through. And what do we find? Our descendants are increasingly like the people we fled from. Yet two of them were lost to us for a short time—sheep strayed from the fold. And then they returned leading a train of refugees from devastated manifolds, like the sighted leading the blind. They were not like those helpless ones. They were more like us. Hard. Unsentimental. Everyone senses it. And your own peers are envious of those qualities."

"How can I be what you say, when I don't even remember that time?" Livia objected. "Hard? Not me—and certainly not . . ." *Aaron*, she almost said; but there was no way she was going to reveal her feelings to this woman, especially not when her own masks seemed temporarily down.

Suddenly angry, she said, "We gained nothing from the crash. Nothing! And yet we've been marked for life by it. It gave us nothing, it took away people we loved."

The lady nodded, unapologetic. "I never said it was a positive experience. On the contrary, it must have been awful. That's precisely what your peers don't understand about it, isn't it? *That nothing good came of it.* Yet that is the very reason why you and Aaron seem the stronger for it."

"I don't understand."

"Of course not. You have no real peers to compare yourself with . . . that you have met prior to today, that is." Lady Ellis smiled in a conspiratorial way. "I have no doubt that people have asked you many times for the story of what happened. No?" Livia nodded. "But has anyone ever told you how the crash affected us? The founders, I mean?"

"N-no." She had never even thought about it. "It was a great tragedy. All of Westerhaven mourned the families that died . . ."

"Oh, so did we." The lady dismissed that with a wave of her hand. "No, the crash itself. How did we react to that?"

Livia looked at her blankly.

"Look." The founder looked down, frowning at the grass. "Inscape has let us create a perfect mask over reality on this world. You grew up in it, so the very notion that there could be something else . . . it never occurs to you. But it occurs to us. We think about it all the time . . .

"Two airbuses of Westerhaven Great Families were circumnavigating the ring-shaped coronal that morning. It was an educational outing for you, wasn't it? But your family remained here. Aaron's went along for the ride. And almost halfway around the world—thousands of kilometers from home—you were suddenly engulfed in a massive electromagnetic pulse. We saw it happen: I was standing outside, I remember a flash of light at the zenith as the mad anecliptic hit the coronal's undersurface and exploded through it. He tore up ten kilometers of forest and left a great hole in the ground, through which the air began to escape. I saw that, too—after the flash, clouds appeared out of nowhere and turned into a vast whirling cyclone on the far side of the world. What I didn't see was that the magnetic shockwave had destroyed every artificial intelligence on that side of the coronal. Inscape was dead, your angels were dead, the manifolds there had crashed—and your buses were caught in a hurricane."

What was that word Lady Ellis had just used? *Anecliptic?* Livia had never heard the word before; the official story was that a meteoroid had pierced the coronal's skin.

The founder continued. "It's fortunate the coronal's healing powers are so great. The puncture was sealed before you could be sucked into space—but the buses crashed and everyone from Westerhaven except you and Aaron was killed. That much is history. But do you know what went through *my* mind when I saw that flash in the sky? Not that the coronal was being destroyed, although that was the rumor for some hours. No, what I thought was: *they have found us.*"

She stood up, and to Livia's astonishment, began to pace. "*They have found us.* I thought that the oppressive culture that we fled, oh so many years ago now, had learned of our existence. That we were about to be pulled, kicking and screaming, back into the embrace of that monstrous empire they call the *Archipelago.*"

She looked down at Livia, and now Lady Ellis's eyes did show her age. "You and Aaron experienced what such a catastrophe would be like, Livia. That is why you are special."

Livia matched her gaze, tight-lipped. "Special? You mean we're not Westerhaven."

"Westerhaven is not about conformity! You should know that. No, it's just that you have the potential to see more of the world than merely this manifold. And that would be honorable, and truly Westerhaven of you."

Livia was troubled. She knew now that she was speaking not just with Lady Ellis, but with the founders as a whole; and the words she was hearing might or might not be coming from this woman standing before her. They had, it seemed, pierced the defenses of her Society, raising issues and incidents she would rather have edited away. Yet ultimately, her private inscape filters would not have allowed the conversation to get this far if they didn't think she would want to hear this. In fact, that was what was most disturbing.

"What is it that you want of me?" she asked. *What am I willing to let you request?*

Lady Ellis had lost her smile. She came and sat by Livia again. "Let me show you something," she said. She gestured, and a square of space in front of them opened to reveal a picture. It was a 3-D photograph of a city, taken from the air. The longhouses of Skaalitch were guarded by tall redwoods, and in the center of the photo several tall, intricate totem poles rose almost to the height of the trees.

"One of our people took this picture about six hours ago," said the founder. *"From the air."*

It took a moment for her meaning to sink in. Then Livia stood up quickly. "Oh! But that's . . ."

"Impossible? Yes, it is." They both stared at the photo.

Taking pictures from the air was simple in Westerhaven. In Raven's world, however, photography did not exist. Neither did flying machines. Inscape and tech locking worked together to exclude inappropriate technological interactions; the upshot was that Raven's world and everything in it was invisible from Westerhaven. The two technology sets were mutually invisible. Lady Ellis was showing her a picture that by all Livia knew simply could not exist.

"The light from the towers reached the camera," mused the lady. "That's to be expected; it would reach our eyes too if we were flying by. But then, the tech locks should have edited it out of the camera's image, just as inscape would edit it out of our sensorium. The pilot said he *saw* this Raven city, Livia. What does that mean?"

She shook her head. An unquiet feeling had started in the pit of her stomach.

"It's like what happened at this potlatch thing, isn't it?" continued the founder. "I hear the diplomats dismissed the event as unimportant. Pah!" She waved away the window. "They were too busy obsessing about Lucius Xavier to pay attention to the real issue. Worse yet, when we confronted them just now with this picture, they all hemmed, hawed, or hid behind their animas. Nobody wants to take this on."

Here it came, thought Livia. "Take what on?"

"Livia, someone has to go investigate what's happened in Skaalitch. That should be obvious. We think it should be someone who's had . . . experience with situations of instability in the tech locks and inscape."

Livia blew out a heavy sigh. It was momentarily amusing to picture Jachman and his cronies going to the founders to manipulate them for this outcome. But they could never have had the authority for it. Nobody did. Which meant either that Ellis was telling the truth about her motives for asking Livia . . . or there were politics here she knew nothing about.

Either way, this conversation couldn't have happened, no matter how strong Lady Ellis's authority, unless Livia was willing to let it happen. That alone was sufficient to guarantee her answer.

"Yes," she said. "I'll go check it out."

5

QIINGI OF RAVEN's people trailed his fingers in the water and looked down over the side of the canoe. Below him, sleek blue beings cavorted. Beneath them, in the depths, the trees and house poles of a half-real city shimmered.

He had come to the center of the bay to find peace. Qiingi had always been able to do that, ever since he was able to paddle on his own: he would glide silently over the hurrying water, watching the mist consume the bottoms of the nearby mountains. That mist was where a being could trade its *ghahlanda* and become something else, as Livia Kodaly had when she visited from the world of ghosts. The mist devoured everything and in it this became that, lost became found.

Today there was no mist. The distant shoreline remained crystal clear under limpid sunlight. He could see the individual rocks along the shoreline, the splashing as the waves lunged against them.

He slapped the water and one of the sleek beings surfaced next to him. "Qiingi," it said, after playfully shaking water all over him. "You neglect your studies."

"I know," he said regretfully. "There are problems in the houses of men. Strangers who have no *qqatxhana*." He no longer thought of them as *ancestors*—that fabrication had fallen in the first day of their visit.

"Yes, we know of them. You must trust them." The being flicked its flukes, dove and rose again. "But for now, we must pick up where we left off last time. Tell me, Qiingi: where does *teotl* come from?"

"It is not ours," he said stiffly. Qiingi's skin was crawling; these beings had never endorsed interlopers such as the ancestors before. "Teotl was the guiding principle of the Nahuatl of Earth," he went on. "Like everything else we have, we stole the idea from someone else."

"Qiingi . . ." The being sounded reproachful. "Good artists borrow, great artists steal. And truly great artists forget that they've stolen. You sound like an adolescent. Is it because you have been polluted by the ideas of the Westerhaven girl?"

"Unlikely," he said, reluctant to talk about the strangers who had visited the day of the potlatch.

"Tell me, what is teotl?"

He scowled at the being for a few moments—but he had come here to find peace. If he was truly to do that, he must shift his worries away from what was transpiring on land. Qiingi sighed. "Teotl is the region of the fleeting moment," he recited. "Ometeotl is the one near to everyone, to whom everyone is near. But teotl can only be a thing, it cannot be itself."

"What? Qiingi, what are you talking about? Are you speaking nonsense?" The being dove under the boat, emerging on the other side.

They did this all the time—teach you something then pretend you were speaking gibberish when you recited it back to them. The being was trying to get him to think about what he was saying, not just recite.

As he focused on explaining what he meant, Qiingi found his thoughts settling. This was what he'd come here for. "Teotl is . . . teotl is that which is always something other than itself. It is everything and everything is it."

"Qiingi, again you talk nonsense. Do you mean that those trees aren't really trees, but something else?"

"No. That would be a lie." He concentrated. "Since . . . since teotl is always other than itself, those trees must really be trees, because if they were teotl they would not be teotl, but something else, and that something else is trees. Teotl can only be by being those trees. That is how teotl comes to be. And yet, the trees are only teotl, and nothing more."

"Very good!" The being spun around and ducked its head, flicking water on Qiingi again. "But, silly human, if teotl is always something other than itself, how is it that it has a *name*?"

With that it dove, and didn't resurface. Qiingi stared down into the depths, pondering, until he became aware of a voice coming from shore.

"Halloooo . . ."

A gull flew by, wings trembling just above the wave tops. "Answer, answer," it cried. "The ancestors summon you."

Qiingi watched it go, suppressing a sharp retort. Seagulls were never smart. The ones around here had fallen for the "ancestors" unreservedly; Qiingi was not about to let one order him about.

But the voice called again. Reluctantly he turned his canoe and began paddling back. He could hear singing in the distance, and the smells of wood smoke and seaweed drifted out to him. As he pulled his canoe up onto the round rocks of the shore, the ancestor sauntered over, looking lazy as always. These beings never worked, but simply plucked what they needed from the mist. That alone made them worthy of suspicion. At least the beautifully masked Wordweaver Kodaly worked.

"I couldn't quite make out what you were talking about out there. Were you discussing the Aspect of Eros or the Pulsation Process of the Absolute?" asked the ancestor. He loomed over Qiingi, radiating health and pent-up energy.

"Neither. And both."

The ancestor laughed. This one was named Kale; he was blond and had a perfectly chiseled face, which he never changed. It was yet another thing that marked these people as strange: they worshiped beauty, and yet they would not change their faces to suit the tastes of those around them.

They had contempt for ghahlanda and for the Song of Ometeotl, Qiingi had learned.

"How can I help you this morning?" asked Qiingi.

"We are holding a meeting in the grand hall," said the ancestor affably. "I was thinking you might like to be one of those in the council circle."

Qiingi's uneasiness grew. Things had been strange for the past few days. It felt like the buildup of tension before a thunderstorm. His cousin Gwanhlin, who always had time to talk, now hurried to and fro, never meeting Qiingi's eyes. Even the forest people, bear, badger, and fox, had begun singing strange songs and congregating in shadowed spaces, always slinking away when interrupted. And everywhere, the ancestors walked and brayed their confident heresies.

"I am not sure what it is that we have to discuss," he said. Despite himself he was intimidated by this big man. He looked like he could snap Qiingi in two if he wanted.

"Things are changing," said Kale. "Very rapidly. Some of your people are adapting with admirable speed. Some are having difficulty. You're not having difficulty, are you, Qiingi?"

"I am a wordweaver, one who speaks to those from over the horizons," said Qiingi, crossing his arms. "I have traveled between the worlds. I do not think I am having difficulty coping with the changes."

"Ah. Good. So—"

"But," interrupted Qiingi, "I am having great difficulty in knowing why you are doing this to us. And how." What he really wanted to say was, *I don't think you should be taking down the walls between the worlds.* But the elders had discussed it; they had decided that the fall of the walls was a metaphor, merely a piece of mysticism.

"What do you mean?" asked Kale. "We explained it all to you." The ancestor began to walk up the beach, crunching dried seaweed. Iodine scent wafted from the weed. "Come, we can talk as we walk."

Qiingi fought with himself as they walked. How much could he say? He sensed the danger of admitting his suspicions, and yet . . . people were disappearing. Not that they didn't do that all the time, vanishing into subworlds or under the waters of the bay. Young people in particular saw other worlds all the time, before they learned to trade their ghahlanda, and sometimes they were seduced away from Raven to a place behind the mists, such as Westerhaven. But they often returned, and very rarely were they impossible to find. But these people—good friends of Qiingi's, stable and full members of the community—they were simply gone. Had Qiingi not known that the totems and spirits of the forest protected his people, he might have thought they had died.

"Kale, some of my people are missing. Do you know where they have gone?"

Kale looked him the eye. "No idea," said the ancestor.

There was a brief silence. "Ancestor Kale, I know that you have told us . . ." At that moment Qiingi saw something and forgot what he was about to say.

"Yes?" Kale looked at Qiingi, then followed his gaze upward.

Swooping low along the treetops that lined the bay was a craft of the air. Qiingi had never seen such a thing, but he knew instantly what it was. The fact that he could see it at all meant that Kale was right: the walls between the worlds really were falling. The elders had said that this would result in the world perceiving the true face of Ometeotl. But that was impossible, Qiingi knew. The old men had mistaken the ancestors' proposal for just another living myth that would, like everything else, use the technology of the Song of Ometeotl. Qiingi doubted that Raven himself believed there could be a single face to Ometeotl. Now, in their zeal to dismantle the worlds, the elders were learning what they had deliberately forgotten: that if you took down the walls of the world you would not see the face behind the masks, but just one more mask.

"Westerhaven has come," Qiingi said. He thought about the subtle men and women of Westerhaven, with their bright devices and ease at manipulating realities. A glimmer of hope came to him then, even as the flying thing made its own wind beneath it and settled in swirling sand and flying seaweed onto the beach.

Kale crossed his arms and smirked at the apprehensive look Qiingi sent him. "Go on," he said. "Talk to her."

Qiingi left him standing in the dappled light of the treeline. He tried not to run down to the flying machine, as its curving mirrored door opened and Wordweaver Kodaly stepped out.

"Qiingi," she said, in some surprise. "Did the forest people tell you I was coming?"

He shook his head. "I was on the waters," he said. "Wordweaver Kodaly, it is good to see you. But perhaps this is not a good time for you to be here."

She narrowed her eyes and looked past him. "The ancestors are still here, aren't they?"

"Yes. And what I told you about on the day of the potlatch . . . it is happening." He did not try to hide the anxiety in his voice. She, he noticed, appeared in Westerhaven clothing, complete with a sword strapped to her side. He should only have been able to see her in traditional Raven garb; it was one more detail that proved the world was ending.

"My people want to talk to these ancestors," said Livia. "Can you take me to them?"

"Yes, one is right here—" When Qiingi turned he saw that Kale had vanished, either trading his ghahlanda, or perhaps just walking away.

"The ancestors are not here," he said.

"Oh. Their qqatxhana . . . ?" She had used another word, but the Song translated for her. Some things still worked correctly, it seemed.

"They have no qqatxhana to call. I'm sorry I cannot take you to them, Wordweaver Kodaly."

She gazed at him for a moment, obviously judging whether or not he was lying. "Well, I can wait. Meanwhile, though, I'm also trying to find one of my people. My leader, Lucius Xavier. He disappeared on the day of the potlatch."

"I cannot comment on that," he said neutrally. "Your world behaves differently from mine." But it did bring to mind those citizens of Skaalitch who had vanished over the past days.

"If you haven't seen him . . . what about the animals? Could I talk to them?"

How could he tell her that the animals could no longer be trusted? "Let us not speak of this here," he said. "We will find a more comfortable place." Kale might return at any moment.

They walked into the forest. Qiingi did his best to lower horizons of privacy around them, but he could not be certain that the invisibility would work in this strange new world that the ancestors had created. So he ensured that there were no masks between them, then drew Livia Kodaly down long winding paths and under the leaning moss-roofed trunks of fallen trees. They passed a set of trees that were being cut down; one small one was almost cut through, but the workmen had left it leaning, a few strands holding it upright. Eventually they came to a hollowed-out stump big as a house where he had played as a child. They stepped inside. "We should be free to talk here."

"What is going on?" she asked impatiently. "Who are these ancestors? What do they want?"

"I don't know," he said. "But I am very afraid, Wordweaver Kodaly. They are doing in daylight what they said they would do in dreams."

"Yes, but how?" she asked. "No one can dismantle inscape. I've been talking to our experts. Inscape is impervious to assaults."

"I'm afraid, Wordweaver Kodaly, that whether it was assaulted or dismantled, or something else, in this place the Song of Ometeotl is ending."

QIINGI SLUMPED AGAINST the mossy wall of the stump, staring at the ground. He didn't even hide his vulnerability behind a mask. The knot of worry that Livia had felt in her stomach since seeing the city from the air was becoming an actual pain. Something impossible and terrible was happening.

"Livia, Livia!" Peaseblossom appeared at her side. "We tried to follow you like always and this time we made it!" The little creature looked inordinately proud of itself as it balanced on a nearby twig. Livia blinked at it.

"You mean you can move freely here?"

"Yes! Isn't it wonderful?"

She leaned away from it in confusion. "Go then—get out of here. Reconnoiter. Tell me what's happening in the city."

"Yes, ma'am!" It saluted and flew away. Livia found her heart pounding; it should not have been able to appear here.

"Your qqatxhana?" inquired Qiingi politely.

"Why, yes. He's . . . rude." Qiingi had seen the pixie, and her interaction with it! It was her own private agent; nobody else should be able to perceive it unless she explicitly willed it. Livia felt exposed, embarrassed and shocked at the event.

She sat down on an outthrust of knotted wood and gazed up at the open ring of bark twenty hand-spans above them. She tried to order her thoughts. "We've been interrogating inscape, I mean the Song of Ometeotl, about this breakdown. It's not even aware there's a problem. Something is deeply wrong, and it's all the doing of these 'ancestors,' isn't it? When did they first approach you? Sometime before the potlatch, isn't that right?"

"A few months ago," he said, sitting cross-legged in front of her. "At first there were only two. They came as visitors, we believed they were from a village under the bay, or from inside a hill. But they preached our own stories at us fluently, and claimed to be our true ancestors—the parents of Raven's people."

"But only Raven created Raven's people," she said.

"Yes—but he did not appear to us to explain or deny any of it. He was . . . strangely absent."

She sat up, eyes widening. "He said nothing about the arrival of the ancestors?"

"The last time Raven appeared he was angry. He said something strange then. That we should not play with . . . what was the word? It was an old word, disused now. Yes: we should not play with *transcendence*. It is possible . . ." Qiingi looked sick. "That he has left us," he whispered.

Qiingi must believe he'd said that behind a mask. Livia was embarrassed for him, and kept on as if she hadn't noticed.

"Have you asked the ancestors about that? You lied earlier when you said they weren't around, didn't you?"

"Livia, I think it would be very dangerous for you to approach them now. They are too sure of themselves, like young men who have staged a successful raid. They might do anything."

She remembered the way inscape had broken down when they first appeared. Her angels had not protected her in their presence. Livia fingered the hilt of her sword, wondering.

"Your animals and spirits aren't helping, are they?"

"They are under the control of the ancestors."

"What about basic inscape services? Memory, communication, querying?"

"The Song of Ometeotl does not include the xhants or qqatxhana of the ancestors. They carve no marker for themselves. But perhaps if we hunt among our own people for your Lucius Xavier, we will discover something about them as well."

She shook her head. "I've already back-stepped through my whole history with Lucius, Qiingi. I didn't find anything."

"*Qiingi?*" It was a man's voice, coming from somewhere outside the stump. They both froze for a moment, staring at the entrance.

"YOU MUST STAY hidden here," said Qiingi in a low voice. "I do not know what the ancestors will do with you." He saw the uncertainty in Livia Kodaly's face; finally she nodded.

Qiingi stepped out of the stump and walked up the path. As he came next to the propped-up tree, Kale appeared around over a hump in the path. "Ah, there you are," boomed the ancestor. "Have you seen our friend Livia Kodaly?"

"She left," said Qiingi.

"Really? That's strange. Her aircar is still here."

Qiingi knew that the stump where Livia Kodaly hid was not visible from where they were standing. Of course, Kale controlled the Song now; he could probably find Livia using the eyes of the forest as easily as his own.

"Well, let's just see what's down this path, hmm?" Kale went to brush past him.

"You're not really our ancestors," said Qiingi.

Kale stopped. "What do you mean?"

"Ever since you arrived, you have been pretending to follow our traditions and practices," said Qiingi quickly. "You say that when the walls between the worlds have fallen, all those in the other worlds will come back to Raven, and we will be pure again. You speak our stories with great familiarity, and you promise a world in which there is only us—only the mountains and ocean and Raven."

Kale nodded gravely. "That is so."

"Do you think we're idiots?" said Qiingi. "Do you think we actually believe that we live on a planet—on *Earth*? That our traditions are some sort of orthodoxy that we all believe like little children? What are we to you, Kale, innocent forest people who know nothing of the wider world?"

Kale simply stared at him.

"Kale, we know who we are. We are the inheritors of a civilization that has conquered the stars. We built this world. We made the soil and the air and the sunlight with our mastery of physics and manufacturing, and then we made the Song of Ometeotl—what Wordweaver Kodaly calls the *manifolds*—to live in. And like every other people within the Song, we are busy with the work of generations, quite deliberate and careful, to build meaningful ways of life for ourselves and our children."

Now Kale nodded slowly. "We are discovering that we misjudged you."

"You fed us a story that fit with our program," said Qiingi. He felt apologetic to be having to use archaic language, as if he were telling a child that he had done something bad. "Since we live so deeply within our own narrative, we wove yours into ours at first without thinking critically about it. But it has been some time now. I have been thinking. I am sure others have, as well."

"Yes," said Kale with a shrug. "But I was hoping you'd thought more than you apparently have, Qiingi. Some of your friends have taken the next step."

"What do you mean?"

"If you know what we're doing here, you know we're ending the Song. We're bringing your people out of their fantasy-land and back to reality. Which is simply the just thing to do."

Qiingi began to back away. "You are no friend of Raven's. You are a disguise of Ttsam'aws."

"Your little pretend-society has already ended, Qiingi. The only issue now is who among you will be leaders, and who will be led. Most of your people still believe in what the animals tell them—they've decided not to see us pulling the strings on the puppets." Kale laughed richly. "They want to be led, so we'll lead them. Some of your friends have decided they'd rather live in the real world, and have come over to our side. They can be leaders in the illusion-free world we're making here, Qiingi; *you* can be a leader. You just have to stop pretending you're something that you're not."

He should be running, Qiingi knew, but the magnitude of what was happening wasn't sinking in. His xhants knew it, but could not convince his body that what Kale was saying was true.

"It was never an illusion," he heard himself saying. "It was the face we saw in the wood we carved."

Kale shrugged dismissively. "Do you want to know where your vanished friends have gone, Qiingi?" He waved a hand, and images appeared in the air. Qiingi saw a land of forest and grass, with great estates and in the distance a shimmering city. All across the land warriors of Raven were walking, spears balanced on their shoulders. There were hundreds of them—thousands, perhaps, taken from all the villages and towns of the land. They were converging on the shimmering city, grim-faced and single of purpose.

"This must be stopped!" Qiingi turned, intending to run for the elders' compound. He felt Kale's hand descend on his shoulder and quickly spun away, aiming a blow at the man's kidneys. His hand was deflected a centimeter from Kale's skin. Now Qiingi saw the faint shimmer around his body; Kale was protected by his totem, of course. When Kale punched him in the stomach, Qiingi knew his own totem had deserted him.

He staggered back, tripped over a root and ended up with his back against a tree. Kale stepped forward, his face ugly with malice. "You could have joined us. Now you're just meat for the process, Qiingi."

Qiingi heard a cracking noise, looked past Kale's shoulder—and heedless of where he was going, dove to one side. He landed on some sharp branches, gouging his arm. He saw Kale turn just in time to look surprised as the tree fell on him.

It was the tree that had been abandoned half cut. Behind its stump,

Livia Kodaly stood with her sword drawn. Qiingi got to his feet awkwardly. "That was a truly mighty blow."

She held out the sword. "Monatomic edge. Normally wouldn't work in this manifold. Cuts through anything." They both stared at Kale, who was struggling beneath the tree, which was as thick as his waist. Blue sparks shot out from the area where the tree was pressing him into the ground. So far, his totem had kept it from touching him, but Qiingi could see that the totem was losing strength rapidly.

"The angel's going to burn out any second," said Livia.

"Or he's going to get up," said Qiingi as Kale heaved himself up ten centimeters, his face a twisted red.

"Then come on!" Livia ran up the path.

"Where? Where can we go now that the Song has ended?"

"Westerhaven! Barrastea! Qiingi, my aircar's still by the shore. We have to get there before the other ancestors come after us."

Qiingi nodded, and without another glance at the fallen ancestor, he followed Livia Kodaly up the path, and forever away from his home.

6

"THIS IS WRONG," said Qiingi as Skaalitch passed out of sight behind some hills. He sat awkwardly in his seat, staring down at the landscape with some complex mix of sadness and loathing in his eyes. With a start Livia realized that he was feeling guilty—guilty at taking the easy way to Barrastea, and not walking.

Livia had summoned her full Society as they ran to the aircar, but something was wrong with that, too. The animas of her family and friends appeared, but they stood listlessly, unresponsive, as if most of their attention were elsewhere. She supposed it was, if Barrastea was the city that Raven's warriors were marching on.

"Speak to me," she said to the Society. "What's happening below?"

At first nobody responded. Then the image of Lady Ellis turned slowly and looked at her. "We have gone into games mode," said the anima. "Join us on the ground at city center, Livia."

She let out a breath in shock. Only two or three times in her life had she been into the war games submanifold of Westerhaven. Parents showed young children how to get there, when teaching them about emergency realities. But nobody went military lightly, or for long.

She wanted all of this to just stop stop *stop*. She needed a chance to think, to find an exit from this strange new manifold she was living in. But the clouds continued to whip past, and a warrior of Raven really sat by her side, in a place that should have been impossible for him.

She made her way into games mode by tuning down certain features of the outside world and amplifying others. "Qiingi, you must come in here with me," she heard herself say; as she worked he had faded to the gray of a nonparticipating noncombatant. She flung him a reticle—a set of frames, icons, and interactive objects that he could use to select the attitudes and focus of the submanifold. After a surprisingly short time he was fully real next to her again; she supposed Raven's people had some counterpart to this place.

The rest of the world, though, had gone hyperreal. Things in her immediate vicinity—the aircar, Qiingi, the closest clouds—were suddenly perfect in their clarity. It was as though she were seeing Qiingi for the first time: every hair, every breath he took registered as a distinct object or event. At the same time, everything beyond this little bubble of hyperreality had been reduced to a wire-frame tactical display. The sky was neutral gray, the land a sketch covered with icons and winking lights.

"Give me a portable map," said Livia. The map appeared, pretending to be a paper object on the dashboard. She unfolded its half-felt leaves until it lay across her lap. Qiingi turned from the simplified outside view, leaning over her shoulder to examine the map. "Is that your land?" he asked. She nodded. "And those little torches?"

Tiny winking lights were scattered across the map's surface. "Those mark where fighting is happening." There were hundreds scattered evenly throughout the manifold.

"You've invaded us," she said in despair. Qiingi shook his head.

"Your lands and ours have always been the same," he said. "Many of our people wander for much of the year, and they know that the lands they walk through contain other peoples, though they rarely see you. Livia, they are our lands, too."

Livia shook her head, but she knew he was right. If the horizons were falling . . . Where Raven's people had communed with life and nature for centuries in silent forest cathedrals and trackless meadows, suddenly they found themselves standing in or next to farms and towns full of blaring machines and swooping aircars. Mobs of people crowded up against them at every turn.

"There have always been lands that are not strongly real for either of our peoples," Qiingi continued. "There, we encounter one another. These places are where we stage our raids, those of our young men happy to war with yours. But it is wrong for that war to be everywhere or involve everyone, as it now seems to."

Livia barely heard him, because the aircar had punched its way through a series of big puffy clouds and there, spread out below them in topographic relief, was Barrastea.

The city was almost unrecognizable in this tactical view—but she could see that it was surrounded by a perfect ring of flickering light. The battle indicated was on a scale never before seen in Teven Coronal. "But this," she whispered. "This can't be your people."

Qiingi saw where she was pointing. "No, not us," he agreed. "We stage raids. We defend ourselves. We don't—"

The world suddenly spun around them. Her inner ear gave no sign of what had just happened; the war games submanifold wouldn't permit sensations such as vertigo or nausea. Livia found her awareness snap away from Qiingi, to the cloud of aircars through which they were suddenly diving.

The sky was full of whirling icons, some the green of friendlies, some red. Something loomed close, was, for an instant, the vision of a tumbling, half-ruined car falling past. Then coming straight at her, filling the sky, was a giant eagle.

Qiingi shouted something in Raven's dialect. There was no sound or sensation to the impact, only a squeezing pressure on her face as she was suddenly nose to nose with the dashboard, the sparking blue stuff of her angel having prevented her shattering her face on it. Just above her right ear, a huge avian claw was widening a hole in the aircar's canopy.

Qiingi stood up in his seat, reciting something in a loud voice. He stood face to face with the eagle, whose beak was the size of his head. The eagle matched Qiingi's gaze, opened its beak and screamed. The scream came right through Livia's military consciousness and took root in her deepest fears. She watched herself whimper and shrink back. But Qiingi didn't blink.

Then the eagle was gone, replaced by a cold gale and the sky and earth, sky and earth flipping by in rapid succession. Even as she realized they were in a spin the car righted itself and went into a more sedate spiral, aiming itself at the Great Library in the center of Barrastea. In this giant stone edifice were stored records and artifacts from all the manifolds Westerhaven had touched. Teven's history was preserved there; so it was fitting that this was where the founders had set up their command post.

Something huge that was all angles blocked the sky. Livia had a confused glimpse of black wings with black eyes on them, a beak with faces carved in it—then they were past and had missed the compound. Tree-tops whipped by just under the car and leaves fanned up behind like spray from a boat. Barely clearing a low stone wall, the aircar slowed at last and bumped to a stop.

"Out! Out!" Qiingi shoved her onto the grass as the black and red thing reappeared. It was nightmarish but recognizable as a living manifestation of a Raven design. Each part of its body was a separate creature, each so distorted as to be unidentifiable. It stood atop a row of trees and roared.

Qiingi dragged her into the shadow of an archway. "We need weapons," he said in a reasonable tone.

For the moment the monster wasn't moving, just roaring, so Livia looked around. The games submanifold swept into strong focus around her: the sky was separated into quadrants, with a giant circular compass rose centered on Livia herself. Different quadrants glowed different colors and different intensities depending on the disposition of forces under them, so that she could see at a glance how the battle was progressing. The sky was crisscrossed by lines showing advances, retreats, and logistics and supply.

They were standing on the edge of Carewon Avenue, a long green mall that extended from the center of Barrastea to the outskirts. It would be a perfect funnel for enemy troops; also a good place for ambushes, dotted as it was with hedges and groves. As she looked down the length she saw people pouring out of distant side ways, running chaotically. Some were pursued by gigantic things that hopped from one person to the next, like a boy stomping on ants.

"Don't move!" She turned in time to see Qiingi being forced to his knees by four Westerhaven youths. Belatedly she realized he must look like an enemy to them.

Livia summoned all her authority and pushed aside the barrel of their squad leader's rifle. "Stop! He's one of ours."

It took some convincing for them to lower their guns; the boys were shaking from what they had seen this morning, and were quite prepared to shoot anything non-Westerhaven. Although Qiingi looked like a warrior of Raven, the war games submanifold had marked him as an ally; that was the only reason he was still alive.

Livia took off her shift and gave it to him. "Tune this to some Westerhaven clothes, Qiingi. And . . . tie back your hair or something."

As he hurried to comply she turned to ask the boys what was happening. "Who agreed they could raid Barrastea?" asked one, his eyes wild. "This is crazy!"

"It's not a raid," she began, but before she could explain further the boys wavered and were replaced by animas. Livia found herself facing the founders.

"We got your message," said Lady Ellis. "It gave us a few minutes' warning. Thank you, Livia."

"A few minutes?" said another of the founders. "Maren, it might as well have been nothing."

"We always knew something like this could happen," said Lady Ellis. "Once we turned our backs on what we'd built . . ."

"It's the anecliptics," said another, fear in her voice. It was the second time Livia had heard this strange name. She raised a mask, partly to hide her astonishment at hearing the founders expressing doubt and confusion; while there, she asked, "What's an anecliptic?" of her Society. Nobody answered.

Meanwhile her own anima said, "Wordweaver Qiingi, may I introduce the founders of Westerhaven." As they nodded to one another, Livia thought back to the party at the Kodalys. Lady Ellis had talked about her fears then; she had worried that *they have found us*. Could *they* be these ancestors, and were they the same as the mysterious anecliptics? These thoughts flickered by momentarily then were gone, unimportant as they were in the face of the current situation.

Qiingi cleared his throat. "I have spoken to the ones who are doing this," he said.

As usual, his understated style worked: the founders gave him their full attention. He briefly described Kale, and what the man had said. "I have been thinking about our conversation. I believe that the invaders think they are doing us a favor. They believe we are enslaved by illusions, and that they are freeing us from the ropes of a dream."

"They seem to be primitives," agreed Livia. "They don't know that reality is always mediated. They see that inscape is a filter between us and reality . . ."

"But they don't see that when you're outside the manifolds you're just living with a different set of filters," said Ellis and nodded. "Thank you, it's good to have some idea of their motives. But it may be too late to help us."

Kale's words had been clear: he believed the people of Teven were using inscape to hide from the real world. But Livia had lived outside inscape; she had seen nothing there that she didn't see within it. It was the emphasis that changed when you changed the technologies mediating between you and the world. Before the accident, her angels, implants, and augmented senses had skewed reality one way; afterward, her clothes, hands and feet, and biological senses had skewed it another. Part of reality had been turned up, other parts turned down or shut off. But neither showed the total picture; one was not true and the other false.

"We have to talk to them," said one of the founders. "Find a way to make them understand—"

Lady Ellis shook her head. "It's too late for that." The other founders glanced at one another. Several nodded grimly.

Livia dismissed her anima and spoke directly to Lady Ellis. "Ma'am, these beasts—the warriors . . . How can we help?"

"You have to reach us at the library," said Lady Ellis, pointing. "The Great Families are trying to save our heritage, and your peers are on the front lines. Unfortunately, we're faring badly. Now that the horizons have been blown, weapons that should only work for Raven's people or Westerhaven work in both. It seems as though Raven's warriors have been training to take advantage of the fact. Our own people . . . it's swords against totem spirits, Livia. Our people don't know how to react, they're getting cut to pieces."

"But surely we have better weapons," said Livia.

"The big guns haven't made it to the front lines yet. You must understand, everything your generation and your elders know about the world led them to expect that rifles and grenades would not work against Raven's forces. But if their spirit-warriors are effective against us . . . Chagrined, she added, "I tried to strengthen Westerhaven against this sort of possibility, but my efforts were too little too late, I'm afraid."

Founder Whyte himself stepped forward. "For now, Livia, you must stay out of the fight. We've sent scouts to the borders of Westerhaven to verify that what's happening here is local, and not a general attack on Teven Coronal. So far the collapse seems confined to this area. That means if things go badly, we can always retreat to another manifold. Because you've got experience outside inscape, we may need you to lead your peers to safety."

Retreat, she thought, *yes, that might be prudent.* Wait—when had she started thinking impossible thoughts? To abandon the very reality that they had crafted for themselves over so many generations . . . She could see the Great Library in the distance—the very heart of Teven, where her family and friends had spent their lives and passions gathering and preserving all the stories, paintings, sculpture, and music of Teven's mortal manifolds. Westerhaven was a celebration of all difference, it was the very soul of Teven. To abandon it . . .

She shook her head, trying to summon some argument that the founders would agree to. "But . . . some of our people won't be able to journey to another manifold." *How could they?* Who could abandon all they held dear, which was what inscape would demand of the traveler?

Ellis nodded sadly. "Those that can't will make a final stand with us. We'll defend the library. Those that can go will need a guide. That's where you and the other diplomats come in."

"But—" The founders had vanished, leaving her standing in the open with the four amateur soldiers.

"Come on!" They ran for the distant marble slab of the library. Thankfully, Raven's monster ignored them as it screamed into the air. As they ran Livia looked around through the war games submanifold and took stock of the situation.

Some of her friends were dead. She had brief moments to contemplate the fact as they paused under bridges or trees, so the realization came and went in random waves of horror. Had she not seen death before firsthand, the knowledge alone might have paralyzed her; as it was, more peers were dying because they simply couldn't believe what was happening to them. They stood in intersections throughout the city, swords drawn, each facing down a charge by up to hundreds of warriors. First their angels, then they were cut down. Their own friends saw them die, and the shock froze them into immobility. They became easy prey for Raven's warriors—no, the *ancestors'* warriors. Livia found herself turning back more than once, shouting warnings, running to help people who were too far away. Each time Qiingi dragged her back, and they continued toward the library.

She was just succeeding in shoving these terrible deaths out of her consciousness when Livia realized where they were; she instantly stopped running. The others crouched down behind a wall just ahead of her; some mythic beast was crunching over the earth no more than a few meters away. "Livia, get down!" shouted one of the squad. She didn't listen, didn't care.

She was home.

The canopies that slanted over the Kodaly estate were torn. Paths and stone sidewalks were clotted with debris; ways that had been at once public and private were now gutted out of human usability by fire and collapse. The shock of it filled her with a kind of cold; she watched herself running, like somebody else's anima, away from Qiingi and the others, through low archways and across parks full of flaming trees. They were running after her, yelling, but she didn't care.

"We're safe, dear, we made it out!" Mother was saying. She and Livia's father floated alongside her, unscathed but not really here. Livia's footsteps faltered. "Let it go," said her father. "You can't save it. We need to defend the library."

Then she came around one last corner and stood next to the statue of Feste. The park/ballroom lay before her, with her open-air bedroom visible in the coignes of the arch opposite. She could see the bed she'd slept in since she was ten; the footlocker open with a childhood's worth of arts and crafts spilling out of it; her clothes scattered and now torn under the talons of a beast like an unfolding flower of black and crimson, its petals grimacing faces and its claws the beaks of savage birds.

It spotted her immediately. Livia swore, and cast about for somewhere to hide. Feste wasn't big enough. She began to back away, even as the monster raised its wings and prepared to leap on her.

She turned to run and there came the beat of giant wings behind her. She drew her sword—little good that it would do—

—And an explosion knocked her off her feet. Blocky pieces of monster hit the ground and one rolled to a stop next to her head. It was a claw the size of a table, and it looked surprisingly like it was made of wood.

She sat up and looked back. The statue of Feste was gone. Black scorch marks extended across the grass, which was dotted with the strange gore of the monster.

Someone reached down a hand to help her stand. She took it and got to her feet, then followed the hand up the arm and saw who it was.

"Rene?"

Rene Caiser was aged by fear and covered in soot, but his gaze was steady as he smiled at her. He had some sort of rocket launcher slung over his shoulder. "Follow me," he said as Qiingi and the others ran up. "The library's less than a kilometer."

Strange, when you could bring back any moment of your life in full color and detail, relive every word of every conversation, hear the buzzing of the insects on any perfect day—strange, for the most important days of your life to be unrecorded. Yet, for Livia there had been times after the crash that were as vivid to her in memory as if they'd just happened. Others . . . whole weeks had been lost, become mythological. She and Aaron had debated who did what and when, but it was pointless. Memory had shattered along with the bodies of friends in the crash, even as she saw the plans and dreams of the peers vanishing now.

At ten years' age, Livia had begun seeing things. Mother was pleased; she explained that this happened to everyone as they approached the age where they could make decisions for themselves. What Livia saw were distant cities, strange flying signs that spoke to her, people who walked through walls, and everywhere words and ethereal conversations that poured and dove around her like the surging waves of an ocean. The visions were beautiful and overwhelming. But she quickly learned that she could summon or dismiss them, or parts of them, as she chose.

One day she ran around the manor with a wand in her hand, pointing and going "poof" at this and that. When she caromed around a corner and met Mother, she pointed the wand at her and said, "Poof, you're a good cook!"

Mother tried not to look annoyed. "Livia, dear, you can't change the real things of the world. You can only change inscape things, and hide or reveal real things. All you can really change is yourself."

Livia thought about that for a moment. She tapped her own head with the wand. "Poof!" she said, "I *think* you're a good cook!"

All her friends were getting into the vision thing. The boys were a little slower than the girls, so for a year or so she and her friends had it all over them in inscape. What was in, and what was out, was terribly, terribly important—not only how you appeared, but what appeared to you signified your place in the girls' nascent Society.

Over time she came to learn that this was indeed a serious game. She was being shown a wider world than Westerhaven, a world of distractions and seductions so powerful that they could mesmerize her for days and shake her sense of self and duty down to its foundations. She was being challenged. She was also being given all the tools she might need to construct as true a version of herself as she desired.

She could choose to turn away from Westerhaven and embrace some other manifold that suited her character and ambitions better. It wouldn't even be necessary for her to leave home to do this; that other world would interpenetrate hers, its denizens becoming more real even as her childhood friends and family faded. She could live the rest of her life on these grounds where she'd been born, yet completely outside Westerhaven. Or, she could embrace the Societies she'd been born into and tune herself more and more in their direction. Accept this, discard that feature of the world until Westerhaven was all there was.

She had come to terms with this strange new world—was beginning to accept it—when one afternoon she found herself crawling out of the burst skin of an airbus, drenched in blood that she could not will away.

None of the blood was hers. The whole world had turned a strange yellow, the sky given over to a pillar of dust the width of a mountain that seemed to rise to infinity. In every direction the landscape was torn and flattened as if giants had rampaged across it. After a while of puzzling, Livia decided that the strewn matchsticks in the distance had once been a forest. In many places the underlying skin of Teven Coronal showed through the stripped soil. These scars were midnight black, and smooth as glass.

She turned, a slow stagger as her legs failed to coordinate. She looked for her Society. "Hello?" There were no human forms visible anywhere. Only what she'd seen in the gash she'd just exited. Human forms—partly. Some still moving where they hung; none alive.

The moment of realization came like white light, like the burn of a flare overtaking reason. Livia ran—

—and here was one of those holes in her memory.

Some time later she huddled with Aaron under the trunk of a downed tree, as rain plummeted around them, fat, oily drops of it. There was no sound except the mindless drumming of the downpour and Livia's own cries as she called over and over for her Society. For anyone.

Neither of them understood it. They tried over and over to switch off the rain. Stand the trees back up. Bring the corpses in the bus back to life. Things changed when you willed it. People listened, the right things happened. Yet all was silence and the world had turned its back on them.

The first thing Livia had said to Aaron was, "Where are we?" Not *what happened;* what happened had to do with where you were in inscape. What happened was what you decided happened. Next was, "Who's doing this?" After all, whatever happened did so for a reason, and it was always somebody's reason in particular.

She supposed that the next few holes in her memory had to do with realizing that none of these assumptions was true anymore.

Later, after jumbled recollections of fear, pain, and hunger, she remembered other survivors. They had wandered like ghosts through the blasted landscape; the story was that Livia had led them, and Aaron, out of the dead zone and back to the manifolds. But about half didn't make it. In retrospect, she could name the things that had killed some: thirst, exposure, shock. But two of the adults had simply *stopped,* without apparent reason. They had struggled for a time to comprehend what had happened to them, and failed.

Years later, she wondered if it wasn't the indecisive realities of adolescence that had given her the strength to guide the others after the crash. She and Aaron were already living in a phase where inscape had come unlocked; it was a huge step from that to having no inscape at all, but still they had been able to take it. Not so the other survivors.

WESTERHAVEN HAD WEAPONS and troops aplenty to withstand any assault by Raven's people. They were part of the games submanifold and were never intended to be used on people, but were still potent. It didn't matter. As the hours dragged on, defeat after defeat changed the zones of the compass-sky over Livia's head from green to red. When it became too much and she couldn't watch any more, Livia left the games manifold to find herself sitting in sunlight in a park full of well-manicured shrubs and exuberant flower beds: the Great Library's grounds. The only sounds here were the zizzing of passing bees and the clear-throated song of a skylark.

She remembered then that catastrophe takes its time as much as any ordinary day. Later, memory would erase this moment, leaving only the pain. For now, this place was real. In wonder and emotional exhaustion, she simply stared at the gardens through the trembling air of afternoon.

She was still sitting that way when the founders returned. They were grim-faced and silent. There was no need to explain the situation; Whyte simply gestured and Livia's Society reappeared, now populated with what was left of the peers. All were running or trudging in her direction while behind them Raven's warriors burned the houses and shattered the towers of Barrastea. Survivors of other generations were rallying behind their own exemplars, some to fight, others to flee.

"As you travel you must leave behind one or two people in each manifold," said Lady Ellis as the first aircars of the evacuation flattened the flower beds Livia had been contemplating. "There must be a chain of people capable of getting messages back to us here."

"All right."

"There's one other thing, Livia." She leaned in and spoke quietly—an action Livia had only ever seen in old movies. "If everything fails, you are to make your way to the aerie. Do you know it?" Livia nodded; the aerie was a Westerhaven outpost built into the south wall of the coronal, high in the mountains. It was reachable only by aircar, or from the Cirrus manifold.

"I've sent Aaron Varese there with his team," said the founder. "I don't know what good he can do, but . . . your peers have workshops at the aerie. And it's in the skin of the coronal. That should make it impregnable. If . . . if this catastrophe is everywhere . . . go there."

Livia wanted to know more about Aaron's part in all this, but in the end she simply nodded, watching as her anima shouted and waved, rallying weary fighters near and far. "Come!" it cried. "Form up and tell us your status!"

Her pixies appeared, sporting little military hats. "We've got our orders!" one said, saluting smartly. "Reconnoiter and report!" It waved a tiny map. "This is your path to safety, Livia."

The map, expanded, showed a flight plan in real space as well as circled points that indicated where she should leave each of four charted manifolds. As she was tracing a trembling finger across it, Qiingi came to stand by her. "I have spoken with your founders," he said glumly. "I am of your family now, Livia Kodaly. My home is gone."

She nodded numbly. For a moment she was tongue-tied, so her anima appeared and said briskly, "All right. You're familiar with travel between manifolds, Wordweaver Qiingi. Can you help me shepherd these people to safety?"

"If safety exists." He frowned at the map. "What are these places?"

"Close neighbors of Westerhaven that don't overlap any of Raven's lands. If the ancestors' warriors aren't there, we can use them to stage a counterattack." She let the anima talk; Livia's own attention was on the increasing flood of arriving aircars and running squads of men and women. "Since these places are so close to our own reality, most of the peers should be able to travel to them without difficulty. If we have to go beyond them . . ." The line on the map continued beyond the neighboring manifolds, but the next circle had a question mark next to it.

Qiingi nodded. "Maybe I will be able to help with those places. Some may be similar to Raven's." She heard a trace of wistfulness in his voice.

She stared in an agony of grief at the survivors who now stood or sat about, or wept on one another's shoulders. Some of the wounded floated unconscious in grayish clouds of angel-stuff. If this war was spreading generally, they might all have to flee far from what they knew. She doubted that all of these people would be able to make such a journey; paradoxically, as with Livia and Aaron after the crash, it might be the youngest peers who would have the least difficulty.

A dozen meters away, a young man was walking between the wounded, comforting them. He was covered in dust and blood, his hair matted and his face grim. But he spoke to each injured man or woman himself, not through his anima. Livia felt a flash of admiration for his courage, and shame at herself for hiding behind her agencies. It was Rene, who had run back into the streets after delivering her here, days ago it seemed.

She dismissed her anima and walked over to him. He looked up as she put her hand on his shoulder. "Livia. Did you find Xavier?"

Livia almost burst into tears, but suppressed the anima that offered to take her place in the conversation. "We just barely got out," she managed to say. "The ancestors are in control of Raven's people . . . Have you met Wordweaver Qiingi?"

Rene looked Qiingi up and down angrily. "You invited the monsters in."

Qiingi didn't reply. After a moment Rene broke his gaze and sighed. "What are we doing here?" he asked.

"We need your help," she said. Briefly she outlined the founders' plan to fall back into other manifolds. The fear on Rene's face became sharper as she spoke; finally he shook his head. "I don't understand it," he said. "Why do we have to do something so . . . suicidal? Abandon our homes? Then they've won."

"Westerhaven isn't its geography," she said, trying to make herself believe it was true. "*We* are the manifold, Rene. That's why we have to make sure we're not divided. Going next door is our only option for now. But it doesn't mean we've lost."

"But to 'go next door' as you put it . . . No, Livia, we *will* lose ourselves. To travel at all you have to reject your own manifold and embrace the ways of another. How can we do that and not lose ourselves?"

Others had heard and were gathering around now. She could see the doubt on many faces. In moments they might reject the idea entirely, and then would even the founders be able to rally them?

It was time to play the card she hated the most, and at this moment Livia wished more than anything that she could do so from behind a mask. Let her anima take over for a while. But they would know if she did that and she couldn't have even one person believe that she didn't have faith enough in the plan to support it wholeheartedly.

Livia adjusted her voice to carry to all the peers, including those not yet here. "You know me," she said reluctantly. "I'm one of the famous survivors of the farside crash. I have lived outside of all manifolds and come back to tell about it. I know I haven't spoken much about the crash over the years. But I did learn something; my survival and return are the proof that I learned it." She took a deep breath, wishing that she really believed what she was about to say.

"We think Westerhaven lies in the way we live—in our Societies, our chosen technologies and systems. But when you have all those things stripped away, you find that you're still of Westerhaven. How can that be? It's because all of this," she gestured around herself, "is only the visible manifestation of what Westerhaven really is. It is what we value—about ourselves, each other, and the world. The Societies, the animas and agencies, these are merely how we manifest those values. When we travel we will find equivalents and recreate Westerhaven in other forms. And when we return we will be stronger for it. Believe me. I know, I have the scars and the knowledge to prove it. I came back.

"Follow me. Follow me now, and I will lead you there and I will lead you back again."

Without masks, she stared down the doubters. And for the first time in her life, Livia knew what it was like to truly lie.

7

No ONE COULD see it; inscape was not transmitting from the vicinity of the Great Library. But the news spread quickly throughout Westerhaven: the library was burning.

Livia had walked those halls many times. She had gazed at exotic paintings from manifolds now erased from inscape—portraits of men and women, of places that had once held all the importance in the world to those who lived in them. She had listened to strange music and wondered what sort of mind could think it beautiful. In such a way she had done what her people prized above all else: she had given her respect to those different from herself.

In one contemptuous gesture, all that abundance was being wiped away. The ancestors were treading on the accumulated treasures of the past, blind to the value of those diverse lives lived before theirs. They thought they knew what was real. That confident and terrible belief would only spread with their success. The circle of annihilation would ripple out from Barrastea and swallow all of Teven, if someone didn't stop it.

But it would have to be someone more heroic than Livia. She had done as Lady Ellis had asked—she had led her peers out of their homeland. But after they had arrived here, one of the peers—a youth she barely knew—had come up to Livia and said, his voice quivering with rage, "I guess you've got what you wanted, Kodaly: no more manifolds."

Now, she wandered the edges of a grassy clearing far from Westerhaven, trying to stay unnoticed. It was all she could do to help direct the setting up of tents and tables for the widening flood of Westerhaven refugees; she flinched whenever someone looked her way.

A dozen citizens of the manifold of Oceanus were easing the wounded out of aircars and into the tents. All wore their own faces, and there was no aura of authority around them to indicate social rank. Esther Mannus was profoundly disturbed by that little detail; she'd had trouble reaching Oceanus and now clung to Livia's arm or walked about the clearing twisting her black hair in her fingers.

This space where they had landed was a hundred meters up the slope of a forested island; below, the trees ended in a sandy beach that fronted seemingly endless ocean. The slope continued up, and up, its sides converging with perspective until the "hill" became visible as the attachment point of a giant cable. As the eye tracked it and it rose into the air, breaking from the ground below with waterfalls and trailing snapped strands, it became something impossible, a highway stretching all the way to heaven.

"Forget about looking *around* the people," Livia was telling Esther, "and look *at* them." She could tell who was important by the actions of the people around them. It was a trick Esther would have to learn.

Esther frowned, staring at the Oceanans. "Th—that man, he's the leader?"

"Good, you're getting it." Oceanus was one of the nearest neighbors of Westerhaven, both geographically and in worldview. Still, this manifold was a kind of idealized oceanic paradise whose citizens often lived their whole lives without setting foot on land. Technologically, they prohibited air travel, Societies, and animas, and Esther wasn't the only one having difficulty with the fact. About half the refugees were still clinging to Westerhaven; when Livia flipped her perspective to Oceanus's, these stragglers faded like ghosts.

Oceanus had agreed to host the wounded, but not the healthy gamers-turned-soldiers or any weapon more advanced than swords. The gamers vanished whenever Livia entered Oceanus's realities. Qiingi, on the other hand, loved it here. Water was sacred to him, so the idea that the Oceanans lived entirely on it appealed to him. He was helping dig a latrine at the lower end of the field where the soil was still thick enough; up here it was already thinning, and a few kilometers higher the naked black substance of the cable began to predominate. Once, its surface had been festooned with life all the way up to the clouds; the crash that had traumatized Livia and Aaron had caused the coronal's cables to vibrate like plucked harp strings, and (Livia had heard) a rain of trees and whole hillsides had fallen from them for days. It would take centuries for them to regain their coating of verdure.

Livia had no time to contemplate the view; people kept asking her questions about what to do, where to put things. She was exhausted. The remaining leaders of the peers were away, trying to explain the situation to Oceanus's founders. So far they were being met with complete disbelief. The locals thought Westerhaven had decided to war with Raven, and could not comprehend that this was not an agreed-upon conflict. Invasion was a word that had long ago become a storytelling term here, unattached to reality.

Rene was organizing a makeshift kitchen in the shadow of a giant oak tree. He had adapted quickly to the technological matrix of Oceanus— no, the usual agencies of inscape weren't available; yes, human labor was valued; no, people were not entirely free to choose what kind of labor they performed. Even now he was distributing money cards to bewildered refugees so that they could "pay" for their food, a concept that was giving them a lot of trouble.

Livia herself was bone weary and emotionally drained. All she wanted to do now was find a cot in one of the tents and collapse on it for twelve hours. She was wending her way in that direction when a half-familiar voice said, "Livia Kodaly?"

She turned, expecting one of the peers. A young woman her own age stood several meters away. Her costume was all Oceanus, voluminous and colorful; but she looked familiar.

"Livia, it's me, Alison Haver."

"Alison!" Her face was that of a young adult, but still recognizable as the girl she had been when Livia last saw her—years ago, now. And they had not parted on good terms. Livia hesitated, realized she had no anima here to hide her reactions, and made herself smile. "How are you?" She held out her hand, and Alison shook it.

"So," continued Livia awkwardly, "you live in Oceanus now."

"Yes, I moved . . . a little while after we, uh, broke up." Alison looked down. "It wasn't you—well, not just you. I decided Westerhaven wasn't for me. The masks, the deceptions . . ."

Livia winced. For some time after her rescue from the crash, Livia had plunged herself into the shifting perspectives of adolescence. She had tried on different roles and identities, often presenting herself as several people at once at social gatherings. At one of these Alison had met a male persona of Livia's, and the two had hit it off. In her need to explore, Livia had let the relationship go on too long; Alison had fallen for the man she thought lay behind the mask. When she finally learned the truth she was devastated—not by the fact that her beloved was actually female, but because of the deception. After the painful evening when Livia revealed her true nature, she never saw Alison again. Livia had believed that Alison still lived in Westerhaven, maybe even next door, and had simply edited herself out of Livia's Society. It was a blow to think that Livia might have driven her out of Westerhaven entirely.

"It's good to see you," said Alison. "Hey, if you need a native guide, just call on me any time."

"Thanks," she said, genuinely grateful. "But I'm not sure we're going to be staying here long."

Alison nodded. "I understand. You want this war over right away. There's some people I know who might be able to help."

Livia shook her head in frustrated anger. "The peers are talking to your founders, I mean government, now. There's nothing more we could . . ."

"This is somebody else. Don't think about it now. Get some rest! You look like you're going to collapse right here. I'll come by tomorrow morning and we'll talk about stuff, how's that?"

The mention of rest made Livia aware that she was, quite literally, swaying on her feet. "Yes. Find me in the morning," she said. Then she stumbled away to her tent, sparing no time to wonder at this strange meeting.

THE HOUR BEFORE dawn was cold and scented with ocean spray. For some reason, the opening bars of "The Thieving Magpie" kept running through Livia's head. She huddled under her blankets for a long time before venturing out; it was a shame this manifold was not one of those that permitted personal climate control. When she finally climbed out of her cot, she avoided anything more than polite hellos to the others who were up. Instead, she walked away from the tent to watch the dawn.

The lands to the east had been bright with sunlight for an hour now. The line of lit terrain rolled down toward Livia, apparently faster and faster. The moment that line crossed you was always startling. A vast wave of sunlit air leapt forward, clouds catching fire under it in flickers of purest blinding white. Livia looked straight up in time to see two narrow lines of brilliance appear at the zenith. In seconds they burgeoned into twin suns: one the ancient sun of humanity, the other a local starlette called Miranda. Of the two, Miranda was by far the brighter.

Now the lands shone in full daylit glory. To the east they swept away and up, forests, plains of gold and green, glittering brooks and lakes merging together in the distance into a white haze. Beyond that, seemingly at infinity, a vast sweeping spire was etched on the sky itself: half of an arch bigger than the world, its surface painted with clouds and land that rose to the zenith and vanished behind the suns. Continuing the circle, its distorted reflection curved back down the western sky and disappeared in the dark hazy quarters where night still reigned.

Livia strapped on her sword, visited Qiingi's new outhouse, then stalked through tall wet grass to the mess tent. Taking her plate with her she retreated to an upthrust of broken cable material in the corner of the clearing and sat down to eat. In the distance, a knot of white sails dotted the horizon—an Oceanan floating town.

She was sitting hunched over her breakfast, heedless of the evaporating dew scenting the air, when inscape chimed. She flinched. The last thing she wanted to do right now was confront her Society, with its terrible gaps. But duty demanded it. She took a deep breath and let the call come through.

Aaron Varese appeared before her—in projected form, not as an anima. Livia blew out her held breath. "Aaron! You're . . . Where have you been? I've been trying to find you for days. What—where . . ." *Why did you abandon me?*

His projection sat on the log next to Livia. "I know," it said. "I'm sorry I didn't warn you. I tried to call you when the attack started, but things were too crazy in the Societies."

"I heard you escaped—well, that you were never in Barrastea," she said. "Maren Ellis told me."

He nodded. "A group of us have been working at the aerie for a while now. Are you coming here?"

"I don't know yet." She was happy that he'd escaped the battle, but couldn't hide her anger all the same. Once, she and Aaron had been inseparable. She'd felt she need never keep anything from this young man who had seen the things she had seen, including Livia scrabbling like an animal to survive in the ruined lands of Teven's far side. Now he was keeping secrets from her.

"But what are you doing up there?" she asked him. "And why the secrecy? You left my Society!"

He looked uncomfortable. "It was the founders. They asked us to keep it secret. At the time, I thought it was because we were playing around with technologies that went against the tech locks. Now, I'm starting to wonder if there wasn't more going on."

"What do you mean?"

"It started," he said, "with an invitation from Lady Ellis."

THREE WEEKS AGO, Ellis had asked Aaron to visit her at the aerie. He had never spoken to any of the founders before, and had eagerly agreed. "I tried to tell you that afternoon," he insisted, "but Ellis's agents blocked me. Whatever I said to you, they'd intervene and change the words. It was . . . frightening, the power they had." Intrigued, but more than a little confused, he had flown out to the Southwall mountains to meet the founder.

"You are to take credit for what we are about to do," Ellis had told him. Aaron told Livia that the founder had reinforced this by later wiping the record of their conversation from inscape. He hadn't known that was possible, but Aaron had always suspected that the creators of the tech locks had resources they kept hidden from their descendants.

"It's right up your alley," Ellis said as they walked along a rocky path at the foot of one of the Cirrus glaciers. Below them, past mountain slopes and broken peaks, Teven Coronal spread out like an ocean of cloud and detail; above, huge cables formed a horizontal grid across the sky.

"Explain," he'd said, putting his back to a rain-slick slab of black rock. "You're somehow opposed to the peers' city project?"

"Not opposed to it," she said carefully. "We want your generation's ambitions to go forward. The city is a worthy project. No, you can view this as a . . . complementary activity."

"So what do you want us to do?" She had contacted some twenty other peers, apparently—choosing those who'd opposed the city project.

Ellis gazed out over the coronal; in profile, she looked very like the young goddess many of the peers grudgingly imagined her to be. "It's pretty simple," she said. "I want you to reinvent science."

Aaron barked a laugh, but she didn't join in. His smile died, replaced by a quizzical frown. "Science was completed centuries ago," he said. "We know it all."

"You *know* nothing," she said dismissively. "Despite the fact that you benefit from the knowledge. It's the AIs of inscape, and the system of the tech locks that know. You only know the broadest outlines of natural science, because your generation doesn't need to know more. You benefit from it without understanding it. But even the application of that knowledge—what it allows you to *do*—is disguised in one way or another by every manifold in Teven. Your generation doesn't learn science, and the locks have hidden much technical knowledge from you."

None of this came as any surprise; long-range radio was impossible in any manifold Aaron knew of. So was space travel, and astronomy was almost impossible because the Lethe Nebula blocked so much of the sky. "Let me get this straight," he said. "We deliberately forget some things in order to create the culture we want to live in; then you, who did this in the first place, tell me you want us to open those books again?"

She shook her head. "We don't want to recover old ideas. Science embodied in a device or object is pure. Science written down and interpreted by humans always comes with historical and ideological baggage. We created the manifolds so you could jettison that baggage whenever you wanted."

"But if all of scientific knowledge is embedded in the tech locks anyway—if we could get it out without violating their programming, we could just ask them for it."

She shook her head. "We want you to *rediscover* it. Reinvent it. Make it yours. Do the experiments. Theorize. Build the missing parts of the edifice again, and put your stamp on them." He remembered her eyes shining as she said this. "We wiped the slate clean when we came here, so that we could start anew. That always included the history of science as well as culture. We're ready, Aaron—that's the point. Westerhaven is confident, full-blooded, and unique. So are some of the other manifolds. We can do this now without falling under the shadow of long-dead thinkers and their belief systems. We can have an utterly Westerhaven science."

He got it then, and the idea flooded him like a benediction. This was something he could do, something worthy of all the restless energy and passion that he'd wasted so long on petty intrigues and face-saving.

Maybe it didn't matter that Ellis had wiped the record of this conversation; Aaron remembered its every detail with electric clarity anyway.

"*THAT'S* WHAT YOU'VE been doing?" Livia asked angrily. "Reinventing things?" On another day it might have seemed a very Westerhaven thing to do. Now, the whole escapade looked trivial and foolish. "Even while Barrastea burned?"

He winced, but held his ground. "I know how it looks, in the face of what's been happening. Unless you look at where Ellis wanted us to start."

"What do you mean?"

"I'll show you: come here." He stood up and held out his hand. Livia took it, and with a shimmer of transition, found her virtual self standing elsewhere.

This place was something like a half-cave hewn out of the side of a mountain, huge, cold, and echoing. The mouth of the cave was closed by a single sheet of cleanly transparent glass or diamond. Outside that vast window was a broad ledge of white metal, and beyond that nothing but an abyss of stars.

The floor of the half-cave was cluttered with lathes, cabinets, and work benches. The place was also crowded with people—and when Livia saw them, she felt a knot in her stomach unwind. "They're alive!"

Many of the peers whose names had appeared on the rolls of the missing were walking and talking here. At least six of Jachman's friends, supposedly staunch advocates of the city project, were physically present. Several were enthusiastically working on what looked like a half-finished boat, planing away at the wood while slinging fragments of ribald poetry back and forth. One saluted Livia.

"So now you know," said Aaron. "I haven't been idle, and I haven't been neglecting the peers. Quite the contrary—you've walked in on something of a conspiracy." He smiled at her undisguised look of astonishment.

"But what are you doing here? What could possibly have been so important that you—that these people weren't there to defend the city? The city, that's now *burning*—" She couldn't go on, but just stood there glaring at him.

Gently but firmly, Aaron took her arm and led her to the huge curving diamond window. "We were under orders from the founders. Maren Ellis commanded us to try something that the tech locks have always forbidden. And we were succeeding. When Raven attacked we were all here, and nobody had time to organize a return to the city before air travel became unsafe."

Something glowed under starlight on the broad metal shelf beyond the window. The shelf must have been fifty meters deep, and against that the barrel-shaped thing looked small. "Is that what you were working on?"

He grinned proudly. "Yes. It's something, Livia, that we cast away over our horizon centuries ago. Something that's been impossible for any manifold for a very long time. It's a device for traveling in space."

She stared at the thing. It looked like a wine cask. Whatever it was, that unobtrusive little object should have been as impossible in Westerhaven as flying craft had been for Raven's people. "How . . . ?"

"I wouldn't have even thought of trying it if Ellis hadn't insisted. I wanted to start by relearning the theory behind the mind-AI interface of inscape. But she insisted that wouldn't work. We had to rethink key technologies in Westerhaven terms, imagine how they could serve our values rather than change us. So the tech locks would ignore them, see? So up here, over the past few weeks, we succeeded in broadening our horizons to the point where we can build things like this.

"We tried various designs before I hit on this one," he continued when she didn't respond. "The locks won't allow anyone to build any of the old space traveling designs because they all require an industrial culture that we don't want. So how do you preserve the technological mix of your own manifold, and still end up with a device to travel between worlds?"

"Is that . . . wood?"

"It is indeed. Sealed with lacquer against the vacuum, of course." The barrel she was looking at wasn't big enough to hold humans. When she pointed this out, he admitted that nobody had taken that step yet.

"But what does it do?"

Aaron crossed his arms and stared at the black sky behind the barrel. "It goes away, and it comes back. So far, that's all. But that's a lot." He turned, and she saw he was frowning. "Though it seems a strange coincidence to me that Lady Ellis should have come to us asking for such a thing, just before these so-called ancestors arrived."

"You think they're not from Teven?" she said jokingly. "And that she knew?"

He shook his head. "I have no idea, actually. But listen, you need to come here, Livia. It's not safe down there."

"Nowhere is safe," she said. "And I have people to look after down here." She was seething with anger at him for abandoning her in favor of this ridiculous project. "Look, I have to go. But . . . I'm glad you called. It's good to know you're okay."

"Look, I'm sorry I couldn't . . ." He saw the look on her face and shrugged. "Come to us," was all he said. Then the vision dissolved and Livia was back amidst grass and morning dew.

PEOPLE WERE TALKING a few meters away; two of the peers were walking through the field. Livia started to hurry away; now was not a time when she wanted to play fearless leader to anyone.

"Ms. Kodaly?" She hunched her shoulders, turned and smiled, still backing away. One of the men stared; the other smiled and, still smiling, steered his companion away from her. For the moment, Livia couldn't care less what she looked like. Just as long as they left her alone.

"Livia!"

Alison was waving to her from across the beaten-down grass. Relieved at the distraction, Livia walked over to her. She took a deep breath and forced her face into a carefree expression.

"Good morning!" Alison looked fresh and untroubled, as if nothing terrible were happening. For her, nothing probably was. "Remember when I said I might know some people who could help? Well, they've agreed to meet with you—only you, though, since they have my opinion of you to go on. Can you come now? Or do you have duties?"

"No, I've got nothing today," she said. "This is good news, Alison. Thank you." She felt a flood of relief—though she wasn't sure whether it was at the possibility of help for her people, or because Alison offered a chance to escape the camp for a while. People looked at her like she was some kind of leader now. Visiting with a lost friend who awakened awkward memories seemed a small price to avoid being singled out that way again.

The mess tent was a strange mix of despondent and exhilarated people. Some of the peers had woken today to find new strength in themselves. Some just wanted to go home. The tensions were spilling into argument, but so far no duels had broken out.

After a tense meal Alison led Livia down a path to the shallow sea. On the beach was a beautiful little sailboat. "It's about a half-hour trip," she said as they climbed in. "Oceanans refuse to hurry anything; it's an important part of our life. Anyway, you and I can use the time to catch up on gossip." They pushed off from the shore and bobbed out into a light breeze.

As it turned out, Alison had maintained many ties to Westerhaven after she left. For the first few years her absence had not been geographic: she had continued to live in her parents' house while inhabiting a different manifold. She came and went as she pleased, but gradually gave more and more of her time to Oceanus. Finally she had moved there physically to be with a new lover. His name was Cam and he was, according to her, perfect.

Livia watched the giant cable becoming smaller and increasingly two-dimensional in the mist-blued air. Instead of the grand estates of Westerhaven, she saw yachts and giant three-masted schooners on the horizon. Alison talked quietly about the values of Oceanus, and gradually Livia drifted into a reverie, thinking how you'd have to feel to measure your days by the breezes and currents of water. As she often did, Livia turned to music to help her imagine her way into Oceanus. Dreaming a slow pavane, with Alison's guidance she began to see across the bright lapping waves the distant sails of a vast seafaring civilization. Oceanus beckoned.

So this was how it felt to live outside of time; Oceanus seemed like a refuge from every possible worry. It was clear why Alison loved it here. For the first time in two days, Livia felt the knot of fear and anger inside her loosen a bit. She could even begin to forget her disconcerting discovery of where Aaron had been all this time.

The hills and forests of Teven had faded away, leaving only dappled waves extending to infinity in every direction. For all Livia knew, she and Alison could be completely alone on an endless, placid sea.

Eventually she realized they were arriving somewhere: a yacht bobbed in the green water, its sails furled and its anchor down. She could see no one on deck, but a number of boats, ranging from sailboats like Alison's to kayaks, were moored at its stern.

As Alison tied up the sailboat, Livia climbed up the yacht's side. She spotted a covered deck beyond the wheelhouse. Someone sat in a wicker chair there, sipping a drink. Without waiting for Alison, she walked over, feeling the deck sway subtly under her.

Lucius Xavier squinted up at her from a deck chair. "Livia! I'm glad you made it okay. Please, have a seat."

She stopped dead in surprise; after a moment of paralysis she realized what he had just said, and warily sat opposite him. Alison didn't approach, but instead went into the wheelhouse, emerging with a tray. She put a glass of lemonade in front of Livia then retreated again. Livia stared at the glass.

This was one of those times when it would have been good to hide behind masks and animas. But Livia had not failed to learn from years of Westerhaven intrigue. Imitating one of her own animas, she smiled graciously and sipped the drink. In moments she had recovered her poise enough to say, "How are you, Lucius?"

He looked careworn. "I'm as good as can be expected, under the circumstances. I hear you led the peers out of the holocaust. Very well done."

"We would have done better if you'd been with us."

He nodded, looking tired. "I know. I'm sorry that wasn't possible. But I've been working very hard . . . behind the scenes, shall we say."

So far behind the scenes that not even the founders had known what he was up to? Or had Ellis known? She made herself nod encouragingly. "You knew about these ancestors before the potlatch?"

He scowled. "Yes, I knew about them. I'm working with the Oceanans on a plan to counterattack them. Anyway, 'ancestors' is just Raven's name for the invaders. They themselves say they're followers of *thirty-three forty*. A leader with a number, not a name. Interesting, no? And I'm pretty sure that this 3340, wherever it is, is not on Teven Coronal."

They have found us. Could it be that Aaron's preposterous notion of invaders from another world was true? No one had left Teven Coronal in Livia's lifetime. No one, she had always believed, had ever visited from anywhere else either. And yet, Maren Ellis had initiated a secret project to study such travel, only weeks ago.

Livia covered her amazement with a casual nod, which made Lucius smile. "You're not surprised, are you?" he said. "You understand, then, what's happening."

"Not really," she said. "I know our way of life is being destroyed. But I don't understand by whom, or why."

"I know parts of it," he said. "I know 3340's followers are from offworld. I know they're human. And I also know they aren't all-powerful.

Their technology isn't any better than ours, they've just caught us napping. We can beat them, Livia, if we strike right away. That's what I'm here to do: organize the counterattack."

She brooded on that. He seemed eager to talk, and there was all manner of ways she could steer her line of questions. It might be best to keep him off balance.

"Lucius, have you ever heard of something called an *anecliptic*?" she asked.

His eyes narrowed, and he took a sip of his lemonade while staring off into the distance. "Sure," he said grudgingly. "I know of them. They're the creatures that built this world, Livia—and all the worlds you see when you look up at night."

"I was taught that *we* built Teven Coronal."

"You were taught that, yes." He smiled at her expression. "You were taught a great many truths that are only Westerhaven truths—not truths anywhere else. But I thought you knew that. I thought the shadow-play of half-true stories we call our history annoyed you as much as it does me."

"So what are these anecliptics?" she pressed. "Are they this 3340? Or is it something else?"

"They're not important. They built this world and a number of others and then abandoned them. As far as the rest of the solar system is concerned, this place," he gestured grandly, "is part of something known as the Fallow Lands. The anecliptics have forbidden anyone to come here. Some say that the founders made a pact with them hundreds of years ago; but I think the founders snuck in. They wanted to be free of any outside control including the anecliptics. Livia, I don't think the anecliptics even know that you and I *exist*. And they have nothing to do with 3340. We'll get no help from that quarter."

She sat back, struggling through the possibilities. Had Lady Ellis deliberately dropped the name of the anecliptics in her conversation with Livia the other day? But why, if Lucius was right and they were irrelevant? Wheels within wheels, she thought dazedly.

With difficulty she brought her thoughts back to the matter at hand. "If this 3340 isn't superior to us, how is it that the ancestors have destroyed Raven's people and Westerhaven?"

Lucius nodded somberly. "Because they know something we don't," he said. "Oh, not technologically; they have an edge here and there, and they leverage the vulnerabilities of whatever technology set they're faced with. A manifold is just a specific set of technologies. You can't have speedy ground cars without highways to run them on—the one technology demands the other. A complete collection of technologies defines a way of life: a manifold. And what's a technology? It's a *value*. If you fly, it is because you don't want to walk: to fly is to make a value judgment.

"Inscape is a values-driven interface to technology-sets. So, to travel between manifolds is to suspend or abandon your values. You and I, Livia, are good at traveling, because we can both suspend our judgments . . . because in the end, neither of us *believes* in anything. Which is what you've never accepted about yourself."

She bridled. "We're talking about 3340 here, not me."

"But you see, 3340 realized something very similar—it realized that each manifold represents a set of ideals. And to break that manifold, all you have to do is push its ruling ideals to the point where they contradict themselves. To the point where they turn into their opposite."

She thought about what Qiingi had told her—how the ancestors had played on the prejudices of the elders and warriors, convincing them that it was their destiny to conquer other manifolds. While at the same time, Westerhaven had reached out more and more to neighboring manifolds, proselytizing through people like Lucius . . . and Livia.

"Thirty-three forty's agents are everywhere in the Coronal," said Lucius. "They manifest differently in every manifold, but what they do is essentially the same. They can't control inscape directly, so they play on the ruling ideals of the manifold. They push those ideals until they disintegrate. With Raven, the logical consequence of wanting to conquer other manifolds is that you open yourself to all of them so that you can reach them all. For Westerhaven, the logical result of reaching out to other manifolds is that you accept them all in. At a certain point the change goes far enough that 3340's people can reveal themselves and apply their technical know-how to dissolve the boundaries between the manifolds entirely. The same scenario is playing out everywhere across Teven. There is no escaping it."

"You know that Oceanus wants to help Westerhaven," she said slowly. "If you're right, then the very act of trying to do that will collapse the horizon between them and us . . . You're working for them, aren't you?" The realization burst on her as she spoke. "They're pushing the manifolds against each other. To fight your neighbor you have to collapse your horizon; to ally with somebody is to collapse the differences between you and them. Anything you do is playing into 3340's hands. And to cut yourself off entirely . . ."

". . . Is merely to postpone the inevitable." He nodded. "You understand—but then you would. Unlike your countrymen, but like me, you believe in nothing. And that makes you strong, Livia, a potential survivor of this catastrophe."

"Why did you change your mind?—about taking me with you, back in Skaalitch?"

He shook his head glumly. "They wouldn't let me bring you over. They didn't trust you yet."

There was a brief silence. "How long have you known?" she asked at last.

Lucius leaned forward, clasping his hands and looking serious. "Six years. I met them a year after the crash that had you living half wild in the bush for so long. But you have to believe I'm telling the truth when I say I am trying to find a way to counterattack them. When they first appeared I recognized them immediately for what they were: the advance scouts of an invading army. At first I thought I should go to the founders with what I knew, but when I learned just how far 3340 had spread before I discovered it . . . Livia, there was no point. This wasn't a war we could win. And if you can't win, the alternative is to negotiate the best capitulation you can. And then fight them from within."

She opened her mouth to say something sharp, but caution kept her silent. This ocean was their place, then; all of Oceanus already was. And that being the case . . . "I don't see what you have to gain by talking to me," she said, puzzled. "If your 3340 has already won."

"It's not *mine,*" he said angrily. "You're here because you have a talent we can use against it. I'm offering you a chance to escape the coming troubles; I can shield you from the changes. Your abilities could be crucial in the counterstruggle."

Livia remembered Qiingi telling her that Kale had made a similar offer to him. Had she not known that, she might have believed Lucius. He had never looked more sincere.

She shook her head. "You call believing in nothing . . . a talent?"

"Absolutely. And you can use that talent to help your people. And, meanwhile, to thrive once all the horizons are down. Or . . ."

"Or what?" She kept expecting the conversation to steer back in an innocuous direction. Shouldn't his or her animas be taking over, smoothing things, preventing the distress she felt building up to an intolerable state?

"You go back to Westerhaven without my protection. In that case, you can't leave, or change your realities anymore. Like all your people. That's the deal."

She stood up. "I'm afraid I have to be going."

"That would be a bad decision," he said. Behind him, Alison bit her lip nervously. "We separated the other leaders from your peers on the pretext of negotiating with Oceanus's founders," Lucius continued. "Your people are isolated and vulnerable now—but they're safe as long as they don't know that Oceanus has been subverted. Livia, I'm not going to use force to keep you here; treat that as a gesture of sincerity on my part. You can go back to the camp if you want, or you can stay and learn from us. But if you go back, you should know the consequences. We can't let the others know what you know."

"You'll do what? Imprison me? Kill me?"

He laughed. "No—you're the valuable one, not them. No, we'll imprison *them*. Or kill them. Now sit down."

She ran around the table. Alison stepped in between Livia and the corner of the wheelhouse. "Out of my way!" Livia shouted.

"Livia, listen, forget about Westerhaven, it's you and I—"

As Lucius made to stand she overturned the table on him. He fell backwards against the ship's rail. Livia shoved Alison out of the way and ran around the wheelhouse.

"Livia, please!" shouted Alison.

"Why are you so angry?" shouted Lucius. "Ask yourself that! I know you, Livia. I know what drives you. Westerhaven was too small for you and we both know it!"

Livia clambered into the seat of one of the kayaks and threw off its anchor rope. The distant shoreline had reappeared, even as the distant sails of Oceanus faded. She would not be able to return there, she knew.

She put all her strength into the paddles, nearly capsizing in her haste to get away.

LIVIA BEACHED THE kayak at the base of the cable. When she stepped onto the sand, she found she could barely lift her arms from the effort of paddling this distance. She was shaking. She had the sick feeling that something terrible was happening in her absence.

There were many fresh footprints in the sand. She ran heedlessly up the hillside, willing herself to act in order not to think.

The forest was deep and she had to pick her way over ancient moss-covered logs and around thick brambles. Tangled as it was, there was no need to call up an inscape compass; though there was no way to tell direction from the permanently vertical sunlight, she could not mistake the way to the clearing. Just follow the sound of screaming and the music of war.

It was only a kilometer, but it took her nearly an hour to fight her way through the thick undergrowth to the edge of the clearing. By the time the last bushes gave way to reveal the field, all was silent.

She stood panting, legs and torso scratched and bleeding, sword in hand; but there was no one to fight. The aircars were gone, the tents overthrown, and the grass trampled everywhere, bloody in places. There were no bodies.

Lucius had been true to his word. She shouldn't have run. The peers were gone, and it was her fault.

8

FOR A WHILE Livia was too devastated to even think. She just stood in the bright sunlight and stared about at the results of her decision to run. Eventually she realized she was an easy target here and stepped back into the trees, leaning against one as if the world were tilting out of control.

She was lost in a hostile manifold, alone and probably hunted. She didn't dare ask her Society for help, because she no longer trusted the AIs that controlled the animas. Also, she didn't want to see how many of her friends and family were now missing from it.

Reflexively, she did the automatic thing her upbringing had conditioned her to do when at a loss: she ran some sims.

While they were going she skirted the clearing, looking for any signs of other survivors. When she finally summoned the courage to step into the field, she found only human footprints. Raven's mythological beasts had not been present. So, the attackers were almost certainly gamers from Oceanus—probably tricked into thinking this attack was some new simulation.

In the ruins of the mess tent she found some ant-covered bread and cheese. She ate while huddling under the one upright corner of the tent. After a while her sims signaled their completion.

The results were not good. She watched herself call up her Society— and immediately be found by 3340. The sims couldn't give her probabilities of escape. She watched herself head out to sea, there to be scooped up by a ship loaded with troops; or confronted by Alison, maybe winning the subsequent fight or maybe not.

She could paddle back to the mainland; but it would take her days to get back home, and then what would she do? Westerhaven was lost.

The hopeless permutations went on and on, until she dismissed them all. She walked out into the center of the field, and sat down in the sunlight.

She was only one person. Maybe it was time to give up.

. . .

IN THE MONTHS after their rescue, Aaron had started acting strangely—taking chances, going on adventures that were uncharacteristic of him. Once, he took a bet to skydive from one of the Teven side cables. A group of unruly peers including Livia had flown alongside one of the great upsweeping behemoths. The peers had landed their aircars ten kilometers up its length where the air began to fail and took ground cars up switchback trails another two kilometers. In the dizzy air high above the mountains they had gotten into their parachutes while perched on platforms welded to the slope of the now-bare cable. Far below, it entered the ground alongside dozens of others that curved away to left and right. Above, it vanished into haze high above the mountains. Hundreds of smaller cables hung off it or stretched away like vast open nets into the distance: the abodes of the Cirrus manifold. Tiny flying specks were all that could be seen of the people who lived there.

Aaron let Livia—only her—ride his sensorium on the way down, and she felt the terror of the drop with him as he stepped into space, falling without air resistance at first. All was silent for that first part of the fall save for the sound of Aaron's breath, which felt like it was heaving in Livia's own chest. She remembered the stiffness of the drop suit and the giddiness of the long fall, as the imperceptible glide through half-vacuum became an increasing rush through heating air. At first the Coriolis effect meant Aaron was falling almost sideways rather than down and he sailed away from Westerhaven, over strange countries and oceans like a bird. As the whisper of air became a violent roar, the swirls of white and mottled green below became cloud and sea filigreed with shorelines, then visibly hills and forests waiting to catch him.

Aaron went into a spin and blacked out long before his chute opened. When his sensorium went dark Livia switched to the view of one of his angels, which paced him a kilometer away. Slowed now by the air, he fell limply, as though exhausted of meaning, and somehow that moment summed up everything about him since the crash. She wept even as his chute opened and he glided toward the silver-touched barley fields that were his target. Naturally he was awake again by the time he reached them and when he staggered to his feet and his Society coalesced, cheering, around him, he laughed as proudly and confidently as ever. Livia smiled as she greeted him, too, though her eyes ached from remembered tears.

That was the beginning of their estrangement. It was also the day when she had realized that, on some level, she had been thinking about whether to give up and *stop,* like the other survivors had before their rescue. And she had realized that she didn't want to—no matter how far she had to fall.

AN INDETERMINATE AMOUNT of time had passed when Livia stood up again. Somehow, in the depths of her despair, something had kept nagging at her. There was something the sims hadn't revealed; she felt it must be obvious, but what was it? For a while she stared around at the ruined landscape, wondering what was hidden in plain sight. There was nothing—and that, of course, was it.

She had looked at the field from within Oceanus, and through Westerhaven eyes. There was no trace of the fearsome beasts from Raven; that suggested that the battle had happened within Oceanus only. And that in turn meant that, at least so far, Oceanus had still not had its horizons collapsed by 3340. Certainly they had been up yesterday, when the refugees from Westerhaven first arrived—otherwise the peers' military equipment wouldn't have vanished when they entered Oceanus.

During the fight here, the Oceanans could easily follow anyone who tried to flee back into Westerhaven. The manifolds were close; Alison had lived with a foot in each, after all. But might there be other places here—places that a warrior of Raven might find, but not a soldier of Oceanus?

Livia tore her gaze away from the trampled, bloody grass. She tried to remember how Raven's people saw things. The grass was not merely grass, it was a gift of Ometeotl. This clearing, it wasn't random, it was a place with some significance, even if that meaning wasn't apparent to human eyes.

She faced the forest and opened her senses to it—feeling the warmth of the air, scenting the grass. You traveled between manifolds by *caring;* could she find the values of some nearby manifold that was like Raven's? It would be tricky, because she might merely summon up the ghahlanda or qqatxhana of Raven itself. The task here was to reject both the social whirl of Westerhaven and the animism of Raven. To look for something new.

She stood, arms raised to the sunlight, and opened herself to the possibilities. And, after a while, she saw something new under the leaves of the forest. It wavered in and out of existence, fading when she worried about the terrible things she was running from, solidifying when, for a second or two at a time, she simply admired its colors.

To travel there she would have to abandon the distress she was feeling. For a long time she couldn't do it; then in one moment she sighed, let it all go, and was there.

The gateposts were tall and candy-striped in red and white. They held up an arching sign that said BLOCKWORLD. The gate was closed by fili-greed gold bars. Livia walked up to it, looked past the gleaming gold, and looked again. Past the gate, the sky seemed, well, mauve. And the clouds were big rounded affairs, all their detail stripped off, more like clusters of balloons.

She blinked and stepped back. Then she noticed something hanging from the rightmost gate pillar. It was an ornately framed mirror with let-tering under it. She went over to it.

CHOOSE AN AVATAR TO ENTER said the sign under the mirror. She looked up at her own reflection.

She seemed wild-eyed and haggard—and as she thought this, her re-flection's eyes widened even more, impossibly more, while her pupils shrank into little dots. She was so surprised she laughed. This just made her reflections' teeth pop all over the place like mushrooming skyscrap-ers, and as she blinked and tried to figure out what she was seeing, Livia found her mirrored self had turned into a cartoon version of her. She had huge buck teeth, her hair was a sweeping wave that plummeted past her big saillike ears, and her body had been reduced to a sketch, except for the outlandishly big hands and feet. The apparition would have looked funny in other circumstances; now, though, it seemed bizarre and threat-ening. She felt her anxiety returning, but by now the manifold seemed to have stabilized.

There was a tinkling click and the big gold gate swung open. Without hesitation she ran through.

The forest where she had stood moments ago was gone. Livia looked around herself, and nearly fell down. Distance was seriously distorted everywhere she looked. Also, the whole landscape was rendered in fluo-rescent primary colors. She had to sit down on the road and stare at the ground in front of her to keep from becoming sick.

It was all simplified, that was it. The dirt was a single seamless sub-stance, with a simple texture and one color, brown. She reached out to touch it, and felt dirt—but her brain wasn't allowing any variation to it, no pebbles, no fines. It was just . . . dirt.

When her head stopped spinning Livia looked up. Now it was obvious what was going on here. The grass with its wildflowers and the rolling hills were all simplified as well. Some things were nearby—like the grass on either side of the road and the road itself—while some were in the middle distance, and some were far away. Her eye was telling her that there were only three possibilities: near, middle, and far. The clouds over-head were *far,* all equally far, just like the distant hills and mountains.

She stood up and walked up the road, taking in the strangely simplified landscape. She had definitely escaped Oceanus; the question was, had anyone else?

It came as no real surprise when she spied a strange figure approaching her from the middle distance. It was hopping. By this time Livia had begun spotting all sorts of detail. The skies were full of gamboling birds. There were jaunty trees here and there with friendly faces plastered on their trunks. They smiled and winked at her as she passed; the feeling of friendly surveillance gave her the creeps.

So the fact that she was being approached by a giant rabbit seemed perfectly consistent with the rest of the place. The rabbit was a pale pink, with three-fingered hands and giant, bent-over ears. Something subtle about its face suggested it was male. It—he—approached in big bounding hops, each one accompanied by a ridiculous *boing*ing sound. He touched down in front of Livia, bounced a bit, then said, "You're new!" in an appropriately big-rabbitish voice.

Livia said, "My name is Livia Kodaly, of Westerhaven manifold. I'm looking for some friends of mine . . ." She didn't finish because what she'd said wasn't what she heard coming out of her own mouth. She heard: "Hi! I'm Livia. Will you be my friend?"

"Okay!" said the rabbit. "I'm Bounder. It's my own name and I chose it myself. I'm going to Centertown. Do ya wanna come?"

"All right," she said, which translated as an enthusiastic "Sure!" Bounder set off, each of his hops apparently covering a dozen meters or more. Livia found she could keep up with him by simply strolling. Movement here was simple: head in the direction of something that was in the middle distance, and *pop*, it became part of the near distance. The disturbing implication was that nothing in Blockworld was more than a few steps away from anything else.

"What do you mean, you chose your name?" she asked Bounder. He didn't answer; instead, a pair of absurdly blue birds spiraled down from above, one landing on each of Livia's simplified shoulders.

"Bounder was born William Mackenzie Casterman," peeped one. "He is forty-six years old," added the other.

"Why . . . uh, why is he pretending to be a rabbit?" she asked the bird-shaped agents.

"He isn't," said one agent.

"Pretending," said the other. "He understands bunnies. He thinks bunnies are people and he feels like a rabbit.

"It's quite simple, really. William was born with subnormal neural processes. You are going to ask why he was not fixed. It is because his parents live in one of the lower-technology manifolds. Their culture does not permit meddling in natural events such as childbirth."

"So they sent William here?" It seemed barbaric.

"William's parents loved him. They were happy to rear him regardless of his mental capacity. Unfortunately he proved to be highly accident-prone. One day he wandered past a river in flood and was caught in it. William's parents believe he died in the flood."

She nodded slowly. "He fell in the water . . . and when he woke up, he was here."

"It was his wish. Despite his love for his family, William wanted to find a place where he fit in. Falling in the river was half deliberate."

Doubtless William had angels. Those entities would have known him better than anyone; better than his parents, probably. They, of all his friends, would have known best what William really wanted.

"William undertook a marvelous journey," said the bird. "He saw many fabulous things. At the end of the journey, he finally came . . . home."

A town that was in the far distance had popped into the middle distance. Bounder pointed. "See?" he said. "Centertown! Come on!" He redoubled his speed.

"Bounder, wait!" He stopped, looked back inquisitively. All kinds of questions were crowding in Livia's mind, but they all involved big words and she realized that big words might be a problem for William Macken-zie Casterman.

"I'm looking for a pal of mine," she said finally. That statement went through without any editing. Encouraged, she said, "He's called Qiingi. Have you seen him?"

"Qiingi!" shouted Bounder. "My pal Qiingi! Come on, I'll take you!" Without another word he hopped away to the left, and Centertown became far again.

SHE FOUND QIINGI and fifteen peers sitting under a giant, perfect oak tree in a stylized grove. They all looked strange, some like child versions of themselves, some animals or fabulous beasts. Qiingi was an animated wooden Indian. She ran and embraced him.

"Livia! We thought you'd been taken like the others."

"No, no . . ." She told them of her meeting with Lucius—slowly and haltingly, because Blockworld kept changing and simplifying her language (instead of "bastards" it had her say "bad guys"). She finally managed to get the chain of events across. "Lucius told me if I didn't stay with him they would attack"—which became "beat up on"—"the camp.

I didn't believe him," she finished. She found she was trembling, whether from relief at finding her people, or anger at Lucius's betrayal, she couldn't tell.

They were all that was left of Westerhaven; they comforted her as best they could until she steadied. Wiping her eyes, she looked around at the stylized landscape. "Qiingi, what is this place?"

He half smiled. "It seems to be a refuge for people with hurt *xhants*. Your friend Esther found it."

Esther was the last person Livia would have credited with the ability to travel. Yet, here she was, appearing as a tiny girl in a canary-yellow dress.

"Esther! How did you do it?"

"It's just like a place we have in Westerhaven," she said with a shy laugh. "Sometimes babies are born wrong, and sometimes their parents choose not to have them fixed. Then places like this are made for them. Adults have a hard time coming here at all, and if they do they arrive without weapons and without strength. I know this because I have . . . well, a cousin." She blushed. "I've been visiting him my whole life. But I never talked about it, you know, in our Society."

Through the awkward interface of Blockworld language, Qiingi explained that it was the Oceanans who had attacked the camp. "They expected us to try to escape by going down to the sea; I took these people up instead. The Oceanans saw and chased us, but I am good in forest paths, and we escaped them. They were sure to find us eventually, though, so we looked for another way. Esther guided us here. I am . . . surprised that you found us."

Livia tried to smile. "I . . . travel well." *I am good at rejecting places* would be another way to say it. She understood that now, to her own sorrow.

"But now that we are here," said Qiingi, "where else can we go?"

Livia thought about the sims she'd run—and before that, Lucius's assertion that 3340's people were everywhere. She shook her head. "There's only one place we might be safe now. We're going to try to make it to the aerie."

They ate their fill of the overflowing berry bushes. Then they faded into the forest, the ghosts of children leaving home.

IT WAS A relief to be alone. Aaron Varese sat on a small cot in an equally small stone cell, its walls rough-hewn out of asteroidal rock. Rust from iron deposits stained it here and there. Near the small slotlike window, the stone was wet from the permanent mists that hung at the aerie's height. When he'd first arrived here, he'd often stepped outside just to admire the slick black surfaces that gleamed like a god's sculpture above and below. Today he simply sat, brooding.

The others were all huddling together, venturing out alone only when they had to. Ever since the general order had gone out that the AI of the Societies was no longer to be trusted, the peers had been miserable in their isolation. Aaron had little time for Societies; he had even less for the real company of his peers right now.

At the moment they were all bickering over the latest news from Westerhaven—or more properly, the total lack of news. For the first time in their lives, these young men and women were cut off from the culture and gossip of Westerhaven's social network. They couldn't believe it was happening. Their responses ranged from simple denial to outrageous and suicidal schemes to retake the fallen lands of Teven.

All that filled him with contempt. It brought back memories that he normally tried to suppress. After the death of his parents in the crash, Aaron had sat with Livia for days, waiting for rescue to arrive. It didn't come, and didn't come, and gradually, it began to dawn on him that no one was looking for them. Inscape had crashed in this part of the world—and that was such a terrifying prospect that nobody from the outside would risk entering here. He had been abandoned.

He had never viewed the duels and posturing of the peers with any respect since then. When he'd needed it most, they hadn't been there. He would never forget that. Worse, he saw the same attitude in the endless discussions and lack of action going on around him right now.

Everybody wanted to know what the bizarre invaders—these "ancestors"—wanted. What were their politics? Were they religious? What scope of freedom would the people of Teven have under their rule?

"Who cares?" Aaron had said again and again. "Catch me one of them so I can find out what technologies they use. That will tell us their true manifold, and it's all we need to know about them." His words hadn't penetrated many of their thick skulls, so now they were engaged in planning some pointless raid into the lowlands thousands of meters below the aerie. It was strategically useless, just a make-work project really.

Nobody would listen to his theory about the invaders. Old stories and movies from the time before the manifolds told that men had once seriously tried to eliminate the boundary between the human mind and artificial intelligences. The only remnant of those early explorations in Teven was the omnipresent implant technology that let people communicate with inscape. He was convinced that much more was possible.

Stories from the Modern period talked of "uploading"—artificial immortality by transference of the human personality into a computing system. Such technology didn't exist here in Teven, doubtless because of the tech locks. But beyond Teven, it must be possible.

"What does this conquest matter if the invaders are in a position to change the very nature of our humanity?" he'd asked his peers. They had returned blank stares. In just such a way must primitive tribesmen have worried over how attacking Europeans would divide the village's goats. "We have to know what they are before we know what they want," he'd insisted. "And we have to know what they want before we know how to fight them."

Idiots. They were losing everything because of their short-sightedness. Maybe they deserved to lose it.

"Aaron!" Francis, the group's military leader, appeared in an inscape window. "There are people coming up the main cable! We think they're refugees."

"Right." He was already on his feet, heart pounding. Could it be Livia? It was a ridiculous hope—but word had filtered out of Wester-haven before all went silent, suggesting that an unusual search for her was underway. Nobody knew why. But she, it seemed, had so far eluded the ancestors.

He raced down stone steps built by unknown hands, and slammed out a doorway into the arctic chill that flooded down from the glaciers. The air here was thin and bracing, its cold almost a taste on its own.

This truly was the edge of the world. High in the Southwall mountains, a giant outthrust of rock stood out like the prow of a ship between two split-backed glaciers. The cliffs behind Aaron rose sheerly for kilometers, finally ending in a seemingly infinite vertical wall of black material. Its mist-wreathed face was streaked here and there by long tongues of ice. The full height of this wall was hidden by thin planes of cloud. The spur of rock where Aaron stood was far above the tree line, too far even for lichen or wildflowers, but terminating on the flat top of the prow were several arrow-straight bridges, supported only by the cables they rode on, that stretched horizontally away into the sky. These cables connected to a whole network of similar lines that made a vast spiderweb many kilometers above the lands of Teven. They were anchored here at the south wall of the coronal, and on their other ends to various of the great slanted cables that rose up from the coronal's floor.

In happier times, Aaron had stood here and contemplated the impossible bridges that seemed to sit upon the air itself. As a boy he had watched his father meet traders from the Cirrus manifold as they stepped tentatively down to stand on solid rock for an hour or two. But he had never ventured up one of those strands himself. His parents had died before his father could deliver on a promise to take him to visit Cirrus.

Behind him were several landing circles for aircars, and then a low entrance carved into the rock face of the cliff. Extending over many levels above and below this spot was the aerie, a Westerhaven outpost and recently Aaron's new home.

He stood stamping his feet and watching the distant moving shapes. They slowly resolved into two parties, one seemingly running in the lead, the other following. Could both those parties be warriors of Raven, come to slaughter the remaining holdouts of the Westerhaven manifold?

The tiny, struggling forms had as their backdrop a vast ocean of sun-lit land and water that spread to a hazy infinity of distance, and curved up vertically to either side. Rows of great cables stood in ranks like delicate flying buttresses in the blued distance. Something flashed in the middle distance and he squinted at the distant dots. One of the people in the lead party seemed to be faltering. As he watched, the figure fell from the narrow bridge, tumbling helplessly into miles of air.

Aaron turned and raced back to the entrance to the aerie. "Defend the lead party!" he shouted at his Society. All around he could see the animas of his peers racing to their posts. At the entrance he snatched up the rifle he'd had fabricated when the invasion began and turned to sight at the incoming refugees.

He tried to count the figures, but they were nearly head-on to him now and the leaders were blocking those behind them. But they were getting closer—not yet in range, but almost . . .

A rock near his foot exploded. Aaron stumbled and fell, almost going over the edge. Loud bangs and ricochet whines filled the air as bullets tore up the ground where he'd been standing. Then he heard answering fire coming from overhead; his friends were firing back.

He heard a distant shout and saw two figures fall from the bridge. He couldn't tell if they were in the lead party or the pursuers. The prey were getting close—enough so that he could see that they were five young people, probably peers of Westerhaven. Still prone, he aimed past them at a pursuer.

A flash of light hit him like a slap. "Ahh!" He dropped the rifle and put his hands to his eyes—too late. That had been a laser. Momentarily blinded, he froze, blinking back tears and trying to see past the ovals of light that persisted in his vision. As he was groping for his rifle, the vanguard of the refugees made it off the end of the bridge and he heard gunfire close by. The echoes were enough to nearly drown out the sound of running feet.

Someone grabbed him by the shoulders. He surged up, trying to throw the attacker off.

"Aaron!" It was Livia's voice. He clutched at the sound and when he felt her reality, hugged her tightly.

"Come on!" she said. "The door's this way."

He turned to go with her. The gunfire was coming so fast that its echoes overlaid one another to form a jumble of intolerable noise. And people were screaming—

"It's coming down!" That wasn't Livia, but the accent was Westerhaven. He blinked again and looked over, glimpsed a face and an arm, hand pointing upward. Aaron looked up.

A wall of sky-blue glacial ice was toppling majestically toward him. It was moving so slowly that it must be terribly far away. Hence terribly big . . .

"Come on!" Livia dragged him the last few meters into the doorway, which was crowded with a knot of bodies all struggling to get through. Before they could get inside the first blocks hit the spur behind them. Aaron found himself flying through the doorway to land on a heap of elbows and knees. Something hit his head and he spun to the floor.

LIVIA HALF CARRIED Aaron along the corridor. He was cursing; behind them the stone itself was groaning from the tons of shattered ice that were settling over the entrance. "Ha!" Aaron slurred. "That'll keep 'em."

Livia looked around quickly. Her party was all accounted for: finally, at least for a while, they were among friends.

An angel flickered into being next to Aaron. "Is he all right?" she asked frantically. To have come so far, only to lose him now—

"He'll be fine. He might have a slight concussion."

"Knew you'd make it through," mumbled Aaron.

"I didn't," she said shakily. "I didn't know I could do it without you beside me."

A flight of emotions crossed Aaron's face: embarrassment, perhaps?—sadness, certainly. "No, not me; it was all you," he murmured, looking away.

Gentle hands unwove Livia's arms from Aaron, but she had to watch while he was carried up a long flight of stone steps and laid out on a pallet.

Then, with nothing more to do, she collapsed on the uneven floor.

After a while the haze of exhaustion and shock began to wear off. Livia raised her head as someone handed her a bowl of hot soup, and she even summoned up a smile. While she was eating Qiingi came to sit next to her.

"So this is the aerie of which you spoke," he said. "I was expecting a camp, or buildings. But we're underground."

She nodded. The aerie was a series of rooms and passages carved out of stone. The mountains had been built out of asteroidal stone, uneven in density and veined in silvery nickel-iron. They sat now in one of its main halls, a lofting space like a long slot cut in the rock. Crude halogen lamps lit the spaces, and the air was cold. Water dripped from the ceiling in places. "We discovered this place a couple of generations ago. We don't know who originally built it, but we use it as a storage depot for trading with Cirrus," she said.

In the cleared center of this hall were various towering devices of wood and brass. Most of Aaron's friends were here, standing or sitting in a semicircle. Several of them stood in the middle, debating. She watched them dumbly for a while, until she realized she didn't recognize the oldest debater. "Who's that?" she asked.

Qiingi let out a deep sigh. He looked stricken, in a way he had not during all their adventures on the way to this place. "Qiingi, what is it?"

"I approached him," he said. "I wasn't sure, because his appearance was very different when he was with us." He met her eyes sadly. "That, Livia Kodaly, is my founder. Raven."

"There's nowhere to go," the old man was saying. "These invaders are spreading everywhere. They're close to shutting down the tech locks. Then they won't need to skulk around anymore." He didn't talk like Qiingi, Livia realized; this Raven sounded more Westerhaven than anything. But she didn't comment on that to Qiingi.

"Somewhere, someone must have a manifold that can resist this '3340,'" said another of the debaters. This was Francis Munari, the best military thinker among the peers; he had apparently arrived here with the remains of the Barrastea rearguard several days before.

Several others took up the thread of his argument. Raven kept shaking his head, but he was drowned out for the moment. With a groan, Livia levered herself to her feet and walked over to the circle.

"It's not a technical problem," she said, projecting her authority as best she could. Heads turned.

"That's why nobody's able to resist them," she continued. "What nobody seems to get is that the manifolds *use* inscape and the locks, but they're not created *by* them. They're created by ideals."

"Make sense, Livia!" snapped Francis. "While you talk, they're digging through the ice to get us. Make sense or give the floor to somebody else."

Raven bowed to her. He had a charming face, a bit satyrlike with a fringe of white hair around his bald scalp. "Livia Kodaly, it's an honor. You've seen what I've seen, haven't you? That the ancestors aren't attacking us through our technology?"

"Yes. That's the problem." Reluctantly, she walked into the circle. "The tech locks seem untouched; if they weren't this form of attack wouldn't be necessary. The invaders have a little control over inscape, just enough to be able to distort messages and meanings. But they can't seem to attack the locks directly. They're probing each manifold to find out what its highest ideal is, then they come and promise a new way to get to that ideal. It's different for each manifold, but the end result is that people hand control over to them."

Francis crossed his arms. "How do you know this?"

"When we set out to find this place, there were sixteen of us," she said. "We ran from manifold to manifold—each time thinking we'd shaken our pursuers. And each and every time, we found they'd gotten there before us. As if they had always been there, hiding in the cracks of the world." Trying to escape pursuit, Livia had led her people through the warrens of a vast, baroque stone city that clung like lichen to the ascending cable, isolate and paranoid. From there they had slipped past cloud cities and arbors that hung in the sky like a dream of angels, and past hardscrabble farms perched on sagging square-kilometer nets of sailcloth that hung in the permanent mist. When they ran out of sky, they walked a length of frayed cable down to the mountaintops and hid in the mazes of a forest-dwelling people who seemed more owl than human. In every place she met some manifestation of 3340; and in each one she lost one or two people.

"I know it was 3340, once or twice," she said. "Catching the stragglers as they tried to open their hearts to a new destination. But more often, it was just too hard for our people to go on. To reject the values of the place where we were resting for a day or two—to embrace new values in order to see a different world." Each new place was a revelation of sorts: an example of a new way to live. A couple of the refugees had found paradise during that long climb, and simply refused to leave it. A couple had found hell.

"Everywhere we went, we tried to warn the people," she continued. "No one believed us. In many places, we couldn't even find the words to explain what's happening—if you tried you would start to fade." She shook her head sadly. "I never knew how many manifolds had turned in on themselves. Even though we all went through the freeing of inscape that happens at puberty, most people no longer seem to believe in any reality beyond theirs."

She ran out of steam. For a while there was silence. Then Raven cleared his throat.

"Some of you are wondering how I came to be here with you." He glanced significantly at Qiingi. "I did not betray my people. But the animals—my spirits—they deceived me. I didn't know about the presence of the ancestors until it was too late. Then for a while I lived as a 'guest' of these invaders."

He looked down at the stone floor. "I only escaped after the Oceanus incident."

"How is it you escaped?" someone asked suspiciously. "It seems a bit convenient. How do we know you're not working with them?"

Raven looked back at the man blandly. "You don't. I escaped because I had help from one of your founders—Maren Ellis. She trusted me, and some of you here trusted me enough to take me in. For that I'm grateful." He raised his voice. "I've seen what these ancestors are doing to our people. They're trying to shut down the tech locks. Men and women of Raven who spent their whole lives learning to work leather, or carve wood, now can get clothing or shelter with a simple gesture. Their life's work is rendered meaningless. And your diplomats and seekers of knowledge have nowhere to go now; all inscape's differences are being annihilated by the conquerors."

"But why?" asked Francis. "If we're going to fight them, we need to know why they're doing this."

Raven hesitated. "I don't know," he said at last. "They don't need human labor. They grow machines for that. They aren't plundering our treasures—they ignore them. And they're not telling us what to do, they don't seem to need that kind of power over people. But they're changing us. Changing the people themselves."

"What do you mean?" asked Francis. A hush had fallen over the crowd.

"We lived in a world that accommodated the human need for meaning," said Raven. "It let us know that our beliefs were valuable in and of themselves. The invaders reject that; they say that our beliefs are only valuable insofar as they serve something else. Something they call 3340 and will not define any more clearly.

"But they are clear about one thing. Those who follow 3340 will gain the power of gods. All we have to do to achieve this power is abandon the realities we've been building all our lives."

9

THE STONE FLOOR shook under Livia. "They're into the corridors!" someone shouted. With that signal, the crowd melted away as humans, angels, and agents all raced to their posts. Qiingi was offered a weapon, accepted it gratefully. Francis shouted orders; massive engines stood up on their hydraulic legs and began stalking after him toward the stairs. In seconds Livia found herself standing with Raven and a few of the refugees. Aaron was awake, and now stood unsteadily, holding his head.

Livia watched the action with a resigned sense of detachment. "Such a lot of effort," she heard herself saying, "for a day or two's reprieve."

Aaron scowled at her. "What else are we supposed to do? If you're right, there's nowhere to run to."

She shook her head. "I never said that." She turned to Raven. "There is an alternative, isn't there? You knew this attack was coming."

Raven shrugged. "We didn't know. We . . . saw some signs. We were worried that we'd gone too far in our isolationism. So we decided to take steps."

"In secret?"

"The other founders would never have agreed to it."

Aaron looked from Livia to Raven. All three of them turned to look past the chaos of running people, to where Aaron's experimental barrels sat in a far corner.

Livia walked over to one of the barrels. When she tapped it, it sounded hollow. "So you and Maren Ellis inspired Aaron here to experiment with space travel," she said to Raven. "Aaron, last time I talked to you it sounded like you'd succeeded." She looked up, expecting to see the light of understanding in his eyes. Instead she saw disappointment.

"Theoretically, yes," he said, shaking his head. "Sure, we've sent cargoes . . . even round-tripped them, but—"

"Round-tripped? What do you mean?"

He gazed at her evenly. "It doesn't matter. You know the difference between running away here, within Teven Coronal, and running away out there? If we run here, we can always change our minds. Always come back. But nobody ever responded to the messages we put in the barrels. We don't even know what's out there." He waved at the glass-walled end of the workshop, where the stars slowly wheeled past.

"Raven knows," she said. "Don't you?"

To her surprise, the old man shook his head. "I know what *was* out there two hundred years ago. I've tried to contact my mother, but only get her anima. And it claims to know no more than we do. We can't help you much, I'm afraid."

"But you know what caused the accident that stranded Aaron and me outside of inscape," she accused. "You all knew, but you never told us. There was a name for the thing that caused the accident, Aaron."

His eyes widened. "Livia, I don't want to—"

"The *anecliptics*, Aaron. You know that word, don't you?" she said to Raven.

The old man shrugged. "I know we bought this world from them. They were our friends. But my mother never told me more than that."

"Your *mother?*"

"Maren Ellis." Seeing their astonished expressions, Raven laughed. "Yes, my mother. We've had our differences over the years . . . I guess you could say Raven's people is one of them. But she's one of the originals, and I'm not. And the originals don't talk about the time before the manifolds. I don't know any more about what's out there than you do."

Livia glared at the barrels. "You'd think she would have told you. Or told somebody what she knew. She knows more about what's happening than she's told any of us.

"The one thing we know, though, is that Ellis and the other founders came from there." Livia nodded at the stars visible past the diamond-glass far wall of the workshop. "They built this world with the help of the anecliptics. Another thing I know is that this 3340 who is attacking us is *not* one of the anecliptics. It's an interloper, a trespasser, where our real ancestors were invited in."

Raven nodded. "Mother told me that the anecliptics agreed to shelter us from outside influences. I do agree that if these so-called ancestors are invaders on our territory that they're also invading the territory of the anecliptics . . . but . . ."

Shouts from below, then tense silence. Then—the deep *crump* of a distant explosion. As dust filtered down from above, both of them turned to watch the stairwells that led to the outer doors.

"What are you suggesting?" asked Aaron after silence returned.

For a moment she was afraid to say it. But they were just standing there; nobody had a plan beyond simple survival. What was needed right now was a countermove whose audacity matched that of the attack against Teven. None of the peers seemed ready to think on that scale, and Livia didn't feel worthy of doing it either. But she had a reputation for heroism—even if she didn't remember being that hero. For her, audacity was permitted.

Her eyes on Raven, Livia said, "We have to leave the coronal. Find these anecliptics. Tell them about 3340. Maybe they'll evict everybody; maybe they'll kill us all, I don't know. But Aaron, I'm betting they won't be indifferent."

They stared at her in shock for a moment. Then Raven shook his head. "Well, Maren and I talked about this kind of travel . . . We commissioned the space-travel research project. But, Livia, leaving Teven is a worse suicide than what we face here. We isolated ourselves in this place for a reason: because the outside world is full of enemies."

It was the old ostrich-head-in-the-sand argument that Esther and the peers had always used on her. It infuriated Livia.

Aaron shook his head. "It won't work anyway."

Gunfire and shouts echoed up from below. Livia grabbed Raven by the shoulders. "Listen! We're out of other options. Anything else we do, 3340 wins. Are you already resigned to that?"

People were boiling up out of the stairwell now. Qiingi came loping over. "Up, up!" he shouted. "They've taken the foyer. Eagles and thunderbirds!"

Aaron looked around at his scattered experiments. "Livia, there's no way to do it. None of the test barrels is big enough to hold a person, much less the supplies and oxygen they'd need. And with no heat source . . . it's sure death, Liv."

But Raven was looking away, his expression troubled. "There might be a way. If we go up," he said to Aaron. "*All* the way up."

Aaron frowned in sudden understanding. "How do you know about that?"

"You forget, I grew up in Westerhaven—before this manifold had that name. I know this place, and its secrets."

At that moment Francis ran over. "What are you doing standing around?" he shouted. "Grab a weapon and get down there!"

"Let me handle this," Raven said to Livia and Aaron. "You gather the supplies you'll need."

"Then you agree?" She ignored Francis.

Raven sighed. "No. But it's a thing to try."

"What's going on here?" demanded Francis. Livia didn't stick around to listen to his confrontation with Raven. She followed Aaron's lead as he grabbed a box and began throwing food and other gear into it.

THE BATTLE WAS reaching a peak. The equipment he'd been using for cover had crumbled under an onslaught of laser fire and Qiingi was looking for a better vantage point when he felt a hand descend on his shoulder. Startled, he looked up. Raven stood over him. The old man didn't say a word, but simply pointed—away from the battle.

Qiingi turned and immediately spotted Livia Kodaly dragging boxes onto an open-sided freight elevator stuffed with crates and pieces of metal equipment. He nodded to Raven and followed the founder over to help with the loading.

Half of the equipment appeared Modern, or even older. The rest was totally new, composed of quantum dots and ganged mesobots. Some of it exhibited the pseudo-life of post-scientific technology; it was all equally repellant to Qiingi.

Qiingi helped Aaron dump several last boxes into the elevator. "Where are you going?" he asked. Livia's friend eyed him suspiciously but said nothing.

Livia looked up from where she was lashing some metal tubes together. "Away from Teven. We're going to try to find help."

Away from Teven. The thought was astonishing, dizzying even. Qiingi didn't hesitate. "I will go with you." Out of the corner of his eye he thought he saw Raven nod.

"No," snapped Aaron Varese.

"This is my world, too," said Qiingi. "Or is it only Westerhaven that you intend to save?"

"But you don't have the skills—"

"What skills, exactly, do you think we shall require?"

Aaron glared at him. Livia watched them both. Then Aaron simply said, "Up!" The huge metal square began grinding its way toward an empty black shaft in the ceiling; icy air swept down from there. Below them the workshop spread out like a game board. On it Westerhaven was playing a losing match.

It was shaming to watch Raven's thunderbirds clawing their way up the stairs through the withering fire. Once Qiingi would have trusted his life to the beasts. Now they were almost upon him. "We're rising too slowly," he said, as calmly as he could. Nobody answered. At any second the invaders would be up the stairs, and then this platform would be the most prominent target in the room.

Aaron was explaining something to Livia, who listened intently. "The first barrels just disappeared," he said. "It took a while before we figured out that the coronals expect to find destination and routing labels on incoming and outgoing packages. Then, two months ago we labeled a barrel and dropped it, and forty days later, it came back! Round-tripped! The coronals, they rotate, and the ones in this part of space are lined up, so if you drop something off one at just the right moment, it heads straight for the next one in line, on a tangent to its rim. And *the coronals know this . . .* they're watching for incoming cargos all the time. They'll pick it up . . ."

One of the stairwells exploded upward. A bellowing monstrosity stood up into smoke and flame and chunks of rock and metal flew everywhere. The concussion knocked Qiingi off his feet. But they were only two meters below the ceiling now . . . one meter, and the workshop was opaqued with smoke. Qiingi let go a long-held breath as the line of light and smoke narrowed and vanished, leaving them alone in a black shaft of rock.

Livia sat disconsolately on a nearby box. Qiingi knelt before her. "Wordweaver Kodaly, are you hurt?"

She shook her head, smiling wanly. "We couldn't save the others." It was half question, half self-accusation.

"Of all of us, who travels best?" he asked. "You should be the one to go on this journey."

Livia tried to brush back her dust-filled hair. "No, I shouldn't. It's precisely because I travel so well that I *shouldn't* go."

". . . It's a whole system," Aaron was saying to Raven. "Like a subway, only it's shut down. Built to take hundreds, thousands of cars a day between the coronals. Surely it'll be able to recognize and route just one . . ."

"I'd been trying not to think about it," Livia said slowly. When Qiingi didn't speak but just continued to look at her, she met his eyes reluctantly. "I mean, how I was able to get us here through all those manifolds. I couldn't understand it myself at first, why some people can travel between manifolds and others can't. Lucius explained it to me, but at the time I refused to understand him. I didn't want to give him the satisfaction of seeing that he was right . . ."

"Livia, what are you talking about?"

"So naturally, the system is designed to take objects of all kinds of sizes and shapes," Aaron babbled. "So you're right, you're absolutely right. Hell, what does a vessel for traveling in space have to look like, anyway? Does it have to be a *vessel,* at all . . . ?"

As they inched their way up the stone shaft the sounds of battle below reached a crescendo. Then silence, empty except for the low scraping noise of their own ascent.

Livia sighed. "The manifolds have a values-driven interface, right? To visit another manifold, you have to suspend the values of your own. So the person who can travel the best, who can go the farthest is going to be . . . the person with no values, no beliefs. The one who believes in nothing." She looked down at Qiingi again, bleakly. "Someone like me."

Qiingi shook his head. "No. It is the exact opposite. The person who travels best is the one who can see the worth of the greatest number of things and people and places."

She shook her head.

"Listen," said Aaron, "you need to adjust your shifts for extreme cold, and gather your angels around you. We're headed for vacuum in a few minutes." Above them, a square of light was widening slowly.

Qiingi followed Aaron's instructions, but kept an eye on Livia. She seemed listless, spent. The sight alarmed him. After a few minutes the lift ground to a stop on a shelf of rock high above the mountains. The thin wind was bitterly cold, and Qiingi's sinuses and ears hurt. As he gasped for breath he felt his totem coil around him protectively, and after a few moments his breath came more easily.

Raven stepped off the platform first; he held out his hand to help Qiingi. Qiingi hesitated. He couldn't deny that he felt betrayed by this man. But he forced himself to nod curtly and clasp the other's hand as he stepped down onto the cold rock.

They started shifting boxes from the elevator to another open cage that sat outside. This one was rusted and ice-painted, and from its crosspiece roof a thin black cable led up and up, apparently to infinity. The car was mounted to the cliff face by only two frail-looking rails.

When they were done shifting the supplies, they all clambered aboard the new car—all except Raven. He stood perfectly still, a little drift of snow starting around his feet. "Go on," he said quietly.

"What are you doing?" asked Livia. "Come on, we need you with us to represent the founders."

The old man shook his head. "You are your manifolds," he said. "And a founder is not a leader. It's better if I stay here and try to aid my people directly. Anyway, somebody has to tell the founders what you're attempting."

"But they'll be waiting for you when you go back down."

Raven smiled wryly. "There's more than one way down."

Qiingi put his hand on Livia's arm. "Come. He has made his decision." Raven nodded to him. Qiingi turned away.

Aaron ordered the new elevator up. They began to rise surprisingly fast. Despite the ache in his heart, Qiingi found his gaze drawn to the vista before him.

Raven stood watching from a narrow ledge on an otherwise vertical plain of rock. A hundred meters below it, glacial ice started and a kilometer farther down the aerie's landing spur was a jumble of blue and green rubble from the avalanche. From there the crags and faces of the mountainside fell away in steps that were veiled in mist and cloud.

Through and between the clouds stretched many fine, threadlike cables, all suspended kilometers above the peaks. The threads dwindled into invisibility where the mountains stretched vast forest-covered fingers onto a distant plain. The land there was just a blue haze filigreed with indistinct detail. It stretched on and on—but not to infinity. At the very limit of sight, an indigo wall stretched from left to right across the north end of the plain. Above it: only sky.

Qiingi found himself standing with his head tilted back, mouth open, looking up and up as the deep blue sky became black overhead. And still the wall they were climbing continued upward as though it cut the universe itself in two.

He had to sit down, clutching the car's rail and trying to steady his breathing. Of course he had known that the world he lived in was a constructed thing; his people were not so foolish as to abandon all true knowledge of their home. But he had been raised not to think of the land this way. Qiingi's understanding was of the habits of fox and otter; he knew the names of all the trees and plants of the forest, and their various properties. Raven's focus was on the human-scale world; that, he claimed, was the only level at which reality could truly make sense to people. Perhaps that was the real reason he was not coming with them.

Yet someone had imagined more. As the elevator rose, faster and faster it seemed as the air thinned, Qiingi tried to enter this manifold, see the world as the coronal's creator must have seen it. He could not.

Down at the spur, the mountains had seemed like giant waves flinging themselves up Teven Coronal's side wall. That wall had stretched off into white haze to either side; there was no sense of scale to it. Now as the elevator rose it came clear: the wall seemed infinite only if he looked straight up. To either side its distant top became visible, a knife-edge with black above it.

All his life, Qiingi had known the four cardinal directions: if you looked north or south you saw these impossible walls, but east and west it was different. Far beyond their blurred horizons stood two pillars of upsweeping blue and white. They curved toward the zenith, narrowing and fading into an ethereal white until they met somewhere behind the suns, an arch bigger than worlds. Qiingi's people called that arch Thunderbird's Door.

He had always known that the arch was an optical illusion; only now did it really hit home. He was rising up the inside wall of a ring two thousand kilometers in diameter and five hundred wide. The walls cupped an ocean of atmosphere and at its bottom lay the carefully sculpted landscape of whole continents.

Was Raven's people really just another carefully crafted segment of coronal shell, five or ten meters thick with vacuum below it? The hills he had climbed as a child, hollow and metal? Of course they were; and it shouldn't matter. He had known this all along, he had *known* it, surely he had. What did it matter to the hawk and the otter that their world was artificial? It shouldn't matter to him, either.

He fought back tears and turned away.

No one had spoken since they began this ascent. Time seemed stretched, as if each second was an hour. But if Qiingi glanced at the wall behind him, it fell past with an uncanny speed.

One of the boxes burst open in a white cloud of ice. Aaron closed it again by sitting on it. "We're nearly at vacuum," he said. "A real workout for our angels." Nobody laughed.

Qiingi thought about what Livia had said. He had believed that her strength came from a belief that the world was wider than any one manifold. Because she knew that, she could put her own world away when needed, and trade her ghahlanda for that of another place. So Qiingi had believed.

He still believed that. But she didn't.

"There," said Aaron. "Our destination." He pointed up and to one side. Qiingi followed his gaze.

Something perched on the very edge of the wall top, which was now only a few kilometers overhead. Unfamiliar with such things, it took him a while to realize that the tiny square object was a house.

Livia stood, her misery temporarily forgotten. "Aaron! That can't be real. Who would be insane enough . . . ?"

Aaron shrugged. "We never found out. Maybe Raven himself. I learned about the place from my uncle. He said he found it thirty years ago. It had been abandoned a long time by then. But it's not the only building on the top of the walls, Livia. There's a whole city on the north side; and there's lots of other places, some like this, some totally alien looking. You can find them with a good telescope, they're usually at the top of the coronal's built-in elevators—like the one we're riding."

They stood watching as the top of the wall approached. The house blazed brilliant against the black sky; it was lit not from above, but from the side. The vertical surface of the wall below it also glowed, fading gradually over hundreds of meters. "See the way it shines," said Aaron. "That house is the first thing you've ever seen that's lit directly by the sun." Qiingi looked up; the suns he had grown up knowing as the most constant of things were now faint curved slits in blackness. For the first time in full daylight he could see the edges of the vast oval mirror that slowly spun in the open center of the coronal ring. Teven Coronal rotated at right angles to the sun, and the oval mirror directed light down onto the ring's inner surface. The mirror itself turned, slower than Teven, to create a twenty-four-hour day. From here the mirror's edge looked crisp and clear, as if it were only meters away. It was at least two hundred kilometers above him.

Then they rose onto the glowing section of wall, and sunlight burst on Qiingi from the side. He looked out over the well of light that was Teven, and saw the true sun of humanity rising slowly over the north wall of the world. His first real sunrise. It declared his entire previous existence a lie.

He couldn't think; couldn't even breathe for a few moments. With a start he realized they had stopped rising. Aaron was opening the metal gate of the cage, his expression resolute.

"I'm glad you convinced us to do this, Livia," Aaron said. "I'd forgotten what it was like up here. From here you can see the truth: 3340 may be conquering every manifold in the coronal, but now it's clear just how small that conquest really is."

THE THREE-STORY TUDOR-STYLE chalet sat on the very edge of the cliff, a kilometer from the elevator. The first thing Livia noticed was that it wasn't alone up here; the top of the wall was littered with junk—opened boxes, broken machines of various technology levels, uprooted and dried plants. They were scattered in a broad arc around the house. Looking beyond them, she saw that the dark surface was about two hundred meters wide, north to south. Its clean edges converged to infinity east and west, with the swirled white-and-blue of the coronal's lands to the north side of it, and utter blackness to the south.

Aaron was hauling some boxes in the direction of the house. Listlessly, she went to join him. "I can't see stars," she commented.

"Too dim to be seen in the day," he muttered. "Damn!" He'd grabbed a crate and frost-burned the palm of his hand through the material of his angel. "Come on, we have to hurry with this stuff."

"But I don't understand what we're doing," she said. "Are we hiding here?"

"We probably could, but for how long?" He shook his head. "No, look: the house isn't attached to anything. It's just sitting on the surface. That's because this stuff," he stamped, "is too hard to be drilled or punctured by normal means. It's woven fullerene—carbon nanotubes— like the whole coronal. Whoever built the house just hauled it up and pushed it to that spot. We're going to push it ourselves, only in that direction." He jabbed a thumb at the fathomless black that ate half the vista.

Qiingi had been dutifully dragging a sack of assembler spores. Now he stopped and peered at Aaron. "Is your xhants ill, Aaron? You are not making sense."

"Sure I am," he said, lifting the crate more carefully. "The house is airtight. It has its own heat source, which we just have to fire up. I've brought supplies . . . you have to get over the idea that we'd be falling if we went over that edge, Wordweaver. If you jump over *that* edge," he pointed at the bright side, "you'll fall fifty kilometers and splat on the mountains below. But if you go that way," he nodded at the blackness, "you're not falling. You're *traveling*."

Livia half listened as they brought the supplies in through the house's airtight foyer, which Aaron called an "airlock." The coronals, he said, were colossal spinning rings and anything dropped off the edge of one, if it was dropped at the right time, would travel through space in a straight line until it gently tapped the underside of the next coronal in line. "And underneath the coronals," said Aaron, "there are landing pads. Those are automatic; they won't let us miss."

Teven Coronal was but one of many. Aaron had used his telescopes to verify that a chain of them led millions of kilometers into the distance— past the heaven-sized pillars of luminous gas that obscured most of the night sky. The chain might lead all the way to the place where the founders had come from. History spoke of a universe outside of Teven holding trillions of people. But crucial details of that wider world had been lost—obscured, she now realized, by Ellis and the other founders.

To people confident of their permanent isolation, such a sacrifice must have made sense; the founders had wanted each manifold to be able to craft its own origin story, consistent with its values. But once that isolation was disturbed, the folly of the plan became obvious.

They knew nothing of where they were going. So either the coronal next door would have its own civilization and be willing to help them; or it was the very home of 3340. In which case this journey was in vain.

The airlock opened and Livia stepped into the front hall of the house. It was shocking in its normality: the floor was pallasite tile, illuminated from below, and an ordinary side table held a green vase containing withered flowers. Faded portraits hung on the walls. She wandered in a daze into a rustic living room with a beamed ceiling. Her feet sank into deep white pile carpet. A long couch and two leather armchairs faced a stone mantelpiece with satyrs carved in it. Above the mantel was an excellent painting of the Southwall mountains. A burl oak writing table sat in one corner, an empty rosewood china cabinet in another.

Everything was covered in fine patterns of frost. It was so cold in here that, without her angel's help, she wasn't sure she could even breathe. As it was, the air that came to her nose was painfully dry.

She walked to the front window and looked down fifty kilometers at the coronal lands.

"What kind of a person would live like this?" She coughed.

Aaron appeared embarrassed. "I don't know . . . I kind of like it."

"Okay," she said, "now we do what? Get out and push the place over the cliff?"

"Essentially, yes." He walked through the oak-paneled dining room and twitched back the drapes; they disintegrated in his hands but he ignored that, pointing to something outside. "I've brought a few kilometers of fullerene cable. We're going to tie *that* to the house, and mount some thrusters to both. Then we see if the tractor my uncle brought up here twenty years ago still works."

She looked where he pointed. Some kind of heavy processing unit squatted on the smooth top of the wall, twenty meters away. "That's the power plant for the place," he said. "I brought our own power source so we don't really need it; but it'll make a great counterweight."

"Counterweight? For what?"

"Gravity."

She sighed, and from then on she didn't ask any more questions. While Aaron and Qiingi clambered under and over the house, enmeshing it in thin cables, she busied herself with the devices they'd brought inside. She found Aaron's power source, and plugged it into the house's feeds. Then she turned up the heat and air, and set about exploring.

The place was huge. It had three floors, four bedrooms, two bathrooms, a kitchen that could serve dozens, and even a library, its shelves empty. Most of the rooms were furnished; on one of his trips through the living room Aaron revealed that his uncle had actually lived here for a while. And so had Aaron, off and on since the accident.

Eventually it was warm enough and she was tired enough that Livia simply collapsed on the living room couch. Through the front window she could see Qiingi's feet; he was standing on a ladder, gluing small rockets to the wall of the house. She stared out over the lands of Teven for a while, then dozed. In her dreams she saw Barrastea in flames, with centuries' worth of sculpture, painting, and architecture being ground under the heels of petulant giants who fought over baskets full of people. She woke disoriented and overwhelmingly sad, to find Aaron and Qiingi stamping and shivering in the front hall. "We're ready," said Aaron. "The tractor works. Livia, don't you want to watch this?"

She stared at him. "No," she said, feeling that she was stating the obvious. She turned over and faced the back of the couch, but she could still hear the two men chattering on about what they were doing. Despite himself Qiingi had warmed to the adventure, she knew. And if they were to travel to another coronal, they had to do this work. She still resented their comings and goings. All she wanted to do was sleep until the stars went out.

Abruptly the house shook. She sat up, fearing for a moment that the thunderbirds had found them. But no—it was only the hulking tractor, which was pressed up against the front of the house and had started pushing it in the direction of the infinite black sky. The motion was slow, and a constant grinding sounded from below. The vibration ratcheted up through every surface. She heard things toppling and smashing in the kitchen.

It all became real to her suddenly. They were leaving. She might never see her people again. Urgently she called up her Society, and they all popped into being around her—parents, uncles and aunts, friends, people she'd admired and tried to emulate over the years. They stood or sat around the room, smiling at her, conversing quietly as though nothing had happened. But they were all animas—there was not a single connection to a live human being among them.

Cicada and Peaseblossom flew over and landed on her knees. "Livia!" said one. "We haven't seen you in days!" said the other. "How are you?"

She started to cry, and at that moment the house tipped and shuddered, and in a chaos of sliding furniture and smashing glassware, she and her agents and Aaron and Qiingi and everyone she had ever loved fell over the edge of the world.

PART TWO

Under the Anecliptics

Institutions are information processing systems created to promote specific values. Once they exist, these systems (club, company, government, or church) become values in and of themselves. Then new systems are created to support them in turn. We call this constant cycling of systems "history."

—from the
Founding Declaration of the Narratives, 2124

10

AARON BUMPED AGAINST the ceiling. Something huge lunged at him in the sudden darkness. He shouted and flailed backwards. The china cabinet pushed gently against his palm and came to a stop.

He peered past the cabinet. Everything was still falling—that was the sensation—but nothing was landing. He'd known it would be this way, but his heart pounded anyway. After a moment of indecisive paralysis he shoved the cabinet aside. Across the living room Livia was curled into a fetal position, and the Raven warrior had braced himself in the archway to the front entrance. All around them floated various pieces of furniture. As he watched, the painting over the mantelpiece gently lifted itself up off its hook and drifted to the ceiling.

This panic was a waste of time. He tried to get purchase on the wall but simply flew away from it. After a bit of bumping and thudding he managed to get to the front window. There was nothing visible outside at all, just a faint pearly glow that rotated around the window frame every minute or so.

"Qiingi, could you get the lights?" he said. His voice sounded properly calm now. "Livia, are you all right?"

She mumbled something from nearby. Aaron put out his hand to reassure her, but somehow couldn't complete the gesture of touching her.

Qiingi sounded apologetic: "I don't know how to light your rooms."

"That's just perfect." Aaron gauged his jump more carefully this time, and sailed over to touch the traditional switch plate next to the archway. The room was flooded with light—and looked ten times as surreal in the steady illumination as all its contents sailed majestically around, like a parade of household gods.

"If you're not going to help, could you at least get out of the way?" The warrior reluctantly let go of the doorjamb and Aaron slipped past him and back to the kitchen. Aside from the table and some floating plates, it was clear in here but dark. He went to the window and looked out.

Aaron gave a gasp of wonder. Here were stars such as he had never seen. The darkness was crowded with them, and he'd swear he could make out different colors. The constellations were drowned in detail.

As the house slowly turned, he saw the source of the pearly glow that had been visible from the living room. The arching inside surface of the coronal formed a sliver of light far above. The rest of the giant structure was invisible in the blackness, but they must still be falling past the sidewall. It was probably a good thing that they couldn't see that endless surface speeding by.

He went to the control boxes he'd clamped to the kitchen counter and cautiously ordered a small burst from the rockets he and Qiingi had attached to the house. For a moment nothing seemed to happen; then he had to grab the counter as the whole room moved to the left.

Five minutes later he re-entered the living room—walking in great slow bounding steps. Livia looked up from where she perched on her toes on the floor. "What's happening?" she asked, fear in her voice.

"I spun us up a bit," he said. "I've given us enough momentum for a twentieth of a gee. I didn't want to do more yet, to let the furniture settle. After everything's back in position we can spin back up to a good weight—say, half a gravity. It's the best way to lose weight," he added with a grin. They didn't laugh.

Nobody spoke, in fact, as they went through the house fetching chairs and beds down from the bizarre piles and configurations they had made. Then Aaron spun them up and real weight gradually returned.

As Aaron adjusted the position of the painting over the mantel he heard Livia drop onto the couch behind him. "Now what?" she asked.

"Well," he said, stepping back and eyeing his handiwork, "most of the work was in timing when to throw us off the wall. There's nothing to do now but wait."

Silence. He turned; both Livia and Qiingi sat bolt upright in their chairs. They were waiting. Aaron began to laugh, all of the tension finally ebbing away as he did. "Weeks!" he said. "The next coronal is weeks away. The house is self-healing, the oxygen and heat plants are the best pseudolife we had . . . there's really nothing we have to do. This is what space travel is like."

They stared at him, uncomprehending. Finally he just shrugged and went to fetch the house's broombug to clean up a spill in the kitchen.

LATER, AARON AND Livia came together in the kitchen. For the first time since her arrival at the aerie, neither was busy with something. They hugged and he gazed intently into her face. "Have I said how proud I am of you?"

She raised an eyebrow. "No, but go ahead. Oh, by the way—about what?"

He laughed. "The others thought we'd lost you after the Oceanus thing. You disappeared at the same time as the rest of the peers. But I kept saying, 'if anybody can make it out it's Livia. She's done it before.'"

Uneasy, Livia broke away. "I'm not special. I was just lucky enough not to be there when they attacked."

"But you led them."

She shrugged irritably. "What does that matter?"

He waved a hand. "It doesn't. It doesn't. As long as you're okay . . . And this Qiingi fellow? He helped you?"

She nodded. "Qiingi's a . . . very special person. Strong. He doesn't seem to know what the word *uncertainty* means."

"Huh." He busied himself with the house controls he'd clamped to the kitchen counter.

"Aaron." He looked over, smiling. "Why didn't you tell me you were going away? I mean, I understand if the founders didn't want you to talk about the specifics of the project you were working on. But you could have *said* it was secret, and left it at that."

He looked blank for a moment. "I didn't want to keep secrets from you. And I didn't want to lie to you."

Livia gave him a puzzled frown. "So vanishing out of my Society was somehow better?"

"Look, I'm sorry. I was . . . consumed with the project. It's all I've thought about for weeks. Besides," he said with a grin, "I'm a big boy now. You don't really need me to tell you all my comings and goings, do you?"

That stung, both because Livia knew she shouldn't have to rely on his presence so much anymore—and because once upon a time, she had been able to rely on it without hesitation.

Does that mean we're no longer inseparable? she wanted to ask. But she kept silent. They continued chatting, catching up as if nothing had happened. But so much *had* happened lately; she couldn't sustain the casual tone of the conversation.

Eventually, talk dried up, and they drifted their separate ways.

THEY GATHERED OVER breakfast to discuss their plans. So far the details had been sketchy: all Livia had cared about was escaping Teven. All it took was an eloquent look on her part for Aaron to understand.

"What do we do next? Well, this was the easy part," he began. "The coronals take care of travel between them. Normally we wouldn't have launched from the top of the wall but from one of the cities under the coronal's skin. The skin's only two meters thick at any point and there're lots of doorways and shafts opening into the undersurface."

Livia paused with her fork halfway to her mouth. "I've never heard of anything like that," she said. Qiingi also looked puzzled.

"I've explored some of them," said Aaron. "There's whole cities hanging like chandeliers underneath our feet. But they're in different manifolds. I thought that some of them might know how to use the coronals' transport systems, but it seems that the founders excluded use of the docking systems from the tech locks. They made travel as impossible as long-range radio and laser-com."

"But why?" asked Livia. "Oh," she answered herself. "Because they didn't want us to be found. They wanted to isolate the manifolds here."

"Yes. Which is a shame because from what I've been able to learn, all you'd have to do to travel between the coronals is walk down a flight of stairs and enter a moving stateroom. At the appropriate moment it gets dropped, and you're away. At the far end, grapples pick you up as you fly by the destination coronal on a close tangent. I found pieces of old cargo boxes in some of the underways, and figured out the basics of their labels. We tried various destination labels on the barrels we dropped, and ones with a particular label were picked up and held at the next coronal. So we know the label, or I guess the name, of that coronal: it's called Rosinius in Old WorldLing.

"The system seems fully automatic; there'd be way too much traffic for a human to oversee. But you see, nobody claimed the barrels at the far end. I don't know if anybody noticed them at all. When they weren't claimed after two days, the system returned them. It's that automation that we're going to rely on to get us to Rosinius."

"And if we don't find help there?" asked Qiingi. "Do we travel to the next one? And the next? Then what? Will we be stranded?"

Aaron hesitated. "I don't know. I didn't want to do this in the first place. Of course, we know the Teven label, so we can always come back . . ."

"If we're not captured by someone or killed," Livia pointed out. Aaron shrugged.

"Same chance we were taking at home."

Qiingi smiled; it was the first time in days he'd done that. Livia smiled back at him. "What next, then? Who is it we seek?"

She hesitated. "The one name I've got to go on is the *anecliptics*."

"What do we know about them?" Qiingi asked. "Are they founders, like Raven or your Ellis? Or qqatxhana?"

"Well, the name is a clue," said Aaron. "If you squint, you might be able to see what I mean." He waved a piece of bread at the window; weak but direct sunlight slanted in. Livia did squint at the sun, but it looked the way it always did: tiny and fierce, with minute thornlike spikes of intense light hanging just above and below it. The spikes made it look a bit like a sideways eye.

Aaron rose and went to the window. He pointed to one side. "Have you ever wondered where *that* comes from?"

Livia craned her neck. He was pointing at the faintly drawn, rainbow-colored clouds that hung across one half of the sky. "It's just the Lethe Nebula," she said. "It's always been there."

"Actually, no," said Aaron. "It was never there during ancient times, or the Modern period. I checked old astronomical records. There's nothing about a seventy-million-kilometer-thick cloud orbiting near Jupiter." He pointed again, this time to the brightest star. Livia knew it was Jupiter; that pinprick of light was the only celestial object other than the cloud and the sun that never moved with the seasons. "And did you know," continued Aaron, "that there's another cloud like this one on the opposite side of the sun?"

Livia shrugged. "It's all one thing," he said. "The sun has two jets rising off its poles. So that's your clue: those jets rise at right angles to something called the *plane of the ecliptic.*"

He dipped his finger in his water glass and drew a wide circle on the tabletop. "All the planets orbit the sun like trains on rails, all the rails on the same flat plane. That imaginary flat surface is called the ecliptic." He smoothed his palm over the wood surface. "The jets we see coming off the sun rise and fall at an angle to that plane."

Livia looked at the circle, then out the window at the sky-spanning iridescent cloud. "That cloud is fed from the sun," she said.

". . . From off the ecliptic," said Aaron and nodded. "So whatever these anecliptics are, they surely have something to do with that process."

Visible on any night in Teven were dozens of starlettes inside the Lethe, and countless infinitesimal sparkles of light—each one a congealed comet of gases from those clouds. "Without Teven blocking out half the sky, you can see big engines working near the starlettes," said Aaron. "They're building coronals and other things even larger. They're all radio silent, but they might communicate by laser. The Lethe blocks any transmissions that might come from beyond it. But those places might be where your anecliptics live."

She shuddered. "They're not mine," she said. She looked up to see Aaron eyeing her; there was something unspoken between them. It was, she knew, the memory of the horrible destruction of the crash that had killed his parents. Lady Ellis had casually said that a *mad anecliptic* had caused it.

"Rosinius Coronal is two million kilometers away," he said. "That's exactly a week's journey at three point three kilometers per second, which is the rotational speed of Teven, hence our traveling speed. If we're lucky, we'll find allies at Rosinius. If not . . . then we collect supplies if we can, and keep going."

They looked at each other. No one had anything to add. For the moment, all they could do was wait.

AND THERE WAS nothing more to space travel than waiting. In a sense, Livia had been traveling in space aboard Teven all her life, and this was no different. She ate, she slept, she stared at the walls. Occasionally before sleeping she would tease back the drapes in her bedroom and gaze outside. Then the stars and the intricate constructions of the anecliptics would be fully visible to her. Yet there was no ground below the house, no horizon and no clouds above. It was only when she saw this that she really understood that their known world lay behind them.

So they padded to and fro like ghosts, murmuring polite greetings to one another in the hall; cooking, tidying, inventorying their supplies, and sitting. Endless sitting in perfect silence and stillness. The house had inscape projectors, but with nothing to project, they might as well not have existed at all.

One evening she was sitting in her room, reading one of the archaic paper books that had been left in the library by the previous tenant. Someone tapped on the door; she looked up to find Qiingi peering around it. "May I come in?" he asked.

She glared at him but he didn't go away. "Surely," she said after an awkward moment. She tuned her shift to the formal black she was wearing these days and slipped off the bed to sit in one of the armchairs. He hesitated over the other chair, then sat cross-legged on the floor.

"Livia, if I have done something to offend you, I would like to apologize—once you tell me what it was."

She stared at him. "Offend—? No, Qiingi, no you haven't done anything. Quite the . . . opposite. You've been very patient, both you and Aaron."

"Ah." He gazed at the wall for a moment. "In that case, I would like you to apologize to me."

"Ap—" She opened her mouth and closed it. "What for?"

"You are behaving in an accusatory and abusive manner," he said calmly. "You snap at myself and Aaron if we so much as smile at you. But ten minutes later you are cheerful and start a conversation. It is . . . wearing us down."

"Oh." She shifted uncomfortably. "Really? I . . ." She tried to remember some such incident, and couldn't. "Things have been hard on all of us," she said at last.

"Hmm." He sat there for a while, picking at the carpet. "There is another thing."

"What?"

"I have not seen you speaking to your Society since we left. It . . . concerns me."

She sighed painfully and said, "I don't believe in Societies anymore."

He rubbed his chin. "I don't understand."

"Qiingi . . ." She tamped down on her anger. "How do we know what's true in inscape, and what's a lie created by these 3340 fanatics? They may have infected inscape—it could be that our animas have been working for them for years. Don't you see? If I bring up my Society, who am I really talking to? The spirits of my family and friends? Or some puppet master?"

He scowled at the carpet, then nodded. "I understand. But that must be terrible for you. To be so cut off from everything . . ."

She hunched, fists clenched. "What do you want me to say? Yes, yes, it is terrible and I don't know how to deal with it. I don't know *how*. You come in here accusing me of stuff and trying to find out where I hurt— of course I hurt! Of course, but what can I do about it? What do you want from me?"

He didn't turn away from her intensity. "To hear you say it, as you're doing now."

"Well," she said frostily, "thank you, but I'm not sure how you can replace an entire Society, Qiingi." She felt the need to say more—words tumbled over one another but she held back—and finally she turned away from him.

"You're not the only one who has lost their loved ones," he said quietly.

She leapt to her feet and as he stood she made to push him out the door. "Damn you, what do you want!" She put her hands on his chest and shoved but it was like pushing a wall. Instead his arms went around her.

Then she was in tears, cursing herself for a weakling. He just held on to her and let her cry.

In her need she found herself kissing him, then pulling him to her bed.

LATER, SHE LAY perfectly calm and stared at the ceiling. He breathed deep and slow next to her. The night felt unreal—things had changed, but how could anything really be different while they were exiles? Love was impossible in this time, she was sure.

Unbidden, memories came to her of the ruins and overturned trees of Teven after the accident. Her recollection of that time was fragmentary, but she knew there had been times when she walked amid the devastation with much the same detachment as now. She had coldly wondered whether she would live or die. That was how you survived, she told herself now: you went past fear and anger and despair and just extinguished your emotions entirely. You lost sympathy for yourself, you stopped dreaming about rescue—you treated dreams with contempt.

Unless there was another way . . . She turned and gazed at Qiingi's sleeping face. He seemed to sense her, and opened one eye. "What?" he mumbled.

"Qiingi, how is it you were able to travel with us all the way to the aerie? The others all dropped away as they found places they couldn't believe in enough to enter. But you walked through every world with us. How did you do that?"

"I believed," he murmured.

"In what?" she said, allowing herself a moment of hope.

"You," he said. "I believed in you." Then he turned over and went back to sleep.

Shocked and confused, Livia lay for a long time staring at the dark curve of his shoulder. Was he just another believer in the stories about her? The thought hurt; disappointed, she finally turned away from him.

Her eyes were dry; quietly, in the dark, she withdrew her sympathy from herself. She let it go, and let go too of her parents, her friends, of Barrastea and her rooms and all the things she had done or wanted to do. They drained out of her leaving her cold and empty. Then she curled under the warm wall of Qiingi's back and went to sleep.

THE WEEK PASSED in boredom and increasing tension. Qiingi came to Livia's bed as often as not, but they continued to spend much of their daytime apart. She supposed they were brooding on their separate losses. He and she were such different people that their intimacy seemed forced anyway.

Aaron was barely polite to either of them. He hid in his room much of the time, building a radio using components he hoped were not contaminated with the nanotechnology of the tech locks. He smelled of copper and oil when they passed in the hall.

Qiingi had fashioned a spear out of scavenged household materials, and spent much of his time casting it in an upstairs hallway. Livia found out about it one day when she awoke to the sound of a furious argument between the two men. Arriving at the scene, she found a wooden pole sticking out of a wall that was peppered with diamond-shaped holes from previous throws. "—Know what could happen if you hit a circuit that can't repair itself?" Aaron had been shouting.

Livia walked away without intervening.

There was a time when she had considered Aaron her closest friend; had he wanted more than that? Did he love her now? He had never expressed such desires to her before. Livia resented his silence but didn't feel that it was her place to bring up this subject. They all began avoiding one another's eyes, and skulking about.

Meanwhile anything could have happened back home—manifolds conquered, people killed or made into quislings of 3340. There was no way to know. Outside the windows the towers of cloud that made up the Lethe turned slowly, revealing deep cavities and slopes within themselves. And beyond the Lethe, something else was becoming visible, day by day. Coronals and starlettes glowed out there, as well as brilliant pinpricks that moved almost perceptibly fast.

Aaron had brought a telescope with him from the aerie, and he spent a lot of time peering at the newly revealed wonders. Once, as they were all sitting in the living room, he turned and said to Qiingi, "Come here."

The warrior looked over at him warily. "Come on. I want to show you something," said Aaron. Reluctantly Qiingi went over and looked through the eyepiece.

Livia had no interest in telescopes, and Qiingi said nothing at the time about what he saw. That night, though, as they lay together, he told her.

"I remember trying to catch mist in my hand, when I was a boy. I had thought that the Lethe would be the same, that it was a kind of fog too insubstantial to see." Instead, when he pointed the telescope at the Lethe he saw, not mist, but a broad distribution of starlike points that only merged to form the cloud at a seemingly infinite distance. Aaron had showed Qiingi how to zoom in on one of the points; up close, it looked something like a dismembered aircar leg was coalescing out of the fog. It hung alone in space, distant sunlight picking out fine detail on one half of it, the other half an unformed smudge. He focused the scope on another pinprick of light; this looked like it would become a bundle of girders, given time. And over there was a curved diamond-glass window, visible only as arcs and lozenges of reflection. Each of the objects was separated by many kilometers from its nearest neighbor—but there were billions, trillions of such pieces. Between them, Aaron had explained, an unguessable amount of virtual matter floated. Its components seemed to drift together over time and spontaneously morph into objects and devices of any sort.

Livia lay there a long time thinking about it, aware that Qiingi was doing the same beside her. The Lethe Nebula was nothing more or less than several civilizations' worth of parts and supplies, drifting slowly in currents and eddies of their own diffuse gravity. According to Aaron, countless fusion-powered ships grazed up and down the vast outer surface of the cloud. Qiingi suggested that this might be the solar system's watering hole: a gathering place for whatever it was that lived beyond all manifolds, beyond the tech locks. Here they—whatever they were—fed off the bounty provided by the anecliptics.

And somewhere within that abyss of drifting machines and parts, the anecliptics themselves might lurk—watchful, alert for anyone who tried to take too much or enter too deeply into what Lucius had called the "Fallow Lands."

Or, perhaps, alert for anyone who tried to leave.

11

THEIR EXPERIENCES AT Rosinius Coronal remained vivid in Livia's memory later; the coronals that followed tended to blur together. Maybe it was because they spent more time at this first stop, or maybe it was that in those first days Livia wondered whether its desolate jungle was to be their home for the rest of their lives.

When the coronal first loomed ahead of them, they talked in anticipation about what they might find there: a culture of manifolds like their own, perhaps—or perhaps a fallen civilization, captured and conquered like their own by 3340. They spent time getting their stories straight, depending on what the people were like and how they were received.

No one received them.

Invisible grapples delicately plucked the flying house's tether and drew them through the skin of the coronal, depositing the house in what Aaron said was an airlock chamber similar to those underneath Teven. The room was big enough to accommodate a dozen houses; giant letters on one wall spelled out ROSINIUS. After an hour of tense waiting, during which hissing and popping sounds indicated an atmosphere being pumped into the chamber, they finally ventured out their front door. Qiingi brought his spear. But there was no welcoming committee in the dusty corridors that opened off the airlock—only soil-clogged stairs that led upward into steaming air and the buzz of unfamiliar insects.

They looked at one another uncertainly, then Aaron grimaced and said, "Might as well see what's up there."

At the top of the half-blocked stairs they emerged in a clearing where some forest giant had fallen long ago, taking many of its neighbors with it. The tumbled logs were overgrown with moss and ferns and up-thrusting darts of new forest. It was bright under the hazy suns—three starlettes—but beneath the encroaching forest nothing was visible but gloom. They walked slowly into this cathedral of trees and stopped, daunted right at the start of their exploration.

There were no landmarks that would make it easy for them to find their way back here. Still, nobody raised the issue; they all needed to know what had happened here. Unspoken was the thought that perhaps this was what Teven would look like once 3340 was done with it.

Then Qiingi pointed. "There is a deer track there," he said. "A track for something, at least; these plants are unlike any I've ever seen."

Indeed, all the vegetation in sight seemed bloated, about to burst with water or sap. There was an unhealthy, fetid stench under the trees. In-sectlike birds flitted under the high forest canopy. The ground here was clear of underbrush, but rows of huge fungi crisscrossed the loam like fences.

"If we follow that track, we return the same way," said Qiingi confidently.

"And what if we get lost?" said Aaron.

Qiingi stood up straighter. "I will not become lost."

"Oh, like that's reassuring. I—"

"Hey!" shouted Livia. "Are we going or not?"

Aaron shrugged breezily. "All right. But I don't see what you hope to find."

They walked in silence. After the first hundred meters Livia was drenched in sweat; she found it hard to breathe this thick air, but she wasn't about to complain. She felt like they were finally doing something. Qiingi took the lead, and for the first time in weeks he looked alert, even happy.

Asteroidal rocks, weathered with time, poked up here and there along the trail, which meandered back and forth but always maintained its general direction. They saw no animal life other than the distant avians. The creatures always stayed high above where stout branches reached out and vines drooled from the forest climax. The air was full of midges, but nothing bit them.

The land became swampy, and the path wound its way in between dark pools. These were fringed with gouts of green vegetation that seemed frozen in some complex fight for space above the water; those stalks and branches that won were turned downward, leaves pointing at the black water. The gargantuan trunks of trees reared up in between the pools, and sometimes the path followed the backs of twisting exposed roots that formed bridges across the still, leaf-paved surfaces. There was no sign of the creatures that had created the path, but as they were crossing one of the pools Livia happened to glance down, and stopped.

"That's odd." She pointed at a distant glow of pastel light that glimmered deep in the water. It seemed like frozen clouds of radiance were trapped down there. There was something familiar about the glow, but it was unlike anything she had ever seen in the forests and pools of Westerhaven. As she watched, the glowing roils moved slowly to one side, as though some great river were flowing beneath her feet.

Then the first stars came into view.

Aaron breathed an inarticulate sound of wonder. A glittering starscape appeared beneath the bridge, delicately shimmering as if trapped in the depths of the pool. "It's a window," said Livia. Qiingi frowned in confusion. "Don't you see?" She pointed. "The skin of the coronal is transparent here."

He shook his head, uncomprehending—then gasped as a starlette appeared below, and bright dawn came to the shadowed pillars of the forest.

The sunlight appeared first in the far distance; it looked as though some giant were lifting the trees away in patches here and there, leaving bright spring-green and yellow shining in shafts of sunlight. A crimson and gold glow welled up in the pool—and the little sun appeared there, too bright to look at. The wreaths of foliage around them were now bathed in full daylight, and the underside of the forest canopy far above was painted bright green.

"This window could be kilometers in size," said Aaron. "Maybe once it was all clear, like a shallow lake. You could have canoed over the stars. But the soil's invaded it . . ."

The strange ground-lit day only lasted five minutes. But its glitter revealed vast distances under the forest canopy, and it was plain that there were no buildings here, no clearings—no sign of humanity.

So, though they made several more forays out to the jungle, they never traveled farther than that very spot. There seemed little point. They gathered large armfuls of various plants to feed into the food processors in the house; they came up at night and scanned the visible ring of the coronal for any signs of a living civilization, and they debated endlessly about what might have happened here. And finally, after four days, they trooped back to the house and Aaron replaced the ROSINIUS sign on its side with the next name on the list of coronals he'd compiled while exploring Teven's underside. Sure enough, after another day of tense waiting, a creaking and popping signaled the withdrawal of atmosphere from the giant airlock—and then suddenly the house was falling, everybody shouting as the furniture flew every which way. Rosinius had released them.

So began weeks of travel and disappointment, as each coronal turned out to be empty—whether jungle like Rosinius, waving grassland like Makhtar, or ice and mountains like some others. Barren as they were, though, with each coronal they visited they came closer to the outer boundary of the Lethe Nebula.

When they emerged from the stairwell in the last coronal for which Aaron had a name, it was to find themselves standing on an island no more than five meters on a side, in an endless ocean choked with ice floes. The sky was full of low, brooding clouds and the wind cut like daggers.

They had talked about what they would do when they ran out of destinations. Aaron had proposed a bold solution, one that might not work. If it didn't, there would be no disastrous fallout. They simply wouldn't go any farther, and would have to retrace their steps back to Teven. But if it did work . . .

He and Qiingi changed the sign on the house to read JUPITER.

A day later, as usual without warning, they fell into blackness. This time, they had no idea what their destination would be. All they knew was that the Lethe Nebula had begun to recede. The glittering complexity of the greater solar system lay ahead, its threats and promises unknown.

BY THE SECOND day of this new journey, something changed. Aaron's crude radio had begun to pick up faint voices.

There were thousands of them, overlapping on all frequencies. It was difficult to pick out and follow any one for more than a few seconds. Some of the complex noises they heard might or might not be human, but many spoke an understandable dialect of WorldLing. Understanding the language didn't help; very little that Livia heard made any sense. She listened for an hour, and the impression that built up was of a vast and vibrant civilization completely concerned with its own affairs, either ignorant or uncaring of the discarded worlds right next to it.

The view out the windows reinforced this impression. They kept the lights off in the living room much of the time now. All took turns sitting in the darkness and watching, as something like a giant scintillating galaxy emerged hour by hour from behind the Lethe Nebula. Countless starlettes of all sizes lit the sides of the nebula from within that tangle of detail. There were hundreds of worlds for every miniature sun: ring-shaped coronals, long oval cylinders, round balls of metal just a few kilometers in diameter, and crystal rods, cubes, and spheres like teeming one-celled organisms. All of space beyond the Lethe seemed to be filled with light and structure, starlettes and mists of worlds receding in layers and sheets, runnels of light raveling and overlapping into an infinity of detail.

Aaron fussed over the radio and finally announced that the transmitter part was working. He actually joined Livia and Qiingi for dinner that night. "We can send voice, but nothing so sophisticated as inscape or even video," he announced. "The question is, what do we say?"

They looked at one another. Qiingi nodded slowly. "We know that our elders' stories about this place are largely true," he said. "The elders speak of a single Song of Ometeotl that encompasses all the gardens of the sun. All the planets and coronals, you would say. For some reason, our world of Teven is not part of this Song. These radio voices do not give any clues as to why."

"Except one," said Livia, waving a fork at Qiingi. "We've heard ships signaling one another and their ports. None of them mentioned Teven, or Rosinius, or any of the coronals we've visited. It's as if those places don't exist to them."

Aaron shrugged. "Beyond their horizon. Nothing unusual there."

"But, the elders have always been adamant about one thing," said Qiingi. "The rest of the solar system does not have horizons. It is all one place. So how could we be beyond its horizon?"

They debated as the evening wore on. Raven's histories were very different than Westerhaven's; each manifold saw the past through a different lens. It was no surprise that they could find few common denominators in the stories.

In particular, the history leading up to and immediately following the self-imposed exile of the founders to Teven varied wildly from place to place. Qiingi claimed that this was natural, because that period constituted the origin, or dreamtime, of all the manifolds. "We each make it our source myth," he explained.

Aaron opened his mouth to make some snide comment, but was interrupted by a squawk from the radio.

Qiingi raised an eyebrow. "Did it just say 'house'?"

They crowded into the bedroom. Sure enough, the radio was saying,

"Attention the house, attention the house. You have no identification beacon. This is a violation of—" *bzzzzt.* The last noise sounded like machine-language.

Aaron grabbed the crude microphone he had built. "Well, what do I say?"

"Say we need help," Livia said. "What's the Old WorldLing word . . . Mayday?"

"Mayday, mayday," Aaron said into the mic. "We are unpowered and unarmed. Can you hear us?"

Rich laughter poured out of the speaker. "If this isn't the craziest stunt I've ever seen!" The voice faded a bit. "Hey, guys, take a look at this thing. Some damn fools built themselves a flying house."

Livia and Aaron looked at each other. "I doubt we're dealing with officials here," he said.

Qiingi was staring out the bedroom window. "What do you think that is?" he said, pointing.

It looked like a little metal star, seven-pointed and twirling sedately. Livia went to the window and shielded her eyes with her hands. In the second or two it took to do that the distant vision had expanded from an intricate speck to button-sized. Then all of a sudden it was on top of them: kilometers-long, sides of white metal, with chandelier cities on the ends of long netted cables slung from its central body.

A shudder went through the house. "We've been caught," shouted Aaron. For a second Livia's inner ear told her she was falling, then things leveled out with a bounce.

She was about to comment on the smoothness of their capture when the bedroom was suddenly filled with vertical yellow bars, spaced about one per meter. These flickered, faded, and were replaced by a set of nested blue spheres. The black outside the window turned to static, and then landscapes appeared out there: a plain of wheat fields, turned sideways; a glittering cityscape; a vista of mountains.

Livia grabbed Qiingi for support. "Inscape failure!" she shouted. She had seen this before, as had Aaron.

And then the house was full of people.

A young man in an outfit of canary yellow and blue appeared in the bedroom doorway. "Fantastic!" he laughed in heavily accented WorldLing. "This is a great stunt, you really had us going there for a while."

Livia could hear a crowd of men and women in the living room pointing at the furniture and laughing. More were arguing in the kitchen. She forced her shoulders out of their defensive hunch. Obviously these people were projections of that large ship's inscape system; this young man wasn't physically here. Not yet, anyway—the house was doubtless being drawn up into one of those chandelier cities even now. She glanced out the window. Space was gone, replaced by an endless landscape of forest, trees, and lakes.

"But how did you do all this?" said the young man. "I mean, the inscape is so strange. Look at this!" He gestured, and suddenly Livia's mother stood before him.

"What can I do for you, sir?" she inquired politely. He laughed, and as Livia watched in horror, Father appeared, then Esther, and Jachman and Rene—her whole Society, summoned for the first time in her life by a stranger.

"*Stop it!*" She gave the command to dismiss the Society, and she saw the confirmation icon blaze briefly in her lower visual field; but the animas of her friends and family remained visible. "What are you doing? Stop!"

The youth cocked his head, examining her as if she were some unusual butterfly he'd just collected. He opened his mouth to speak, but was interrupted by shouts from the living room. It was a female voice, saying, "Out, out! Shoo!"

The young man turned and said, "Wait—" then vanished. Suddenly the house was quiet.

"What just happened?" asked Qiingi. Livia shook her head, then froze as she heard something move in the living room. Together they slipped out into the hall and peered around the edge of the archway.

Bright sunlight streamed into the living room. Curtains thrown back, the big picture window showed a close-clipped lawn outside and, in the distance, the fairy towers of a city.

Contemplating this view, chin on hand, a young woman stood by the coffee table. She wore baggy overalls and her brown hair swept back in a disordered pageboy cut. Livia stepped into view, and she turned, smiling.

"Welcome to the Archipelago," she said. Livia shook the virtual hand she offered.

"Pleased to meet you, ah, miss . . . ?"

The young woman smiled brightly. "I have many names. But most people around here just call me the Government."

12

"SORRY FOR THE riot," said the inscape agent that called itself the Government. "This is nominally an Archipelagic warship you've docked with—but the boys are a bit..." she waggled her fingers, "undisciplined. It didn't help that your inscape implants are decidedly nonstandard." She cocked her head as though she were looking into Livia's skull.

"This Archipelago," said Livia. "It is the nation that controls the solar system?"

The Government looked at her archly. "You don't know? But then, you did come from the anecliptics' storage depot."

"Storage depot?"

The being gestured out the window. "The Fallow Lands. You know: a few trillion cubic kilometers of volume that is off-limits to everyone but them."

"These anecliptics," said Aaron eagerly. "What can you tell us about them?"

The Government strode toward the front door, saying, "You have questions, I have questions. Let's cooperate. Firstly: what are you doing here?"

Livia hardly knew where to begin; she looked at Aaron, who appeared similarly nonplused. Qiingi stepped forward and said, "We are fleeing people who've conquered our coronal. We need help to recapture our lands and free our people."

"Your coronal is..." The Government nodded at a point somewhere behind them. "In the Fallow Lands?" Qiingi nodded.

"Then I can't help you."

"Wait—"

"Why not—"

Again it held up its hand. "Not my jurisdiction. And technically, you're not my concern." Its expression soured a bit. "But since you are refugees, I'll cut you some slack. Come on." It opened the front door, and sunlight poured in. Outside, birds twittered on a green lawn that now surrounded the house. Farther away were more houses and beyond some hills, the towers of a city. It was all an inscape view, but highly convincing. "The first thing you should know," said the Government as she stepped outdoors, "is that your inscape is insecure as it stands. Until you get it fixed, other people can steal your records and histories. The guys started plundering yours as soon as they found you," she said, glancing back at Livia. "So don't be surprised if your agents turn up under other people's control."

Livia had been looking around herself, but now stopped in shock. Her Society stolen? "But . . . you say you're some sort of government agent. Couldn't you prevent that sort of thing?"

The young woman stopped and turned. Her eyes blazed with some powerful emotion, and she seemed to grow a few centimeters as her voice deepened. "I am *the* Government," she said. "I am a force of omniscience and unparalleled power within the human part of the Archipelago. I am a public-domain distributed artificial intelligence. I have made all human institutions redundant, for I am the personal and intimate friend of each and every one of the trillion humans under my domain. I am the selfless advocate of each of them, from the lowliest to the greatest.

"The only problem is . . . Well, nobody listens to me much anymore." She shrugged apologetically. "We all have our problems. I have little control these days. You're lucky the guys who picked up your ship don't believe you really came from the Fallow Lands, because if they did, what just happened would look like a polite tap on the shoulder compared to what they'd do. You must keep your origins to yourselves."

They stood silently, but none of the three spoke. After a moment the Government sighed, its aura evaporating. "What I mean," it said, "is there is no law here other than your will, enacted through me or the other agencies of the Archipelago. All may do as they may attempt. I will not let anyone kill or abuse you; but I can't be responsible for your property. Look to it yourselves.

"You'll need to use inscape, of course; in fact, you won't be able to get along without it." She indicated the parkland and city. "This is one of the typical views of the Archipelago. You'll find this landscape goes on for millions of kilometers in every direction—it's a virtual aggregate of all the colonies, coronals, ships, and starlettes in the solar system. Most people here don't like to be reminded that they're living on artificial worlds. Many have forgotten or don't believe it anymore.

"The other thing you need to know is that I'm going to have to impound your house." The woman-shaped agent put its hands on its hips and glared at the building. "It's full of dangerous nanotech—so are your clothes, in fact. It'll all have to go. I'll compensate you for the mass and energy you've lost. You can use that to set yourselves up here."

"All right, but if you can't help us, who can?" asked Qiingi.

The Government hesitated. "Granted where you come from . . . Well, just talk to people. Maybe you can generate an adhocracy to help you out. Or appeal to the Good Book or the votes."

"What about the anecliptics?" asked Livia.

The Government shook its head. "You'll get no help there." Then it winked out of existence, leaving two trim footprints in the grass.

THEY GATHERED THEIR few things, and left the house at a walk. There were some people in the distance but otherwise the brightly lit parkland seemed very empty. If inscape, it was particularly convincing. Livia plucked an orange from the low-hanging branch of a tree as they passed by. It seemed real; she peeled it, and felt the sharp flavor as she popped a piece in her mouth. "It tastes real," she said. "How is that possible?"

"Are you addressing me?" asked the orange. She almost dropped it in surprise.

"Well . . . I suppose so."

"Just switch views a few times, and you'll see where I came from."

Livia obliged, calling up an inscape reticle around the tree. She tracked down the translucent menu with her eyes, and the parkland vanished, replaced by a towering cityscape. Where the tree had been was some sort of dispensing machine.

She tried another view. They now stood in a public market crowded with people. The tree had become a fruit-vendor's stall. The vendor himself waved from behind his counter. "Come back any time!" he said.

"What are you doing?" asked Qiingi.

"Aren't you seeing this?" she asked. He shook his head.

"There's no tracking on inscape in this manifold," said Aaron wonderingly. "Everybody can see whatever they want, however they want even if it contradicts what the person next to them sees."

Livia shuddered. "But that's madness. Where's the common view?"

"That's what I'm saying. There is no common view."

"No common view . . . and just one tech set?"

"I'm in a technical view right now," said Aaron. Some inscape address icons glowed faintly around his reticle like an aura; they were different from her own, she realized. "It's beautiful," said Aaron, gazing around himself. "I'm querying . . . did you hear that? It says it doesn't know what I mean by tech locks."

"Who are you talking to?" asked Qiingi. "A qqatxhana?"

"Uh, yeah. An inscape agent. You can't see him?" Qiingi shook his head.

They wandered on, experimenting. Livia found that after a few queries and after flipping through a few views to try to find something, her local view was beginning to anticipate her. The parkland mutated spontaneously, showing paths, buildings, labels, and reticles indicating rest stops and fountains; and people began appearing. The first few were serlings: inscape agents designed to help search for information. She asked one of them who the other people in her view were.

"People who share your interests or activities," said the man-shaped agent. "Or who just like the same places. When you use inscape you accumulate a profile based on what you've done and where you've gone. Inscape locates people with similar or complementary profiles and brings you close." It moved its open palms together.

"Not physically close."

Now it looked puzzled. "What do you mean, physically?"

"They're not really here, all of them, are they?"

It frowned for a moment. "If you mean, would you see them if you fell out of inscape, no. But don't worry, you can't do that."

Within an hour Livia, Qiingi, and Aaron were sitting in a restaurant surrounded by a crowd of affable strangers. Food came; people told jokes and let the three newcomers pester them with questions. Feeling cautious, they took the Government's advice and told no one that they had come from the Fallow Lands. But after the fourth time that someone asked just where they *had* come from, they went into a huddle to get their story straight. Once again, a serling appeared to assist in the discussion. When Qiingi asked it to name a plausible place of origin far enough away that no one here could have visited it, it said, "How about the planet Ventus? Nobody knows much about it, but it's a real place."

From then on they told people that they came from Ventus.

By the time their chosen view slid toward nightfall, they had a better understanding of this place—enough to know that a real understanding might not be easy to get. This Archipelago customized itself to your every thought and action. There was no base reality here, at least not for anybody inside inscape—and that was everybody. The irony was that now that Qiingi and Aaron could tune one another out, they seemed to be getting along at last.

Livia faded out their new acquaintances as well as the restaurant; the other two followed suit. For a while they wandered along a broad boulevard, their few salvaged possessions bobbing in virtual matter fogs behind them. Finally Aaron asked inscape where they could find a place to sleep, but he was a bit behind Livia, who had started yawning a few minutes before. As far as she was concerned, all three of them now stood in a luxurious apartment with deep beds and full amenities. Of course, the place must be, in part or whole, an illusion—but the plumbing and beds were real enough. A serling told Livia that the amenities were built up of programmable matter and certain pieces flown in by microbots as soon as the apartment was requested. This technology was like that which made up her angels back home, only taken to an almost absurd degree.

The whole place was also moving somewhere, though you couldn't tell unless you queried. But wherever they were, it was out of the way of heavy traffic.

Lying in tonight's bed—the first, she thought, of many—Livia listened to the silence, imagining she could hear the two men through the walls. The idea that they were there was reassuring, but even the walls could stroll away in the night if they chose to.

What world would be waiting for her in the morning? And would Aaron and Qiingi still be in it?

LIVIA STUCK HER head out the aircar's window, letting the rush of air whip back her hair. She was so happy to finally be free of that stale house, and to at last be doing something—even if the issue of their urgent mission still hung over their heads. Maybe today's meeting would hold the answer.

She had good reason to be hopeful. In the several days they had been here, none of the three had found any overt evidence of 3340. Inscape had adapted to their needs by bringing close anyone and anything that knew something about invading or aggressive forces throughout the Archipelago. No one they'd spoken to had heard of a numbered movement to subvert inscape. And if so, if it were not the godlike power of the Archipelago itself that had attacked Teven . . . then maybe they could find help here.

"Livia," said Cicada, startling her out of her wind-blown reverie. The little faerie hovered in the air outside the car.

"Is our inscape repaired?" she asked him. He nodded.

"Almost. We put together a repair adhocracy with some of the house resources. But inscape still can't steer your bodies; give it a few hours. By the way, we checked into the theft of your archives. We think we succeeded in encrypting a bunch of them in the microseconds before they were stolen. The thieves only got some memories from before the attack on Barrastea."

Which was enough of a violation in itself, Livia felt.

Peaseblossom appeared, nodding vigorously. "But you don't have enough processing power in your implants for us to run sims of this place." He crossed his arms petulantly. "How are we expected to do anything really useful?"

"Look through my eyes, and learn," she said.

"Hmmf. Okay." He brightened. "Hey, do you think that's our host?" Peaseblossom pointed.

Walking across the sky toward them was a striking woman dressed in flames and white vapor. Her face was silhouetted in a golden glow, and behind her spread a vista of dazzling white clouds, like a tunnel, with light pouring from its far end. She walked easily on the air, one hand held out before her in greeting.

"You must be my new guests," she said. "My name is Sophia Eckhardt. Welcome to my narrative." Livia stood up—the view of the aircar dissolving—and reached to take her hand.

"Alison Haver," said Livia. They had decided that until they knew for sure 3340's agents weren't from here, they would use false identities. The Government didn't seem to care.

As light welled up around Sophia's face, Livia saw that her dark, aquiline features were crisscrossed with black tattoos, apparently physical. A fan of them swept back from each eye like feathers. Livia wondered what significance they might have; but inscape here was not so convenient as to let her query it discreetly while letting an anima talk for her.

"We're delighted to meet you." Livia introduced her companions to Sophia. "Georges Milan," said Aaron; "Skyy," said Qiingi—as unique a name as Qiingi, but, Livia supposed, there was really no hiding his differences here.

"But tell me," said Sophia, "why this traveling view?" She gestured at the aircar. "It's terribly crippleview of you. You're not *versos,* are you?"

Livia tried to look embarrassed. "I'm afraid I don't know what that is. We might have chosen not to experience the flight," she added, "but our inscape implants are slightly incompatible with yours. We don't seem able to completely separate our consciousness from our bodies yet." She didn't add that, as a matter of principle, Qiingi would never do such a thing. "Anyway, we didn't know if it would be considered rude to arrive virtually at the . . . narrative . . . before our bodies caught up."

Sophia frowned for a moment, obviously considering something. "You really are aliens, then. How wonderful, you'll be a big hit. Sit down for now, and we'll put you into my narrative in your seats. Just remember not to stand up and try to walk about or you'll find yourselves back in the aircar."

Livia nodded; they sat; and then she found herself reclining on a divan in a sumptuous, marble-pillared garden. The place was jammed with people—tall, short, human-normal and stylized, half-animal, elemental, ethereal. They crowded together, talking and laughing, waving drinks, musical instruments, neural stimulators, and other unidentifiable things. Clouds of bots and inscape agents flitted to and fro. Pulsing music shuddered through the floor; a slowly rotating inscape reticle near Livia's right hand showed dozens of iconic buttons indicating other possible views of the party. "My humble narrative," said Sophia as she sat on a moss-covered ottoman nearby. "Now, where were we? Ah, yes: it would be considered rude not to leap ahead of yourselves. We don't much tolerate old views here—like 'objective reality' and physical bodies and such. Those are just relics of ice-age programming. Why take the crippleview when you don't have to?"

They all nodded as if this made sense to them.

"As to the versos," Sophia continued, "I'm amazed you haven't heard of them. Tell me, where are you three from?"

"Ventus," said Livia. "We're from Ventus."

"I'll have to visit a sim some time," said Sophia. "Did you bring any personal locations with you?"

"Unfortunately, no."

"Well, anyway, versos are people who don't want inscape to weave a coherent narrative of their lives for them." said Sophia. "They disable inscape's narrative function and do horrid things like allowing accidental events to happen to them. Some of them even try to live in a single consistent view their whole lives." She shook her head in disgust.

"Oh, I see," said Livia. "Well, we're not versos. Just foreigners." She remembered how her surroundings had slowly begun to look like Barrastea yesterday, until she intervened and deliberately switched views. In all likelihood, Livia decided, she *was* a verso.

"What brings you to the Archipelago?" Sophia leaned forward, looking indulgent.

Qiingi smiled at her; he had lost the shell-shocked look he'd had for the past days, and now looked completely self-assured. Livia felt a swell of pride at seeing him rally.

"We are looking for your . . . authorities," he said. "We would call them founders where we come from: people with responsibility, decision makers. Those granted power by the majority."

"Leaders?" said Sophia helpfully.

"Yes. But other than a brief and confusing encounter with something that called itself the Government, we've met none of this Archipelago's leaders. I suppose you're our first."

"Me!" Sophia leaned back, affecting alarm. "A leader? But of course your questions didn't turn up anything. We don't have a government here, after all. Only the Government. And the votes. And nobody pays much attention to *them* anymore."

Livia was about to ask more about that, when she heard the aircar's voice say, "We have arrived."

"Just a moment," she said to Sophia. "We're here—I mean, our view is still stuck in the aircar. Awkward, really. We'll just exit the car and meet you in person, if that's all right?"

Sophia looked amused. "If you want."

The garden vanished, and they stood up out of the aircar, which sat on a broad platform hundreds of meters above the glittering lights of the city—virtual or real, she wasn't sure—known as Brand New York. A fantastical tower like spun sugar spiraled above them; outthrusts of glass or more likely diamond cradled long oval residences. The nearest one was full of light and sound and the movement and laughter of people. "That would be the place," said Aaron as he set off toward it. "Work the crowd?" he said, glancing at Livia with a raised eyebrow.

"You take the technical questions," she said. "I'll do our host."

He nodded. "Some of the people here looked like AIs, or at least animas of a sort. I'll try to learn more about how they use inscape. And why it looks like there's no tech locks here."

Livia turned to Qiingi, who was watching this exchange intently. "The other essential is how we're going to live here," she said. "That and . . . who can we trust? You're good at assessing people. Can you find out about Sophia for us? Discreetly, of course."

"I will be charming," he said, "but discreet."

The process that had led to their invitation here was somewhat mysterious. The invitation had arrived the first evening; Livia had initially assumed that the Government itself had contacted Eckardt. When she summoned it to thank it for the service, it denied having done so. "Nobody issued the invitation," it had said, "it just *emerged.*" Livia had been too tired to pursue the matter. After that conversation, though, she'd begun to notice new things about this place. Life seemed tightly organized yet nobody consistently kept roles—customers became shopkeepers to other customers; people in restaurant views cooked, served, or ate as the whim took them. She'd put it down to the fluidity of inscape eliminating the need for stable identities. But that didn't explain apparent strangers—who were not encompassed by the shared reticle that indicated they were in the same view—exchanging items without consultation. She saw people tap one another on the shoulder and issue cryptic statements that were then passed on, like in a child's game. There was something going on outside of the Archipelago's consensual realities, it seemed.

As they entered the submanifold that Sophia Eckhardt called her *narrative,* they split up. Livia made her way in the direction of Sophia, who stood chatting with a striking, slender woman dressed in mirror-bright metal. As Livia walked she listened to the swirling conversations in the submanifold. The names were different, but the topics were mostly the same as at home: art, gossip, relationships, sports. She didn't overhear any political discussions, though, unless the excited talk about something called "Omega Point" counted.

Several small groups of people were huddled around what looked like copies of an actual paper book. One man was showing another a page, and as Livia passed he said, "You see? You were Phoenix up until we met, but since I'm currently Priestess, you become Charioteer." The other man nodded grudgingly.

As she was rounding a small pool Livia heard sounds of heated argument off to the left. It was unfamiliar enough—the sort of thing that animas would have smoothed over at home—that she stopped and looked over.

He was a total contrast to the rest of the narrative. Where they were dressed in light and impossible garments such as the butterfly-swarm flitting strategically around the woman next to her, this man was garbed in stolid gray cloth. His sandy hair was not augmented by light or motion; the lines in his face appeared real. He held an ordinary looking glass with some amber liquid in it. Just now he was glaring at a tall, multilimbed thing that might once have been human.

"Don't you think it's wrong, if not downright creepy," he said loudly, "that inscape can take over your autonomic nervous system, make someone who's standing right in front of you invisible and then *steer* your body around them? Don't you think we're being violated in such moments?"

The many-armed thing dismissed this line of reasoning with a laugh. "More than nine tenths of all our thought and action is unconscious, Respected Morss. Why should such petty issues as avoiding tripping over somebody be allowed to take up that last fraction in which we are aware? And why should I make any distinction between the unconscious processes going on in here," it pointed to its head with two arms, "and those going on out there on my behalf?"

Livia entirely agreed, but this Morss grunted derisively. "Because *I* am *this*," he said, pointing toward his body, "not this." He gestured at the swirling party. "This is just a fantasy-land for people who've forgotten about reality. You can keep it. I prefer to live in the real world." As he spoke his eyes drifted away from the being he was speaking to. His gaze alighted on Livia, and she saw his eyes widen slightly.

Of course: she was not dressed in any illusions, was in fact only in her shift which had been scoured clean of tech lock nano and most of its programming. She had not yet found out how to interface with other people's inscape to craft the kind of fabulous confectionary costume that the rest of the submanifold wore. So, she and the other refugees were the only ones in the place who looked as plain as this Respected Morss.

She smiled at him politely and walked on by. She spotted Sophia again and waved; her host energetically gestured for her to come over.

"This is Lady Filament," said Sophia. The woman in rippling silver smiled and held out her hand. She appeared human except for one feature: her eyes glowed with inner light, a subtle and entrancing gold. "She is a *vote*."

"Oh." Livia shook her hand. "Tell me, what exactly is a vote?"

Filament's eyes widened in surprise. She looked at Sophia as if to confirm the joke, then laughed. "You *are* from far away. I'm the aggregate personality of a particular constituency within the Archipelago. Just an average person, in the most literal sense." She grinned and Livia smiled, a bit uncertainly.

"You're an AI?"

"An old term, and crude . . . call me an emergent property of inscape itself."

"You were asking how we ran things here," Sophia said at Livia's obviously puzzled smile. "So I thought I'd introduce you to Filament. She's one of the ways. In the modern and ancient ages they used to vote in humans to run their institutions, but you could never guarantee that the person you voted for really had the same agenda as you. Aggregate personalities like Filament solve that problem. They really *are* the constituency, in a sense. So when they get together, you know your interests are being looked after."

"Thank you," said Filament, "that sounds very flattering. But it's not really a top-down thing. Inscape is designed so that like-minded people doing similar things form stable nodes of activity. When such a node becomes large enough, a vote spontaneously appears as a high-level behavior of the network. There's one of us for each interest group in the

Archipelago. And the entity that emerges out of *our* interactions is called the Government."

She smiled at Sophia. "But I'm really just a relic of the past, aren't I? Sophia here represents the new way: an emergent government that doesn't use the inscape network at all."

"The Good Book," said Sophia.

"The invitation for you to visit Sophia emerged from a self-organizing system," said Filament, "but not one that lives in inscape. For more than a hundred years there's been no way for the human citizens of the Archipelago to govern themselves except through people like me—"

"Until the Book," Sophia nodded.

"—Which is exactly that: a bound, old-style book. Its pages contain simple rules of interaction. If enough people follow these rules most of the time, a network intelligence emerges from the social connections between them. It's independent of inscape, see? So the Book operates outside the control of the Government."

Livia's head was spinning. "But you're a vote. Doesn't that make you an enemy of this Book?"

Livia's host simpered. "But the votes don't have an agenda of their own—only *our* agendas. If I choose the Book, my votes choose it, too."

Gamely, Livia tried to keep up. "So you use the Good Book—is that the significance of your tattoos?"

Sophia's eyes widened. "You mean you don't know—" Now it was her turn to look shocked, while Filament grinned. Sophia quickly composed herself. "I've never had that question before."

"I apologize if I've offended you—"

"No, no, I'm just surprised. I thought the soundtracks were known everywhere."

"You're . . . a musician?"

Sophia nodded. "I'm a soundtrack. A soprano."

"Not just any soundtrack," interjected Filament. She proceeded to describe what Sophia did, only about half of which Livia understood. The tattoos were apparently proudly-born marks of an ordeal Sophia had undergone years ago. In a carefully constructed virtual world (basically a submanifold, although they didn't call them that here) she had allowed herself to be starved, tortured, and terrorized for weeks. She had emerged with a psyche ringing with anxiety and rage, her days full of bad memories and flinch-reactions. With the use of drug and neuroimplant therapies she could easily partition off that side of herself and so live a placid life. But when she performed at assigned times in other people's narratives she let it all out, and her rawness and pain lent emotional power to whatever key event was occurring in that person's life. It was all orchestrated by inscape, of course.

"Passion is a rare commodity these days," said Filament. "When everyone can have all pain, mental or physical, treated and removed instantly. And when everybody can have their vocal tract altered to give them an ideal singing voice, how do you stand out? Here," she pointed to an inscape panel, "you can find a sample of Sophia's lovely work."

Livia tuned in for a moment. The voice she heard shuddered and begged, raged and commanded, all in a language she had never heard before.

"Is there much work for, uh, soundtracks, here?" she asked without thinking.

"Do you sing? Almost nobody does," said Sophia, "simply because, as Filament said, everybody *could*."

Livia thought of the many songs of the Fictional History that she had learned as a child. They wouldn't know anything of that cycle here. "I might . . . have a unique contribution," she said.

"Go ahead then," said Sophia. "Let's hear you."

Livia hesitated; but she was actually in pretty good voice lately, from singing to Aaron and Qiingi during the long days of their journey here. She decided on a particularly difficult run from the *Opera of Chances* that she'd been practicing lately. She began to sing, feeling her confidence soar as the words poured from her mouth. Of course, the language was Teven's language, Joyspric, but even so she could see she was drawing a crowd. She closed her eyes as she came to the chorus—

—and was interrupted by a loud splash from nearby. Everybody looked over, to see the strange spectacle of a multiarmed man flailing about in the reflecting pool.

Gray-clad Respected Morss stood on the edge of the pool, looking down at the wet guest. "Oops," he said with heavy irony. "Lucky thing that's not real water. Oh, and I suppose you're not really sitting about on your ass in it, either."

"Excuse me," said Sophia. She scowled and edited Morss out of their view. Before he vanished he grinned unashamedly at Livia.

Things were getting just too strange. "If you'll excuse me," Livia said to Sophia and Filament. "I should find my people." She bowed to them both and hurried off to find the others.

THE THREE REFUGEES summoned up a quiet apartment of their own in a corner of Sophia's narrative. Then they sat down together to decide what to do next.

Livia described her conversation with Sophia, and her introduction to Filament. "There are no founders here," she said. "And apparently, no stable institutions as we'd understand them. Everything's an adhocracy, even the government. Sophia was picked to meet us and introduce us to Archipelagic society, but nobody chose her, her name just emerged from the process. And yet there's the Government AI, and these votes. I'm not sure they'll help us. But it seems like all we have to do is *want* help, and it'll appear from somewhere, because the inscape here tries to make a narrative—a story—out of whatever we do. I think that's how it works, anyway."

"If it worked that way," commented Qiingi drily, "we would be on our way home with a fleet of ships already."

"Hmm." She wouldn't let him puncture her good mood. "What about Sophia? Did you learn anything about her?"

"She is apparently a singer of old songs, which is probably why inscape brought you to her attention—you share a common interest. Also, she is a passionate believer in something called 'The Good Book.' I do know that the Book is *not* part of the narrative process you just described, Livia. Beyond that I learned little, except that the people here find us exotic and fascinating. But they have not guessed where we come from."

She frowned, thinking. "We may have to decide whether to ignore what the Government said, and reveal ourselves." She looked at the other two; Aaron was remaining strangely silent. Livia frowned at him. "What about you, Aaron? Did you find out anything?"

"Well," he said reluctantly. "I started out with some discreet inquiries about the anecliptics. The guests were just confusing on the subject, but I had a couple of good conversations with serlings about it. It seems," he took a breath and let it out heavily, "this whole area of inhabited space is near the boundary of the Lethe Nebula. Nobody crosses that boundary into the Fallow Lands. The Lands are off-limits to everybody except the anecliptics."

"The Government said that," said Livia impatiently.

Aaron shook his head. "But I don't think you understand the implications. Nobody gets in or out of the Fallow Lands. *Nobody ever has.* These people hate those restrictions—so it's a good thing only the Government seems to know we came from there."

The *annies*, as the anecliptics were called, were apparently AIs of transcendent power. They seemed to have taken over much of the function of blind nature in the Archipelago. They had complete control over the Feeds, those two twisting bands of precious matter radiating out from the sun. They doled out matter and energy to the various human and nonhuman civilizations that encircled the sun. But the annies themselves were answerable to no one. They existed outside of all human law and influence.

Qiingi seemed unsurprised at this. "They are like thunderbirds," he said. "Mediators between Man and the Great Spirit."

"Well. I wouldn't put it that way," said Aaron. "They're more like the local equivalent of the tech locks. Apparently they were created to prevent any one group from taking over the Archipelago—in particular, post-humans. They ruthlessly limit the technology and resources available to anybody in the Archipelago . . . Which is not to say there aren't beings of a great power out there, and more being created every day. One serling kept talking about 'gods.' It took me a while to realize he wasn't being metaphorical. If not for the annies, humanity probably wouldn't exist anymore. We would all have been replaced by post-humans.

"Anyway, the Fallow Lands belong to the annies," he continued. "They're rumored to be experimenting with new life forms there. But nobody gets in or out, not even the Government." He looked at Livia somberly. "And that's very bad news. Nobody's going to believe we're from the Fallow Lands—and nobody's in any position to help us go back. No human power exists that can safely return us to Teven."

Livia shifted in her seat. "No, there must be someone. And anyway, we got out, didn't we? So you must be able to get in."

Aaron just looked at her.

"Aaron," she laughed, a little nervously, "we've only been here a few days. We need to know a lot more before we jump to this sort of conclusion."

"Maybe." He summoned a reluctant grin. "I guess."

That ended the conversation. They sat silently, surrounded by sumptuous, virtual luxury. Livia felt her hopes slipping in the face of her companions' gloom. *It can't be true,* she thought. Thirty-three forty's people came from somewhere—but she refused to believe they were employed by one of the anecliptics. Maybe they were from elsewhere inside the Fallow Lands—but no, it would do no good to believe that, either.

"Actually, our next course of action is obvious," she said after a while. "The followers of this 3340 got into the Fallow Lands somehow. Find out who they are and where they came from, and we find out how to go home."

The men looked at one another. Aaron nodded, and seemed about to reply when inscape chimed. "Yes?" said Livia quickly.

Sophia Eckhardt appeared, seated on the air next to Qiingi. Livia could hear the continuation of the party behind her. "Alison, dear," she said, "I'm so sorry about the interruption earlier. Your song was lovely— you have a wonderful voice. Everybody's saying so."

"Well, that's very nice—" she began. Sophia cut her off.

"In particular, one of the most powerful and influential humans in the Archipelago said so." She smirked. "You had no idea I had guests like that at my little bash, did you?"

"Well, no, we—"

"Anyway, dear, you've received an invitation! Well, we both have. To sing for some special guests of Doran's on board his worldship. It'll be an important gig for me, but for you, I can hardly believe it! Not that I'm jealous, I'm proud of being the one to discover you. Will you do it?"

"Um." She glanced at Aaron and Qiingi. Both were smiling at her; Aaron nodded. "What does it get us—me?"

"Access to what they used to call 'the corridors of power.' Influence. Resource. Oh, and a certain amount of fame, I suppose."

"All right," she said hesitantly. "Who—who's this Doran person, again?"

"Oh, you saw him in the narrative. Doran Morss. He's the one who so rudely interrupted your little audition."

13

CLOUDS DRIFTED AWAY from the sun and shafts of white burst out to illuminate Doran Morss's private world.

Having never been able to travel to Earth, for all his wealth, Morss had recreated part of it in his worldship: the exact topography and foliage of Scotland drifted by beneath Livia's window. Sophia still insisted on seeing it laid out flat within the consensus space of the Archipelago, like the original, but Doran Morss apparently preferred to see his lands through crippleview and so to be polite, Livia did, too. This view showed the lands to be rolled up into a tube that was capped on the ends to keep out the implacable vacuum of space. Huge diamond windows in the caps let in sunlight that reflected down from conical mirrors floating at the axis of the cylinder. The east and west shores of Doran's *Scotland* nearly met where the North Sea and Atlantic combined into a thick band of treacherous water on the far side of the world. He had so designed the place that it was full of cloud and mist most of the time; even without inscape's intervention, you could only tell you were in an artificial world on the sunniest days.

High above the rugged landscape of Morss's *Scotland* swung a chandelier city in bolo configuration, its two tethered halves separated by kilometers of cable. At the bottom of one glittering tangle of buildings hung a vast domed ballroom, its walls patterned like lace in opaque white and transparent diamond. After performing her songs, Livia had drifted over to one of the transparent panels, seeking a vantage point from which to watch the proceedings.

Doran Morss's party was both a surprise and a relief to Livia: it wasn't a swirl of half-real inscapes, like nearly every other event she'd seen so far in the Archipelago. Indeed, everything here was refreshingly solid, as were the people, who were all physically present. Sophia was deep in conversation with one of the visiting post-humans. She seemed uncomfortable around the rest of the guests. For the moment, all Livia wanted to do was stay out of the way, however much her Westerhaven training told her she should be shmoozing and picking up gossip.

Almost all of the guests looked like human beings, with notable exceptions such as the nonsentient brody that squatted like a living tank near the drinks table. These weren't humans standing about with drinks in their hands, however. The ballroom was crowded with votes, and Livia was witnessing a meeting of the government in the Archipelago.

Each vote was the embodiment of some value that had once had its own institutions, buildings, cadres, and followers. Some churches stood over there, chatting and munching canapes; here sporting fraternities and paramilitaries swapped anecdotes; and farther away, the arts were bickering. Apparently, while their personalities were the average of the values of millions of humans, these beings were required to conduct their business with one another on the humanly accessible levels of conversation, innuendo, back-room dealing, and treachery. It was part of something the locals called "open-source government."

The votes didn't intimidate Livia; nonetheless, her performance had been difficult. Not technically—she was in voice and well rehearsed. No, it was a fight with Aaron and Qiingi this morning that had her distraught and distracted, fumbling through her song. Luckily no one had seemed to notice.

"I know you're upset, but stay, please," Sophia had told her. "You can't help your friends until all of you calm down a bit." So Livia stood by the wall, arms crossed, waiting out the rest of the entertainments.

Finally they were done, and Doran Morss stepped to a podium at one end of the dome. A cylindrical cloudscape wheeled behind him as he said,

"Welcome to my humble abode," to general laughter. "You particular constituencies have been summoned here by the Government to discuss the Omega Point crisis. I hope that while you're here you'll see some of the sights in my little world and hopefully drop by to see me as well."

The crowd made polite noises. Morss accepted them with a nod, then simply stood there and waited, his arms crossed. The crowd quieted. Morss stayed still, gazing out at them.

What's he doing? Livia felt the tension in the room grow as the seconds stretched on, and Morss didn't move.

"So it's come to this," he said at last. The words were spoken very quietly, but by now the ballroom was utterly silent. All faces were turned toward Morss.

"Not so long ago," he continued, "there could have been no Omega Point crisis. If a trans-humanist movement sprang up during the rule of the monoculture, it would have been quashed before it encompassed a hundred people. But of course, the monoculture ultimately failed, didn't it? And you were born in its place. Some of you are old enough to remember the first years of the Government." He nodded to the small crowd of churches. "You remember a time when you would have channeled the people's energies back into some more useful pursuit. Inscape would have changed their narratives' plotlines and led them back to sanity. But that didn't happen this time."

"Hello again," said someone next to Livia. She turned to find the Government standing next to her. It wore its guise as a young woman, this time dressed as a waitress. "How are you?"

"I'm fine," Livia said curtly.

The Government was carrying a tray of canapes. "Then try the calamari," it said with a smile. "It's fine, too."

"This worldship is on course to the Omega Point Coronal," continued Morss. "The cultists have expelled or killed the remaining human population and have barricaded themselves inside the coronal. We're supposed to be meeting to decide how to deal with their creation as a newborn post-human entity—you, as votes, me and other outsiders as representatives of anecliptic interest."

He waved a hand negligently, half turning away. "Sure. Let's spend a few hours trying them for crimes against viability. Fat lot of good that'll do, now that they've killed everybody around them.

"I'd much rather talk about when this is going to happen again!" he shouted. "And what are we going to do to prevent the next outbreak? Before you were born, the monoculture tried to stem the tide of post-human transformations—and failed. Are you here today to say that the

Government has failed, too? Is that the real message we're going to send the human race?"

"I was hoping he'd do this," whispered the Government. "Doran's a reliable ally."

"Ally? You speak as though he's your equal. Isn't he just another citizen?"

The Government shook her head. "He's an independent nation. As such, he *is* my equal."

Livia nodded, not quite comprehending. "What does he have to do with the Omega Point thing?"

Sophia had talked about the Omega Point crisis on the way here. To Livia, the thought of an entire coronal uploading their minds into a machine was outrageous. "Sophia thinks Omega Point are heroes," she added, nodding in the singer's direction. What had disturbed Livia most was Aaron's reaction. He also seemed excited at the prospect of people doing such a thing.

"Doran has authority as a traditional human," said the Government. "Many people supported Omega Point, including many of the votes here. People see embodied humanity as a dead end, and post-humanism as the only way out from under the anecliptics. Doran's wrong about one thing, though; we're not here to debate the right or wrong of it. The question is, is Omega Point's creation *viable*?"

"What do you mean by that?"

"Can it survive and find a place in the Archipelago?" said the Government. "That's all it means. It's the ultimate question for any entity—bacteria or god."

"You're victims of your own success," Morss was saying. "Government happens so seamlessly now that most people have abandoned public life entirely. They're drowning in inscape—we see it every day. Every day there's more outbreaks of post-human expansionism from within our own ranks. As a human who is outside the jurisdiction of the Government—hence independent—I'm one of the few individual humans able to talk to you all on an equal footing. And I have a simple message, from humanity to you: forget about Omega Point. Don't shoot the messenger. Look to yourselves for the problem and the solution."

"Now I didn't expect him to say *that*," mused the Government.

THE GOVERNMENT HURRIED off to speak to a knot of votes. As Morss wound up his speech the votes were arguing and chatting, like any conference or colloquium. Livia had intended to stay so that she could petition the votes for help; but right now she just wanted the day to be over.

This morning's argument had begun almost as soon as Livia sat down. Qiingi had said, "Why are you not physically present, Aaron? These meetings are important."

"Of course they are," Aaron had snapped back. "That's why I'm making the best of my resources. I've got sixteen animas out there right now, tracking down leads. But I don't see you copying yourself at all." He wasn't just present as an anima, Livia saw; Aaron registered as a veritable tornado of information-density in her reticle. His view of the Archipelago was intense and multichanneled.

"It is not our way to divide ourselves," Qiingi replied awkwardly. Aaron had laughed at him.

"Whose way? Who is this 'we' you're talking about? Are you part of this expedition or not, Qiingi? Are you going to pull your weight?"

Qiingi winced. "But this . . . this is not my teotl—my technology—"

"Maybe it wasn't when you were back on Teven, but it is now." Aaron appealed to Livia. "Tell him, Liv. He's got to get with the way the world works here. Otherwise he'll just hold us back."

"Get with the way the world works?" Livia stared at Aaron. "You mean abandon your own technological mix for somebody else's? Since when has anyone of Teven Coronal done that willingly?"

"Oh, stop defending him, Liv."

"I do know what you mean, Aaron—but please," she had said, "this isn't the time. Why don't you tell us if you've found out anything since yesterday?"

"Me?" He glared at her. "What about you? What have you found since yesterday? Or have you spent yet another day doing nothing but chatting with your new friends?"

Before she could respond he'd said, "I'll tell you what I found. Nothing. Nothing at all. A thousand adhocracies willing to build armies to help us—until they hear the words 'Fallow Lands.' And not a whisper anywhere of anything called 3340."

Livia chewed a nail now, staring at the vast concentration of political power before her. She had to do something, so at last she sighed and walked through the mass of votes, wondering who best to talk to. She finally decided on one of the churches.

"Excuse me, can I ask you something?"

She approached the subject obliquely, using a cover story they'd agreed upon: that a group of people from Alison Haver's supposed homeworld of Ventus had vanished into the Fallow Lands. She needed to rescue them.

As soon as she said this the vote held up a hand. "Your people are outside of our realm of influence. We're not an absolute power within the Archipelago, you know."

"But the Government—"

"Its job is to balance influence between individuals and groups; we weigh a single voice as equal to a million voices in our decision making. But that power counts for nothing in the Fallow Lands, or anywhere that the anecliptics control. It doesn't seem to count for much anywhere, lately, since people have largely stopped paying attention to us."

"But how can that *be?*"

The church, which looked like a kindly old man, patted her arm sympathetically. "Let me tell you a little story. Once upon a time, human beings were mere equals of all the other life forms on Earth; they fit into their niche in the ecology. Then they discovered machines, and began to think of themselves as separate from nature. They genetically engineered new sentient species, and AI came to pervade everything mechanical.

"Now picture the result: a world where every species has become conscious and fully technological—and so have all their technological creations. The lamb wars against the lion, and their machines rebel against both. We've come full circle: humanity is again just one of many species competing in an ecology out of its control.

"Today, you have the anecliptics on the one hand, and the realm of sentients and blind powers they cultivate on the other. You can picture the anecliptics as the solar system's equivalent of the carbon cycle—the bedrock of predictability that is necessary for an actual ecology to flourish. They mete out resources to all the viables in the solar system according to a rigorous plan. Without this artificial nature, there'd be a destructive collapse of the ecology."

"But surely someone deals with them—someone has access to the Fallow Lands—"

The church shook its head. "The anecliptics maintain their power by remaining utterly aloof from all our power struggles. In practice that means they don't even talk to us votes, much less individuals like yourself. All they care about is the ecology they maintain."

Livia crossed her arms. "I don't understand why you keep talking about ecologies. This is just politics."

The vote sighed. "No, it's not. Humanity is just a species with a particular ecological niche, as it was a hundred thousand years ago. In the

Archipelago of the anecliptics, real power is no longer possible—or meaningful—for individual human beings. Many of them blame us, although we're in the same position with respect to the annies. So people have starting finding creative ways to work around us, like the Good Book and its imitators. They think they're defying the anecliptics this way, but the annies don't care. As long as the ecology functions, they don't care what we do or how we do it."

"So what you're really saying," said Livia, "is that you're unwilling or unable to defy the anecliptics. You'll never help us."

The vote shook its head sadly. "I'm sorry. But no human power can help your friends."

Feeling helpless and frustrated, Livia drifted through the crowd, ending up near another of the filigreed windows of the ballroom. For a while she stared out at the clouds. This was a beautiful place, but it wasn't home. She longed for the ancient trees and sweeping sails of Barrastea with an almost physical ache. The pain had been tolerable when she led her people out of Westerhaven, and even while sitting idle in the flying house it had not overwhelmed her. At least there had been a purpose to that waiting.

But to never return to Teven; and if there were no leads to this 3340 in the Archipelago, to never learn what had befallen her friends and family, or why . . . She turned and leaned on the transparent wall, staring down at the bleak moors below. She didn't weep. Tears wouldn't express what she felt.

"Ms. Haver?"

It took her a second to remember that this was the name she was going by here. Livia took a deep breath and turned.

Doran Morss stood there, for the moment without hangers-on or votes near him. "Are you all right?" he asked. "Did you have friends or family at Atchity?" That was the coronal that Omega Point had ruined, she recalled.

"No—no connection there. I'm fine. Just . . . a little tired after my performance." She summoned a smile, wishing for an anima in its place. "But I'm afraid I missed the end of your speech."

"That's okay," he said, turning to scowl at the crowd. "They didn't buy it anyway."

"What do you mean?"

"They've decided to send a punitive expedition to wipe out Omega Point. They want me to go along."

"Oh. What does that mean for you?"

He raised an eyebrow. "You really don't know who I am, do you?"

"I'm not from the Archipelago," she said, just in time to be overheard by a small group of votes who had wandered over.

"How lucky for us!" one of them said. "Just when we were trying to locate a baseline to round out the expedition."

"Not a chance," snarled Morss.

"What?" said Livia.

The vote cocked his head, amused at Morss's reaction. "Have you asked her? Or have you just been chatting her up?"

"I came over to compliment you on your singing," said Morss, now looking a bit desperate.

The vote bowed to Livia. "I hope you don't think me rude, dear, but have you taken the cliff test?"

"The what?"

"She's a performer and a guest," Morss snapped. "I don't think it's our place to press her into any kind of service."

"It is when there doesn't seem to be a human other than yourself within twenty million kilometers who can pass the test," said the vote.

"Of course there isn't," said Morss. "So why should you expect this one to—"

"You said you're not from the Archipelago," the vote said to Livia. "Where are you from?"

Wary, she said, "What is this cliff test? And why should I be afraid to take it?"

"Oh, it's nothing to be afraid of," said the vote. "In fact, it'll only take a second. May I?"

Morss stepped between the vote and Livia. "Now wait a minute—"

Livia thought about their lack of progress on any front. A stray thought came to her: what would Lucius Xavier do in this situation? "Go ahead," Livia said past Morss's shoulder.

"We're much obliged," said the vote. He waved his hand even as Morss said "No!"

Livia stumbled. She looked around; somehow in the press of people she'd ended up with her back to the diamond-glass wall. She put out her hand to brace herself against the impenetrable substance—

—And it shattered.

Reflexively she grabbed for the edge as she fell, and swung out and then back, slamming against the side of the wall below the level of the ballroom's floor. Above her was a gabble of concerned voices and several arms reached down, waving futilely just out of reach. She slid down a centimeter, then another, and made the mistake of looking down.

Clouds wavered past, kilometers away. Below them, nothing but cold ocean.

She screamed, feeling the jagged edge of broken window cut through her fingers, then she had to let go and she fell—

—And was standing again in the ballroom. She stumbled and this time when she leaned against the unbroken diamond wall, it held. She looked at her hands; there were no cuts.

The votes were staring at her with a creepy intensity. Doran Morss looked angry.

"Told you she'd pass," said the vote Morss had been arguing with. He swore at it and walked away. The vote turned back to Livia.

"My apologies for the . . . unexpected nature of the test. It's to see whether you still have normal human responses to threat situations. Most Archipelagics who suddenly found themselves hanging from a cliff would assume it was just another inscape experience, and would not struggle. They'd have had no adrenalin reaction; yours on the other hand was strong."

"What does that mean?" Her heart was still pounding in her chest, and she was angry, but unsure at who or what.

"It means you might be useful to us," said the vote. "Ms. Haver, would you like a job?"

Aaron had accused her of being idle. It was hard not to be when every avenue that might lead home brought you in circles. If only for her own sanity, she had to do *something* that produced results.

"Yes," she said to the vote, "I'll take your job." *Whatever it is.*

THE SOLAR SYSTEM pinwheeled around Aaron. For hours he had swept like an angel through inscape visions of the Archipelago, trying to learn everything about everything. He loved it, loved this place and the ocean of information. But his back was starting to ache and there was a persistent pain behind his eyes. Worse, he was feeling guilty. He should have spent his time searching for ways back into the Fallow Lands, instead of catching up on two centuries of science. But he couldn't help himself.

For a while he had hovered over the sun, amazed at the detail of the boiling Hadley cells like rice grains on its surface. Even down in that incandescent chaos, Archipelagic machines grazed. Vast tethers swung down and up, harvesting material from the inner orbits of the sun in an intricate dance. Farther out, the heavy-metal asteroids known as the vulcanoids had been taken apart and made into giant arching machines that focused the outpouring solar wind into discrete streams. These hurricanes of energy were directed with pinpoint accuracy throughout the solar system, where they acted like trade winds to push cargoes, and even whole coronals, from port to port.

The closer he looked the more detail there was. Each of the thousands of coronals had its own history and local flavor, all open and visible in a way the manifolds had never been. True, everyone could live everywhere at once through inscape so there were few real cultural distinctions. Automatic translation hid any language differences; and since any coronal could have its own mile-high waterfalls or any other wonder imaginable, natural beauty was kind of redundant here. Qiingi and Livia kept complaining that this place lacked the overwhelming abundance of Teven's manifolds.

There was more here than could be learned in a lifetime, though. Couldn't they see that? With a heavy sigh he wiped away the inscape view. Now he stood in a sumptuous apartment somewhere in Doran Morss's chandelier city. Outside the French doors to his left was a wide balcony that currently looked out over a view of the drifting sands of Mars. Once or twice he'd tuned it to see the blasted heaths and hills of Morss's *Scotland*. That was his physical location, after all. It made no difference; when he stepped out of this apartment he could just as easily view the streets of Brand New York or an aerostat city on Venus. He could be anywhere—except Teven Coronal.

He stalked into the kitchen to find an analgesic patch for his neck. While there he saw that one of his discussion boards had filled up with comments. He had generated dozens of agents to comb the Archipelago for any clues to the identity or location of 3340. While doing this he had often succumbed to the temptation to spin off queries about his various passions in science and technology. One agent had led him to this board, where amateur AI designers compared tricks and techniques, and speculated on topics that he'd wondered about his whole life.

Why such a horror of trans-humanism? he had asked in a recent posting. *People who try to improve themselves in the Archipelago seem to be persecuted for it.* Before they came here, he had sometimes daydreamed about the wider world beyond Teven. Without the deliberate tamping-down of the tech locks, he assumed, people would remake themselves however they wanted. And why not? Why not grow wings to fly, or new senses to see microwaves and hear the hiss of radio? Imperishable bodies, networked minds—these had been his fantasies for years, because such things were banned in Teven. Yet they were banned here, too.

One person had posted several replies, he noticed. They were signed *Veronique. Many of us feel as you do,* Veronique had written. *But it is difficult to speak out right now, because of the Omega Point crisis. It makes us all look bad.*

"But why?" he asked the board. "What did they do?"

They tried to become gods.

He stared at the reply. He'd always known it was possible; there were entities within the Archipelago that had such power—and not just the annies. But as he reread the words, he remembered the devastation of the farside accident; remembered the corpses. One gray and awful day he had come upon the body of a woman dressed in some fabulous costume from a manifold he didn't recognize. Her face had been like porcelain, perfectly clean and composed. It had hit him then: she could still be alive. The technology existed, the angels were a small example. People didn't have to die *at all,* anymore. Or if they did, they could be resurrected. But he was cursed with living in a place where such mercy wasn't permitted.

There had been nothing he could do about it then. He suppressed the rage and grief. He'd kept it locked away ever since.

"The votes are talking about Omega Point right now," he said to the board. "My . . . friend . . . says that they're going to wipe it out."

A reply came instantly this time. *How do you know that? Isn't that meeting happening off-line?*

Aaron frowned. Was he interacting with an agent, or was this the real Veronique now? "I'm there now," he said. "In Doran Morss's *Scotland.* We, I, were invited."

And do you agree with them? Should Omega Point be destroyed?

Aaron frowned, gazing out the window for a while at drifting dust devils. "I don't know," he said honestly. "Somebody on this message board said that's why the annies were originally created. To fight an outbreak of trans-humanism that ended the monoculture."

That's the official story.

He stared at the words in surprise. In a civilization without government, where anyone could say or do anything they wanted, how could there be any such thing as an "official story"? The annies were supposed to be unconcerned with the daily affairs of humans; so at least he'd come to understand in the days he'd spent exploring the place.

He hesitated, then said, "And what's the real story?"

There was a long pause, which often meant that an anima was being taken off-line while its owner prepared a personal response. Then: *Do you want to meet?*

This time the signature was Veronique's, unmediated by any agent.

All thoughts of the search for 3340 were forgotten; so was his tiredness and sore muscles.

"Where?" said Aaron. "And when?"

14

"I THOUGHT I was supposed to be working for the Government?" said Livia. She settled herself into the acceleration couch next to Doran Morss.

"It hired both of us," he said with a touch of annoyance. "It was in your briefing." He reached up to slam the hatch of the small aircarlike vessel.

In the several days since she had been "hired"—a quaint term whose implications she had yet to explore—Livia had encountered Morss several times. One thing she had noticed was that even a slight hint of irritation on his part was enough to make most of his hangers-on cower. These hangers-on were referred to as "servants"—another old term she'd never heard used in reference to human beings. The man was a tyrant, she had decided; she did not like him. This morning he had shown up unexpectedly at her door and announced that the Government wanted them both to visit the devastated Atchity Coronal, where Omega Point's forces had just been routed.

She was thinking about how to answer Morss's comment—she'd read the briefing, but hadn't understood much of it—when the floor fell out from under the little spaceship. They were leaving the *Scotland* via a hatch in its outer skin, just as Aaron's house had exited and entered Rosinius and the other coronals. So it was a familiar enough experience; still, Livia hissed involuntarily and grabbed at the arms of her chair as they fell into black space.

"See, that's why they hired you," said Morss, unperturbed by the sudden fall. "Sophia Eckhardt wouldn't have reacted like that. To her, it would be just another shift of realities in inscape. Her kind doesn't understand that there's a real world underlying all the fantasy visions they cram into their senses." He sounded contemptuous, almost bitter as he said this. Out the windshield, Livia watched the black underside of the worldship rising away like an iron cloud. Stars specked into view around them as the dark hulk dwindled. She shook her head.

He half turned in his seat, gazing at her as if she were a suspicious fruit in the Barrastea market. "You really are a foreigner. I get that. You obviously have no idea how bad things have gotten in the Archipelago. Haver, Sophia's quite tolerant for her kind, which I suppose is why the Good Book put her on to you. But the rest of humanity's turning into a race of fucking sleepwalkers. Those of us who believe in the existence of a real world are in a shrinking minority. Most people think inscape is all there is. They're more and more out of touch with reality; whole coronals have started failing the cliff test."

Their little ship—which consisted of the cockpit they were in, and a large fusion engine behind it—leveled out and the power kicked in. Livia felt some weight return; the experience was no more dramatic than lying on her back and looking up at the stars.

"But that still doesn't answer my question," she said. "Why did they hire me?"

"You're what we like to call a *baseline,*" said Morss with a shrug. "Your nervous system encodes the sorts of behavior patterns that we evolved for—what they dismiss here as the 'cripple' view. Hence the cliff test. If you fell in a virtual river you'd hold your breath and try to swim. Natural human reactions for somebody from Ventus, maybe—but you have to understand, many people here get their inscape implants while still in the womb. Generations have grown up now completely inside inscape. When they fall off a cliff, they laugh and flap their arms. When they fall in a river they just keep on breathing—because they don't have the experience of a stable and dangerous reality to ground them. They lack the baseline human reactions you still have. You've got an almost pure set, by our readings. You and your two friends form a kind of behavioral standard that's getting increasingly rare. We can use that standard to judge how viable a person or inscape is."

Oddly enough, that made sense: Morss wanted her to judge manifolds, something she'd gotten quite adept at just before leaving Teven. At least, that's what it sounded like he wanted.

In the distance Livia saw a thin arc of light emerging from the endless sky: a coronal. "Is that Atchity?" she asked. Morss didn't answer. He was talking quietly to a blurred inscape figure in front of him.

She tamped down on her annoyance, and watched out the windshield for a while. The coronal was beautiful: a fat ring or short can with open ends, its interior surface brilliantly lit in swirling cloud and blue by a round mirror angled in its central space. But as the ship's trajectory took it toward the sunward side of the coronal, the light shifted to reveal something else—something that took up so much of the sky that Livia hadn't even seen it.

The two-thousand-kilometer-wide ring of the coronal was half cupped in the arcing metal claws of something that dwarfed it—something planet-sized. So this was an anecliptic dreadnought: a vast nightmare of machinery, its outstretched arms the size of continents. It looked like nothing so much as a mailed fist ready to crush the delicate ring-shaped world.

The sight was extremely unnerving. Livia needed to look at something else, so she pulled out the copy of the Good Book that Sophia had given her as a gift.

The Book was a physical object, a rarity for Sophia. Bound in vat-grown leather, it held a pleasing odor. Its hundred or so chapters used parables, stories, and poetry to describe particular "roles" such as Phoenix, Priestess, or Pack-Carrier. "Pick a role, any role to start with," Sophia had said. "That's you—for now." While you were acting in a particular role, you were supposed to try to emulate its qualities as closely as possible. At the end of each chapter were a few pages of rules about what each role should do when encountering people playing other roles. You might take charge of that person for a time; your own role might change to something else; so might theirs.

There were over a thousand pages in the book, and it was heavily cross-referenced and indexed. She flipped to the back and looked for any index entries that might say *Annoying People, dealing with*. She couldn't find one.

"The Good Book's not a religion." Sophia had laughed. "The Book started replacing local adhocracies about seven years ago. It's just a bunch of simple rules: if this happens, do that. People have had systems like it for thousands of years—you know, the Ten Commandments and the Categorical Imperative, that sort of thing. But those systems weren't based on systematic testing. The Good Book is the result of massive simulations of whole societies—what happens when billions of individual people follow various codes of conduct. It's simple: if most people use the rules in the Book most of the time, a pretty much utopian society emerges spontaneously on the macro level."

The Book was like magic. Sophia had wanted Livia to try it out, so she did to be polite. Using it was like play-acting; Livia found she could slip easily into some roles but had more difficulty with others. One day she was the Courier, and people came to her with packages for her to deliver until she met someone whose role changed hers. The next day she was designated the Tourist, and she did nothing but explore Brand New York until she met a Visitor, at which point her role changed to Tour Guide. That was all very simple, she thought; any idiot could have designed a system like this. But every now and then she caught glimpses of something more—something extraordinary. Yesterday she had run through a chain of roles and ended up as Secretary. Reviewing the Secretary's role in the Book, she found that she should poll inscape for anyone nearby who had one of the roles of Boss, Lawyer, Researcher, or about five other alternates. She did, and went to meet a woman who had the odd, unfamiliar role of Auditor.

Livia met the Auditor in a restaurant. Five other people were there, too; all had been summoned to this meeting by their roles, but nobody had any idea why, so they compared notes. One man said he'd been given the role of Messenger three days before, and couldn't shake it. He was being followed by a small constellation of inscape windows he'd accumulated from other roles. When he distributed these, they turned out to all relate to an issue of power allotment in Brand New York that the votes were dragging their heels on. Suddenly the Auditor had a task. As Secretary, Livia began annotating her memory of the meeting. In under an hour they had a policy package with key suggestions, and suddenly their roles changed. A man who'd been the Critic suddenly became the Administrator. According to the rules of the Book, he could enact policy provided conversion to Administrator was duly witnessed by enough other users.

This was amazing. After a while, though, Livia had realized that far larger and more intricate interactions were occurring via the Book all the time. It was simply that few or none of the people involved could see more than the smallest part of them.

Eventually she slipped the Book back into its carrying case and looked up. The coronal loomed huge in front of them. Morss had ended his private conversation, so Livia turned to him, opening her mouth and closing it several times as she tried to think of a way to broach the subject of 3340. She was still unsure of how much to reveal about herself; but she remembered a conversation she'd had the other day. She had discreetly asked one of Morss's servants how it was that Morss could be so rich in a place where each citizen's potential for wealth was controlled by inaccessible, outside forces. "Somebody told me that you're not a citizen of the Archipelago," she said now.

"That's right. How do you think I'm able to keep that?" He jerked a thumb at the now-tiny worldship behind them. "My *Scotland* was built with cometary materials I scavenged myself from outside the solar system. Took me many years to bring it in; you can do that, you know, but you have to get the stuff personally and ride it home yourself for your claim to be valid. Took years . . . Anyway, I came back with a few quadrillion tons of raw materials that the annies didn't own. There's only a few humans in the Archipelago sitting on that much resource—everything else comes from the annies. Of course, they disapproved; they wouldn't let the Government work for me anymore. Said I would be putting too much resource into the 'human niche,' I might upset their precious ecology. They designated me a 'distinct entity.'" He laughed. "I'm on a par with the human race as a whole in terms of my rights. But there are precious few places where I can spend what I've got."

"The annies again?" ventured Livia.

"That's right. I'm a little speck of chaos in their deterministic machine. So they load me down with obligations to keep me busy—though they haven't taken my wealth away from me."

Livia had the distinct feeling that there was a much bigger story here, and was about to ask for more details when their ship flipped over in a stomach-lurching way. "We're on final approach," said Morss. And then he busied himself with his virtual conversations and left no anima to continue speaking with her. She sat back, crossed her arms, and watched the impossibly sharp curves of the coronal slide slowly past beneath them. Moments later they were whipping past the knife-thin edge of its south sidewall and without warning, plowed into atmosphere as thick as water. Red flame burst outside the windshield as they were jolted back and forth in their seats by deceleration. After some tense minutes of this they had shed the differential of their velocity with the coronal; as the diamond windshield cleared of flame, retaining only a wavering heat-distortion, Livia gazed down on a landscape unlike anything she had ever seen before.

The whole surface of the coronal looked like a circus that had been half drowned in a mud slide. Bizarre buildings and towers of jewel poked up everywhere out of long runnels and sluices of pale beige. The beige substance had a kind of texture to it—almost familiar . . . "What is that stuff?" she asked.

"Paper, mostly," said Morss. "Books of the old physical kind. I'm told they're chiefly novels, every one of them unique. There's also film scripts and symphonies. Billions and billions of them." He waved a hand at the strange buildings. "As well as oil paintings, sculptures, architectural forms, new fashion styles, shoes, quilts, tiling patterns, and furniture and cutlery designs. Blown across the whole damn coronal like dust. All part of the propaganda blast."

"Propaganda blast?"

"We wouldn't have been able to get this close a week ago," said Morss. "This whole area was contested—mines and lasers, disassembler fogs and so on, on the side of the last few humans defending their homes—and art bombs on the side of Omega Point. Throw a missile at 'em, they convert its mass and energy into a thousand new operas and throw 'em back at you. All of them with Omega Point's people as heroes, of course. Hell, they've rewritten the history of the world a million or so different ways to make themselves look like the culmination of everything. It's disgusting. Luckily the anecliptics came—along with Choronzon himself—and cleared it all out of the way for us."

"Who's Choronzon?" she asked.

"You'll meet him," was all Morss said.

Morss brought the ship around and they settled toward a particularly devastated part of what might have once been a city. They stepped off the ship's landing leg onto a surface composed entirely of paper sheets. Livia knelt and looked at several. They were neatly printed, and seemed to be pages of some rather tawdry adventure novels. The phrase *mad anecliptic* came unbidden to her mind, and she hid her hands, which had begun to shake.

According to what she'd read prior to embarking with Morss, this coronal had once housed a billion people. Its citizens had always been a bit extreme in their use of technology. By the time of the post-human efflorescence, most of the moderates had fled. Lucky thing, judging from the psychotic overflow of creativity that had ruined the land.

"There it is," said Morss, pointing past the aft end of the ship. Livia walked under the hot pinging metal and looked.

A thing like a metal tree sat entirely alone in a fire-blackened plaza a hundred meters away. Instead of branches, the tree thrust blades into the air at all angles; some were visibly red-hot. Several human figures stood about the tree, along with the tanklike shape of a semisentient brody. Morss headed in their direction.

Morss shook hands, then Livia stepped up to do likewise. These people were mostly votes, but the Government was here, too, in the guise of a young man with calloused hands. In addition, there was a thing like a swirling cloud of virtual matter, which introduced itself as a Zara—whatever that was—and a pair of otterlike biological beings that might be true aliens.

". . . And here comes Choronzon," said Morss, nodding in the direction of a nearby, half-built colosseum. A tall man was sauntering toward them, dusting off his hands and smiling. As he got closer she found herself staring; he had intense eyes and black hair, and he moved like a panther. His beauty was almost mesmerizing, in fact. *Some inscape trick,* she told herself, with a twinge of resentment. But she didn't look away.

"Alison Haver, the god Choronzon."

Choronzon grinned at Morss, clapped more dust off his hands and held one out for her to shake. "Nice to meet you," he said in a deep, resonant voice.

Sophia had talked about the gods, but in the manner of distant beings she never hoped to meet. Here was a viable post-human in the flesh—or pseudo-flesh—and he looked like nothing so much as a sim actor.

"So you're our baseline," he said. "I trust Doran's briefed you on what we're doing here?"

"No—yes," she said, and found herself inexplicably blushing. "I'm a bit out of my depth," she admitted.

"That's okay," he said quietly. "So am I."

There was an awkward pause.

"Has it said anything?" Morss asked the Government. They were standing near the metal tree, looking it up and down.

The Government nodded. "It's radiating news stories on all frequencies—thousands of self-serving docudramas per second. But that's all reflex action. There's been no communications from the thing's core at all. See for yourself: you can enter its inscape by walking under the, uh, branches there."

Livia regarded the smoking tangle nervously. Six days ago, a Government agent had overflown the coronal to find out what had happened to the people who had won the post-humanist civil war. He had flown in on a stealth-craft and cruised up and down the coronal for days before spotting the tree. By that time he was thoroughly rattled by what he'd seen: cities eaten and regurgitated by architect-dreamer machines; inscape hallucinating entire new civilizations; everywhere the stink of dead plants and animals. The lakes had been drained out and stored as ice on the underside of the coronal, and even the soil replaced by some unknown industrial process. Omega Point couldn't tolerate the idea of any nonconvert coming within a thousand kilometers of this strange metal tree.

"Now that we're all here," said the Government, sounding for all the world as if it were chairing a meeting, "let's go in and see if anybody's home." He turned to Livia. "Your task lies there." He pointed to the building Choronzon had come from.

"What's there?" She peered nervously in that direction.

"I am," said the Government with a smile, "so don't worry. No, it's just some of the humans who survived the recent war. They wandered into this zone after Choronzon wiped out the Omegans' defenses. They need someone to talk to."

"Talk to?" But the Government and the others, including Morss, had turned and were walking toward the bizarre metal tree. Livia shook her head and walked toward the building.

DORAN MORSS FOUND himself hovering in an endless sky: the inscape representation of the metal tree's core. Avatars of the other Archipelagics floated nearby. Sourceless illumination lit them a soft, sunset rose color. Choronzon was scratching his head, looking unimpressed.

"Listen to that," said the god. Morss heard nothing. He said as much.

"That's what I mean," said Choronzon. "We're interfaced with a system that's supposed to contain the downloaded minds of millions of people. We've attacked them and knocked out all their defenses, leaving them totally vulnerable to us in the real world. Shouldn't there at least be somebody manning the door?"

They looked around uneasily, but the blue sky went on forever in all directions, empty of promise. Finally the Government said, "All right, nobody's meeting us. Choronzon, you and I will crack the system." The god nodded. Nothing more happened—the two simply stood there on the air, staring at nothing, while presumably their agents made an all-out assault on the information processing systems of the metal tree.

Their distraction gave Doran the chance he'd been waiting for. He quickly muttered a number of commands under his breath—commands that had been given to him by an Omega Point evangelist he'd sheltered, in secret, on board his *Scotland*. The commands were supposed to unlock a set of interfaces to the core of the tree. If all went well, he should be able to access the genetic code for Omega Point's eschatus machine.

Omega Point had explored many options for self-deification. The eschatus machine was a single-person device, so they had never built it, but had instead elected to implement a collective approach that they claimed would allow all of their members to achieve a state of absolute consciousness. The evangelist had assured Doran that the plans for the eschatus machine were complete, however. Doran had paid the nonhuman brodys to build it and Omega Point had promised to give him the machine's genes if he appealed to the votes on their behalf.

With the eschatus machine, Doran Morss could in one second transform himself into a being like Choronzon—a god.

He had given the passwords. There was nothing to do but wait. If Omega Point believed in his honesty—frankly, if they cared at all at this point—the eschatus machine genes should automatically download into the capacious data store he'd hidden under his shirt. Meanwhile the Government and Choronzon had lost their distracted looks and were frowning at each other.

"What's the matter?" Doran asked innocently. "Can't get through?"

"Oh, we got through all right," said Choronzon. "It was just what I said would happen," he said to the Government. "There was never any other possibility."

"What's going on?" asked a vote.

The Government shrugged. "It was pretty much a foregone conclusion. The fact is, there's no such thing as an ultimate state of consciousness. It's a myth; sentience has meaning only insofar as it's connected into the physical world. We always knew the Omegans were going to be disappointed."

"All a cosmic wank," said Choronzon.

"We have full access to their systems," said the Government. "If you'd like to see it, here's a view of the Omega Point." It gestured to open a large inscape window in the sky. Instantly Doran's head was filled with an undifferentiated roar: white noise matched in the window by endless video snow.

Choronzon laughed. "The more information there is in a signal, the more it resembles noise. You're looking at infinite information density, gentlemen, a signal so packed with information that it has *become* noise. These idiots pushed so far in one direction that they ended up at the opposite pole. It's not like I didn't warn them."

"Then they're gone?"

The Government nodded. "All gone. Dead."

"You could call it the most elaborate act of self-entombment in human history," said Choronzon with another laugh. "Come on, let's get out of here so I can dismantle this thing." He vanished from the inscape view. After conferring for a while the votes followed. Doran hung for a while longer in front of the big square of gray snow, listening to the roar of infinite information density. He almost thought he could hear voices in that monstrous basso hiss, but then he'd heard the same in the sighing of the night breeze. Perhaps the fanatics of Omega Point had gotten their wish, but if so they had been mistaken in thinking that the Absolute was something that hadn't been there all along. Absolute meaning, it seemed, was no different from no meaning at all.

He shuddered, and left them to their hypertechnological tomb.

"THEY REFUSED TO leave," the Government was saying. Livia knelt next to one of the human refugees who huddled inside the ruins. Ovals of light like spotlights from holes far overhead picked out one or two of the young-looking people. They sat listlessly, not apparently in distress, but not speaking either.

There were about thirty of them. Sixteen had gray patches where skin had been replaced by some substitute; one had an all-gray arm. Choronzon had healed their physical wounds with this stuff, according to the Government. Their psychic state was another matter.

"What am I supposed to do?" Livia asked. "I'm a stranger here, I don't know these people or what they've gone through . . ." She heard the rising note in her voice and stopped herself. She shook her head and looked down.

"It's all right," said the Government gently. "You're already doing what we brought you here to do. Look."

She looked up. The refugees were staring at her—not angrily, or with hope, but intently, almost with fascination. "What is it?" she murmured. "What do they see?"

The Government sighed. "They see something they may never have seen before: a normal human reacting normally to a traumatic situation. Livia, these people have been insulated within inscape their whole lives. They have lived in a world where their merest whim could be granted with a thought. Reality has always conformed to their desires—never the other way around. Now they find themselves in a world that obstinately refuses to change itself to fit their imaginations. They literally have no idea how to respond."

Livia remembered her conversation with Lady Ellis—it seemed like years ago now. Livia was special, the founder said, because she had gone through the crash, seen people die, and learned that *nothing good came of it.* For that very reason she was stronger.

Of course these ruins resonated with memory. Livia could remember huddling under broken eaves with Aaron, watching rain she could do nothing to dispel. After inscape crashed here, these poor people must have undergone just what she had.

She shook her head. "But I come from a world very like this one," she said. "With inscape . . . and all." Even as she said it she knew it wasn't quite true. On Teven, the tech locks anchored the reality of each manifold. Inscape was not a means to wish-fulfilment there.

"There's something different about your home," confirmed the Government. "I'd love to know what it is. Meanwhile, you have a useful role to play here. As an example to these people of how to *feel.*"

"Surely there's other, uh, baseline people around."

"Oh, millions," said the Government. "Whole coronals of people who'd qualify, in fact. But I've had to disable long-range inscape, and none of those people are within a week's journey of this place. We need you *now,* Livia."

"All right," she said. "But I still don't understand."

"Just do what you do," said the Government.

Livia thought for a while. Then she began to walk among the refugees, and she sang for them an ancient song she'd learned as a girl, but never understood: "The Dark Night of the Soul."

O night you were my guide
O night more loving than the rising sun
O night that joined the lover to the beloved one
Transforming each of them into the other . . .

As always, she came to feel the emotions of the song as she sang it. The words were uplifting, a benediction that had weathered the test of centuries. By the time she left, there were tears on the cheeks of several of the Omegans, though they neither smiled nor spoke; but the Government smiled.

EXHAUSTED, LIVIA LET her feet guide her in the direction of Morss's ship. She had talked to a number of the refugees. In different ways, she had asked them all the same question: Did the evangelists of Omega Point come to you? Did they promise you the things you'd always dreamed of?

They had not answered the way she'd expected. The cultists only had one name for themselves and they never promised anything other than a merging of all identities in the Omega Point. Unlike 3340's agents, who adapted themselves to every person's vulnerabilities, Omega Point were charmlessly direct.

She couldn't prove it, but it seemed that Omega Point had not been 3340.

Evening had fallen, but as she walked she could hear no crickets or night birds, just the slow exhalation of a breeze through the gap-toothed buildings. As she neared the ship, though, Livia could make out voices.

"Do you know how an eschatus machine works, Doran?" It was the self-made god, Choronzon. He and Morss stood on the opposite side of the ship; she could see their feet underneath it. Livia paused to listen.

"It's basically a hydrogen bomb," continued the god, his voice silky and calming. "But a bomb so finely made that every atom in it has been carefully placed. When it explodes and the pulse of energy comes from its heart, the energy is filtered and modulated down to an angstrom's-width as it surges outward. It's a controlled burn, you might say, turning what would normally be chaotic and destructive energy into creative power. In a millisecond you go from having a bomb to having . . . well, what, do you suppose?"

"I have no idea," said Morss. He sounded irritated—nothing unusual in that.

"Well, a newborn god is one possibility. A coronal might be another. But I think I can guess which might interest you more."

"I have no idea what you're talking about."

"Of course not. Certainly I wouldn't be talking about the fact that you fought us every step of the way on whether we should shut down Omega Point. You—the most vocally anti-god human in the Archipelago, defending them? Strange.

"Of course, strange behavior might be explained if one knew about the eschatus machine that the Omegans designed before their hasty departure from this mortal coil—the machine whose plans you downloaded earlier today."

There was a brief silence. Then Morss said, very quietly, "What do you want?"

"Nothing. I'm just intrigued by your change of heart, that's all.

"You know I was once a human being, too, Doran. I remember how hard it was to marshal all the resources I needed to cure myself of the affliction. I also remember, quite clearly, how I always told people I had no interest in self-deification. It was a useful and sometimes necessary shield against interference."

"Blow off," said Doran. "Unless you have some specific threat you want to use on me."

Choronzon laughed. "Not a threat. Just curiosity as to why someone so violently opposed to improving on the human model should decide to go against all his principles."

"Sometimes," said Doran icily, "mature people do things they don't want to do. It's called following higher principles. But someone without mortal concerns, say, like yourself, wouldn't understand that."

"I know you blame me for not doing enough—" began Choronzon. Morss cut him off.

"I do. These people needed a champion. I didn't have the power to stop them destroying themselves. So yes, I took their side, because I saw a chance to *get* that power—too late for them, but maybe not the next Omega Point."

There was a brief silence. Then Choronzon said, "You'll make a fine god, then—you already have the necessary urge to meddle."

Livia heard the god's footsteps crackling away over the paper landscape.

Livia made sure her own footfalls were audible as she walked around the ship. Doran stood there, staring off into the evening gloom with an unreadable expression on his face. As she approached he snapped, "Where've you been?"

"Working," she said. "What have you been doing?"

He just grunted. Suddenly he looked very tired. Over his shoulder

Livia could see the flicker of orange flames: the remnants of the Omega Point tree were collapsing in on themselves. As she watched, Choronzon stepped forward to reinsert a heavy piece that had fallen out of the fire.

"Let's go," said Doran. "There's nothing more for us here."

15

WEEKS PASSED WHILE Livia, Aaron, and Qiingi settled into life in the Archipelago. Livia still felt urgently driven to seek help for her home, but whole days went by now when she did nothing about it. She was distracted in her new role as baseline.

It was a simple enough job: guide lost people out of the sometimes baroque realities they had walled themselves into. Doing this involved, as Doran put it, "mostly just showing up." She had to tune her view to that of the people in question. The Government advertised her coming and those who were interested could, with her help, tune their realities back toward the human baseline—though no one ever came all the way back to "crippleview."

Her experience traveling between the manifolds of Teven suited her well to this role; so she felt useful.

Though Doran Morss had few permanent residents in the *Scotland,* he allowed Livia to stay, and so was obliged to let Aaron and Qiingi remain as well. It was a small imposition, since they had thousands of square kilometers of open land to roam aboard the ship and could come and go as they pleased.

During this time Qiingi came less and less to Livia's bed. She thought she understood: they had been cooped up together for so long, first fleeing through Teven's cultures, then within the house. He needed to establish himself in this place as much as she did. So she didn't think much of it when she didn't see him for days at a time.

Later, Livia would realize that her own distraction had prevented her from seeing the effect that the Archipelago was having on him, and on Aaron.

Of course, by then it was too late.

"SO YOU'VE COME," said Aaron. He stared glumly at Livia and Qiingi. He looked like he hadn't slept in days.

"Are you going to invite us in?" asked Livia. Aaron started, and stepped back to let them into his apartment. The view was of some outer planet's moon. Livia seemed to be stepping onto a powdery white landscape with a close horizon, a black sky and stars blazing overhead. It was bleak, and empty; typical of the places Aaron loved.

As Qiingi moved past Livia she smelled wood smoke. The scent gave her an aching memory of home.

"We haven't met in over a week," Aaron was saying as he nervously summoned up a couch and some chairs. "I just thought . . . we should."

"I'm sorry," she said, touching his arm. "I know you've been working hard, Aaron. I've been sidetracked, but it's for a good cause, believe me: I'm worming my way into the corridors of power. Doran Morss seems to have a relationship with the annies. If I can convince him to let us talk to them . . ."

"Yes, yes, I understand," said Aaron. Livia had sat down; Qiingi stood with his arms crossed. Aaron chose to pace. "I'm still looking for 3340," he said.

"Have you had any success?" asked Qiingi.

"Have *I* had success? What about you? What have you been doing?"

"I have been sitting by my fire, and thinking," said Qiingi. He had recently moved out of the chandelier city, settling on the moors in a sod hut he'd built himself.

Aaron snorted contemptuously. "You've given up, haven't you?"

"We could destroy our souls attempting to do the impossible," said Qiingi quietly, "or we can choose the possible."

"What are you talking about?" Aaron shook his head. "We have to find a way to help our people. Don't you care about your friends and family? Or that *we* care about ours?"

"There may be no way to help them."

Qiingi's words hung in the air like a death sentence. They had all been thinking this, Livia realized; it had run like an undercurrent under all her recent choices. But she didn't want to admit that. Not to these two men after all they had done and seen together.

"There might still be a solution," she said. "We have to keep hunting—"

"For what? We don't know what we're looking for." Qiingi shook his head. "Don't you see the increasing desperation of our search? Very soon now it will cease to be a rational thing, and become an obsession. We will fixate on trivial hints, pursue them in denial of their falseness. Maybe we have already begun to do this," he said, gazing levelly at Aaron.

Aaron went white. "*How dare you,*" he whispered. "You, who do nothing but sit like a fat parasite in your—"

"Hut," said Qiingi with a half smile. "This is a fine apartment you have, Aaron Varese."

Livia jumped to her feet. "Stop it! You're both behaving like children." She rounded on Qiingi. "And you! What are you doing, deliberately provoking him?"

"I am doing nothing, apparently," said Qiingi.

"Well you just admitted that—" started Aaron. Qiingi shook his head.

"Like you, I came here to find a way to save my people. But I no longer believe we can find those who attacked our homes. And we cannot go home. If we cannot save the bodies and minds of our people, we are left with preserving their spirit. I am determining how to do that. You," and now he pinioned both of them with an accusatory gaze, "are the ones who are doing nothing."

Livia shrank back. She'd been happy, the last few days. Traveling with Doran Morss, singing to the confused and lost, she'd finally felt like she was doing something useful. Qiingi was telling her that she'd been lying to herself.

"Qiingi, that's not fair. What do you expect us to do? I'm sorry, but it really does sound like you've given up."

"Your hand must let go of one thing so that you can grasp another—"

"Not another proverb!" Aaron laughed derisively. "Spare us! You're useless, Qiingi. So what the hell are you doing here?"

Raven's warrior stood stiffly. "Nothing, other than telling the truth." Again, the words hung there, but now both Aaron and Livia were glaring at him. Qiingi sighed heavily.

"I will leave, then," he said. "When you have taken your search to its logical conclusions, you know where you can find me." He walked to the door with great dignity.

"Qiingi," said Livia, "who are you walking out on?"

He didn't reply. It was only when he closed the door that she realized how far apart they'd drifted. Instantly she wanted to take back everything she'd done in the past while, but all she could do was sit there, paralyzed. There was no anima to mask the past.

Behind her, Aaron was stalking up and down, cursing furiously. Bereft, she turned to look at him; his anger was astonishing. It had been building for months, she realized—or more likely years.

Swallowing her own fury, Livia stood and went to him. She held out her arms and he folded himself into her embrace, hugging her fiercely.

"What is it?" she whispered. "Tell me."

"It's . . ." He hesitated. "Livia, have you considered that maybe you're working for the enemy?"

"*What?*"

He grimaced. "That came out wrong. I don't mean 3340; but you know it's the annies who are keeping us from ever going home. They're the ones who've kept us—all of Teven's people—locked away like zoo animals for two hundred years! And the whole human race is under their thumb, too. And you're working for them."

"I'm working for the Government," she said, her face hot.

"Which works for the annies."

"Aaron, I'm helping people. I'm not doing it for any outside agency, I'm doing it for those individual people."

He shook his head sadly. "Sometimes you're the most cunning of players, and sometimes you're frighteningly naive. Can't you see what you're doing? You're part of the Government's program to convince people that the status quo is working. You're hiding the bodies, Liv. Sweeping the contradictions of the place under the rug, so that the greater society doesn't notice them. Is that *good?*"

"Why are you saying this?"

"I know you have the best of intentions. But we should be encouraging people to push the limits of human nature—we shouldn't be holding them back! Of course some will crash—that's natural selection. But if we don't try to improve on our design, how is humanity ever going to match the annies? And if nobody confronts them, how are you and I ever going to get home again?"

She gaped at him. "Confront them? But that's . . ."

"Impossible? So was leaving Teven, if you'll recall. I don't think it's impossible. In fact—" He hesitated, then shrugged and looked down. "I just want to know which side you're on here."

She looked down at the powdery grit inscape was telling her lay under her feet. "I should have thought that was clear," she murmured.

After a moment she realized Aaron was standing over her. Livia looked up. He had the oddest expression on his face.

"Liv . . ." He bit his lip. "Stay here tonight," he blurted.

"What?"

"Stay. With me. Tonight."

"Oh . . . Sure. I can just summon a bed for myself, and—"

"That's not what I meant." He looked terrified at what he'd just said. Realizing what he did mean, Livia felt supremely uncomfortable.

"Oh! Aaron, I . . . I can't."

"You're not still with him? After what he—"

"No!" She stood up, twining her hands in distress. "At least, I don't know. I'm not *not* with him. Aaron, this . . . this just isn't the right time for us to have this conversation."

Something changed in his face—a shuttered look as though he'd replaced himself with an anima. "I see," he said coldly. "It seems it never was the right time, was it?"

"Aaron." She went to him, but he shied away from her touch. "You know me better than anyone else. You've been my best friend ever since . . . well, you know. And we've never in all that time had this conversation. Maybe we should have—"

"It's okay, I understand." He turned away, his shoulders hunched. "I'll see you later, then. Don't worry; I'll be all right."

"Well no, wait a second. This is serious, Aaron. How long have you been thinking this?" *Wanting me?*

Still not looking at her, he plodded toward a distant cloud of inscape windows. "We both have work to do . . . To save our people. It's no time to let our emotions run away with us."

"But you brought this up, Aaron. We have to deal with it."

"Not now." He vanished into some view inaccessible to her. Stunned, Livia stared at the spot where he'd just been standing.

She didn't know what to do. After several long minutes, she turned and left the now-empty apartment. Summoning up Qiingi's footprints, she stared at them for a long while. Then she walked the other way.

DORAN MORSS WATCHED his newest employee from under the shadow of some trees. He had come here to confront Alison Haver about some irregularities in her work for him. From the size of the crowd here in her narrative, she was obviously thriving in her dual roles of soundtrack and baseline. So now he felt foolish at walking over there and confronting her. He fidgeted, trying to think how to justify his presence here.

Haver's narrative was set in an open-air parkland. The buildings all had a 1950s rocket-ship chic that she seemed to have fallen in love with. In inscape, her estate was currently docked next to one of Doran's trouble-spots: a coronal whose population had just revolted against the anecliptics. They'd been put down, and now boiling resentment was pushing a lot of people toward post-human experimentation. Doran had sent her there to work as a soundtrack; her real job was to act as a Government baseline.

Doran had insisted that her narrative be *stable*. On his way by the drinks table he saw that she had taken his advice. The drinks were served on a table by a human-shaped agent; the liquids came from bottles; the bottles came from crates at the agent's feet. Any link in this chain could have been interrupted—customized into something inconsistent, such as having the bottles snorted out of an elephant's trunk. Most people's personal narratives had many such breaks because they had never lived in an environment where all objects had consistent relationships. Haver seemed to know intuitively what a seamless view would look like; thus, the very act of visiting her narrative should be healing for many people exhausted by the arbitrary dreamworlds of their own inscape.

He'd had few opportunities to speak with this highly capable young woman since the Omega Point incident. When they did speak, he found her disarmingly direct, apparently unafraid of his power. Whether it was this or something else about her that put him off balance, he didn't know. But around her, he always seemed to forget whatever he was about to say. He wasn't used to that kind of weakness, and he inevitably ended up saying the wrong thing.

It would definitely not help matters if he revealed that he had been investigating her use of his inscape agents. Haver was sending them on errands all over the Archipelago. She and her two friends seemed to be searching for something, but they were being damnably secretive about it. They wouldn't even tell the agents—*his* agents—what they were after. Their cavalier use of his resources was galling.

But every time he spoke to her, it ended badly. And he didn't like that fact, either.

He cursed and walked toward Haver. As he did, Sophia Eckhardt converged on her from the other direction. Eckhardt got there first and Haver, not yet noticing Doran, greeted her warmly.

"Welcome to my narrative," she said to the soundtrack. "I'm currently the Sage—though I don't feel very smart today."

Sophia smiled at her, pursed her lips in thought, then said, "Well, Sage and Minstrel cancel. I believe that makes us both the Student. What's wrong?"

Haver looked down disconsolately. "I may have just broken my oldest and most precious friendship."

Doran had been wracking his brains for some clever opening line and was thrown by the realization that Haver might be pursuing a romantic life he knew nothing about. Consequently his mind was now a blank as he walked up to the two women. "You'll have better luck if you stop playing dress-up with that damnable book," he heard himself say.

They both turned to glare at him. Doran mentally kicked himself for being a clod, which made him even angrier. He glowered at Sophia, acutely aware of Haver's gaze on him. He desperately tried to recover. "And how's the other you today? The . . . non-book side?"

Haver's smile was coldly polite. "Well, Respected Morss, *publically,* I'm very well, thank you. If you have no interest in other sides of me, then we can leave it at that."

Doran knew he should stop, retreat, that this whole conversation was a slow-motion crash. What he said was, "That's a laugh. There is no public life anymore. Only private life, ridiculously intensified. Isn't that what we're fighting against?"

"Well," she said seriously, "that would certainly explain the sense of claustrophobia I've been feeling ever since we got here."

Was she humoring him? He was used to people doing that—ignoring or absorbing his anger. But he hadn't expected Haver to do it, and somehow that just added to his sense of humiliation. "It's like there's no wider world outside my own garden," she said. "I've been trying to get a handle on the big picture here in the Archipelago. But every time I think I get it, it turns out to be just another view." She looked up at him expectantly. *She's throwing me a line to save myself,* he suddenly realized. Not because she was afraid of his anger, but because she was more adroitly diplomatic than he'd ever imagined.

He nodded gratefully. "Yeah, you can't see the big picture because there is no big picture. There's just individual people—and the annies. The Government, the votes, the narratives—they're all *personal.* There's no public life."

"Except in the Book," said Sophia coolly.

"Ah, yes. Of course," he said with an awkward smile. "Well, anyway, I just thought I'd drop by and say hello. I'll see you later, ladies."

He walked away quickly, face burning. What kind of a lout had he turned into? He couldn't even have a simple conversation with an attractive young lady anymore. Too many years of loneliness and political paranoia had disabled what grace he'd once had.

Or maybe he'd just been thrown by the fact that Haver treated him like any ordinary man—and not like the larger-than-life, richer-than-gods figure he'd turned himself into. He swapped out Haver's pleasant narrative for a noisy and crowded cityscape, and just walked for a while letting the bustle and detail wash over him. Anonymity, however, just made him even more lonely.

That evening Doran paced his small suite of rooms, fighting with himself. Finally he sighed, summoned an inscape menu, and said to it, "Show me a list of popular sims."

If anybody knew he did this he'd blow his credibility in the narratives that needed most to trust him. Doran Morss was dedicated to reality; he had vocally and dramatically condemned escapist sims many times over the years. And yet, on nights like this he risked the presence of spybots and, for a few hours, left his own complicated life behind.

He had never told anyone that he did this.

After making his selection he found himself in a pleasant parkland; it was late evening here, and the arch of a coronal swept across the sky, very crippleview and reassuring.

A black-haired young woman stood hipshot near a tall hedgerow. She saw him and smiled. "Doran! How are you? I haven't seen you in ages."

With a sim, he could be himself. He needn't second-guess its motives, needn't be on constant guard against plots and conspiracies. Sims weren't intimidated by him, nor were they judgmental. He felt the knot of tension between his shoulders relax as he shook the young lady's hand. And he hated himself for it.

"It's good to see you, Livia," he said sadly. "I seem to remember that the last time we met, you promised me you'd give me a tour of your city."

The sim looked pleased. "Let's go, then. Night's the best time to see Barrastea."

THE HOURS OF the night seemed to last forever. Aaron lay in his bed, staring up at the ceiling. He couldn't help endlessly replaying his argument with Livia and its disastrous end. How was he ever going to show his face to her again?

Nothing had gone as planned; not just now, but ever since the day that the airbus crashed. Seeing his father's dead face had nearly unhinged Aaron at the time. Never learning what had happened to his mother proved to be worse in the long run. He felt like he'd been knocked off balance and ever since had run forward full-tilt, always on the verge of toppling.

And fall he would have, if his self-humiliation before Livia had been the only thing he could think about. It was intolerable and he needed oblivion to cure him of the pain. There were amnesiac drugs he could take, sedatives . . . but none could take back what had actually happened. He couldn't undo his life.

Yet he had one last straw to grasp—if he could just make it to morning. He thrashed and tossed and turned, and sat up cursing, but promised himself he would hold on, just that little bit more. In a few hours a visitor would be arriving. Things would have to change then; they would have to get better.

At five A.M. he abandoned sleep and padded out to the balcony to stare down at the mist-shrouded highlands. The gigantic louvers on the worldship's end cap were starting to peek open, letting wan beams of sunlight in. Aaron sipped a coffee and thought about the scale of the world he now lived in: trillions of people, all under the thumb of the same implacable power. It made the problems of Teven look petty by comparison.

At nine o'clock an iris opened in the worldship's end cap, way up at the airless axis. A tiny bright dot glided in and some time later docked at the chandelier city. Aaron was tidied up and waiting when the elevator doors opened and Veronique stepped out.

There were six of her. All greeted Aaron warmly, in minutely different ways. He'd been warned about this aspect of his new friend: she maintained numerous artificial bodies, and flipped her sensorium between them at will. Those bodies not currently inhabited by her were run by the Archipelagic equivalent of animas.

She had confided in him a few days before that she sometimes lost track of which body was hers because her five senses were all transferred. Only internal states of distress still anchored her to her own flesh. "I have indigestion to thank for keeping me human," she'd said with some embarrassment.

It was an instant party. Veronique's selves talked and joked not only with Aaron, but with each other and even with random passersby. The experience reminded him of animas, so he felt quite at home; and having her attention from so many different points at once filled the void of loneliness he had been lost in all night.

"But why did you come in person?" he asked, when they were finally ensconced in his apartment.

Veronique's selves gathered around, one sitting on either side of him, another perched on the arm of the couch, the other three seated opposite. They adopted a serious look.

"I don't trust inscape," said the one on his right. "I use quantum encrypted channels between my selves," added the one on his left, "but I rarely get access to long-range links. And my creations can't travel at all."

"Don't trust inscape?" He looked around at her skeptically. "But isn't inscape fundamentally secure? It has to be, or all sorts of things could happen—"

"Inscape is not something that serves us," said the one on the arm of the couch. "I believe we serve it; and that it serves the Government and the annies."

He frowned. "Can you prove this?"

She looked uncomfortable in six different ways. "Do I have to prove it to you?"

He thought about it. "I can't believe that having the annies lurking in the background of everything hasn't twisted things up somehow. But what can be done about it?"

Now some of her smiled. "Let me tell you a story. Ever since I can remember, I've been fascinated by inscape agents. When I was a girl I generated simple agents and set them puzzles in artificial worlds I made for them. By the time I was eighteen my narrative had grown to include some of the best architects in the solar system. By that time I was so good at designing minds that I could create sentient entities that mutated and divided and struggled with their various versions, like bubbling cell lines in my synthetic realities.

"They were too primitive to have any sense of self, or feel pain or anything. One of them . . . It could converse so well you couldn't tell it wasn't human—but it couldn't manipulate the simplest object in inscape. It had no sense of physical reality.

"More fundamentally, I learned that I couldn't trade my creations with the other designers. Anything we sent across inscape became garbled in transit, to the point of uselessness. At first this was just annoying. Then it became frustrating. I couldn't trade my mind genes with anybody—it was as if we were being held back deliberately. The older people in the narrative shrugged and said I was being paranoid. Inscape is designed this way: they call it a *whisper network*. No message can be relayed across the Archipelagic data nets without the semantics of the message being reinterpreted by countless stations along the way. If you try to create direct, clear-data routes, you're apt to find the anecliptics coming down on you with both feet."

Aaron shrugged. "The annies are threatened by anything that might become like them."

Several Veroniques nodded. "Yes. But listen to this. About a year ago I began catching hints that others were as frustrated as me. It was nothing overt—that was the point. A real movement to fight back against the network restrictions would have generated a narrative, or a vote—or both."

Aaron chuckled. "And since it's *always* easier to use the services of the vote than to continue struggling without it, even the most anti-Government group would find their movement absorbed into the Government itself."

She all nodded vigorously. "It's like if you and your friends struggled to build a road, and then inscape hands you wings. Pretty soon the road just seems pointless . . .

"I eventually figured out that there *are* other people out there trying to find a way around the network's semantic transforms. The problem is, they can't collaborate overtly without having the network organize itself to help them: they walk a fine line between independence, and the generation of a vote."

Veronique couldn't even investigate whether she was right about the existence of the others. She just had to have faith that they were there, and send out hints about her own work. People who were savvy enough could figure it out and help without having to talk to her directly.

"For nine months now I've been laboring on the components of a new kind of inscape-virus." One of her stood up and began pacing. "The thing has frightening power. It's designed to take complete control of inscape. Yet, I don't even know whether the whole thing exists. I've been eaten up by doubt—do the other conspirators even exist? Maybe this is all just a particularly paranoid narrative playing out. It's so hard to know what's real . . ."

Aaron started. *Real* was not a term he'd heard much lately.

"I'm not sure," admitted another Veronique, "because the pieces are distributed among so many people. But I think the virus is ready. All we needed was an entry point from which to inject it into the Archipelago. The big problem was, it had to gestate outside the Government-controlled part of the network."

Aaron laughed, only slightly disappointed. "Doran Morss isn't an Archipelagic citizen. So the *Scotland* is outside the Government's inscape."

"Yes. You see now why I had to come . . . why I leaped at the chance to meet you. Morss allows very few guests. But his guests can have their own guests, within limits." Some of her looked down contritely. "I wanted to meet you anyway, because you're an exotic, I mean I've never met anybody from outside the solar system. I hope you're not angry to learn I had an ulterior motive."

He laughed again. "I assumed you had one. But it's one I like."

She grinned at herselves. "Then you're not angry with me?"

"On the contrary." He leaned forward, clasping his hands on his knees. "When were you planning on taking down the Government?"

16

QIINGI TRIED TO avoid staring as he sat down in the verso house. He could see that the roof was about to slide off, and the wall had been patched but the stones were still crumbling here and there. The stove was improperly placed and most of its heat would leak out before it reached the cots. Politeness kept him from saying anything about these matters, but perhaps he could volunteer to help around the place. Then he could discreetly fix some things.

Qiingi had been sitting cross-legged on the shore of Doran Morss's ocean, weaving twine from grass, when she'd come walking up out of the fog: a young woman of Archipelagic perfection, dressed in uneasily patched cotton. She'd stared hungrily at his hands as he continued to work. "Show me how you do that," she had said, even before introducing herself with the unlikely name of Ishani Chaterjee.

"There are doubtless inscape tutorials that will teach you better than I could," he had said mildly.

"But I want to know how *you* do it," she'd insisted.

"...And this is my housemate, Lindsey," Ishani was saying now. Housemate Lindsey wiped hands covered in chicken grease on her apron. "Would you like some stew, Qiingi? It's my own attempt at a highland recipe."

He was skeptical at the smell coming from the pot, but he smiled widely anyway. "That would be very welcome."

Ishani had talked a great deal about her new friends during the several craft sessions he'd had with her. She had tried for years to come to Doran's *Scotland,* but he could sense the unhappiness in her voice at finally being here. Qiingi had been amazed to hear it—among Raven's people, such discontent would not have arisen. Ishani would either have come to love this new home, or Ometeotl would have provided a world for her more in keeping with her spirit. As it was, Ishani could summon any view she wanted through inscape—but she seemed unable to commit to any of them.

The two women sat with him and Qiingi choked down some of the flavorless food. "Ishani says you're new here," said Lindsey after a silence that Qiingi had felt comfortable, but which he sensed she thought of as awkward.

"I apologize if I am encroaching on your land," he said. She laughed.

"This whole world is owned by Doran Morss. It's not our land, is it? Besides, we're happy to have a neighbor. What brought you here? You're a verso, obviously . . ."

He shook his head. "I am unfamiliar with many of your terms. WorldLing is not my first language."

"Verso," she said uncertainly. "Someone who does . . . well, this." She gestured around at the stone walls. "Someone who's turned away from the insanity of the narratives. Returned to the old ways—pure ways of living."

Again, he shook his head. "My people did not turn away from anything. We turned *to* something." Her face eloquently expressed her incomprehension. "I am not from the Archipelago," he said reluctantly.

"Oh! An alien," said Lindsey. "Or a colonist? That explains . . ." She gestured at his recently-made clothing. "But this is fascinating! Ishani, the things you find."

"So what are you doing here?" asked Ishani. "Are you working for Morss?"

"No." He frowned at the black hulking stove, an abomination of heat-pump technology where a fire should be. "I am doing nothing," he said at last. "Because I do not know what I could do to help my people. They have been destroyed. Many of my kinsmen and friends are dead. The rest are enslaved to a power I do not even understand." He had no reason to tell these people any of this. But Qiingi found he couldn't stop talking now that he had started. "I came to this place to be alone, away from your Archipelago of illusions. To mourn."

Lindsey sat back, clearly unsure whether to act appalled or admit to being in on the joke. "Your people . . . They're dead?"

"Many of them, I'm sure."

Her look of skepticism was infuriating; Qiingi knew she could have no idea what he'd been through. Suddenly spiteful, he said, "Those that are not dead will be slaves now. And our cities and canoes, our long-houses and our great Song of Ometeotl are gone. Our animals speak for the invaders." Lindsey glanced uncertainly at Ishani, who was gazing at Qiingi with wide eyes.

Qiingi grimaced. "We came to your worlds to find help for our people, but no one will help us. We cannot find anyone to defy your anecliptics."

"The annies?" Ishani looked puzzled. "The annies attacked your coronal?"

Qiingi didn't answer; he felt tears welling up in his eyes. He glared at the tabletop, feeling a surge of deep helplessness. It was a familiar feeling, one that had come upon him daily ever since he had left the Song. These people could never understand what he was going through.

Surely he was being unkind. Yet, everyone he had met in this forsaken place seemed to lack some essential spark that he had known at home. He glanced miserably around the room, wondering why this hut, so similar in many ways to those in Skaalitch, felt like a parody of a reality only his people had known.

"*Qiingi* . . . that name is familiar," said Lindsey. "Oh, where have I heard that, it's on the tip of my tongue, I'm tempted to do a query." She laughed at Ishani's expression. "I won't, of course. But Qiingi, you said *we* just now. Ishani said you were living alone."

"True. My friends have . . . lost their way. One is mesmerized by the wonders of your science and technology, and the other has thrown herself into the service of Doran Morss. They neglect our search for allies. Every day they seem to remember less why we came here." He tried to express the depth of his feelings of betrayal and pain at Livia's absence, but all he could say in the end was, "I do not understand."

Ishani shook her head sympathetically. "It's the narratives. They're making sense of your friends' lives; that's what they *do*. It's insidious, you don't even know it's happening. I'll bet they've both found causes they can believe in. They've even met people, haven't they? . . . Beautiful men or women who hold out some hope of completing them, of being their match . . ." She sighed ruefully at his expression. "It's true. Narratives will do that. And what they find for you is genuine, and emotionally fulfilling. It's just that it's been given to you, you haven't made it yourself."

He looked around the cabin, suddenly frightened. "And have the narratives given me this?"

"No. If you're here on the ground of the *Scotland* you're outside the narratives' influence. This is Doran Morss's ship, and he's not part of the human Archipelago. That's why *we*," she gestured at Lindsey and herself, "can be ourselves here."

"I came here to respect the loss of my people through isolation and genuine sadness," he said after a while. "Why did you come here?"

Lindsey brooded for a moment. "Because," she said, "everybody's looking for a way *out*. Out of the smothering comfort of the narratives, away from the impossibility of change. Since the anecliptics took over the Archipelago, things are safer—there's been no billion-casualty wars in a long time. But people are starting to realize that the price is too high. They can't change the world around them, so they try to change themselves—like Omega Point. But that's no answer. We have to look to the past for models of how to live."

"That's very interesting," he said politely. "But what I asked was, why are *you* living like this? I don't understand how anyone lives in this Archipelago, it is a strange place where people do not follow their . . . spirits. I merely wondered if that was what you were doing. Following your spirits."

Ishani frowned. "I don't know how to answer that."

He swallowed more of the horrible stew, then said, "In my country, we did not have sims or books or other entertainments. But on cold nights we would sit around the fire, and tell each other our stories . . . I see from your expressions that you do not know that tradition. I'm sorry I assumed too much."

"No, wait," said Lindsey, reaching to catch Ishani's arm. "I think that's a great idea, don't you? Ishani, why don't you tell us your story. How you came to be here."

Ishani sat back, looking shocked. "You mean, not by rewinding a memory, but by talking?" She started to grin, then laughed. "Like Charon did . . . All right, but I haven't organized my life as a *narrative,* you know. I'm not sure you'll understand."

"As listeners, we are not required to understand," said Qiingi. "Only to care."

"Ah. Well, then here goes."

MY PARENTS CAME from an average background, six generations all living together in an extended estate on an ordinary coronal. My first memories are of running and laughing on gigantic lawns among miles of parkland. The parks were full of fabulous animatronic creatures who staged tableaux and intricate dramas for us kids. The whole coronal was like this—paved with the grand estates of dynasties that had their roots in fabulous distant places like Mars and Mercury.

As I grew older and received my inscape implants I discovered other worlds that overlaid this one. There was a city, a fabulous place of whirring aircars and towering skyscrapers full of light—but it was entirely virtual, not a single brick of it physically existing. Yet everybody who was anybody had an apartment there. As a young teenager I would spend whole nights out with my friends in the crowded thick air of the city's alleys. Then to bug out and find myself sitting quietly in my room, where in fact I'd been all along.

It was at a party in this virtual city that I met the Wild Boy.

His name was Charon and he came from far away in the outer solar system. He'd grown up in an aerostat city in the frozen skies of Uranus, where the air's perfectly still for centuries at a time and the young people entertain themselves by rappelling up and down the vast curving sides of their cities above an endless abyss of air. He'd seen comrades fall to their deaths during such adventures—had spoken to one ten minutes into her descent, as she calmly related the sensation of the black tightening around her like an invisible serpent a thousand kilometers below him.

Charon was so gray and serious, like Death at a dinner party; but his stories held us fascinated, and not only because he told them to us verbally—like this—rather than just rewinding a memory for us to walk through. We loved his melancholy darkness—but we never let him know it. When we discovered that he refused to edit his inscape feeds, we took to pestering and teasing him mercilessly, playing tricks on his view, that sort of thing. I was very much attracted to him, so I'm afraid I was the worst.

He came to see me in my studio one day—I was a pretentious little girl and fancied myself a painter. I'd had a real studio built for me by the house bots, high up in one attic of the main building. I wore an old-style Parisian painter's cap and a white smock while I worked, even though I would never in a million years have touched *real* paint. I was working in airblocks when Charon came in, moving sculpted shapes of opacity and colored translucence around to create a light sculpture. I remember I'd called up a shaft of sun to spotlight myself and my work on the blond wood floor—totally artificial light, it was cloudy outside, but you get the idea. Charon took one look at me, and burst out laughing.

"I came here to yell at you for that last trick you played," he said; I can still remember the nasal tone of his accent. "But I can see now that it isn't necessary."

As clearly as I remember that, I can also remember my stunningly clever reply:

"What?"

"You're not much more real than that stuff you're playing with, are you?" he said. He was angry, but I wasn't sure why. Sure, I'd done something to his inscape again, but it was just inscape—and if he'd been hurt, well, hurts could be healed with a little pill or a few minutes with a sympathy agent.

I said something inane, I think it was about his interrupting important work. He walked slowly up to me, looking the sculpture up and down, and a sly expression came over his face. "I've noticed," he said, "that you and your friends are so used to inscape that you ignore most of it. You stick to the little parts that are fashionable and you never poke your head outside them."

It was true, but so what? In those first days after you get your inscape implants, the whole universe seems to be waving and trying to get your attention. You learn to tune it out; and I said so.

"Well, I've been exploring," he said. "Let me show you something." And right next to my light sculpture, he opened a window.

Visions unfolded in that window like flowers opening in the sun—first dozens, then as Charon's query raced through the worlds of the Archipelago, hundreds, thousands of subwindows floated in an infinite space next to my sculpture. They rotated in and out of focus at the front of the field. And, in each one of them, a young woman stood in front of a half-finished light sculpture.

"This is what's happening right this second, all across the Archipelago," said Charon. "I simply asked inscape to show me all the publically accessible feeds from girls who are working with airblocks."

The particulars were different—some of the girls stood outside, some inside, some in virtual spaces; some had white faces, some black, some blue and with any variety of genetically varied combinations of features. But out of trillions of people, it was inevitable that some large number of girls, basically human, all basically my age, would right now all be doing precisely what I was doing. I had never really understood that before.

"It gets better," said Charon. "Let's do a query on how many of those sculptures are *just like yours*."

"Stop," I said, but he went ahead with it, opening a second window—and there they were, dozens of girls making *my* sculpture.

"And even better," he continued, enjoying the look of horror that must have stolen across my face then, "let's see how many of those girls are being mocked by a friend who's doing queries next to their work—"

"Stop it!" I tried to hit him, though of course the etiquette fields of the house prevented the blow from landing.

"Don't you get it?" he shouted as he retreated to the door. "You're wallpaper, Ishani. You can't have a thought that a million other people aren't having, you can't do anything that a million other people aren't also doing. It doesn't matter what you say or whether you live or die because a million other you's are there to take your place. So why should I care what you do to me? You're wallpaper. Wallpaper!" And so he fled.

Of course he did care, but I was too young to see that. But he had opened a pit at my feet. I stopped working on the sculpture and stared aghast at the windows. I never painted again.

"That's terrible," said Qiingi. "I can see why you turned away from your world."

Oh, no, that's not the horrible part. It's what came after that made me realize what kind of place the Archipelago really is. You see, *I got over it.*

Several months later, the whole incident had receded and become trivial. I didn't even remember the shock and dismay I'd felt; it was like a dream. And then I met Charon again, who slyly asked me about that day. I proudly told him that I didn't care about what he'd shown me. And he laughed.

"Of course you don't care," he said. "Your narrative steered you away from the edge of that cliff. That's what it does. I bet you had some nice heart-to-heart talks, got gifts, a nod of approval here and there, new interests and people flooded into your life . . . It's been an eventful time, hasn't it?"

I hesitated. Yes, it had been an eventful season. I hadn't even had time to think, really.

"The great commandment of the narratives is that *your life must be meaningful*," said Charon. "If knowing the truth strips the meaning away, then the truth must be suppressed. Do you even remember what it was I showed you, that day?"

I opened my mouth to put him down, and at that moment I realized what was happening. Since the day that Charon showed me the truth, my view had been manipulated to soften the blow. Who I talked to, what was said; where I went, what was there . . . all were filtered and revised on the fly by inscape. All to restore my mental health.

The engines of my narrative had caught and begun laboring, making sense for me. Because they assumed that in the world of the Archipelago, no human could do that for herself.

And so, as understanding dawns, heaven slowly turns into hell. I began to realize that I was living in a labyrinth without exits. My parents had very carefully kept themselves ignorant of the true mechanisms behind the Archipelago. The ignorance is necessary or you'll go mad, you see? You realize that you have a choice: either exist as wallpaper, and accept that there's nothing you can do that hasn't been done before, nothing you can say that hasn't been said, nothing you can think that a million others aren't thinking right this second . . . or else, allow inscape to craft some unique, fulfilling, and utterly unreal fantasy world for you to live in. Any attempt to fight the system becomes *part of* the system. There is no escape.

I became a verso that very moment, though it was years later that I discovered others of my own kind. We're trying to live without narratives, and the only way we know is by going back to the way things once were. When everything you did had real meaning. I thought that by coming to Doran Morss's *Scotland* I would find the perfect place to find that meaning.

Funny thing, though. I may have escaped the narratives, but the Archipelago's pursued me here. I can't seem to escape it, not even by leaving Archipelagic soil. Maybe there really is nowhere to escape to.

ISHANI STOPPED SPEAKING, looking bleak. Lindsey seemed a bit shocked at the way the story had ended.

The two women rose to clear the table. Qiingi offered to help, but they protested that he was a guest; so he sat back to contemplate Ishani's story. As he was thinking, Ishani went to the stove, and cranked a dial on it. Warmth flooded off the squat metal thing.

"In my homeland," he said slowly, "we have something you do not have in the Archipelago. We call it *tech locks*."

"Yes?" said Ishani. Her back was turned as she scrubbed the plate; she seemed embarrassed for some reason.

"The wisdom of the tech locks is simple," he continued. "What we know is that you can't have just one technology. Like you can't have just one silverfish in your house. Technologies come in families, like people, and when you invite one into your home, the whole family will eventually move in and they won't leave."

Both women were now looking back at him.

"And even if you don't let the rest of the family into your house, they will camp out on your doorstep and pester you whenever you go by. The one inside your house will constantly remind you of the ones outside. And each family of technologies comes with a particular *way of life*. To invite that family in is to accept their way of life. To invite just one member in is to be constantly reminded that you could be living another way. It brings doubt into your house.

"Think of your stove, which does not burn. Is it not a reminder of everything you are trying to forget?

"Knowing this, our ancestors drew the family trees of all the technologies. And then they made a . . . a meta-technology that was able to suppress any of the others. It is easier for me to call this Ometeotl, for that is the name I was told as a boy. This great spirit knows what way of life—what family—each technology belongs to. Like people's families, technology's families shift and overlap. So it is never easy for a person to know what family he is inviting in when he adopts a new tool. But the spirit knows. You tell it the way of life you want to have, and it evicts the family members that go against that way.

"I tell you this: you cannot be happy in the life you are trying to make here, if you only evict one member of a family. You must evict them all—all serlings, agents, and helpers. You must leave inscape behind.

"You must throw away that stove."

LINDSEY SUDDENLY LAUGHED and clapped her hands. "I know where I've heard the name!"

Qiingi and Ishani stared at her.

"It just came to me," said Lindsey. "*Qiingi*—you got that name from the *Life of Livia!*"

Qiingi nearly fell off his chair. "*What?*"

"Am I not right? Are you a fan?" Lindsey slipped into the chair opposite him.

"How do you know that name?" he asked apprehensively.

"See?" Lindsey waved Ishani over. "I was right. It took me a while. See, Qiingi is one of the characters from the *Life of Livia*." She turned back to him. "You adopted his name. That's very interesting."

"Qiingi Voicewalker is the name Raven gave me when I was born," he said. "I did not adopt it. But tell me, what is this *Life of Livia?*"

Lindsey looked uncertain. "It's just seconds-new. Everybody's talking about it. It's the perfect verso sim, except it's not as interactive as a narrative. More like an old-style game. Livia Kodaly is this woman, she lives on a coronal, only it's not any real coronal, more like a mix of all of them. The *Life* is packed with scenes from all different parts of her life, mostly her childhood, and they're much more realistic than most sims. The characters are so real—I mean, any competent AI can mimic Archipelagic minds, but these people are different. Not part of the narratives at all. And so strong in what they believe . . . People are just eating it up."

"I hadn't heard about this," said Ishani.

"Well, you've been avoiding inscape," said Lindsey. "Which, if we listened to 'Qiingi,' here, the rest of us should be doing, too. Except that he obviously isn't, himself . . ."

Qiingi was so astonished he could barely speak. "Show me this *Life.*"

As inscape winked open and Qiingi watched an unfamiliar young woman walk the calm streets of Barrastea, he thought furiously about what must have happened. Livia's xhants had been stolen in those few moments after the flying house was picked up, and before the intervention of the Government. Whoever had done it had repackaged Livia's personal records as an entertainment and was distributing them throughout the Archipelago.

"Who is that?" he asked, indicating the young woman.

"That's Livia, the protagonist."

Most of the people Qiingi had met in his brief stay with Livia's peers now looked different; Aaron and Qiingi himself were idealized, almost caricatures. "How much is there?" he asked worriedly. Lindsey flipped through memory after memory, and Qiingi felt his heart sink. Not all of Livia's history was here—much less than half her years, perhaps. And it ended just before the attack on Barrastea.

But her agents were here, and many people's animas as well. Her whole Society, in fact, though Lindsey hadn't known they were there and was astonished when Qiingi called up Livia's mother and spoke to her briefly.

Finally he closed the window and put his head in his hands. "This is a catastrophe," he murmured. "What will she do when she finds out?"

Lindsey stared at him. "You're not telling me . . ." An expression of delight came over her. "The *Life* is real?"

"Real," he said with a deep sigh, "and stolen. A violation of my dearest friend's privacy and soul. Poor Livia, this will destroy her when she learns of it."

But Lindsey stood up in a fever of excitement, knocking her chair over. "But don't you understand?" she said. "This changes everything! If the *Life* is real, and contemporary, then maybe a real verso world is possible. Not just a playground version like this one."

She and Ishani began talking, their WorldLing going by too quickly for Qiingi to follow. For a while he stared at the damnable heat pump stove, mourning for Livia's private existence.

After supper he excused himself, refusing Ishani's offer of a pallet by the fire. He walked out into the drizzle, head down, letting the worldship shed its tears for him.

17

DORAN MORSS LOOKED across the table at the play of candlelight in Livia Kodaly's eyes. The towers of Barrastea glittered behind her. Blinking lights of aircars cruised the sky, and a sigh of cool evening air drifted in over the window's open transom. Livia lifted one side of her mouth in a coy smile. "Having fun?" she asked, swirling her wine.

"You have no idea," he said, digging into his roast duck with gusto. The duck and the wine were the only real objects in this sim, and he was determined to honor their reality by enjoying them to the full.

"I rarely visit a sim more than once," he said past a mouthful. He gestured at her with his fork. "Testament to your design."

"You think I'm just an anima?" she asked. *Anima* was a special word in this place, he'd learned. The sim had a whole vocabulary of its own, which might have been pretentious had it not been so consistent.

"That's not supposed to matter in Westerhaven, is it?" he asked astutely. She shrugged. "So tell me, are you based on a real person?"

"I am a real person," she answered.

Doran was disappointed. The entities in this simulation were not cagey enough to retain an understanding of the world outside their own milieu. That would certainly limit his ability to interact with them. A little self-awareness could make an artificial mind so much more interesting.

"Your own reality seems to weigh heavily on you," Livia said suddenly. Doran sat back in surprise. His mind was gloriously blank for a few seconds.

"If that were not so," continued Livia, "then you could not travel here, could you?"

"What do you mean?"

"To travel you have to value. And un-value." She looked away sadly.

Doran chewed angrily. "What's real is what's valuable. Everything else is just an illusion." *Just like you.*

"So you see yourself as someone who shatters illusions?"

He nodded warily. "If not me, then who?"

She smiled dazzlingly at him. "But what if it were the other way around—that what's valuable is what's real?"

Doran cursed and stood up. He dismissed the sim with a wave of his hand and everything—windows, cityline, music, and entrancing young lady—all vanished. All except for one chair, a small table, and a plate and wineglass.

He stood in his stone bedchamber, alone.

Sims weren't supposed to challenge you like that. They adjusted to your narrative, after all. Livia Kodaly should have provided Doran a quiet evening of relaxation and witty conversation. He needed rest from too much planning. He needed to forget for a while that he had to make a decision about the eschatus machine.

Doran's chambers were unadorned—stark, even. He knew his servants and the versos he indulged didn't understand. They thought he was an ascetic at heart. But it was just the opposite. To Doran Morss, the ability to see the world unaugmented, as he did now, was the ultimate luxury. Alone in these quarters, he could revel in the simplicity of his own five senses.

At least, he should—but instead found himself wallowing in these senseless sims when he should be making decisions. Would he ever again be able to see the world in this simple way if he used the eschatus machine? Or would the virtual overwhelm the real at last?

The brodys had delivered the machine two days ago. It waited now in a scan-shielded grotto hidden deep in one of his mountains. Twice now Doran had walked down the wet stone steps that led to its resting place—a place he couldn't help but think of as its *altar*. Twice he'd trudged back up those steps without having touched the thing.

He felt ashamed of himself. In the past, he knew, men had been capable of making hard sacrifices. Countless soldiers had died for causes they knew to be false. Doran had spent decades preparing for this moment. Why, at the last minute, should he balk at throwing down the gauntlet to the anecliptics?

The seconds ticked on in silence and solitude. Finally, he sat down and took up his knife and fork. But he no longer tasted the food as he ate it.

A faint vibration reached him through the floor. He kept eating—but seconds later, he heard distant shouts. Doran cocked his head, annoyed. Somebody's loud party had spilled over into crippleview, apparently. He gestured open an inscape link to one of his servants and said, "Can you find out who's—"

He stopped. The inscape link wasn't open. Puzzled, he tried again. Nothing.

Doran stood and walked to the door. The shouts were closer now. He opened the door in time to see one of his people round the far corner of the arched, balconied hallway. "Sir! It's gone down!" The man appeared positively frantic.

"What the hell are you talking about?"

"Inscape! Inscape has crashed!" Doran could see the whites all the way around the man's eyes. He was practically wetting himself in terror.

"Out of the way." He ran down the corridors, passing several open doors. People stood slack-jawed here and there. One woman had her nose to the wall and as he passed, she placed her fingers on the surface, and reached out to tentatively lick it.

"Was it some kind of accident?" he shouted back to his man as he bounded up a flight of stairs. "Is it just the city, or has the whole world-ship gone down?"

"I . . . how should *I* know?" Doran looked back at him. The man splayed out his hands, shrugging. "I can't link to anybody."

"You're in crippleview now. Talk to people. Find a window and look for incoming aircars. See if any have crashed. Go on! I'll be in the plaza upstairs."

He raced up the stairs to find himself in the diamond-domed central plaza of the chandelier city. Glittering towers loomed high on all sides, their apexes joined by flying buttresses in a complex knot half a kilometer up. Doran stopped at the entrance to the plaza, stunned.

A field of bodies lay strewn for a hundred meters in every direction.

One person remained standing in the center of this tableau. It was the new baseline, Alison Haver.

LIVIA HAD BEEN talking to the votes to distract herself from Aaron's continued refusal to speak with her. She'd gotten comfortable with several of the ones that had retained bodies aboard the worldship after the Omega Point fiasco; they were sufficiently different from human beings to temporarily take her away from her worries. Today the votes were as usual arguing and debating in a great scrum in the central plaza, when suddenly all of them fell over as if on cue. For an absurd second she thought she was the object of some strange joke, or maybe another cliff test. Then it hit home that she really was the only one left standing.

It was obvious what had happened. Inscape had failed. Strange, that she could coolly and analytically reason this out, while in the distance other human citizens of Doran's city were beginning to scream and run blindly.

For a while she was paralyzed by indecision—and memory. The field of bodies reminded her of the airbus, seen as she and Aaron staggered away from it. There was the same random quality to the out-flung arms and tilted heads surrounding her now.

As she was thinking this someone appeared in a nearby archway. It was Doran Morss, looking disheveled and breathing heavily. "Haver!" he snapped. "What the hell is going on?"

The spell was broken and she found herself actually laughing. "Maybe it was something I said."

He swore and turned away. "Wait!" she called. "I'm fine. Those others," she pointed at some distant wailing human figures, "are going to need our help."

He looked past her, chewing his lip. "Right. It's a place to start."

"There's probably no way to find out what just happened," she said as she gingerly stepped over the fallen votes to reach him. "Not until inscape comes back up. Meanwhile it's a safety issue."

"Right. Right." He nodded vigorously, eyes wide. "So . . . we should start with, uh . . ."

"We have to keep people from hurting themselves or others," she said.

"Right. So . . . how are we going to do that?"

. . .

HOURS LATER, LIVIA walked back to her apartment through the eerily silent city. She weaved a bit as she walked; she was dead on her feet. For a day that had felt like a week, she and Doran, and some versos who happened to be in the city, had fought the rising hysteria of people thrown out of inscape for the first time in their lives. They had used words, fists, ropes, and stun weapons to subdue knots of rioting people. Most individuals had seized on any instruction and allowed themselves to be docilely led back to their apartments. Tonight everything was locked down, and Doran's people patrolled the corridors of the city. A concerted effort was being made to communicate with distant parts of the ship; it seemed the city was not alone in being affected. Just what had happened, though, was anybody's guess.

She entered the grand gallery that led to her rooms, her breath steaming ahead of her. The gallery looked down over kilometers of open air to the cold moors, and without the networked environmental controls, the city was starting to cool down.

Something caught her eye. A small bonfire was burning near the gallery's rail. She hesitated, wondering if she should call for fire fighting assistance.

Then she spotted the man warming his hands near the heap of burning furniture. Doran Morss looked up as Livia approached. He smiled.

"You're welcome to share my fire," he said. "It's all I've got right now . . ."

"Any leads?" she asked as she came to stand next to him. It was utterly quiet except for the crackle of the flames, and darkness ruled beyond this small zone of light.

He shook his head. "I'm sure the systems will come back on line soon. Meanwhile, I just want to get warm." He stared at the flames, and muttered under his breath, ". . . Can't get warm anymore . . . Not for years."

"Are you all right?"

He sat down on the marble floor, and seemed to shrink into himself, staring into the fire. "This? This is nothing. I'll get over it. And you, how are you holding up?"

"Exhausted. I'm going to bed."

Doran grunted. "I can't do that. Not until I find out what the hell is going on."

"What will you do when you do find out?"

"Throw whoever's responsible off the tallest tower of the city,

I think." He shrugged. "For now, I'm sort of enjoying the peace and quiet."

Livia sat down wearily next to him. "Me too," she said, a bit surprised at herself. It *was* peaceful, knowing that at least for now, there could be no inscape-driven interruption to your thoughts.

They sat together companionably for a time while the wind sighed over the balcony, teasing the flames back and forth. Livia felt a deep and wistful melancholy settle over her. Drowsy, her limbs heavy, she just wanted to lie down here on the stone floor and sleep.

Doran looked over at her. "You're a strange one, Haver."

She nodded back to full awareness. "Why do you say that?"

"You live like a verso, but you spend all your free time talking to the votes. Don't deny it; you're using my resources to do it, and I keep tabs on such things. I found you today in a heap of votes, didn't I? So what is it that you're looking for so passionately that it's all you can think about?"

Livia thought of Aaron and laughed humorlessly. "Well apparently I'm no good at seeing what's right under my nose." Should she tell Doran the truth about her origins and quest? It would be good to finally drop the caution advised by the Government.

Doran stared into the flames. "I don't know exactly what you're doing here," he said finally. "But I know you're expending a great deal of effort and energy working on the same levels where I used to work— among votes, between narratives. Doing things that in another age used to be called *political*. I just hope it doesn't turn out to be as futile an exercise as my own attempts to reform the Government."

"Well . . ." Comfortable in the moment, Livia decided to tell him everything. She opened her mouth to begin—

Light welled up around them. She blinked at the disappearance of the cloudscape beyond the balcony.

Doran leaped to his feet. "Finally!"

She turned to look behind her. Though this avenue wasn't large, suddenly it was crowded with inscape phantoms. Throngs of humans and semihumans chattered as they walked by; sentient gases and weird glow-in-the-dark aliens sailed buzzing overhead; a line of chanting monks left footprints of gold behind themselves, while rioting agents set loose by irresponsible adolescents reappeared right where they'd left off, spraying virtual paint in virtual letters across virtual kiosks in the center of the aisle.

The bonfire seemed small and almost invisible in the face of all this.

Doran glanced down at it, sighed, and said, "Back to work, I guess. See you, Haver." He walked away.

Livia sat there a while. She was too tired to move—too tired to query inscape about what had caused the outage. She wanted nothing more than to summon her bedroom around herself and fall asleep. Ordinarily, she could have trusted herself to wake in the real bed by morning. But what if inscape went down again? She could find herself stranded in the corridor in a cube of utility fog.

She dragged herself to her feet and walked slowly to her apartment.

She thought about her men as she flopped onto the bed. There was nothing she could do to salvage her relationship with Aaron if he wouldn't talk to her. And she longed to feel Qiingi's strong arms around her. He would probably laugh at what had happened tonight—but she could never tell him about Aaron. He was no doubt completely unaware and unaffected by all that had happened, sitting down there in whatever hut he'd built for himself on the bleak moor.

It seemed that the three of them had carried a great freight of personal baggage all the way from Teven to the Archipelago. They were never going to breach the walls of history and attitude that separated them, and maybe trying was wrong.

She flung an arm over her eyes. How could she have been so blind as to miss Aaron's attraction to her? The whole fiasco filled her with guilt—but she had tried to reach Aaron, and he was shutting her out. Just like he'd shut her out in the weeks leading up to the potlatch and the invasion.

Just how responsible did she have to be? She had done her best by him and by Westerhaven. She had exiled herself to save her friends and family and she would if given any chance at all, find a way to heal her bond with Aaron.

And if she failed in all of it? Would she deserve punishment then? Or might it be all right if she took some enjoyment from life, something for herself and not others for a change?

She fell asleep before she could really think about it.

AN INSCAPE CHIME awoke Livia. She lay there for a few seconds, disoriented, then groaned and sat up. "Yes, what is it?"

"Respected Haver? May I speak with you?"

Livia blinked and gradually took in where she was. Apparently, it was late afternoon; she'd slept most of the day. Whoever was calling her—she didn't recognize the voice—was apparently right outside her door. She staggered out of bed, summoned some clothes and said, "Just a minute!"

When she opened the door it was to find two women standing there. Still fuzzy-headed from sleep, it took her a minute to realize that they were identical twins. "Yes, can I help you?"

"You're Alison Haver?" asked one. The other was glancing up and down the gallery with a worried expression. "You're a friend of Georges Milan?" That was the name Aaron was using here.

"Yes, I—well, come in, sorry to keep you standing in the hall, uh, Respected . . ."

"Veronique," said the other woman. They both stepped into the apartment and Veronique shut the door after peeking outside.

"Is he here?" asked Veronique's twin.

"I'm sorry, I didn't get your name," Livia said to her.

"Veronique," she said. "I'm both Veronique. I know, it's hard to understand when there's only two of me. And I'm really sorry to bother you, but I have to find Georges—"

"He's not here." Livia crossed her arms, frowning at the two women. "I don't know where he is."

"Oh." The twins looked deflated. "Oh, this is terrible."

"What's going on?"

"He talked about you a lot, I just thought if he were going to go somewhere it would be here . . ."

He'd been talking about her? "Sit down." Livia indicated her couch. "You're obviously upset—would you like some tea? Maybe a nice tropical view . . ."

The women shook their heads. "I have to find him. Morss is after us, I'm afraid he might have caught up to Georges already—"

"What do you mean Morss is after you?" Even as she said this Livia figured it out; this whole situation, the collapse of inscape, the chaos, Aaron's cryptic pronouncements. "You were part of this, weren't you? You engineered the inscape crash. And he was part of it, too."

Both Veroniques nodded. "But it wasn't supposed to come off like this. We'd built a supervirus, it was supposed to take inscape away from the Government and narratives, give it back to the people . . . It wasn't supposed to crash the *Scotland*'s defensive systems—"

"What? Slow down—and sit down!—and tell me what you're talking about."

Veronique sat, and gradually Livia got the story out of her. She described how she had, on very little evidence, convinced herself that a conspiracy of AI hackers existed—a diffuse group determined to fly under the radar of the votes and narratives. She had contributed her skills to a project barely hinted at, certainly not controlled from any discernable point. With Aaron as her sponsor, she had come to the *Scotland* because it was the best place from which to launch the virus she imagined she was building. Yesterday, after months of effort, she had done it.

"Our little AI clawed its way through the *Scotland*'s system, deteriorating as it went. Like in any whisper network, its message packets got garbled as it tried to propagate itself. But just when it was about to disintegrate, it hooked up with another entity coming from, well, somewhere! You can't imagine how I felt! The conspiracy was real! We cheered and danced around when we saw that. Georges and I watched as the two AIs merged and grew and the new entity went on. It found more components, one after another, and got stronger and stronger. Twenty minutes after we let it go, it woke to full power and took over the whole worldship."

The entity sent out queries to the rest of the conspirators before the anecliptics even became aware of it. Veronique's face lit up as she described it. "We established error-free links and the code flooded in. While inscape was going down here, a new AI was being born in Morss's network. The plan had gone off without a hitch."

And that, Veronique now knew, should have been the first clue that something was terribly wrong.

"We sat up all night in a state of exhilaration, waiting for the system to come back. It was so eerie, silent, only the distant shouts of birds from far below the window, and the cold creeping in slowly in the dark . . . When inscape did return, I knew, there would be no Government in it, no votes—no anecliptic presence. We talked about what we would say, the announcement we would make, and we debated about how people would react.

"And then the moment came—hours too soon. Everything hummed back into life around us; inscape windows popped open, virtual objects reappeared, and the heat came back on."

Some parts of the network were still down—including the worldship's asteroid defense and outside traffic control. "While Georges and I were combing through the data, trying to figure out what had happened, a knock came at the door."

Aaron had opened it—warily, but with a look of proud defiance on his face. There, slouching in the hallway, was a short, shabby-looking man with amber eyes. He was a vote.

Veronique buried her face in her hands. "But he wasn't just any vote. Do you understand? Do you know what happened next?"

Livia sat down next to her. "He was *your* vote."

The AI introduced himself. He was, he said, the representative of Veronique and her conspiracy—a mind brought into existence by tonight's attack, the very attack that had sought to wipe out the Government. "I even incorporate your virus!" he had said proudly as he shook Aaron's hand.

"And do you know what he said next?" Veronique's voice rose to a wail. *"I'm here to help!"* Both of her burst into tears.

Livia patted her hand, bewildered. After a while one of Veronique calmed down enough to say, "Well, you can see the effect it had on me. But I think it was worse for Georges. He turned white as a cloud when he realized what had happened. And then he ran out of the apartment. I haven't seen him since."

Livia didn't know whether to be worried, or to laugh out loud. She was still trying to sort it all out when the door chimed again.

Veronique leaped to her feet. "Maybe that's him!" She ran to the door and pulled it open.

Doran Morss stood there, a number of his loyal servants crowding the gallery behind him. Standing between two of them was Qiingi, who was looking very unhappy.

Doran took in the vision of Livia and Veronique standing together. "Well," he said with a scowl. "Doesn't this look incriminating."

AARON VARESE STOOD on one of the chandelier city's highest balconies. It was icy cold up here and the air was thin. The dizzying feeling reminded him of Cirrus and the vast landscapes of Teven Coronal. What he now looked out upon was incomparably bigger.

He had his inscape view tuned to the consensus version of the Archipelago. It stretched out before him as an apparently infinite plain covered with cities and oceans, parkland and the occasional mountain range. Mars was visible by its color, a patch of sandy red off to the left; Earth's skies were a particular shade of blue to the right. In between, and stretching far beyond both, were the patchwork landscapes of countless coronals.

Aaron had come up here to convince himself that what seemed impossible, really was so.

The vista that opened out below him was breathtaking in its scale and detail. That very size bespoke an impossible inertia. At any moment millions of people were being born and millions more were dying. Humanity was huge and powerful and unstoppable. It was a cage so big that its bars were invisible with distance; but it was still a cage. And after the events of the past day he now knew that he would never escape it.

192 ∞ Karl Schroeder

Aaron was not given to dramatic gestures; he wasn't about to jump off this balcony. What he felt would happen was much worse. In moments, or hours, he would take a deep breath, and let go of everything he had ever believed in and wanted. He would throw away the bedrock of determination that had kept him going for years. He would surrender. After that, no matter what happened, his future would hold nothing but different shades of failure. He'd drift like a ghost through his own life, smiling at all the right jokes, getting up every morning, going to sleep every night. And nothing would ever matter again.

He heard a sound behind him. Maybe Doran Morss's people were here to throw him off the worldship. Almost eager for that, he turned.

She leaned in the tower's doorway, her eyes the brightest thing in the shadows. "They're looking for you," she said.

"What does it matter?" He shrugged and turned back to the view. "Anyway, you're a vote—aren't you going to turn me in?"

"Not at all. In fact, I greatly admire what you've just attempted. More people should be trying such things."

"Why?" he said bitterly. "Nothing works."

"Well, nothing's worked *so far*," she said. At this Aaron turned, to see the vote smiling mischievously.

"In order to stage a credible attack on the anecliptic's empire, you need a staging area that's free and clear of the Government's influence." She sauntered out onto the balcony. "Doran Morss's worldship was a good idea, but as you discovered, it's not far enough removed from the Government networks."

He snorted. "And I suppose you know of a better place?"

"As a matter of fact," said Filament, "I do."

18

QIINGI WATCHED THE little boat pop up to the tops of waves and then disappear into the pits that rolled after them. It was only a kilometer away from shore now; he was surprised it had made it this far. Behind it stretched a gray expanse of sea that curved slowly up until the shoreline of Doran's Scapa became visible, a mottled gray-green scab in the haze.

Either a couple of fishermen from Scapa's verso hamlet were lost, or this was some kind of a rescue party. Did they really think that they wouldn't be caught? He shook his head in grudging admiration at the sheer determination they were showing. But in the week that he and

Livia had been stranded here on this rocky isle, no one had made it to shore here.

In his fury over their supposed part in the attack on the *Scotland*'s systems, Doran Morss had exiled them here in an inscape-free part of the worldship. The woman Veronique had been sent to another nearby island. Doran had declared that he would summon them all to account for themselves soon. But even he seemed to have forgotten about them.

Squatting on the sand, Qiingi idly drew a circle with a cross inside it. Everything moved in circles, the elders had told him; everything was made of teotl and so was hurrying to become whatever it was not. Teotl might be just a story, but it was a story about a real thing. It was the story of how men and women made sense of their lives.

Teotl was inscape, he knew. It made a story out of life. And the great spirit Ometeotl was the tech locks. Inscape could tell the tale—as it did in the Archipelago—but only the locks could make the narrative of life both meaningful and true.

He watched the waves roll in and out. They didn't change at his whim. Qiingi felt a laugh build up in him; shaking his head he walked back up the beach.

He was humming as he pushed open the driftwood and pine-bow door. Livia looked up from where she was coaxing more heat from the fire. "You're uncommonly cheerful today," she said.

"I was just thinking," he said. "Doran Morss does not know it, but he did us a favor by stranding us here."

"A favor?" She squinted at him. "How?"

"His rules have become our tech locks," said Qiingi. "As the days roll on, my mind clears more and more. I'm beginning to understand every-thing that happened to us. Without this stable manifold," he gestured at the walls, "I could not have done that." He sat down on the flat stone bench that was the only piece of furniture here other than their rude bed.

She smiled ruefully and shook her head. "Lucky for you that the place is so similar to where you grew up."

"Of course, you must miss your Society." He took her hand. "But at the same time, there is a marvelous silence here that I haven't felt since I left Raven's people. Don't you feel it?"

"I feel cut off and helpless," she said, hugging herself. "But I was starting to feel that way even before we were stranded here. Doran was right—public life isn't possible under the annies. Anyway, what would we be doing if we were free? Just wallowing in our narratives like every-body else."

"Maybe—but the Archipelago no longer intimidates me," he said with a shrug. "These people think they have access to every answer humanity has invented to explain life and the world. They believe they can pick and choose, but it is not so. When there are too many explanations for something, its meanings are lost."

She frowned at him. "That's unusually cryptic, even for you."

He sighed. "We suffered a great loss. We are refugees. I know you struggled long against accepting that. The narratives helped you do that, by fitting everything that happened to you here into a meaningful story with you at its heart. You tried not to be deceived, as did I—but as long as you could even change your *view* of this Archipelago, you could find some new way to put off facing our loss. Would you have done that back home? I don't think so. You can only run so far in a manifold."

She turned away. "You're saying Teven was real, and the Archipelago is an illusion."

"Yes. And I am saying that we have lost Teven." She looked at him again, her face still as a statue. "Perhaps the time for grieving is over," he continued quietly. "It is time to feel awe and pride at what we once had; accept that we have it no more, and move on."

"And how do I do that?" she asked.

He quirked a smile. "I don't know. But Livia, there is a tiny boat out in the bay. It seems to be trying to make it to shore."

"Oh!" She jumped up and ran to open the door. "Think they'll make it?"

"No." He looked over her shoulder; she needed a bath, he thought idly—but then, so did he. "Look there."

A hair-thin black line had appeared below the clouds: a skyhook, lowering down over the bay.

"A week ago you would have run down the sands to see if it was Aaron returning to you," said Qiingi. She had waited for Aaron for the first few days; she had stood by the shore and watched for boats. But he had not come, nor had Doran Morss's agents delivered him as a prisoner. She had not spoken his name for two days.

She winced. "Are you asking whether I've finally stopped struggling? If I've accepted our situation?" She returned to the fire and sat by it, clenching her hands in her lap. She peered up at him with stark intensity. "You're asking me to accept that we failed our mission. That we've let down our friends, our families—everyone who ever meant anything to us. You say they're gone forever. And I need to accept that."

He watched her sadly as she struggled to breathe around these words.

Finally she looked down at the dirt floor. "I can do it, you know. I can let them all go. It's just that . . . once I've done that, what will I have left?" Her eyes held agony.

"I don't know," he said softly. "But learning that is our task now." She nodded, her shoulders slumped.

Several minutes passed. She remained sitting, head bent, and he stood by the door. Then she looked up, a ghost of a smile on her face. "Go on," she said.

"What?"

"You're dying to go down to the shore, just to see what's happening, aren't you?" Qiingi crossed his arms uncomfortably. But she was right. "Oh, go on," she said with a weary wave of the hand. "I'll be all right. And I'm sure they'll appreciate knowing that you saw them." He smiled, and left the cabin to trudge back to the beach.

He raised his hand to the little boat, and was rewarded by a wave back. The skyhook resolved into a black cable with a nest of grappling arms at its end. Its claws were big enough to pick up the entire boat and it seemed determined to do just that. Qiingi watched with interest and some regret. It would have been good to know what was happening elsewhere in the wide world.

Suddenly some kind of wooden arm shot from the bottom of the fishing boat. A whirling net flew straight up and entangled the descending hand of the skyhook. Qiingi gave a shout of surprise, then laughed. They had seen this coming; the versos were not so naive as people assumed—himself included, apparently.

The fishing boat shot forward. They had some kind of engine in there. Now it left a white wake behind it and the nose tilted up with the force of its push. "Livia, you should see this!" he shouted, knowing his voice probably wouldn't carry inside the cabin from here.

The skyhook clenched and unclenched its spider fingers, trying to dislodge the net. Above it a second one popped out of the clouds and plummeted at the boat. Doran must have an endless supply of those things, and they would be wary of the nets now.

A brave attempt by the versos, but doomed to failure.

A shimmer just offshore caught Qiingi's attention. The waves there seemed skewed, out of synch with one another in one—no, in two spots. The horizon became clipped and rose up and down just over the waves; then he understood what he was seeing.

Two man-sized, man-shaped things had just stood up out of the water. They were nearly invisible, but the view of the waves behind them was updated just a fraction of a second late, making the sea and sky jerky in those spots. The two nearly-invisible men splashed out of the surf and ran toward Qiingi.

He backed away, frightened but aware that it was far too late for him to try anything. Irrationally, he wondered whether one of those figures was the false ancestor Kale, come to pay Qiingi back for dropping a tree on him.

"Come on!" said a male voice as a half-visible arm waved at him. "We need to get inside." The two forms raced past Qiingi and he found himself standing still for a moment, staring. Then he ran after them.

"The boat," he shouted. "It was a decoy!"

"Yeah, aren't we brilliant?" Both human-shaped blurs were waiting at the hut's door. One gestured for Qiingi to precede them. "After you, Voicewalker."

"How did you know—" He pushed in ahead of them. Livia stood up, eyes wide. "Livia, we have visitors, I—"

"Who are you?" she said. Qiingi turned.

As the door shut the two men became visible. They looked like brothers, similarly tall and slender, with elfin faces and delicate jaws. They were sopping wet and had identical, ridiculous grins on their faces as they high-fived one another.

"Ha, I knew it would work!"

"No you didn't, you whined about the plan all the way—"

"That was just to motivate you."

"I'll motivate *you*, just wait."

"But Livia, here we are! You didn't think we'd leave you helpless, did you?" The man puffed out his chest with pride.

"It can't be," muttered Livia.

Qiingi looked from her to the men. "What? Who are these people?"

She swallowed and shook her head. "If I'm right, you've met them before, Qiingi. But you were never formally introduced." She walked up to the first man. "Qiingi Voicewalker, this is—"

"Peaseblossom!"

"And I'm Cicada!" And they stuck out their hands for him to shake.

THE LADS PROFESSED to be hungry, so Livia brought out one of the loaves of bread that occasionally fell from the sky. "Are these bodies biological, then?" asked Qiingi politely, as the agents piled cheese and raw onions on big slabs of bread.

"Oh, no, we just like to eat," said Cicada.

"Give me that!" Livia grabbed the sandwich away from him.

The momentary annoyance—somehow reassuring because it proved to her that these really were her faeries—finally made Livia snap out of the state of shock she'd been in since they arrived. "But what are you doing here? And how did you get . . . these?" She indicated their robust bodies.

"Some of your fans made them for us," said Cicada. "Along with some supplies; and when they heard that Doran Morss had kidnaped you, the whole bunch of them went together and got us a ship. It's waiting outside." He pointed down.

"Fans? What fans?"

"Well, you know," said Peaseblossom around a large mouthful. "You're a huge celebrity now so there's thousands of people willing to kick in to support whatever you do."

"Celebrity?" She stared at them, then noticed that Qiingi was looking guilty. "Why? Tell me."

"Well." Qiingi looked to the others for support. Cicada whistled and examined his fingernails. Peaseblossom just grinned.

"Remember when we first arrived in this place," said Qiingi reluctantly. "Our inscape was unguarded. Your own data stores were raided by data-thieves . . ."

She paled. "Oh no."

"Many of your recorded experiences were stolen in those few seconds. We didn't know. And . . . Livia, we just found out about the *Life of Livia*—"

"The *what?*"

In a state of horrified disbelief, she heard Qiingi tell her that her memories had been distributed as an entertainment; millions of people had seen them. As the vast depths of the data began to become obvious, he said, the *Life of Livia* had recently taken on a new significance. There was enough of Teven there for people to become intensely curious about the manifolds. Versos and even mainstream citizens had begun styling themselves after Westerhaven fashions, and adjusting their narratives to resemble the Societies of Livia's home.

"But this is—it's impossible!" She couldn't stay still, but paced up and down the narrow confines of the cabin, wringing her hands. "It's like rape! How much do they know? What have they seen?" She felt physically ill at the thought. Finally she rounded on Qiingi. "Why didn't you tell me?"

He shrank back from her intensity. "I did not think you were prepared to hear it in the right spirit," he said. "It would have been one more confirmation that your public life has been stolen from you."

"It's not that bad," said Cicada, patting her arm. "When people copy the *Life,* they also unknowingly copy us, and we've been guarding the stuff you wouldn't want anyone to see."

"We even changed your looks—"

"We've been talking to the other copies of us, so we could coordinate it—"

"And we hide the important stuff."

She shook her head. "That was not your decision to make! You should have told me! So . . . so how many copies are there?"

"As of now?" Cicada leaned back, cracking his knuckles behind his head. "Well, about seven hundred million, I'd say."

Screaming seemed too weak a reaction at this point. Livia slumped down in a corner, hating them all.

"It's the versos," said Qiingi hurriedly. "It's not you they're interested in—well, except insofar as you're what Mr. Morss called a 'baseline' for them to emulate. No, it's Westerhaven they're fascinated by. And Raven's people, and the other manifolds. There is nothing like them here."

Cicada nodded violently. "There's this huge movement to try to make manifolds, but they don't know how to do it, because the plans for the tech locks weren't included in the *Life.* People know about tech locks now, but they're having trouble making them—"

"Because the key to the locks is this giganormous database," said Peaseblossom, "that cross-references a thousand years of anthropological data on how technologies affect culture."

"We looked into this database thing," said Cicada. "The data were compiled centuries ago by scientists in the monoculture. A huge effort. But all existing copies were corrupted in the Viability War that ended with the anecliptics coming to power."

"There were rumors at the time that a clean copy of the database was saved," said Peaseblossom. "By one of the main researchers. A woman named—"

"Ellis!" laughed Cicada. "Maren—"

"—Ellis." Peaseblossom glared at Cicada.

"And anyway," pouted Cicada, "everybody's coming down hard on the versos who are trying to build manifolds. They say that tech locks would be disastrous—"

"Who says so?" Qiingi stood up in sudden excitement. "Do you know who it is that's so opposed to creating locks?"

Cicada shot him a reproachful look. "Well, I was just getting to that, wasn't I? It's certainly not the Government, though it doesn't approve, as it made *abundantly* clear to us the last time we spoke." He nudged Peaseblossom and rolled his eyes.

"There's all kinds of people against it," said Peaseblossom. "Lots of the votes—basically, churches and any social groups that are trying to expand. They've figured out that tech locks equal horizons, in the long run. And horizons would prevent them from expanding, see?"

"And don't even get me started about the Good Book people," scoffed Cicada.

His words somehow penetrated Livia's cocoon of misery. She looked up. "The Book isn't connected to any political movement," she said. "It's just an emergent system."

"Yeah, but what emerges?" asked Cicada. "Not just a utopian human society, but all kinds of solitons and other high-level constructs that you can't see from the human level. The Book's an insanely complex system on the macro level. And that macro level sends orders back down to the bottom; it's a feedback loop, like your own brain." He pointed at her head.

"The thing is, the book relies on open communications," said Peaseblossom, "except that it needs to communicate through different channels than inscape. Any hint of a manifoldlike horizon would fragment it. It would be the network equivalent of a stroke."

Livia barely heard him. Her head was still rattling with the idea that millions of people had ransacked her private records.

Cicada was saying, "You'd have to write a new version of the Book for every manifold, because technological differences change the way the roles interact. Not that people seem to mind doing rewrites. Apparently," Cicada leaned forward conspiratorially, "they've been adapting the Book to nonhuman species in the Archipelago. Trying to make the anecliptics obsolete by creating an emergent civilization that includes the post-humans."

To shut him up, Livia reached under the rock shelf that served as a bed, and brought out her copy of the Book. "Sophia said she was giving me the very latest version." She tossed it on the table and went back to fuming.

"Really?" Peaseblossom flipped through the Book. "Oh, yeah, the text is changing—I think it's trying to figure out what class of entity I am." He stuck out his tongue at the book and slammed it shut.

Livia took it from him, but didn't put it away. Instead, she flipped distractedly through it. She hadn't looked at it since their exile here; the rules of the Book were pretty irrelevant to a society of two.

"So there's lots of versions, are there?" she said indifferently.

"Yeah. It's easy to verify," said Cicada. "With printed books, they always put that information right in the front."

"Hmmph." None of it mattered; all this talk of politics was just a way to avoid the real question that was eating at her. She nervously flipped through the Book as she summoned her courage. Then she asked, "What about Aaron?"

Cicada and Peaseblossom glanced at one another. "I'm sorry," said Cicada. "We haven't been able to find a trace of him since the inscape virus."

"Ah." Blinking, she looked down, to find herself staring at the first page of the Book. She was too bereft to think, or to really take in the column of words there, the descriptions of where it was updated, according to what sims and when.

And then some lettering near the bottom leaped into focus:
Revision No. 3340.

"THERE'S BEEN ANOTHER breach, sir."

The words came through an old-fashioned speaking tube that ran up through the ceiling of the tunnel where Doran stood. He put it to his mouth and said, "Anybody we know?"

"It's Haver and her friend. They've got visitors."

"From the fleet?"

"Apparently not, sir."

Doran shrugged. "Then forget them. We've got more important things to worry about."

He'd opened an inscape window earlier today to watch a veritable cloud of ships that was approaching his *Scotland.* They were of all sizes and shapes—yachts, cityships, shuttles, freight bots, and one-person sun-dancers. All were crowded with people who individually had no idea why they were here—except that the Book had told them to come. They'd all been given roles like Warrior and Scout. One man Doran had spoken to had excitedly explained how some sort of feedback loop had set in: he couldn't change his role anymore. Every other user of the Book this man met reinforced his role as Herald.

Collectively, they had decided that their new status had something to do with Doran Morss. Now their makeshift armada was preparing to besiege the worldship—and, coincidentally or not, the *Scotland*'s defensive systems were still off-line.

He paced down the stone steps that led deeper into the caves. This tunnel led to one of his clean rooms—an area of the worldship free of nosy anecliptic nano, and totally lacking inscape projectors. Officially, the place didn't exist. During the chaos of the past week Doran had felt himself under a microscope; even the annies might be watching after the fiasco with inscape. So for the past week, he had been unable to come down here and confirm with his own eyes what he already knew must have happened.

He rounded a corner and the great cavern opened out below him. This was a natural space, discovered in one of the asteroids he'd dismantled to build the *Scotland*. Doran had kept the cavern and shaved away the rest of the asteroid from around it. He liked the bizarre twisting shapes the stone made overhead; the overall impression of the place was forbidding. The last time he'd been here, brilliant spotlights had pinioned a strange object that nestled in the very center of the cavern. Now he let his breath out in a whoosh as he looked down on the empty cradle where the eschatus machine had sat.

As he'd thought. The attack on his inscape had been a cover operation. The real target was to steal the eschatus machine. With no working inscape, none of his ordinary servants could prevent the theft. The versos said they'd seen lights here that night, but what could they do? All they had was a few boats.

Doran clattered down the last few meters of catwalk and approached the empty metal cradle.

He should never have hesitated. He should have just stepped inside the machine and let the overhead cranes slam home the plug. Once the seams had grown together, the thing would have been ready. A single command from him and the process would start. The machine would drop out of the *Scotland* and once in free fall and well away from the worldship, it would explode. This particular machine peaked at fifty megatons.

If he'd done that, he would have transcended his human form instantaneously. The energy of the explosion wouldn't burst out randomly, it would be channeled, down to the microscopic level, into a creative reorganization of the machine's matter. Doran's body and brain would have become a template for a new, vastly more sophisticated and powerful entity. An equal to Choronzon. Eventually, perhaps, he might have become an equal to the annies themselves.

Faint sounds drifted down from the speaking tube. It sounded like someone was trying to get his attention. Doran hunched his shoulders, glaring at the empty cradle. Humanity needed a champion, it was as simple as that; and no merely human being could be that champion any more. The annies must be opposed. But despite decades of careful planning under total secrecy, somehow he'd been found out.

"Choronzon," he murmured.

"Good theory," said a familiar voice. "But wrong."

Doran started, cursed, and looked up. The vote Filament stood on a catwalk near the entrance of the cavern. She was cradling some sort of projectile weapon in her arms.

"The thing about an eschatus machine," she said as she strolled down the steps, "is that every atom of it has to be placed just so. Shake it up a bit, God forbid put a *crack* in it, and it can't organize its energies anymore. It's just a very big bomb." She hefted her weapon suggestively. "It's always best to move them when there's nobody around who might object."

"Why have you done this?" he snapped.

"But Doran, we haven't spoken in days," she said with a smile. "Not since my fleet appeared. It seems you've been avoiding me."

Doran had always known that Filament was the Good Book's vote. Despite his contempt for the Book, it had never been an issue. She was a vote, after all; ultimately she worked for the Government. And the Government had no jurisdiction over Doran Morss.

"You set this up, didn't you?" he asked as he backed away from the cradle. Filament sat down casually on a metal step, her amber eyes bright in the shadows. "Did the Government put you up to it?"

"The Government knows nothing about it," she said. "It was the Book's plan."

"The Book? How can the Book have a plan?" He shook his head in anger and frustration. "It's not a *thing*."

"You know that doesn't matter," she said. "Anyway, you should be saying, 'it's not a thing *yet*.'

"Because with your help, very soon it will be."

"I'VE NEVER SEEN her jump like that," Peaseblossom was saying.

"There was that time when she was ten, and the wasps came out of the treehouse—"

"Oh, yeah!"

Livia and Qiingi were sitting on either side of the fire, with the Book open on the hearth between them. They had been staring at it for a while now, not knowing what to do or say. Livia felt like some primitive faced with her first radio. The thought made her giggle incongruously. "Where are the little men who make it go?" she asked, lifting one leaf of the thing to peer under.

Cicada misinterpreted her. "There's no central authority behind the Book—it's open-sourced. It's compiled by testing new rules on simulated societies. If the majority of people act a certain way, what happens? The sims are open to everyone to examine."

"The Book is one thing," said Qiingi. "The behavior of its followers is another thing entirely." He looked, if possible, even more shocked than Livia felt.

She glanced up at him. "You think the Books' users are behind the invasion of Teven? But anybody who's fanatical about the Book is so because they refuse to organize any other way . . . How would they coordinate such an attack? Through the Book itself?" She shook her head. "I don't think it's that specific in its commands."

"Oh, it can be," said Cicada.

"But they wouldn't have to use it," said Peaseblossom. "After all, just like every other interest group in the Archipelago, the Book has its vote."

Livia and Qiingi both sat up straight. "Let me guess," said Livia. "The Book's vote is named—"

"Filament," said Qiingi.

Peaseblossom stood up suddenly. "Uh oh."

"Are you thinking what I'm—" said Cicada.

"Yeah. Okay, people, we gotta go."

"Go? How?" Qiingi looked from one agent to the other. "What do you propose we do? Run into the sea with you? Fly away? Or become invisible as you were and hide among the rocks? Doran Morss will find us anywhere aboard this worldship."

"Yeah, that's why we're leaving it." Cicada and Peaseblossom began clearing an area of hard-packed earth in the center of the hut's floor. "We're not going out, or up. We're going down."

Cicada then did something very unsettling. He opened his shirt, reached his right hand over to the left side of his chest, and pulled. His whole chest hinged out like a door, revealing a large cavity inside. He pulled several packages out of the space and slammed himself shut again. Behind him, Peaseblossom was doing the same.

"Activate these," said Cicada, tossing two translucent packages to Livia and Qiingi. "Emergency angels, Archipelagic style. They'll keep you going when we hit vacuum."

Peaseblossom knelt down and began pouring some sort of liquid in a big circle on the sand. "Sealant," he said. "It'll keep the hole from collapsing for a minute or so while we leave. You two had better step outside for a second. We're about to blow the roof off your happy home." He hefted a metal sphere about the size of a fist.

Livia and Qiingi hastily left. Outside it was getting dark, and a chilly wind was blowing in off the sea. The illusion that they were on a planet was pretty good at this time of day, but there was no way she could believe in it now. Nervously, she pressed the emergency angel against her throat and it blossomed around her like a solid mist. Beside her, Qiingi did the same.

Nothing happened for a minute or so. Qiingi paced in an agitated circle around Livia. She was about to ask him what was wrong when a fearsomely loud *bang!* knocked her to her knees. She watched in fascination as the hut's roof did indeed fly away. The hut's stone walls leaned out drunkenly and one collapsed. A ripple of leaping dust spread out to sea and inland up the rocks, as the skin of the worldship bounced from the explosion.

"Okay!" Peaseblossom—or Cicada, it was hard to tell—opened the door, which promptly fell apart. "Your ride is waiting, Lady!"

There was a large hole where the hard-packed floor of the hut had been. A whirling tornado stood over it, and sandwiches, bedding, spare clothes, Qiingi's tools were all being sucked into it. One of her faeries took a nonchalant step and was yanked down and away. And there went the Book—

She lunged for it, managing to snag one corner before she realized she was over the hole and being pushed from behind by what felt like a giant's hand. Livia had a split second in which to curl into a defensive ball, and then she was in the hole.

Stars whirled around her. Peaseblossom's face came into view then swung away again. She saw the flat black surface of the worldship and the hole, which was rapidly sailing away from her; now Qiingi appeared through it, blazing sunlit on one side and blackly invisible on the other, a half-man. Fog swirled around him.

Then someone grabbed her leg and she was hauled unceremoniously into an airlock that had appeared suddenly out of nowhere. The others bumped in after her and Livia staggered to her feet in a nauseatingly different rotational gravity.

"Thank the Book!" said Sophia as she slammed the hatch shut. "You're safe!"

PART THREE

The Good Book

*Politics will eventually be replaced by imagery. The
politician will be only too happy to abdicate in favor of
his image, because the image will be much more
powerful than he could ever be.*

—Marshall McLuhan

19

"WHY ARE YOU looking at me like that?" Sophia was backing away from Wordweaver Livia. Livia glared at her with such intensity that Qiingi thought he should step between them. "I came to rescue you," said Sophia, appealing to Qiingi. "Livia, it's me, Sophia."

The city of Brand New York shone in sunlight outside the windows. A few of Sophia's friends—the hangers-on of her narrative—lounged around her apartments. Several were intently scanning copies of the Book. Had Qiingi not just seen a vision of whirling darkness and stars, he might have thought he was really there. As it was, the sight brought back all his distaste at the illusions of the Archipelago. Better a sod hut on the beach than this.

"Did you bring Sophia into this?" Livia asked Peaseblossom. Her voice had that metallic quality it got when she was angry. "Or did she find you?"

Peaseblossom toed the floor. "Actually, she found us."

Livia opened her mouth, closed it, then visibly took control of herself. "I'm sorry, Sophia," she said. "It's been a day of shocks, and I'm afraid it's not over yet. I'm going to have to ask you to do something for me that you won't like." She looked around the tiny room. "Who is the captain here?"

Peaseblossom shrugged. "Sophia was the ruling human until you arrived. But we all agreed to see what you would do once you got out. Where do you want to go?"

"I don't know. But could you shut down all our outside communications, please? Immediately?"

Sophia gaped at her. "But that would cut us off! The only reason I agreed to come along physically on this mission was—"

"Because you could do it and continue to live in your own narrative, I know. Peaseblossom, Cicada, do as I say." She walked over to Sophia. "Here's the part you won't like. I'd like to shut down inscape entirely, at least for now."

Their words washed over Qiingi, a gabble of noise. He knew he should be trying to catch up to everything that had just happened, but his mind couldn't stop whirling back to one terrible question:

Had he been wrong? Had he given up on their mission too soon?

Sophia was staring at Livia as if she were insane. "Why are you doing this?"

"I'll explain in a minute," said Livia. At that moment the sumptuous apartment disappeared from around them. Qiingi now found himself standing in a rather cramped plastic room. It had several doors and, in the floor, the big metal panel through which they had entered. Qiingi looked around the place in sad distaste.

"Turn it back on!" yelled Sophia. "Things are happening—important things! I need to be in the loop!"

"You've been in touch with other users of the Book all through this, haven't you?" asked Livia. She seemed coolly accusatory.

Puzzled and angry, Sophia nodded. "Of course I've been in the loop. I'm trying to help! Why else would I be here?"

Qiingi finally roused himself from his bewildered misery. He put a hand on Livia's arm. "Moderate yourself," he said. "None of them know."

"Kale knew," she said, shrugging him off. He frowned and retreated to a corner. He knew he should argue against what she was saying—but he couldn't think right now.

Nonetheless, Livia seemed to relent. "I'm sorry," she said to Sophia. "We . . . have reason to believe that we're being tracked through our in-scape connections. Until we get to the bottom of it, we need to run silent."

Sophia seemed devastated—but not with the shock of an inhabitant of the manifolds suddenly thrust out of them. Hers was more a pro-found distaste, as if she had learned that all her friends were low-born criminals. Silently she led the way into another of the ship's rooms; she stared around at the place as though seeing it for the first time, as in fact she was.

This place was quite large, and Qiingi supposed someone already out of touch with nature might consider it luxurious. There were actual oil paintings on the walls, and a deep artificial carpet that he instinctively hesitated to step onto. Livia collapsed on a couch in a boneless pose, and Qiingi had to smile; he did understand her relief at having a surface softer than sand under her for a change. Still, for him it was sufficient to have a wall to lean on.

Livia seemed spent. Qiingi knew he should think about what was happening, but he didn't know where to start. He turned to glowering Sophia. "You said 'things are happening,' " he said. "What things?" Sophia was staring around at the walls as if she'd been thrown in prison.

"Skyy—uh, Qiingi—you need to see it," said Sophia. "You have to be involved! You too, Livia. That really is your name? We really need to be connected right now, because the votes—the Government—they're being dismantled! All over the Archipelago. It just started happening spontaneously, like an adhocratic sort of thing."

Livia looked up wearily. "It's the Book." Sophia nodded vigorously.

"Yes. We've reached critical mass—that's what people are saying. Nobody knows for sure, of course, it's not like you can talk to the Book directly . . . but it has its votes, you know."

"But what started it?"

Sophia smiled. "That inscape virus that came out of Doran Morss's worldship. It knocked out the Government on a bunch of coronals, but you see, the Book wasn't affected. People started flocking to it, and it's suddenly issuing very clear directives . . ."

"So . . . it was the Book who put you in touch with Cicada and Peaseblossom?" he asked her. His head was starting to hurt.

"No. It was the Government. One day she came to me and pressed me to visit some sims. No explanation—but then she likes to play it mysterious. On a whim I started exploring the *Life of Livia,* because it's become part of a lot of narratives. I met a copy of your Cicada in a sim of Westerhaven; he was disguised as an old gardener. When he found out I knew *you,* he let me in on everything."

Livia lay back, flinging an arm over her eyes. "*What* is going on?"

Qiingi realized that he had somehow wedged himself into a corner of the room. "Does any of this matter?" he asked desperately. "We still cannot return home."

Livia stared at him in a way he hoped was not accusatory. "We don't know that anymore. Do we."

He sat down on the floor, shaking his head unhappily. "I am sorry. I gave up too soon."

"No, Qiingi, don't think that—how could we have known this would happen? Anyway, it's too soon to know where we stand." She yawned spasmodically. "And I don't think we're going to figure it out right this second."

She sat up. "We need to sleep. Boys, are we safe?"

Cicada poked his head around the doorjamb. "Nobody's coming after us. A bunch of ships are converging on the worldship. Either Doran Morss is gathering reinforcements, or he's in big trouble, too."

"Then let's get back to Brand New York while we can," said Sophia.

Qiingi looked over at Livia; she was nodding.

"*No!*" he said, levering himself to his feet.

He had everybody's attention now. "No," he repeated. "We are not going back to the narratives. We are not going back to the Government and we are not going back to the Book."

"Where else is there?" asked Sophia in annoyance.

"Home," said Qiingi forcefully. He stood up and stepped out of his corner. "Teven Coronal may be officially off limits to any Archipelagic ship, but obviously the Book's followers found a way to get there. If they can do it, so can we."

Livia bit her lip. "But where do we even start—"

"We will *start*," he said loudly, "by getting as close to our goal as we can. Cicada, set a course for the Fallow Lands."

IT HAD TAKEN the flying house weeks to pass the border of the Lethe Nebula and enter Archipelagic space; Peaseblossom and Cicada's little ship traversed the distance in a matter of hours. For the bulk of the journey, Livia lay asleep on a bunk in one of the ship's cramped little cabins. Qiingi checked in on her from time to time, but she didn't even roll over.

Qiingi sat in the cockpit with the lads (as Livia called her agents) while they plotted their course and bickered endlessly about what to do. The ship's cockpit was purely superfluous, of course; but the lads loved sitting in retro-style flight chairs with a big instrument panel in front of them and a broad diamond-glass windshield through which they could watch the approaching Lethe.

The flying house had avoided the denser clouds on the way out of the nebula. Now they were steering directly for them. Above the glowing instrument panel, the light from the Lethe was delicate, almost invisible against the blackness of space itself. But if Qiingi looked closely he could see vast curves and billows of rose, green, and palest white hiding the stars. As a boy he'd been told these Night Clouds were reflections of the distant campfires of the thunderbirds. He supposed that wasn't too far from the truth.

Remembering the thunderbirds brought Qiingi to thoughts of home. Was it possible he would walk those forests again, and commune with their enchanted inhabitants? He had given up on such hopes—yet here they were, arrowing closer to Teven by the second.

He didn't allow himself to hope yet. They had a plan now, but he doubted it would succeed. It was, in its own way, too obvious an idea to work.

The nebula grew over the hours until its curves took up the entire sky. Finally the little ship approached a wall of pale mauve that stretched to infinity above, below, and to both sides. It seemed close enough to reach out and touch.

"No," said Cicada with a laugh when Qiingi suggested it. "We're still a million kilometers away."

The little ship reduced its velocity somewhat; still, when they shot into the cloud, Qiingi half expected to feel some sort of impact, diffuse though he knew it was. He sat in the cockpit for a while watching it slowly solidify behind them.

Then came the message they had been waiting for. Suddenly light bloomed ahead of them in a rapidly fading sphere: an explosion? Simultaneously every instrument on Cicada's board squawked or blinked.

A deep voice spoke out of the air. "Archipelagic ship: alter your trajectory or you will be destroyed."

Peaseblossom looked pleased. "Well, that's a clear directive!"

"Should I wake Livia?" Cicada asked Qiingi. He shook his head.

"Not yet. We'll do what we discussed. If it doesn't work, at least she doesn't have to watch it fail."

Peaseblossom nodded. "Here goes."

He and Cicada had spent the previous evening hacking into parts of the *Life of Livia* that would never have been controllable back in Teven. This had been Livia's idea; after walking through the *Life* for a while with Sophia, she had returned thoughtful, even a bit excited. "The anecliptics don't know us," Qiingi had pointed out. "They will turn us away. How can the *Life* change that?"

"Something the lads said yesterday got me thinking," she said. "Peaseblossom? The copy of the *Life* that's out there ends at the arrival of the ancestors, right?" Peaseblossom nodded.

"And you changed everybody's name and appearance in the sim."

"I can't speak for all my versions," he said. "But we always changed you. Not everybody else," he added guiltily. Qiingi nodded; his face had not been changed, at least not in the version Lindsey had seen.

"But it's likely that agents of the anecliptics could have looked at the sim and not recognized anybody."

Peaseblossom looked puzzled. "Who would they know to recognize?"

"One person," Livia had murmured, wide-eyed at her own idea. "They only need to recognize one."

Now, Cicada poked at some of the controls and inscape blossomed back into being around them. Everything looked the same—except that someone else sat where Peaseblossom had been.

She stood up and leaned forward over the instrument panel to flip the manual speaker switch Cicada had insisted on installing.

"I'm not an Archipelagic," she said. "This is Maren Ellis of Teven Coronal. You know me, though we haven't met in two hundred years. I request permission to return to the coronal you gave me."

For a few seconds there was no response. Then, not words, but a flow of numbers across one of the cockpit's archaic display screens.

Peaseblossom/Maren turned to Qiingi, a triumphant smile curling his/

her lip. "They're coordinates," he said, still in Ellis's voice. "We've been invited in."

LIVIA CAME UP to the cockpit when the ship began to decelerate. She felt impossibly weary, and nervous at the same time. Everybody was crowded into the little room; Sophia quickly slid out of the way when Livia came up behind her.

Qiingi also made room for her. "It could be something other than an anecliptic," he said. "We found it hiding in the deeps, emitting no information stream. It's very cold."

"We're ten thousand kilometers in," added Peaseblossom. He still looked like Maren Ellis; the sight made Livia ache for her Society. With an effort she looked past the disguised agent. No stars were visible out there, just a faint, iridescent curve that rose from left to right.

"Is that it?" she asked. Peaseblossom/Maren shook her head.

"As best we can tell, that's a new starlette they're building in here. It's a big geodesic sphere, hundreds of kilometers in diameter. No, we were kind of thinking it might be that." He/she pointed.

Silhouetted against the faint gleam of the unlit starlette, at first it looked like nothing more than a stray grain of rice, hanging in darkness. But Livia's heart skipped a beat. "Magnify that," she said tightly.

The thing expanded to fill her vision.

She remembered once laughing with Aaron's parents. It was seconds before their deaths. Livia had glanced away from them, her gaze caught by something happening outside the airbus's window. She had leaned toward the glass, puzzled.

They were a thousand meters above the waving grasslands of Teven's far side, yet somehow a white tower higher than them had grown up in an eyeblink. The tower was translucent, more like an expanding cone of light than something solid. Balanced on its very top, disintegrating even as she glimpsed it, was a white oval. It wiped away the clouds around it, giving some sense of scale in that instant: it was huge. Hundreds of meters across, a kilometer long. And the tower was gone; where it had been, a wall of fading white rushed outward like a ripple in water. A split second later the shockwave hit and Livia was raked by swirling flinders that had been the window. After that: jumble, pain, and screaming.

She turned away, feeling sick. "That's it," she said unsteadily. "An anecliptic."

ABOUT THE ONLY encouragement they got from the silent anecliptic was the fact that it hadn't trained any weapons on them. It was festooned with them, according to the ship—enough firepower to burn off a small planet. But the lozenge-shaped vessel had no windows or hatches, and remained obstinately silent for the next day.

Then, unexpectedly, the black billows of the Lethe lit up in the distance. A long flickering spear of light tunneled through the millions of kilometers, sliding to a stop right next to the anecliptic. There it hung, a small incandescent point like a man-sized sun. When Cicada showed Livia the recording, it seemed like the anecliptic glowed for a moment; then a slot-shaped hatch opened in its back and the brilliant bead drifted into it.

"And that's it," Cicada said with a flourish. "Whatever it was, it's inside now. And the door's still open."

"So we better go," added Peaseblossom.

". . . If we're going to get inside."

"Because it sure isn't talking to us out here."

So after a solid lunch that Peaseblossom insisted on, he, Livia, and Qiingi jetted away from the frost-rimed hull of their little ship toward the curving wall of the silent anecliptic. It was hundreds of degrees below zero out here and their shifts couldn't keep up, so for the first and hopefully last time in her life, Livia found herself totally encased in a metal contraption Peaseblossom called a "space suit." It was like medieval armor upgraded with lights and Plexiglas—no less uncomfortable, but easy to use in free fall.

"I don't like this view," Qiingi muttered as they crossed the infinite abyss between the ships. "I would almost prefer the illusions of the Archipelago." He sounded as anxious as she felt.

"It's not a 'view,' Qiingi," she said, for distraction. "This is reality."

"No," he said. The man-shaped blot to her right—she'd thought that one was Peaseblossom—waved a gloved hand. "We are not truly experiencing the vacuum and cold. We are inside a manifold mediated by these suits."

She frowned at the approaching anecliptic. Of course he was right. *I've been spending way too much time around Doran Morss.*

They arrived at the dark entrance to the anecliptic. "Let me go first," said Peaseblossom.

"Yes," Cicada said in their earphones. "He's expendable."

The figure on Livia's left shot forward and down, disappearing into the dark opening. For a few seconds there was silence, then a space-suited head popped up again. "You'll never guess who's here!"

Curious, they followed him in. At the bottom of the slot—which was about five by thirty meters, and about ten deep—was a simple, diamond-glass door. Light shone from the other side; as Livia approached she saw what looked like a red-walled apartment, with a few chairs, a canopy bed, and a kitchen area off to one side. They were upside-down with respect to it, its *down* oriented to the outer hull of the ship. Two human figures hung in midair in the center of the room.

One was a young woman. She had nondescript features, and was dressed in a sparkle of flashing diamond light—a typical Brand New York fashion. Livia was pretty sure she had never met her before, but recognized the significance of her amber, glowing eyes. She was a vote.

The other person, though . . . Black hair, high cheekbones, piercing eyes—Livia immediately recognized the self-styled god, Choronzon. He nodded and crossed his arms when he saw them. The glass doors slid back and Livia and the others entered.

"Give us a minute to bring some air into the room, then you can take off your suits," said the god over radio. Then he peered more closely at Peaseblossom, frowning. "So you're not Maren Ellis after all. We suspected that, of course . . ."

Livia took off her helmet. "No. A friend of hers." She turned to the young vote. "I haven't had the pleasure . . . My name is Livia Kodaly."

Choronzon nodded again, smiling slightly. "Alias Alison Haver. It's all starting to become clear."

The woman bowed to Livia. "Emblaze."

"What are you guys doing here?" asked Peaseblossom. Livia shot him a sharp look. It seemed he knew both these people.

"Our host summoned me after hearing from someone he hadn't spoken to in two hundred years," said Choronzon. "I took it upon myself to invite Emblaze along since I suspected she'd want to talk to this 'Maren Ellis.' . . . Would you like some gravity?"

Hesitantly, Livia nodded. Remembering the flying house, she grabbed the back of a couch while the ship slowly began rotating.

"So Maren is still alive?" asked the god, pulling himself into a chair to wait out the spin-up to full gravity. Livia and Qiingi did likewise. Peaseblossom remained standing behind them, still suited up.

"Maren was alive when we left her," said Livia. "But I don't know if she still is."

Choronzon looked puzzled. "What do you mean?"

"If you know Maren Ellis, then you know Teven Coronal," she said. She felt a surge of triumph—and relief—as Choronzon nodded. "Teven Coronal has been invaded," she went on, watching his eyes.

He had the good grace to look surprised. "By whom?"

She hesitated. She wasn't here to explain things to Choronzon, but to learn what she could from the annie. "I think you know. It's true, isn't it, that the anecliptics aren't without their internal struggles? I'm sure you're aware that one of them went rogue a few years back."

Now Choronzon really did look startled. "He was destroyed. I . . . saw it done."

"So did I," she said drily. "Yet, not long after that, strangers came to Teven Coronal. It's possible that the anecliptics let them in, but I don't believe it. If the annies had wanted to move against us, they'd have done so directly. No, these people snuck in."

"Invaders?" He shook his head. "But they couldn't have gotten in—"

"Unless they were able to get past the annies," she finished for him. "Which allegedly is impossible. Unless they came from some distant star where technologies have exceeded even the Archipelago's. Or . . ."

"An anecliptic gave them a way in." Choronzon stood up; the room had stabilized at about a half gravity. The woman Emblaze hadn't moved; she stood silently with her feet planted wide. "You're saying he's still alive," said Choronzon.

"No. But I think I know what this rogue anecliptic did before he died. Please, Choronzon, I don't mean to be rude but . . . I came here to speak with the anecliptics. Not to you."

He laughed. "You *are* speaking with them. Through me. They won't talk to you directly—not out of contempt, but they've learned to be very cautious about all communication. Many times, trans-human entities like myself have tried to infect their datanets using seemingly innocuous messages. Nowadays the annies live in a kind of dream-time; their interfaces recast and randomize any signal from the outside world, hashing it to the point that no Trojan horse programs can survive. What's left reaches their minds as distant whispered music, if at all. Getting their attention is an art, not a science.

"This entity," he gestured around them, "is the one who opened the doors to Maren Ellis and William Stratenger, back in the days when the annies sometimes disguised themselves as humans and walked the Archipelago. You can call this fellow Gort." He smiled at some private joke.

Livia frowned. "I have to confess that I'm suspicious of you, Choronzon," she said. "You could be here to prevent us from telling this Gort what we know." He simply shrugged. "Yes, I know," she said irritably. "We do have to trust you, don't we?"

"I can give you a token of my faithfulness," he said. "You see, I remember Maren from the old days. I'll unreel a few of those memories, if you'd like."

This was the perfect opening, so Livia took it. "Oh, I suspect you have memories that are a bit more recent than that, Choronzon. Isn't it true that you visited Westerhaven after the mad annie was killed?"

After a moment he said, "She told you this?"

"No. But she used the phrase *mad anecliptic* to describe something I saw but never described to anyone—something she never saw at all. How did she know what blew up over the far side of Teven, unless someone told her?"

Choronzon grinned. "Very astute. Okay, yes, I did visit Maren after the incident. She told me there were two Westerhaven survivors, as a matter of fact. Would you like to see our meeting?"

Livia opened her mouth to say yes, then closed it. She reached around and found Qiingi's hand; he put it on her shoulder, a warm reassurance.

"Thanks," she said after a long pause. "I'll review it later. We have more important things to talk about right now. As I said, I know what the mad anecliptic did. I know who attacked Teven Coronal. What I don't know is why."

"Then tell us the what, and I'll see about the why."

Livia told him—about the invaders of Teven and how they claimed allegiance to something called 3340. She described their escape from Teven; Emblaze listened to this account with visible fascination. Livia went on to tell how she had been given a special edition of the Good Book when they arrived in the Archipelago. When she revealed that its version number was 3340, Choronzon slumped back in his chair, shaking his head.

"What?" she said anxiously. "I'm wrong?"

"No," he said, "you're right, that's why I'm upset. We didn't see it."

"But what am I right about? That the mad anecliptic created the Good Book? That it's some sort of emergent intelligence that seems to be replacing the Government?"

"Yes, and yes," he said. "But without knowing that Teven was invaded by 3340, we had no reason to make a connection between the two. And we could be wrong . . . it might just be a coincidence that this number pops up twice. In a place the size of the Archipelago, coincidences are inevitable."

"But I don't understand," she said angrily. "None of it. Why the Book? What was this annie trying to do? And why invade Teven?"

Choronzon sat still for a while, staring at nothing with a frown on his face. Then he said, "About Teven, I don't know why they're there. I have a few ideas . . . As to what the annie was trying to do—what the Book is trying to do—that's clear." He thought for a moment. "Do you know what the ruling principle of the Archipelago is?"

Livia shrugged. "Agonistics," said Peaseblossom behind her.

"And what is agonistics?"

Her agent spoke again, as if reciting a dictionary entry. "You can compete, and you can win, but you can never win once-and-for-all."

"Exactly. It's the same principle the great democracies used back in the Modern period. You could become president, but you couldn't *stay* president. You could build a big corporation, but you couldn't become a monopoly. But the Moderns didn't apply agonistics to everything. They couldn't, because they didn't have a good model for it."

"And you do?" She had no idea where this was going.

"We do." He nodded. "The problem is that whenever you build a large, well-interconnected system, you take the chance that it'll end up in a critical state."

"And what is a . . . ?"

"Imagine you're at the beach. If you've got a pile of sand and you drop grain after grain on it, one after the other, most of them will just land there and stick. But every now and then, one will cause an avalanche. Usually it's a small avalanche. But sometimes it's a mother of all avalanches that takes down the whole pile. A sandpile is a system vulnerable to critical states: states where change is poised ready to avalanche."

"Okay," said Livia impatiently. "So what?"

"Well, a couple of things. First, you can't predict the size of the next avalanche in a system at criticality unless you have absolute knowledge of every particle in the system. In practice, that's never possible. Second, human society as a whole is balanced in a whole variety of critical states. Instead of avalanches, though, humanity has wars, economic collapses, social crises . . ."

"So we're at the mercy of blind forces we can't control? Tell me something I don't know," she said with a laugh.

"Oh, you're often at the mercy of blind forces," he conceded. "But you can often control them. The trick is you can redesign some systems so they don't have critical states. You can flatten the sandpile. Forest fires follow the same power law as human conflicts: any given fire is twice as likely as one twice its size. But you can reduce the likelihood of the big ones dramatically by changing the nature of the forest. A forest is an interconnected system. Break the interconnections and fires can't spread."

Two hundred years ago, Choronzon told her, a viral AI had wakened to consciousness on a sunny July day in Jamaica. Within seconds it had taken over the island's data networks and after ten minutes it had overwhelmed the global net. Inscape became its toy. As it leaped off the Earth to infect the rest of the solar system it made a personal paradise or hell for each and every man and woman on Earth, according to whims or standards that no one would ever understand.

After an hour of expansion it hit the colonies of the post-human and trans-human entities that had seceded from humanity decades before. And when it tried to pry open their datanets, it got its fingers burned.

Two hours after that it was on the run. By the end of the day it was dead—devoured by a new entity hastily cobbled together by beings like Choronzon as well as the humans of Mars and the outer planets.

This entity was the Government. Its creators gave it the motivation of stopping the network attack; but, in the full knowledge of what might happen, they motivated it to want to prevent any such attacks from succeeding in the future. Even attacks by itself.

Now Choronzon smiled, like the cat that had the canary. "When she was a child, too young for inscape implants, Maren Ellis saw her parents driven mad in the attack by the Jamaican AI. She and I talked about firebreaks a lot, before she moved to Teven. It was obvious that we needed to prevent dangerous critical states like that one from arising again. She didn't like using the word *firebreak,* though. She liked the word—"

"—Horizons!" said Qiingi.

"Horizons," Livia murmured. "Horizons keep the manifolds from communicating too far."

"Exactly. They were supposed to prevent any kind of condition from spreading too easily—from economic changes to cultures . . . to wars." He shook his head. "I think they went too far. But this, you see, is the mathematics of agonistics—a trans-political principle for preventing disastrous wars and economic catastrophes. Or for preventing one political or religious system from taking over once and for all. Unfortunately, Maren and I differed on how to apply the principle. She believed that you had to build firebreaks at all levels—social, technological, even perceptual. Otherwise, some unforeseen new kind of critical state might be possible. From what you've told me, it was just such an unforeseen critical state that 3340 exploited to take over Teven."

"So Maren came to Teven," Livia said, "and set up the manifolds. Then, what are the Archipelago's horizons?—Let me guess: the anecliptics."

"On one level, yes. They help enforce the firebreaks by preventing any economic ripples from spreading too far. But there are countless other ways to dampen down critical states. The electoral system in the old democracies was one—it prevented tyrants from consolidating power, by forcing leaders out of office at regular intervals. The Government's another part of it. Even inscape isn't a unified system, you know, it's the emergent identity of billions of networks of differing kinds, many of which can't speak together directly. There is no perfect reproduction of any data transmitted across it, so viral attacks like the Jamaican's can't spread. Everything about how the solar system is organized militates against the development of critical states." He sighed. "Or, it did. Until *he* came along."

"The mad anecliptic."

"The very same. First he tried to subvert the other annies. He failed. But if you're right, he had a backup plan, called the Good Book. It's a network intelligence that runs on human interactions. Since it doesn't use inscape directly—or any of our data systems, in fact—it was able to propagate and connect across the whole Archipelago, slipping past all the barriers and firebreaks we spent so many centuries building into our networks. It causes an emergent behavior in its users that sniffs out and exploits critical states—as seems to have happened at Teven.

"And now the last grain of sand has fallen on the sandpile. It's taken two hundred years, but now an avalanche of change is spreading across the Archipelago, and I don't know how big it's going to get."

20

LIVIA WAS PRACTICING scales in her cabin aboard the lads' ship when she felt the room flip around her in an especially nauseating way. "What's going on?" she shouted at the ceiling.

"It's leaving!" answered Cicada.

"The annie?"

"It's headed off into the Lethe! I think they agreed to help us."

Choronzon confirmed it when he called a few minutes later. "We promised to protect your people two hundred years ago," he said as his image leaned on the metal doorjamb. "Reputations are at stake here."

"And what about us?" she asked. "Can we go home?"

"Come and go as you please," he said. "The annies won't stop you."

"Thanks." She closed the door on him. It wasn't that she was ungrateful, but Livia really would have appreciated having an anima to front for her right now. She went to sit on the bed.

If she started singing again right now she'd cry. She didn't know whether it would be from relief, or fear.

After her conversation with Choronzon, they had returned to the ship to await the anecliptics' decision. The vote Emblaze had asked to come along, and Livia had reluctantly agreed; but she could only play the gracious hostess for a short time before retreating to her room. Sophia had reluctantly agreed not to contact any other users of the Book so inscape was back on. Given the choice, though, Livia found she preferred to limit her own interactions with the ship to crippleview. Maybe Qiingi was right, and she needed a stable world in which to organize her thoughts.

She sat and looked around the room. Everything was silence; nothing moved. As the seconds dragged by she wondered when she was going to feel triumph that their mission into the wider world had succeeded. She was going to free Westerhaven! Mother and Father, Rene, Esther, and all the rest, would soon be walking the streets of Barrastea again, together and laughing.

Except that they wouldn't. This was what she'd refused to face up to all this time: like any manifold, Westerhaven was fragile. Irreparable. At least in ancient and modern times there had been stable institutions such as the Church and State to pick up the pieces after a war. In Teven, that stability was maintained by the tech locks. So Livia would never again walk the streets of the Barrastea she'd known, never again taste the Societies in their full flower. Whatever came after Westerhaven, they would have to build it from scratch.

She'd been telling herself for the past few hours that she didn't care—that she would try to do her duty by her people, but that she was happy to be free of the manifolds. She could storm Teven with the anecliptics' cavalry and free the ones she loved. And then settle where she chose, whether in Teven or somewhere in the seductive, wonderfully rewarding narratives of the Archipelago.

Except that the Archipelago was tearing itself apart, too. Its freedom was only the freedom to realize just how insignificant you were—how pointless any ambitions were next to the anecliptics and the gods next door. How had Qiingi described it? *Wallpaper:* endless repetition of the same streets, same people, same art and intrigues.

Livia groaned and put the heels of her hands to her eyes. This was crazy—she should be happy! Instead, she was miserable.

Someone knocked on her door. Livia gestured for it to open.

"Hello, Respected Kodaly," said Emblaze. "May I come in?"

Too weary to refuse, Livia waved her in. Emblaze held out her hand to shake.

"So," said Livia. "You're a vote." Emblaze nodded. "What's your constituency?" Livia asked, feeling a painful sense that her social graces were about to fail her.

"Well," said Emblaze, "there hangs a tale." Seeing the expression on Livia's face, she hurried on with, "Look, I know you have a lot on your mind, but I may be able to help. But your question's a bit . . . awkward . . . for me to answer."

Both intrigued and annoyed, Livia stood and motioned for her to sit. "Why? I should have thought that it would be straightforward. You're a vote; whose vote are you?"

"I'm yours, Livia Kodaly."

Emblaze sat there gazing at her as if expecting some sensible response. "Huh?" was all Livia could muster.

The vote looked away, frowning. She held up her hand, examined the back of it. "We arise," she said eventually, "when the traffic in inscape intensifies and knots up. When the nodes of heavy usage are stable and large enough, an AI is compiled. It doesn't matter to inscape what the traffic is about—so there's votes for pet lovers, gardening, Shakespeare appreciation, the reinvention of obsolete crimes . . . every imaginable human interest. You know there's a vote for the Good Book."

Livia nodded, remembering Veronique's story. "Yes. Her name's Filament, right?" Emblaze nodded. Livia began bustling in her little kitchenette. "Would you like some tea?"

"Thanks. The point is, Livia, I'm a vote but that doesn't mean I had a . . . strictly political origin. I'm the representative of all the people who use, or are interested in, the *Life of Livia* sim."

Livia dropped the cup she had been holding. Laughing, she retrieved it. "You're the vote for *my* stolen memories?"

Emblaze looked uncomfortable. "I prefer to think that I contain the aggregate feelings and values of seven hundred million people. They just happen to be those people inspired—or outraged—by your recordings of life in Westerhaven."

As she poured some water for tea, Livia thought about what that might imply. The lads had said they'd gutted the sim. It was full of holes, some of very personal memories, some containing strategic information such as where Teven Coronal actually was.

She shot Emblaze a suspicious look. "So I guess you're curious about some things . . . like the tech locks?" What would a vote be willing to do in order to satisfy its constituency?

Emblaze shook her head. "It's not for me to act in place of my people. I'm their advocate, not their proxy."

"Like Filament?"

To Livia's surprise, Emblaze blushed. "I sum to my constituents' ethics, true. They would never harm you, or even pester you, so neither would I. Most are fascinated by the mechanisms that run Westerhaven—these 'manifolds' you and Choronzon were talking about. They'd love to know how they work, especially the tech locks. But a very large number of people are also just interested in you. They saw the way your life changed after that strange accident, and many are concerned for you. And your agents disguised you pretty effectively, but now the cat's out of the bag."

She took a deep breath. "Livia, people want to help you."

Livia had one of those little shifts in perspective that were happening all too often lately. "I guess this is your ship, isn't it? I thought Sophia supplied it, but she works for the Book . . ."

Emblaze shrugged. "She has multiple allegiances, like anybody else. And yes, this is one of my ships—meaning, it's owned by the Government. That's not what I mean about helping, though.

"Livia, your archive has been laid open to us except for the most private of moments, the ones you edited out as you went. Your whole public life is there for all to see, excepting minutes or hours here and there—but there is one span of eighty days that is completely missing. You know the time I refer to."

Livia felt a cold flush of adrenalin. "After the crash."

Emblaze nodded. "It seemed from your behavior after that time that you couldn't remember crucial events. And when my people looked at your records of that time, they were a jumble. Your implants were damaged by the magnetic pulse of the explosion, apparently. But they weren't completely shut down. There were fragments and a constant, low-level murmur of data trickling into the system. Nothing any ordinary data processing system could make sense of. But a few million of my people came together in an adhocracy to comb through the bits by hand. It was incredibly tedious work, but they did it willingly. And now they're finished."

"What are you saying?"

"Livia, we've recovered inscape's memory of your experiences after the crash. It's my gift to you, in thanks for the inspiration you've brought to my constituency."

Livia stared at her for a long time. Then she said, tightly, "Get out."

"But, this is a gift of healing. It's—"

"Out. *Out!*" She practically lunged at Emblaze, who jumped out of her chair and bolted for the door.

When it slid shut Livia collapsed on her bed and laughed. Then she just lay there. After a while she cried.

THE PROCESS WAS silent. Almost unnoticeable, from here. But if Doran stood on his balcony and watched the giant glass face of the *Scotland*'s sunward cap, he would be rewarded every few minutes by sighting a tiny flicker of light appear there: a ship, entering his realm.

Hundreds of them clustered like flies in the weightless axis of the worldship. Thousands of people were riding skyhooks down to the barren moors and lochs. They chattered like tourists, happy and excited at this new turn to their lives. They had followed the edicts of the Book and it had brought them here. Few if any knew that the worldship had been hijacked; he doubted if most would understand the concept.

He heard someone moving in the apartment behind him. Doran braced himself for a moment, clenching the balustrade. Then he plastered a carefree smile on his face and turned.

"Filament! What a surprise."

She returned his smile without irony. "You'll be happy to know," she said as she draped herself on one of his couches, "that I've managed to locate all the versos. They're being relocated now. There's been no violence so far."

"Well, there wouldn't be." He stood at parade rest, not disguising his anger now. "They're civilized people."

"Hmm." She dismissed his jibe with a wave of her hand. "Have you thought about my offer?"

"You mean your *offer* to allow me to escape like a rat from a sinking ship—" She raised her eyebrow at the unfamiliar metaphor—"if I turn the keys over to you?"

"Yes," said Filament levelly.

"Ah well, as to that," he said, smiling again and sitting down comfortably opposite her. "How about 'no.'"

"We need your ship," she said, leaning forward and clasping her hands sincerely. "The god will need a forward base from which to operate for a time. He won't be able to direct the takeover of the Archipelago from within Teven."

Teven? Doran wondered why that name sounded so familiar, even as he shook his head. "Yes but you see, for all its faults, I am loyal to the Archipelago. Humans may not have very much freedom here, but they'd have less under 3340."

"How can you say that?" she snapped. "You've seen how efficiently the Book organizes society. No need for the apparatus of government— not even Government. Even *I* am obsolete here."

"And I treasure that small consolation," he said, "believe me, I do. But overjoyed as I may be over your obsolescence, it's not enough for me to consider betraying the annies."

"I don't understand you," she said crossly. "You fought your whole life for the kind of power we're taking now." Then she sat back, looking sly. "Ah. So that's it. This is simple envy, isn't it? Because we did what you could not." She laughed and stood up. "No matter, anyway. We'll let the *Scotland* fly on its current course for a while. When 3340 arises he'll be able to unlock the controls."

She walked toward the door, then turned and motioned for him to follow her. "You, however, don't need to be here for that. We have a more important lock to attend to. And that one, you will open for us, alive or dead, sentient or driven mad by pain, it's all the same to me."

She meant the eschatus machine, which he had glimpsed being loaded into a fast cutter the day before. He glared at her.

"Look," she said, "we can discuss this matter further during the trip to Teven, but for now you must come with me. If you don't move, I'll have to send in the large gang of unsympathetic men who are loitering in the hallway. They've beaten many people senseless in sims. They're all eager to try the skill on a living person."

"Fine," he said. "Send 'em in then."

"You're such a *boy*," complained Filament. She turned and swept out.

As Doran stood to meet the pack of grinning, feverish-eyed men crowding in through the door, he remembered where he'd heard the name *Teven*. The surprise slowed him down just enough that after he was encircled, he never got a punch in.

LIVIA KNEW SHE was hiding, but she wasn't about to justify herself to anybody. So she stayed in her room. Every now and then, though, she would make a window and peek at events unfolding outside.

The dazzling arc of a coronal approached. The billows of the Lethe visible beyond it were exactly those that she had lived with her whole life. They were so familiar she could have painted them from memory.

Watching home approaching again after so long, though, reminded her of her duty to her people. Even if she closed the windows and lay there pretending that the rest of the world didn't exist, her conscience came around to bother her sooner or later. Soon they would be home. She needed to know what Choronzon and the anecliptics were planning, at least; and maybe somewhere in there was a plan that would include Westerhaven. She could just call Choronzon and ask, of course. But she didn't feel ready to confront him on anything if she didn't like his answers.

She was lolling there uselessly, running through imagined conversations with Choronzon in her mind, when she remembered that he also had given her some memories. Livia sat up, frowning. Hadn't he said something about there being records of Maren Ellis?

She didn't really care about those memories, but maybe she could absorb some decisiveness from Ellis. She laughed at herself, and called up the memory.

Livia blinked at the sudden strong sunlight. She stood at the rail of a balcony somewhere high above the plains of a coronal. Leaning out, she saw that the balcony perched atop a tower that itself hung among the clouds. Other towers and buildings were dotted throughout the near and far air. If she squinted, Livia could make out the fine thin threads of cable, a vast endless spiderweb, on which they sat. This must be Cirrus manifold.

Behind Livia someone shouted in delight. She turned to find Maren Ellis embracing Choronzon like an old friend. "But what are you *doing* here?" cried Ellis, leaning back in the god's embrace. "Wait—that explosion last week . . ."

"Partly my doing, I'm afraid." He grinned at her. "But there's no danger to you or your people. It's all done with, but since I was in the neighborhood I thought I'd drop by."

She laughed, and drew him over to a couch where they sat.

"I can't believe it," gasped Ellis. "It's literally been centuries . . ."

"And yet you still move among your people as if you were an ordinary mortal," he said seriously. "I don't know how you manage it. My own attachments . . ."

"Were never that deep," she said, "if you continue to insist on thinking of yourself as more than human." She shook her head. "I'm not a god, Choronzon. I'm just a very, very old woman. The people here know that. And I don't pretend to be more."

"And Stratenger?" asked Choronzon. "Is he still with us?"

"Yes—though I rarely see him these days."

They continued to chat about old times, but though Livia pulled up a history serling to help, she couldn't follow half of what they were saying. But as she listened, it became clear that Peaseblossom had been right: Maren Ellis was more than just one founder among many. From the way she and Choronzon talked, it was clear that she was *the* founder of the manifolds.

Ellis suddenly said, "Last time we met, you asked me a question."

"Maren, that was two hundred years ago. You expect me to remember—"

" 'How does humanity govern itself when each person can have any-thing they want?' " she quoted.

He smiled. "That was the subject, yes."

"The subject of the war that separated us; the subject of our final ar-gument. Sure you remember. And it's been the subject of all my work for the past two centuries." She frowned at him, her deceptively young face momentarily betraying the ancient mind behind it. "But you know what? It was the wrong question. It should have been: 'How does hu-manity govern itself when nature no longer exists?' "

He looked away from her, out over the pillowing clouds to the hazy distances of the coronal. "Is that why you let these 'horizons' of yours get so out of control?"

Before she could answer he stood up and walked over to the railing—right next to Livia's virtual self. He scowled unhappily at the sky. "I can't believe what you've done here. You've used our firebreaks to deny people their history, their science, all the fruits of humanity's work! You've doomed your people to stumble down one blind alley after an-other for all eternity, searching for a utopia that already exists, if you'd only let them see it. If I'd known you had this in mind when we parted . . ."

Ellis watched him closely from where she sat curled in the corner of the couch. "I'm looking out for them," she said languidly. "And this 'stumbling' you're so contemptuous of is the privilege of every human being: to invent and discover, even if it's reinvention and rediscovery. Now that everything's been learned and everything's been done, the manifolds provide the most control a human being can have over their personal reality and still be human. *You* can have bigger ambitions; you're not mortal. But for someone who is? What does our world offer anymore to the merely human? What can they make for themselves that's truly theirs, in your precious Archipelago?"

Choronzon clenched his hands on the rail. "I wish I'd never helped you design the tech locks."

She laughed. "It's done, love."

"Maybe." He half smiled into the air. "The anecliptics are leaving; I have to go with them. But Maren, if I ever get a chance to return, I'm go-ing to take them away from you." He turned to look at her. "Some toys shouldn't fall into the wrong hands."

"I hope, then," she said coldly, "that you never return."

The record ended without warning, leaving Livia sitting bolt upright on her bed.

Take them away from you? Had she really heard that right?

She stood up to pace the narrow confines of her cabin. Choronzon had threatened to overthrow the tech locks. A few years later, a force from outside had come to Teven Coronal to do just that. Maren must have assumed it was Choronzon following through on his threat.

Was it Choronzon?

She shook her head. No, 3340 was a separate entity, she was sure of that. And if it were Choronzon, why should he have given Livia this recording? Unless he didn't care what she knew . . .

Livia sat down, a bit shaken. Instead of inspiring her with a sense of purpose, seeing Maren Ellis as she really was had made her feel even more helpless. At least now she knew what Choronzon *wouldn't* do when he arrived at Teven.

He wouldn't help Livia or anyone else restore the tech locks.

And was that just? Livia half agreed with Choronzon; she half agreed with Maren. So now what? Livia's hope that she was surrounded by allies was disappearing. Choronzon wasn't on her side; Maren Ellis had her own agenda, as did the anecliptics. Livia felt separate from all of them, the only true human who was a confidante to all of them.

I'm supposed to be this great leader, she thought. *So how do I lead?*

There was only one way to find out. She made sure she was comfortable on the bed and surrounded by lots of pillows. Then she backstepped into the memories Emblaze had given her.

"Wake up!" Aaron pushed insistently at her shoulder. Livia opened her eyes to a sideways view of an ashen-gray mud landscape that stretched into indeterminate hazy distance. She sat up and said, "Where are we?"

"Do you remember your name?" asked Aaron worriedly.

"Of course I do, it's me, Livia."

He sat back on his haunches, breathing a sigh of relief. "That's better than yesterday, anyway," he said.

Livia was looking past him. "Who are all those people?"

"They're the . . ."

—She was standing up, someone was bringing her a roasted black strip of something that might be meat. "How much do you remember?" Aaron was asking.

Livia heard herself say, "We fell out of the sky. Everything was burning . . ." She looked around fearfully.

"Livia, that was six days ago. The fires are all out. Do you remember anything that happened after?"

"No, I . . ."

—Stumbling along with the others. The wooden branch she was using as a crutch was worn in a certain spot, and she had blisters on her hand where she grasped it. "Where are we going?" . . .

"—Aaron, where are we?" . . .

"—Where are we going?" . . .

"—What do you mean you." . . .

"—Do you remember your name?"

"Just leave me alone. Yes, Aaron, I remember my name. And I remember you asked me this yesterday."

"I didn't have to ask you yesterday. It's been three days since I had to ask you anything."

She sat up . . . —Calluses on her hand where she gripped the stick. "Weren't there more people than that?"

Aaron lowered his voice. "Why are you reminding me of . . ."

"—Aaron, I don't understand."

He sighed and suddenly everything snapped into focus. They stood on a plain of burnt grass; patches here and there were still green. Behind Aaron were about thirty people, some sitting morosely on the grass, others standing, a few talking. Most were watching Livia . . . no, their eyes were fixed on Aaron. Although his clothes were as ragged as theirs, he stood tall and clear-eyed. The look he sent Livia was indescribably sad.

"I'm all right," she said.

"Sure," he said.

"No, really," she insisted. "I was hurt, wasn't I?" She touched her bruised temple. "I hit my head. It's done something to my memory."

Aaron looked hopeful. "Your implants have been . . . spasming, is all I can call it. You've been drifting in and out of consciousness."

The enormity of where they were and what had happened seemed to hit all at once. Livia found herself crying and hugging herself. "Why are all those people staring at us?"

"They're just scared, is all."

"Up and at it, everybody!" That was Aaron's voice. She rolled over, in dim dawn light, and saw him walking among the survivors, cajoling, joking, murmuring. He shook one shoulder and was rewarded by a fiercely thrust arm, a snarl.

"You have to get up."

"Go away."

"Please, Daria. We'll get through this. I know you're hurt, I know you're sore . . ."

The figure on the ground rolled away, and just lay there. Aaron talked to it; others came by and made entreaties. Eventually they just stood there over the still form, staring at one another glumly.

Aaron walked hesitantly toward Livia. "Are you . . . ?"

"I'm fine." She stood, embraced him. "Come. Let's wake the others."

"I CAN'T GO any further. I can't." It was Livia's own voice, but more ragged and thin than she'd ever imagined it could be. She sat huddled around herself as a thin drizzle fell on her shoulders.

There were only a dozen of them left now. They stood around her like silent ghosts, casting a familiar look back and forth. She recognized that look. It was the same one they'd shared when Daria refused to get up. Daria—and others.

"Do you want to die?" Aaron stood over her, his arms crossed. He hadn't asked the question rhetorically, he simply wanted to know her intentions.

She mumbled something. Aaron knelt beside her. "Aaron, I don't even know why *you* don't want to die," she croaked. "Why don't you want to die?" She rocked back and forth, keening.

"Livia, listen to me." He took her face in his hands. His eyes were desperate. "There's only one thing keeping me going, do you understand? The only thing that's getting me through this is getting *you* through this. Maybe you want to die. Do you want me to die?"

She became totally still. "No. I—I guess not."

"Then *stand up*," he hissed.

She stood up.

"AARON, WHERE ARE we?"

"Don't worry about it, love." He sounded infinitely tired and sad. But for a while he walked alongside her, holding her hand . . .

"—Why are you looking at me like that?" she asked.

He blushed, and looked down. "I was just wishing I had your problem right now."

"What problem?"

"Memory. I was wishing that I couldn't remember the past few weeks. It would be so much better . . ." For a while he stared off into the distance. "You really don't believe in yourself, do you?" he said finally.

"Is that so much of a surprise?"

He shrugged. "I never had an opportunity to find out before, I guess."

"Aaron, I could never be a hero, like you're being. I don't have the strength. I don't have the courage."

He shook his head. "I don't believe that. You could be so much more than you are, Livia. The only one who doesn't believe it is you."

"It's easy for you to say. It's you who's been keeping us all alive, isn't it? You really are brave, and strong."

He was quiet for a long time. Then he said, almost inaudibly, "I would give anything not to be."

BRILLIANT LIGHTS SPUN in the sky. She heard shouting. Two of the people near her cried out in relief and joy—and then disappeared. Others were blinking out of view even as she reached for them.

An ordinary, solid-looking aircar crunched into the soot a few meters away. People dressed in Westerhaven fashion leaped out of it, ran toward her. She glimpsed the diaphanous shapes of angels unfurling in her direction. Beside her, Aaron was weeping.

"Aaron, where are we?"

"How did you survive?" someone asked. "None of our sims predicted it! And those other survivors—" He waved to where they had been, but it was too late. The others who had followed Aaron all these days had already crossed their own horizons. Now that they were back in the embrace of inscape, they would be found by their own people within hours.

"—DON'T KNOW HOW she did it. She talked to us, encouraged us, beat us when we tried to lie down and die . . ." Who was Aaron talking to? Livia stroked the warm, dry upholstery next to her, trying to sort out what was going on.

"—Damage to the implant interface. It's likely that the amygdala suffered some . . ."

"REST. YOU'RE A hero, everyone's talking about it. How you led them all out. How you suffered so they didn't have to . . ."

"Aaron?

"Rest, Livia. Just rest. I'll be right here."

LIVIA SHUT DOWN the memories and just lay there among the pillows. Curiously, she felt nothing at all—as if she had known all along that it was Aaron, and not her, who had saved them.

Aaron who had loved her—for how long? Aaron who had made her into the person she was now.

The minutes ticked on. She waited for a change to occur—for her identity to unravel completely in the face of this revelation. Part of her was ringing with shock, but she realized that another part was continuing on as though nothing had happened. Coolly planning what she must do when they reached Teven. That part of her went on about its business as though nothing she had just learned mattered.

I am what I was made to be, she realized: a leader, not prone to paralysis. It didn't make any difference if that trait had been woven into her personality by others. Her feelings for Aaron had deepened to a fathomless sorrow and yes, there was anger there, too. But it was he who'd left in the end, and she had had enough of tears.

She would have time later to wonder at the irony and strangeness of it all. Right now she had to plan how to hide her real purpose from Choronzon and the annies, and Maren Ellis and 3340. Eventually, thoughts and disguises composed, she called Qiingi and said, "Come talk to me. We need to get back to Teven before the annies. And we need a plan for what we'll do when we get there."

21

A LONE FIGURE moved slowly down the leaf-strewn avenue. There were few people out; most moved in a trance, their senses overtaken by some inscape vision inaccessible to the lone walker. This person wore drab clothing and a hood to keep out the autumn drizzle. She seldom looked up from the rain-glossed street, but if she did, she saw the towers and sails of Barrastea restored. Then she would touch something clipped to her ear and quickly look down again.

Not everything was as it had been. The sky above Livia's city had once been open and bright. Now, a fine web of cables spiraled up from the city center, disappearing into the gray haze of the lowering clouds. Here and there triangles of white sailcloth poked down from the clouds like frozen wings, implying another city hovering above the one she knew. In those cables, Livia recognized the work of Cirrus manifold.

Just what they were doing in the capital of Westerhaven she couldn't yet tell.

She had been cautious so far. Emblaze's ship had docked at Teven without incident; no one was watching for visitors, it seemed. Livia and Qiingi had only to walk up a flight of stairs and step out of a disused, vine-covered door, and there they were: on the outskirts of Barrastea.

Qiingi had left her reluctantly. His mission was to find Raven, so in the end he turned and walked into the woods without looking back. Livia had never felt so alone and had entered her city with reluctance, expecting to see ruin and bodies. To her surprise, whoever now controlled the place had rebuilt it to something approaching its former beauty. Somehow, that fact upset her more than anything; perhaps it was because where once she had owned the avenues and parks here, now she was entering the city as a spy. She no longer belonged.

Livia did not allow herself the luxury of sorrow. She examined the faces of those she passed, gauging their health and happiness. She assessed the buildings, loitered for a while watching some bots rebuilding a house, and poked her head in a few restaurants and bars. People ignored her—often, she knew, because the little earpiece Emblaze had given her jammed any inscape signals sent her way, making her invisible to many here. Though they were oblivious to her, the people seemed relaxed and unhurried. Indeed, there was no sign that Barrastea was a conquered city. Her vision of the city was that of crippleview, but she couldn't help but wonder if what she saw now had always been the crippleview version of the city. Even the cableways of Cirrus might have always been here.

But no; she knew people who'd traveled in Cirrus. There had never been a net thrown over Barrastea before.

She listened to people talk as she walked. Mostly they gossiped, just as they always had. Every now and then, though, someone would say something like, "Oh, but I'm the Postman today. That makes you a Relay." The terms and phrases of the Good Book had insinuated themselves into Westerhaven's speech. Subtle though its influence might be, there was no doubt that version 3340 of the Book was in control here.

As evening fell Livia sat down on a public bench and aimed a little laser at a particular star twinkling above the Southwall mountains. "I'm here and okay," she transmitted—mostly she imagined herself speaking to Qiingi, but he was incommunicado while he investigated Raven's people. Emblaze and Sophia and the lads would be listening, though.

"There's not much to see," she continued. "They say that when people use the Book properly, a utopia results—and that's happened here. But we thought we lived in a utopia before, didn't we? It's not so different now—so *why*? Why attack us? I don't understand. I mean . . . there's no sign of why Teven was so interesting to 3340; they had to kill the tech locks to make the Book work here at all." She heard the bitterness in her voice, and lacking an anima, could do little to suppress it. "Anyway, things are back to normal—almost, anyway. I guess you could say the conquest is complete." She blew out a heavy sigh. "I'm safe for now. I just have to find a place to sleep. I'm going to . . ." She bit her lip for a second, momentarily losing her signal lock on the distant star. "I'm going to see if my old bedroom still recognizes me."

Bad idea, she told herself as she paced increasingly familiar avenues leading into the heart of the city. Even so, the quiet of the city lulled her; as evening fell she found it easier and easier to pretend she was back in the old days. Barrastea surrounded her in all its centuries-old grandeur and peace. She could imagine the flutter of social manifolds surrounding her again like the breathing of a god, and she would run home . . .

She stopped, scowling at herself. This was foolishness; yet she was only a few blocks from the Kodaly estate now. And though she had told herself not to, she couldn't help but wonder if her parents were there, and safe.

Her footsteps took her unerringly in that direction.

Committed now, she began to relax. After all, she was hardly the lone agent she appeared. Just before they arrived here, Peaseblossom had shown Livia a telescopic image of the deep clouds of the Lethe. At first she thought she was looking at a navy of ghosts—just the smeared wavering outlines of ships coalescing in the dark. Then Peaseblossom had zoomed in and Livia realized what was happening. The trillions of parts and supplies that made up the Lethe were not, it seemed, entirely unpowered and dumb. At Gort's command, rod and girder, plate and lever were sailing together, clinging and forming larger pieces of machinery. These too precipitated and self-organized—a process, Peaseblossom said, that required but a few rules of construction, and no overseer. Out of the limitless resources of the Lethe, in a matter of days, a fleet of dreadnoughts capable of subduing the entire human Archipelago was condensing like dew.

Soon that navy would arrive. They might appear overhead, but more likely they would encircle the spinning coronal like the spokes of a wheel. They would be invisible from inside; but they could vaporize Teven in an instant if they chose to.

Livia only hoped that Choronzon would interpret the ancient pact of protection for Teven in a way that left the humans of the coronal alive after it was liberated.

A spiral of cables lofted into the sky from somewhere in the Kodaly estate. Otherwise, the buildings and sails looked the same as they always had; only the glittering lights of the Cirrus city overhead signaled the difference. Livia felt a deep ache in her breast and her steps faltered as she came to a long, ivy-wreathed gallery that encircled her parents' main residence. Lights shone there, warm as roses in the deepening twilight. Somewhere, music played.

She had danced in the courtyards here. She had sung for family and friends, and even for audiences of shimmering, half-real animas visiting from distant points. The dark undersides of the canopied trees should be lit like pavilions with flickering Societies; a murmur of timeless life should permeate everything. But there was none of that.

Livia hesitated, then reached up and removed the metal clip that shielded her inscape implants. She braced herself for an onslaught of changes—but the gardens remained the same.

Only when she looked up could she tell that she was back in inscape. The sky rotating overhead looked much like the tactical display of games mode. The firmament was divided into sectors in a vast Mercator projection, each sector filled with letters and numbers. Twirling in the sky in their thousands were what looked like tarot cards—each one, she realized with a start, the visible sign of a major role in the Book. Threads of light connected them, interweaving with and obscuring the networks of Cirrus.

Livia was so busy staring up at the intricate patterns that the polite cough right next to her made her jump. She instantly fell into a defensive posture, then recognized the figure standing in the darkness next to her. It was the House's servant AI, Capewan.

He bowed, as he always did when he greeted her. "Livia, it's good to have you home."

She burst into tears. He stepped forward to embrace her, but he was only real in inscape; her shift could give the impression of his arms around her, but there was no solidity behind it. "My parents—" she croaked. "Are they safe?"

"They're here, Livia. Come, I'll take you to them." He stepped back and took her hand. She pulled away.

"No—don't tell them I'm here. I don't want them to know."

"All right." He smiled in his usual genial way, and she wondered whether the intelligence behind his bland face was still that of the Kodaly's ancient servant. Quite likely he was now a tool of 3340, like Raven's animals.

"Can I see them?" she asked after a moment. He put a finger to his lips and led her into one of the buildings. This was a place like a stone filigree, its walls pierced by thousands of openings that let in air, as well as ivy, birds, and squirrels. Livia padded up a flight of worn stone steps and passed through a barely felt weather barrier, into warmer, dry air and the smell of books. Light shone through an archway in front of her. She crept up and peered around the doorjamb.

Livia's father and mother sat in deep armchairs under the towering bookshelves of the Kodaly library. The volumes arrayed around them were all unique, all hand-lettered and bound individually: book as artform. Livia had only read one or two—but she had held, paged through, and admired hundreds over the years.

"... The crowd is growing," her father was saying. Since her parents were facing away from her, Livia felt brave enough to take a step into the room and crane her neck to see better. The Good Book lay on the low table between the armchairs; around it, piled up, opened and bookmarked, were many other volumes. Livia could read several titles: the *Holy Bible,* the *I Ching,* the *Little Red Book.*

"... What they're doing," said her mother. "It's supremely creepy. All those people, just standing there ..."

Her father laughed humorlessly. "And how do you suppose we'd have looked to somebody outside inscape when we had our Societies?— talking to people who aren't there? No, it isn't the silence and stillness that bothers me."

"Well, what then?"

"Why are they all together? Jammed in like that? That's what bothers me."

She shifted impatiently. "But why doesn't the resistance do something?"

"They can't influence inscape on that sort of scale," her father said. Mother didn't answer, and the silence dragged out. Livia began to feel exposed.

She slipped out the doorway. Livia was practically panting, and had to lean on the wall for a moment to compose herself. Just the sound of their voices had been enough to pull up a storm of emotions—relief, sorrow, fury at the changes that had happened. She couldn't settle on how she felt, but staggered down the steps and outside, gulping the fresh air miserably.

"My room," she said to Capewan after she'd gotten some control of herself. "Is it still there?"

"Repaired, my lady. It was somewhat damaged in the ... recent troubles."

She set off in the direction of her room, but didn't object when Capewan followed her. All that could be heard was their footsteps, and cricket-song.

She couldn't face her parents right now. If she once spoke to them, she felt, she wouldn't want to leave this place again. Just being home would be enough that she would turn her back on everything else—Westerhaven, her unwanted role as savior to her people—and, like them, simply live on, spending her evenings sipping tea in the library. And damn the rest of the world.

Round three turns and there it was: the park/ballroom lay before her, with her open-air bedroom visible in the coignes of the arch opposite. There was her bed; her footlocker was open; her clothes were piled neatly where last she had seen them scattered and torn under the talons of a beast like an unfolding flower of black and crimson. All she had to do was climb up the ladder worked into the stone of the arch, and she could flop down on the bed as she'd done a thousand times before, safe and home. In the morning she could climb down and bring breakfast to her parents.

She pressed a combination of stones at the base of the arch, and a hidden locker opened. There were her clothes, and a favorite sword.

"One question," she said to Capewan as she strapped on the sword.

"Yes, Livia?"

She wanted to ask about this "resistance" she'd heard her parents mention, but that might not be discreet, considering she was speaking to an entity intimately hooked into inscape.

Instead, she said, "There are no more manifolds, are there?"

"No, ma'am."

"But people—my parents—they don't seem unhappy."

"No, ma'am."

"Why is that?"

"Some people say that the Book has made the manifolds unnecessary."

"Is that what you believe?" she asked.

He hesitated, his face shadowed under the trees. Once again she felt a prickle of unease at who this might be she was speaking to. But she had to ask the question.

"I believe the conquest has shown us that no matter how different the manifolds we lived in, we were always one people—in that we believed in our differences, if nothing else. We are united in our sorrow at having lost them . . . In my opinion," he said.

Livia's shoulders slumped. A terrible tension left her with a deep sigh. This was the same Capewan as before; he was unchanged despite all that had happened. Somehow, knowing that made her feel that she really had come home at last.

"Thank you, Capewan. Don't tell anyone that you saw me here."

"Of course, Livia. I'm glad to know you're still alive."

"And I, that you are, too." She wiped her eyes and, turning away, walked under the arch and up the paths, and back onto the streets of Barrastea.

THOUGH SHE WAS tired and her feet hurt from walking, Livia drifted on through the dark streets. The Red Quarter was trying to be as lively as it had been before 3340—the streets here were full of revelers and drunks. In the old days, there would have been thousands of animas here, too, men and women trying on the other's masks for a night, the fat becoming thin, the old temporarily young. These masks were gone now, a fact to be mourned.

Now that cool night had fallen, the wealthy and fashionable of Cirrus began to make an appearance. Taut networks of glowing cable descended and they walked down them, not even bothering to put their arms out for balance. Though none would set foot on solid ground, they came to within a few meters of it and perched like birds, tossing confections and toys to the crowd below in return for bottles of wine lobbed carefully back.

Capewan might be right. Westerhaven and Cirrus talking and laughing together was extraordinary to see. Despite their differences, they had been made one manifold by 3340. And it seemed they were happy.

As she walked, though, Livia began to see others venturing out into the streets. Shrouded figures, for the most part, darting from shadow to shadow, usually in tight groups. Livia followed a couple of these and caught glimpses of outlandish costumes made of hand-knit materials or hides. She heard strange accents in the strained and hushed whispers these new people traded.

She thought of the drummers; of the elders of Raven and all the other manifolds that had banned machinery. For them, there was nothing familiar or easy about this manifold 3340 had forced them to live in.

She had been walking in silence for twenty minutes when Livia began to spot the standing people.

At first they were just dots in the distance, like stones in a stream—all solitary, none raising its head to acknowledge passersby. No one in turn spoke to them. As Livia approached the nearest figure, she saw why. He stared through her with sightless eyes. Either he saw nothing, or she was invisible to him.

As she walked she spotted more—first ones and twos, then small groups together. They wore rags, and while a few moved, they shuffled slowly, like sleepwalkers. She had seen such distraction before, in people who were fully immersed in some inscape vision. All of these men, women, and children were held fast within some manifold she couldn't perceive.

Livia turned a corner and found herself facing a street full of silent figures, still as mannequins. She hurried past the expressionless figures, deliberately not looking at their faces.

For a while she had been too distracted by the unnerving sight of these silent people to pay much attention to the direction her footsteps were taking her. Now Livia looked up to see a set of tall domes rising above the trees ahead. They appeared intact, but as she broke into a run and the Great Library grew closer, she saw that the building was sealed up.

There had been some attempt at repair, but it was haphazard and obviously done without the aid of bots. The doors were chained shut and autumn leaves had drifted around them. Not that it would be difficult to get inside, since many of the great stained-glass windows were missing, and there were even holes in the walls.

For some reason seeing the library like this reassured her. This place, at least, did not deny the violence of conquest.

She found a low gap in the wall and shimmied through. Dropping to the marble floor of the library, she looked around. It was a heartbreakingly familiar place; she had been in this very room many times as a child. The bones of the mastodon had stood proudly then, rather than leaning in a charred jumble; and the dinosaur skeletons had posed as if sizing up the visitors for lunch. Now the precious artifacts of Earth lay toppled like dolls.

At least, she thought with a wry smile, she had found a place to sleep.

She knew the hidden fleet of the anecliptics loomed somewhere beneath her feet; it was still hard to believe she was not alone here as she paced through the blackened, roofless chambers of the library. In fact Livia felt oddly angry—offended, somehow—that such hidden power should be available to her now, when she hadn't even known it existed the first time she stood in ruins on Teven. Then as now, vast anecliptic forces had lurked beyond the landscapes of the coronal, and Choronzon himself had walked the streets of Barrastea. But none of those powers had come to save her.

She stopped suddenly. The scent of wood smoke had wafted to her from somewhere ahead. Now that she was still and concentrating, she could hear voices coming from the building's rotunda. As quietly as she could, she crept up to the archway and peered inside.

Orange flames leapt up from a marble waste receptacle. Seven people sat around it on broken benches or chunks of stone. They were dressed well enough, in shifts tuned to somber black and brown colors. But all looked thin and careworn. They were talking together but she couldn't hear what they were saying.

Livia was just debating whether to make her appearance known when a strong voice behind her said, "Hands up! Turn around slowly."

She raised her hands and turned back to the darkness of the corridor. "Check her for weapons," said the voice, and an indistinct man loomed out of the darkness. He frisked Livia efficiently and took her sword.

"All right. March in there where we can see you." Livia walked into the rotunda, feeling exposed and more than a little frightened. She still had her hands up. The people sitting around the fire shouted to one another and several jumped up as she appeared.

"She was watching you, Ross," said the man who had caught her. "Recognize her?"

One of the men from the fire came over and peered at Livia. "Haven't seen her around the city."

"Okay. Well, sit her down and let's look at her." Rough hands pushed her down onto a chunk of stone. Ross stood over her with his arms crossed as the other man emerged from the shadows, firelight glinting off his pistol.

She recognized him. This was one of the peers, albeit of a crowd a few years older than Livia's had been. She couldn't remember his first name, but his surname, she was sure, was Bisson.

"Who are you?" he asked brusquely.

"My name is Livia Kodaly," she said. "Perhaps you've heard of me?"

She saw a flicker of surprise cross his face, then he veiled it with a sneer and a shrug. "Could be," he said curtly. "Then again, why skulk in the shadows? Besides, I've seen Livia Kodaly before, you don't look a bit like her."

She met his eye and managed a small smile. "Well, I did change my clothes while I was away."

He didn't laugh. "How much could she have overheard?" he asked the people by the fire. As he turned away Livia noticed that there was an ugly scar behind his ear. She looked at the man Ross, who was still standing over her. It was hard to tell from the angle, but it looked as though he had a similar scar.

The bone behind the ear was where inscape implants were usually embedded.

One of the men shrugged and said, "We were talking about Esther."

Livia sat up straighter. "Esther Mannus? Is she all right?"

Bisson stared at her for a few seconds. Then he said, "We'd best find out what this one knows, anyway."

She opened her mouth to object, but any argument would be a distraction at this point. After all, she'd come here for a purpose, one that had very few hours left in it. She had to take the chance that she had found the people she was looking for. "I'll only tell my story to Maren Ellis," she said.

Bisson crossed his arms and raised an eyebrow. "Oh, will you now?"

"But meanwhile I've some harmless questions of my own," she said. "Like: who are those silent people in the streets? What's Cirrus doing in Barrastea? What happened to Kale and the other ancestors? Is anybody in charge here anymore, or is it all the Book?"

They were looking at one another with varying expressions of surprise and suspicion. "She's just trying to convince us she doesn't know anything," said one.

Her heart leaped at that. "What would I know?" She looked from face to face. "Are there places in Teven that still aren't conquered? I've seen people skulking about after dark, looking like lost souls. Are you like them? Just hiding here from 3340? Or are you doing something about it?"

"Shut up!" Bisson grabbed her wrist and twisted hard. She gasped. He let go, and she pulled her hand back.

"Is this what the peers have become?" she said coldly. "Bisson, I've come to help you."

He blinked. "How do you know my name?"

"Take me to Maren."

A long silence ensued. The others were watching Bisson. Finally he nodded curtly. "Bring her."

They filed out of the library through a gap in the outer wall. Nobody was watching, yet Bisson took them by hidden ways through the city. Much of the journey was underground, through echoing caveways that had once been broad brightly-lit avenues underneath the streets. Above ground, they hugged the sides of buildings or walked beneath lattice-growths of bush and tree.

While they walked she repeated her questions about what had happened. Bisson threatened her halfheartedly the first few times. Finally he started answering, apparently just to shut her up.

Just why he and these others were hiding out here he wouldn't say. Nor would he explain the scar behind his ear. But the recent history of Teven was an open subject, and he talked about it eagerly. So eagerly that

Livia realized he must truly want to believe that she was who she said she was.

Thirty-three forty's attack on the manifolds had accelerated after the fall of Westerhaven. It seemed as if a chain reaction set in, or perhaps that the tech locks shut down as the carefully crafted interfaces between realities disappeared. Bisson did not describe it that way, of course; for him and for most people in Teven, it was not that the manifolds had disappeared: it was that one manifold that allowed all technologies to coexist had absorbed all the others.

Some people could live in this manifold; certainly it was compatible enough with the values of Westerhaven, Cirrus, and a few other civilizations. But for the majority of citizens of Teven, this new reality was chaos.

Into this chaos had come the Good Book. Kale's forces ruthlessly stamped out any other organizational system, and they soon enlisted passionate new converts from the population to help them. Those people who could adopt the roles of the Book flourished; but whole microcivilizations remained shell-shocked, their citizens reduced to ghosts wandering the streets of the larger cities. The users of the Book tried to help them. Although Bisson did not say so, Livia knew that many more must be engaged in trying to rally them to fight back. She had no doubt that it was such a group she had stumbled upon in the library.

Where one of the great towers of Barrastea had fallen, hundreds of meters of white sail material lay draped over the lower buildings. Bisson brought them underneath a tall fold of the stiff material. Livia heard voices up ahead; then they emerged into a campsite built under the pale tenting. There were about twenty people here, all as ragged as Bisson and his companions.

Livia saw her immediately. Maren Ellis's face stood out from those around the fire—a serene blossom amongst the sunburnt, thin visages of the others. Just now she was surveying the others as they talked, her eyes glittering.

Bisson went over to her and bent to whisper something. Even as he did, she looked up and her eyes met Livia's.

Livia glanced around the camp, looking for a familiar face—and immediately saw one. Rene Caiser was standing up, brushing his hair back nervously. When he saw that she'd spotted him he grinned shyly. Livia laughed and shouted, "Rene!"

Ignoring the suspicious stares of many of the others, he ran around the fire and embraced her, lifting her off the ground in his enthusiasm. "You're back!"

"We don't know it's her," muttered Ross sulkily.

Bisson was arguing with Maren. She stood up, brushing him aside, and walked over to Livia and Rene. Circling Livia she looked her up and down. "...Or a very good likeness," she said to Bisson.

Livia was tired of all this suspicion. There was one simple way to end it, and she took it: looking Maren Ellis in the eye, she said, "Choronzon is coming. He's going to destroy the tech locks once and for all."

22

"WHAT DID YOU *say* to her?" Rene and Livia watched Maren pacing back and forth in front of the fire. She looked like a caged tiger; watching her move, Livia wondered how she had ever thought Maren Ellis was an ordinary human being.

"Livia..." She looked over. Bisson had an abject expression on his face. "I'm sorry I was rough on you. But since the horizons fell... it's hard to know what's real."

"Real..." She half smiled, remembering how that word had once held meaning for her. "I don't blame you." Then she remembered the scar over his ear. She reached out to Rene's own hairline. "Your implants..."

"Inscape's dangerous," he said with a grimace. "Thirty-three forty uses it to build these huge temporary scenarios—as if the whole coronal were suddenly put into games mode. Geography, time, people—it all gets mixed up, and then everyone has to use that damned Book to sort it all out again."

"Really? How often does that happen?"

He smiled ruefully. "It was once every couple of weeks to start off. Then it started accelerating, until the whole place was going crazy. That was about a month ago, and since then it's calmed down gradually. Only now we have the sleepwalkers..."

"The what?"

"I don't even know how to describe them. You'll see. Anyway, when things got out of hand we had to cut our links to inscape or go crazy; it's okay as long as you use the Book, but if you resist... There are days when I almost believe I'm better off without the implants. But it's not true. Those of us who don't use the Book live like animals. Some of us are here in the ruins. The rest are in camps scattered across the coronal. No manifolds any more, no tech locks—everybody mixed together."

"It sounds bad," she said, "but is it really the manifolds you miss?" He stared at her like she was insane. "What I mean is, would you really want it all back the way it was? I mean, bring back the manifolds, sure—but would you want the horizons back, too?"

Now he just looked puzzled. "How could you have manifolds without horizons?"

Livia nodded at Maren. "She would say you can't."

"And you would say . . . ?"

Maren walked over. "Tell me what happened after you left here," she commanded.

Livia sat down and began recounting the story of their journey to the Archipelago and back again. She had carefully rehearsed what she would say; she glossed over many of the details, and for the rest watched Maren Ellis's face carefully. She was especially careful when recounting her encounters with narratives and the Good Book.

"The Book appeared shortly after the mad anecliptic was destroyed," Livia explained. Most of the camp had gathered around to listen, and from the blank expressions it was clear that *anecliptic* was still not a word anyone here had heard. Even in the depths of Teven Coronal's worst crisis, Maren Ellis was hiding things from her own people.

Livia pretended not to have noticed the incomprehension amongst the audience. "According to Choronzon," she continued, "3340 was made by the anecliptic for some sort of fall-back plan, one that involved Teven somehow."

"Do you believe him?" Maren asked sharply.

Livia had no intention of revealing what she thought. She said, "The other possibility is that Choronzon himself made 3340—that he's trying to do what the anecliptic could not—change the balance of power in the Archipelago."

"But why us?" Maren shook her head emphatically. "It makes no sense."

"Actually, it does make sense," said Livia quietly. "Teven Coronal has been isolated for two hundred years. It's the only place in the solar system free of the Archipelagic control systems. That makes it the only place where something like the Book can really cut loose and grow."

"Grow? Grow into what?"

Livia hesitated. "That I don't know."

"And the anecliptics are coming to destroy it?"

"So Choronzon says. But while they're doing that, I'm pretty sure he means to destroy the tech locks."

The founder cursed. "It fits—unfortunately. All except for the idea that 3340 is strictly an emergent system. If it were, how do you explain Kale and his bosses?"

"The ancestors?" Livia shrugged. "We think they were slotted into particular roles semipermanently by the Book. I'm sure they've made a lot of the critical decisions, maybe they decided to invade Teven on their own. The Book doesn't decide, it's not a thing; it's the roles that decide."

"If so, there's a hell of a role just arrived," said Rene. "We have it from our man inside—some people came from this 'space' place—" He gestured vaguely at the sky.

"I think I know who," said Livia. "Listen." She turned to Maren. "Do the tech locks still exist?" Maren nodded.

Livia let out a sigh of relief. Her journey here might not have been in vain after all. "You have the keys to them, don't you? You and only you?" she asked.

Maren nodded again, more warily this time.

Livia crossed her arms and looked away from the founder. "We can still save the legacy of the manifolds," she said slowly and carefully. "The key is to protect the locks, which I assume is what you've been doing since I left." Rene nodded.

"You won't be able to protect them from Choronzon," said Livia. "You need a new plan."

"And you have it?" asked Maren. Her eyes still glittered in the firelight, coldly now.

"There's two alternatives," said Livia. She and Qiingi had gone over the possibilities on the way here; if he'd found Raven, he would be presenting the same options to him. "One," she said, bending back a finger of her right hand, "we enter into a defensive alliance with the Good Book."

The crowd around the campfire looked shocked. After a moment people started muttering angrily. Maren didn't even blink. "What can we offer it?"

"An end to resistance, and cooperation until it achieves whatever it came here to achieve." Nobody looked happy at the idea. "I know," said Livia. "Before we can deal, we need to know what it's doing with Teven. If it's something with a definite end—that isn't going to destroy us all— then we could do it. But we need to know what it is."

Maren scowled into the fire. "And the other option?"

"Make a copy of the locks and run for it," Livia said bluntly. "I have a ship that can do it. But we'd have to go now, before Choronzon arrives."

"Run where?" Maren laughed. "Back to the Archipelago? They're why we came here to begin with." She shook her head. "No, easy as that solution seems, Livia, I'm afraid it's out of the question. We're going to have to go with your first choice.

"We will have to cut a deal with 3340."

IN PREDAWN LIGHT, Livia sat in a deep armchair perched incongruously atop a patch of rubble. She was plotting her next move. Stars showed through a gap in the tenting overhead; earlier, she had aimed her com laser through that gap and reported her situation to the ship.

Qiingi would be in Barrastea in a few hours—along with Raven, whom he had found helping disoriented refugees from some of the neo-primitivist manifolds. From what the lads had (and hadn't) said, it sounded like Qiingi's return to what was once Raven's people had been a saddening experience. She felt a little of that sadness too as she waited for the avalanche of light that was dawn within a coronal. With daylight, decisions would be necessary. And things would change, again.

Someone coughed discreetly. She looked over and saw that Rene was standing at the foot of the rubble mound. "May I approach the queen?" he asked with a flourishing bow.

She laughed. "Come here." He came and sat on the stones at her feet. "You should be sleeping," he said.

She shrugged.

"What you said earlier about having manifolds without horizons—that's what this is all about, isn't it?" he asked. "This person, Chonzon—"

"Choronzon. And he's not a person. He's a . . . well, in the Archipelago they call him a god. He knows Maren from way back. And he doesn't like what she's done in Teven."

"What *she's* done?"

"Rene, Maren Ellis isn't *a* founder—she's *the* founder." She told him what little she knew about how Teven had come to be colonized. Rene expressed some surprise at learning how old Maren really was—but not as much surprise as Livia would have expected.

"So she's the keeper of the tech locks," he mused. "And she never told us."

"And there lies the problem," said Livia. "Maren Ellis, Choronzon, the Government, the anecliptics, 3340—none of them are human. Human beings don't control their own destiny anymore. But the question is, could we?"

"You think the locks are the answer? But why? I should have thought the annies, or this Government—"

She shook her head. "Too much goes on that's simply not on a human scale anymore. Humans could never control the distribution of re-sources in the solar system, for instance—it's too complex a problem. But we should be able to control those things that are on a human scale."

He nodded slowly. "So that's what you're up to."

"What?" she said innocently.

"You want to take the locks away from Maren." She said nothing. Rene laughed quietly. "And that means that everything you've said since you arrived—about Choronzon, and 3340 and so on—could be a lie intended to get Maren to give you the locks."

Livia sat forward. "And if it was? Would you tell her?"

"Well, I don't—" Rene was saved from having to answer by a flurry of activity at the edge of the camp. Someone had arrived, it seemed. He stepped down to look and Livia leaped to her feet, thinking it might be Qiingi, and jumped down the side of the rubble pile.

Maren Ellis was talking to a man who stood leaning on a fold of sail material. "I don't know what 3340's really up to any more than you do—but I know what it *says* it's doing," said a familiar voice. "Would that do for a start?"

Livia stopped in her tracks, shocked; Rene bumped into her. Maren Ellis turned and saw her. "Livia, there you are. This is our agent inside 3340's camp. Livia Kodaly, meet—"

"Lucius Xavier," she said, holding out her hand for him to shake. "Yes, we've met."

Lucius looked into her eyes uneasily. "How are you?"

She sighed. "Older, and less easily offended. And you?"

"I'm no better a person than the last time we met," he said with a faint smile. "But I've never been your enemy—as I believe I told you once."

"You did," she said, letting go of his hand. "But back then, your authority mattered to me."

His eyes widened, but before he could reply Maren Ellis said, drily, "I'm glad you two know each other. But, can we get back to the matter at hand?"

Xavier sat down near the fire. He made a show of warming his hands over it. "We've all wanted to know what 3340 is doing here," he said. "During my long association with 3340's people, I've never stopped trying to find that out. The problem has been that even the Book's people don't know. They follow their roles and are rewarded for it—that's as much as they know.

"But four days ago a vessel for traveling in space arrived in Barrastea." He glanced shrewdly at Livia. "Were you on that?" She shook her head; her little ship had only arrived at the coronal yesterday.

Lucius looked disappointed. "Anyway, this vessel brought some important roles with it, as well as the first person I've seen whom I might consider an actual leader."

"Filament?" said Livia.

"Uh, yes. Yes, that's her—or its—name."

"We need to speak to this Filament," said Maren. "Can you arrange that?"

Lucius looked uncomfortable. "Our resistance doesn't have a very high priority with the Book at the moment," he said delicately.

"Tell her that I'm here," said Livia. "That should get her attention."

"Hang on," said Lucius. "You asked me if I had learned what 3340 is doing here. Didn't you want to hear what I've found out?"

"I'm sorry, Lucius, please continue," said Maren smoothly.

Lucius looked unhappy. "None of this has turned out . . . like I expected," he said, glancing at Livia. "This vessel brought something else with it. It's a . . . I don't know what it is.

"But they say it's here to turn the sleepers into a god."

"I'VE SEEN THIS place before," said Doran Morss, wondering at the streets and plazas that glowed under sunrise. "That way is the park, isn't it?"

The young woman walking next to him looked surprised. "When were you here? Teven's been locked down—only we have the keys to get in and out."

They were trudging up a leaf-strewn avenue. In the distance dawn light painted open parkland gold. Here and there people stood about in the street. Their silence and air of distraction was disturbing.

"In a sim," he said. "I've been here in a sim."

The woman leading him nodded as if his explanation hadn't actually raised more questions than it answered. She was dazzlingly beautiful, but it was the ridiculous physical perfection of the body-sculpted; that suggested to him that she was from the inner Archipelago, where such things were currently fashionable. Judging from the clunky way she walked, she had once been short and stocky, and had never quite adjusted to the tall willowy build she had now.

She was one of 3340's advance guard in this place, and might have been here for years by now. She probably had no idea what was going on in the outside world.

Doran's kidnapping had been remarkably polite—after his beating at the hands of Filament's thugs, that is. There was little need for violence once he was on board her ship. He could escape into any Archipelagic view he wanted, it wouldn't change the underlying situation. And there was nothing and no one for him to fight; any adversary would dissolve into inscape if Doran so much as glared at him or her.

But he had finally been allowed to disembark from the ship, only to find himself in a place he'd thought existed only in an online fantasy. It didn't matter. Now that he was dealing with real people again, things were different. He might be able to actually do something here.

Suddenly the woman dropped back to walk beside him. "That sim— the one where you visited here—who made it?"

Doran chewed his lip for a moment, thinking. Then he said, "A local named Livia Kodaly. One of yours, I assume. I suppose she was part of a propaganda mission of some kind? To interest users of the Book in coming here?"

"Maybe." She shrugged. "The Book's strategic moves often aren't visible to us on our scale. It's probably got millions of projects on the go."

She walked on, serenely confident. Doran sized her up, debating whether he could knock her down and just run for it. Probably not—he could see the faint shimmering outline of a virtual matter shield around her, what the locals called an "angel." He couldn't disable her.

On the other hand, Filament needed him alive and cooperative. And, cooped up as he'd been for the past days, he hadn't had any exercise.

So, as they were passing a narrow alley, he simply turned and ran. It took her a full five seconds to notice what he'd done; her startled shout made him laugh out loud as he dodged and jumped the debris in the alley.

He came out onto a street that he'd never visited in the sim, and quickly looked left and right. She'd catch him any second now—or call in the reinforcements that he had no doubt were lurking around somewhere nearby. So it didn't matter which way he went; might as well pick the most scenic. He went left.

Her pounding feet sounded behind him. Again she shouted for him to stop. Doran kept running, reveling in the feeling of the crisp autumn air in his lungs and the pounding of his feet on pavement. For a few seconds it didn't matter where he was or what this was all about. There was just him enjoying the run.

Then he looked up. He had come to the end of the buildings. And standing there in his way was a wall of silent people—thousands of them packed shoulder to shoulder and blocking his way.

He stumbled and went down on one knee. The Book's agent puffed up behind him, cursing, but Doran ignored her. He was staring at the crowd.

His initial impression had been that they were there to block his escape. But they weren't looking at him; hell, they weren't *looking* at anything at all. They simply stood there, uniformly sightless and silent—no, not silent. Doran could hear a faint sighing sound that he'd at first thought was the wind. But the air wasn't moving. It was breathing he heard—a million, two million inhalations. And though the crowd was still ten meters away, it was palpably warmer here.

"Hell of my fathers," he whispered. "What have you done to them?"

Thirty-three forty's agent clapped her hand on his shoulder and dragged him to his feet. "We've done nothing," she said. "Not yet. But these people are why you are here."

Doran thought of turning and running from this vast multitude. He might have, even though 3340's people would catch him again—but stopped as he thought about the sheer helplessness of these men and women. They were no danger to him; he was probably more danger to them.

He forced himself to examine the scene clinically. If he looked closely he could see faint geometric outlines—virtual matter—drifting over the crowd. Knowing what was possible even within the narratives, these things were probably feeding, watering, and cleaning up after the silent people.

"Is this what the Book does to its slaves?" he asked after a while. "Paralyzes them to make them more efficient? I assume these people's minds are off in inscape somewhere, playing out its little role-games."

The woman took his arm and started walking forward. The crowd parted miraculously as she approached. "It's not paralysis," she said. "And they're not slaves—they're elite users. Volunteers. They're the best at using the Book from all over Teven, and they're true believers in its goodness. They're very busy right now, assembling a new processing kernel for 3340."

Any one person in Teven had more character in their face than any ten Archipelagics. But the faces they passed, each so unique, were all equally blank. "A new *kernel?*"

"They're building a bounded version of 3340 that can operate in isolation from the rest of the network."

Belatedly, Doran realized that the crowd was sealing itself behind them as they proceeded. He'd lost his last chance to cut and run. He instinctively edged closer to the woman, feeling, under the weight of all those empty gazes, as if he were five years old again. "You're going to make a new book?"

"Of course not," she snapped. "Version 3340 is perfect." She looked over at him. "I was told that you knew what we're going to do."

Now, belatedly, he understood.

About a kilometer ahead of them, some of the strange nets and cables that hung above the city drooped down almost to ground level. Where they converged, Doran glimpsed the gleaming blue curve of the eschatus machine, nestled like a spider at the heart of its web.

Yes, he knew what 3340 was about to do. He'd just refused to accept what he was seeing.

"But why do you need the people?" he asked weakly. When the eschatus machine went off, this whole park would be within its blast radius. "Surely a machine could work the processes of the Book a trillion times faster than this crowd . . ."

"Nonusers often ask us that," said his escort. They were making steady progress through the sea of people. "But it's a mistake to think of the Book's roles as being separable from the people who perform them. The Book relies on human perception and intelligence to make sense of those roles. Thirty-three forty's program can't just be transferred into sims or animas and run that way. It can only emerge from embodied minds—minds for whom the roles have an experiential meaning."

"So these people are going to be . . ."

"Incorporated into a new, unified body for 3340. Their consciousness will exist in a virtual world that is infinitely adaptable. This world will be a paradise, and their minds will experience it thousands of time faster than you or I can think. They will never die as long as the new body survives. If it lasts a thousand years, they will experience a million years in heaven. That is why they have come here."

Doran felt sick. "But they'll never be allowed to stop using the Book, will they?"

She looked puzzled. "Why would they want to?"

"So why aren't you standing here too with your mouth hanging open?" he snapped. "If you think it's going to be so great?"

She blew out a heavy sigh. "I'd like to be. I really would. But the Book hasn't assigned me a role in the new body. I suppose I'm just not as good a user as I should be."

"But . . ." Doran's brain seemed to have stopped working. He tried to speak several more times, and finally just said, "Why?"

"Why does 3340 need a new body?"

He nodded dumbly at her. She shrugged. "To directly oppose the annies, 3340 needs to be able to think at least as fast as they do. You see, that's its one vulnerability right now: its processor runs at the speed of human interactions—"

"You actually think 3340 will save us from the annies?"

"The solar system is controlled by the most powerful players," she said. "It's ecological. Humans aren't the top predator any more. We tried creating AIs that would be our servants; I know, I grew up under the Government and the annies just like you did. But how can you deliberately create something that exceeds you in all ways, and still control it? It's impossible."

Doran looked away. He didn't want her to see how that point had hit home. He agreed with this assessment; it was why he'd built the eschatus machine for himself. "But it's not a solvable problem," he argued.

Now her eyes held the fire of true missionary zeal. "Unless you could build a system that exceeded humanity in all the right ways, while still being *made up* of humanity. A system in which ordinary humans were so integral that it couldn't exist without them. Where human aspirations were channeled into creating a being, an entity, powerful and wise enough to take on the annies . . ."

They were approaching a rope ladder that led up to where the eschatus machine sat in its nest of cables. Someone was standing on the strands, waiting. Doran couldn't quite make the figure out, but he knew it must be Filament.

"Your argument's perfect, except for one thing," he said bitterly. She raised an elegant eyebrow, indulging the question. "Once he's got this body you're building for him, 3340 doesn't need you anymore. He doesn't need an embodied humanity at all."

She didn't answer. Filament waved to him and Doran climbed the ladder, emerging onto the gently swaying meshwork surface where she stood.

As always, Filament looked relaxed and happy. Doran debated whether to punch her in the chin. But she didn't need angels, not being human. She probably wouldn't even feel it.

"You now have two choices," she said to Doran. "Surrender the pass phrase for the eschatus machine, and you can walk away before we set it off. Or, I will comb through your brain synapse by synapse and locate the information that way. It'll be painless, you'll still be you at the end of the process; but I'll leave you here to be incorporated into 3340 along with the rest of these people. You might want to stay anyway, you know—it'll mean immortality, in a heaven of your own design."

He crossed his arms, looking around for some hint of a means to escape. It was hopeless; he could leap off the meshwork, but the fall might kill him; and he'd probably kill whoever he landed on as well.

His moment of freedom when he ran from his guide now seemed like a childish indulgence. Doran was ashamed of himself—*but I didn't know what was really at stake*, he tried to tell himself. *I thought it was just my life . . .*

"What about it? Answer now." She stepped forward, her face grim.

Doran's shoulders slumped. There really was no choice here; he could have bravely faced up to real torture, but he had no doubt that she could extract exactly what she wanted from him if she chose. It might take her hours, but the end would be the same.

He should have used the eschatus machine himself. And after Filament captured it, he should have killed himself to prevent her getting the pass phrase. Surely he could have devised a way. But it was too late to do it now, and he knew in his heart that he had deliberately chosen not to act. When it came down to it, he'd simply been afraid.

"The pass phrase," he mumbled, "is 'even the gods fight boredom in vain.'"

Filament smiled. "That's really quite humorous," she said. "Thank you. You're free to go. It's going to take us some time to reprogram the eschatus machine. If you leave now, you should be safely outside the blast radius by the time we set it off."

Doran didn't look at her again. He climbed down the ladder and walked away, barely noticing the crowd that parted for him. He simply took step after step, as purposeless under the autumn sky as a man walking to his execution.

23

"I DON'T BELIEVE it." Maren Ellis shook her head. "Such technology can't exist."

"But I heard Doran Morss admit he was trying to get one," Livia repeated for the tenth time. Morning was well advanced now; Lucius had been gone for several hours. While the leaders of Maren's guerilla army waited for him to report, Livia continued to try to convince her to change her mind. "Look, the people Lucius deals with believe it. The people gathered in the park believe it. Why is it so hard to accept?"

Maren turned away, hugging herself. "It's a nightmare. You don't know . . . If such machines can be made, why should anybody remain human anymore? Just flick a switch, and you can become like him." By *him*, she could only mean Choronzon.

Lucius had described the great mob gathered in the park, and the blue marble set in its center. Through some cataclysmic event, those in the crowd expected to be united in godhood with 3340. Remembering Omega Point and Doran Morss's secret arrangements, Livia had a good idea of what that blue sphere was.

"If 3340's here to make a body for itself, then what do you have to bargain with?" Livia had made this argument in a dozen different ways over the past hour. Like all those times, Maren simply shook her head. "Maren, we have nothing it needs. Once the eschatus machine goes off, it won't need Teven anymore."

"No. No!" Maren glared at her. "We can't hand the locks to the enemy. Think what horrible tyranny they could impose if you combined them with the narratives!"

Maren's lieutenants—who included several other founders—watched this exchange with varying puzzlement, incomprehension, or simmering anger. As far as any of them knew, the locks were not so constituted that copying them even made sense. The guerillas had some limited control over them, but they remained a distinct and inhuman force as far as these people were concerned.

"We have to deal with 3340," insisted Maren.

"What you're really saying," Livia said in an undertone, "is that the locks are yours alone, and you won't give them up."

"Someone escort Ms. Kodaly back to her bedroll," snapped Maren. "I believe she needs a rest."

Bisson stepped forward, an apologetic look on his face. Before he could lay a hand on her, Livia stepped forward and hissed in Maren's ear, *"I'll tell them who you are."*

Maren sneered at her. "What do you know, really?"

"I have memories I could give them," hissed Livia as Bisson took her arm. "Those who haven't carved inscape out of their heads at your request. There's one recent scene I could replay; it involves you standing on a balcony in Cirrus, not long after the farside explosion. It starts with you welcoming Choronzon like an old friend. You want me to tell you how it ends?"

Maren turned white. Livia had never seen such fury, but not for an instant did the founder lose her legendary self-control. No one standing more than a few meters away could have told that Maren Ellis was in a murderous frame of mind.

"Maren!" Someone ran up panting from the other end of the high tented space. "We got the signal from Lucius. This Filament person will see you."

"*Now,* Maren," murmured Livia. "I will take them and go, I promise. Consider it a wise backup plan." The founder stared at her. "He *is* coming, Maren," said Livia.

Maren looked around at the uncomprehending faces of her lieutenants. Her shoulders slumped. "All right, then," she hissed. "Take them and go."

To her waiting lieutenants, she said, "I just realized I didn't thank Livia here properly for her bravery and . . . well, sheer audacity in leaving Teven to bring us help. Make sure you grant her full authority here—give her anything she needs," she added to a now thoroughly confused Bisson. Then she leaned in close.

"Remember, girl," she whispered, "this is my world." She smiled brightly, took Livia's hand and shook it—

—And columns of faint light leaped up behind her and all around, signaling the download of some tremendous amount of data into Livia's implants. "Th-thanks," Livia stammered as an inscape serling popped into existence beside Maren.

"The data you are downloading is too big for your existing storage. Would you like to delete material to accommodate it?"

"Yes," she said under her breath. "Go ahead, delete it all." *It's just my memories. Just Westerhaven.*

But what Maren Ellis had just handed her was incomparably greater.

Maren stepped back. She gave Livia a little squint, a kind of gentle "do as I say now" warning that seemed to hold no anger; then she turned and walked away with her delegation.

"Think the negotiation will work?" asked Rene from behind Livia.

"No." Livia crossed her arms, to hide the way her hands were shaking.

"Huh." Rene watched the small group leave. "But when this Choronzon comes, he'll drive out 3340?"

Livia nodded absently. "Oh, he'll do that; he'll be following the orders of the anecliptics—the ones who made Teven, and the Lethe. But he won't give us the manifolds back, Rene. I think the annies consider kicking out 3340 to be their only obligation to us. I'm very much afraid that we will be at the mercy of whatever utopian experiment Choronzon might have in mind for us."

"So what can we do about it?"

"A great deal." She grinned at him. "I've got a part to play. So might you—but listen, I have to check to verify that Maren gave me what she promised. Give me a few minutes."

She retreated to a quiet corner and sat down. Once she was sure she was alone, she checked the memory in her implants. It was full, but it only had one object in it. Nervously, she told inscape to open the file.

She saw a tangle of glowing threads like hair spilling into existence in front of her. Livia shut her eyes to sharpen the image, and found herself immersed in a whirling vortex made up of sharp lines, almost like arrows that pointed and rotated. She reached out her hand and grabbed at one.

Towers of data flickered into being around her. The arrow flattened out, broadened, became a plain. Thousands of other lines stood up out of that plain, like a forest.

She moved her virtual body through the forest, checking the tiny labels on some of the lines: *Resistance, Capacitance,* said one; *Condensers, designs and uses,* said another. Instead of a forest, she imagined she was sailing across a sea of technologies, able with a gesture to pull any invention or principle to herself and, as if she was hauling a net full of fish, come up with all the other technologies that it necessitated. She grabbed one at random (*Ballistics,* it said) and pulled.

With it in hand, new options appeared as floating reticles around her. The tech locks were a multidimensional database, and the technological dependencies were just one way to cut the data. If she chose another view, she could see the anthropology and politics that spears, bows, and cannon each entailed. She dropped ballistics to explore more; to her surprise, even the five senses were listed here as technologies. They led her to the politics of the human body, and of other body plans: four-footed, winged, finned. The tech locks made no distinction between biology and mechanism.

Each technology equated to some human value or set of values, she saw. She'd known that. But on Earth, in the Archipelago and everywhere else, technologies came first, and values changed to accommodate them. Under the locks, values were the keys to access or shut away technologies.

"But how do you work?" She dismissed the database view, and found herself looking at a set of genetic algorithms, compact logical notations. They didn't describe particular machine designs, but rather specifications; in practice, sims would evolve machinery for particular cases and according to local conditions and resources. The locks could work anywhere.

The specifications were the key. They relied on the database and couldn't be duplicated without it. They told how and when to employ energy fields to suppress various powers and macro effects. In Teven, the sims seemed to evolve machines to manipulate programmable matter. Raw materials couldn't be dug out of the ground in a coronal, since the ground only went down a meter or so. What metals or inorganic compounds were available were actually composed of bulk quantum dots which mimicked the qualities of the real thing: with a single command, a chunk of virtual iron could be transformed into pseudo-sulphur or silicon, or given characteristics that no natural element possessed. To disable any device, all the tech locks had to do was change its material composition. And all this required was a command sent through inscape.

The locks proclaimed that there were no neutral technologies. The devices and methods people used didn't just represent certain values— they *were* those values, in some way.

The system was self-consistent and seemed complete. And yet, though she searched through the database for a long time, nowhere could Livia find the one thing she was looking for.

She left inscape. Rene was standing over her, looking concerned. "Livia?"

"They're not there!" She laughed in relief and delight. "I was right!"

"What are you talking about?"

"*Horizons,* Rene. Horizons were not part of the design of the tech locks!"

"What do you mean—" But she had jumped to her feet, laughing, and embraced him.

"I'd always felt it, you know that? It was the one thing that seemed unnatural about life, the way the other manifolds were so totally inaccessible to us. For Raven's people or the others to be invisible, that was one thing; for them to be *impossible to find*—that's the crime!"

"What crime?"

"Maren Ellis's crime. The crime of assuming that the manifolds were so fragile that they had to be separated from one another by invisible walls. In the end, Maren didn't trust any of us to be able to resist the temptation of other ways of life."

"But there's adolescence—the horizons dissolve for a while when you hit puberty."

"I bet she had to do that, or everything would stagnate." Livia shook her head. "Remember what we used to say in Westerhaven?—'The manifolds preserve abundance in human culture.' But what good's abundance if nobody can experience it?—if all we can see is our own little tile on the grand design? There's got to be a better way."

Rene laughed sadly. "Well, maybe. But that's all water under the bridge, isn't it? The manifolds are gone."

"Are they? Your people have been staging attacks on the ancestors using the locks, haven't you?"

"Yes, but the ancestors have been dismantling them. They have bots digging up the streets and boulevards all over the city . . ."

"Including under the park where that big crowd is gathered?" He nodded. "They're trashing the machinery?" she asked.

"Most of it. Some of it they've taken to a storage depot near the edge of the city. They're studying how the locks work, I guess."

"Hmm." She gazed sadly at the wedge of scar tissue visible above Rene's ear. "Rene, how many of the peers do you think would do something if I asked them? Something that's not, ah, sanctioned by Maren Ellis?"

He frowned. "You're still a hero in a lot of people's eyes—those who don't think you cut and run when the ancestors started to win." She winced. "Why?" he said with a faint smile. "Is there something you're going to ask us to do?"

"Well, it's about this negotiation with Filament. Negotiation is all about strength, isn't it? Leverage?"

"Leverage . . ." He grinned. "You want us to steal the tech lock machines that 3340's been studying." She smiled encouragingly. "And . . . ring the park with them," he said, now not seeing her at all but some vision of his own. "Even inscape is under the locks' control. If we could threaten to shut it down for the sleepwalkers—"

"Now that would be leverage," Livia said with a grin.

"We'd have to let Maren know what we'd done somehow." He scowled. "Why didn't she think of this to begin with?"

Livia sighed. "Maren can't accept that Teven was conquered just to provide a staging ground for 3340's transformation. She still believes the Book has some grand plan for the whole coronal; I'm afraid Maren has too high a view of her own value to believe that all of this," she gestured around to take in the city, the manifolds, and the whole coronal, "could be expendable."

"And when she does realize it . . ."

"She'll need to have the tools to do something about it."

Rene nodded curtly. "Right. I'll round up the others. Where should we meet, or are you going to come with me?"

She shook her head. "I have something else I have to do, which is just as important." When he looked doubtful, she put her hand on his shoulder. "You can do this, Rene. You'll be a fine leader, today and in the future."

He grinned and saluted her. As he walked away he was already waving somebody over. Livia watched him fondly for a few seconds, then jogged for the encampment's exit.

Qiingi was waiting in a doorway three blocks from the encampment. He looked haggard, as if he hadn't slept since she'd last seen him.

She kissed him. He said, "I thought it better to wait for you here."

She laughed. "My friends don't bite."

They walked in silence for a while, passing people out strolling, or working on rebuilding the city. It seemed quiet and peaceful, and no one paid them any attention.

"What did you find when you returned home?" she asked after a while.

He sighed. "Nothing. Skaalitch is almost abandoned. Why live in a hide hut when you can have central heating? And yet, my friends and family, they are still there . . . and they long for the old days."

"They begged me to stay with them," he added after a while.

She looked away sorrowfully. "As soon as Choronzon arrives, he'll destroy the locks, both the physical machinery and all copies of the plans—including ours. The only way to preserve the locks is to leave with them now."

"I know."

"But." She stopped. "You don't have to come with me," she said in a low voice. "Qiingi, these are your people! Why don't you stay with them?"

"I think you know why."

She frowned. "You mean when you told me that Teven was real, and the Archipelago an illusion? And you said that we'd lost Teven."

He nodded.

"You know," she said pensively, "even a few days ago, I thought we were coming back here to save our homes. You never thought so, did you? So why did you come? Not simply to be with me?"

"While I was home," he said, "I told our story to the elders. About our flight from here, and our time in the Archipelago. Livia, I left Teven with you not to seek allies for a war, but to seek meaning for the changes in our lives. I was not idle, while we were in the Archipelago. I was putting together a story to tell my people, one that would fit with the myth cycle Raven and the elders crafted for us. I told my tale while I was home. That will do my people more good than any technology."

She wondered about that as he put his arm around her and slowed her to a stroll. For Qiingi's people, his solution doubtless made sense. He wasn't denying that the tech locks had made his people possible; but she had to admit that Raven's people had very different ways of coping, because of what the locks had made possible. That reinforced the huge gulf she knew lay between Qiingi and herself. But gulfs, she had also learned, could be crossed.

Barrastea looked deceptively like it always had. In other days she might have started singing as she walked, entertaining whoever might pass by with arias from the Fictional History. But it was enough, for now, to be walking the streets as she once had.

Some of the moving sidewalks had been restored, so it only took them a half hour to reach the edge of the city. As they exited the slide-walk Livia could see their destination: a craggy spire of the carefully designed Roman ruin that someone had built here ages ago. Spikes of tall grass, yellow now in the autumn, poked up between big weathered stone blocks. The structure was roofless and exposed, and perhaps for this reason the refugees from lost manifolds had not settled in it.

One large plinth of stone sketched a walk-in fireplace. This structure concealed one of the many entrances Aaron had discovered to the coronal's spacecraft docks. Livia and Qiingi had stepped out of this door only a day ago, and already they were leaving again.

As they rounded the broken wall that hid the fireplace from the road, Livia was surprised to see Peaseblossom sitting on a stone block. They had left the lads, and everyone else, in the ship below. And there was Cicada, standing now as he saw her; and Emblaze and even Sophia.

"What are you doing up—" Livia stopped as she saw who was standing with them.

It was 3340's servant, the self-styled "ancestor," Kale. Two others of his kind stood next to him.

Livia drew her sword, hissing "You go left," to Qiingi—but to her amazement and anger Qiingi put a hand out to stop her. "What—" she started to say. Then she recognized the man next to Kale.

It was Aaron.

"AARON!" SHE LAUGHED with relieved surprise and started to run—but her footsteps faltered after a couple of meters. There was something about the scene, the way people were sitting, the placement of Aaron and Kale, as if Aaron were standing *with* Kale and not with the others . . .

"Aaron . . . what happened?" It was a question for all of them, but Livia saw only Aaron. She couldn't believe the vision he presented.

It was as though some classical portrait artist had been hired to paint an idealized version of her dearest friend. All his imperfections had been smoothed away: where he'd had a slight slouch, now he stood straight and tall; where his cheeks had been a bit thin, now his jaw was square and strong. His eyes, which had once been a colorless gray, were now blue. But overriding all of these physical details was the sense that someone else now lived in the body that had once been his.

He strode through the tall grass and stopped a couple of meters away from Livia. A gentle, apologetic look suffused his features as he said, shyly, "How are you?"

She gaped at him. "How—I, I don't know. Aaron, what happened? How did you get here? And what are you doing . . . *here?*"

"Livia, I wanted to tell you about it, of course. But . . . I guess if we'd wanted to face up to things, we'd have known that politics would someday come between us. I mean, you and I believe different things but it never mattered before." He took a deep breath. "What I'm saying is I'm sorry we had to meet again like this. This wasn't the role I wanted to be playing when I saw you again."

"*Role?* You mean you're working for *him* now?" She glared at Kale.

"Actually, he's working for me." At first Livia didn't realize what he'd said; as she was trying to formulate a response, he added, "I'm afraid we had to confiscate your ship." Again he looked away, unhappily but not, it seemed, with any sense of guilt.

"Why?"

He shrugged. "Politics. We'll give it back, just not in time for you to warn anybody in the Archipelago about what's going to happen."

"And what is going to happen?" asked Qiingi.

"Freedom," Aaron said seriously. "We're going to free the Archipelago from the anecliptics. So that human beings can finally reach their full potential."

Kale cleared his throat. "We're wasting time. She wanted us to bring them immediately."

"Yes," said Aaron. "If you'll come this way . . . ?" He gestured politely for Livia to precede him.

Her fingers itched to draw her sword, but nobody was making any effort to disarm her; doubtless this kind of weapon would do her no good. She and Qiingi joined her friends and they walked out the back of the ruin to a grassy area where several aircars sat.

"Want us to take 'em out?" murmured Cicada loyally. "We're expendable, after all."

She glanced sidelong at him. "You might once have been. Having a body's changed you. I wouldn't want anything to happen to you guys now."

"Oh?" He looked surprised, and pleased.

Despite her loud objections, Livia was separated from Qiingi and placed in the aircar that Aaron would be piloting. She shrank away from him. He noticed, and frowned.

"Whose side do you think I'm on?" he asked, with a trace of his old sullenness.

"Well, I don't know who you are, so I couldn't say," she said. "I once knew a man who looked like you, but he wouldn't be working for the enemy."

He guided them into the air with an expert hand. "What enemy is that?" he asked casually.

"You know. Thirty-three forty. The Good Book. The thing that destroyed our world and killed our friends."

Aaron shook his head sadly. "There's no such thing as this '3340' you're so angry at. We didn't know that when Teven was invaded, of course; you can name a thing even if it doesn't exist. There is no 'Good Book' except the physical object with that name. There's only people and the things they've done. Like you and me, for instance. But standing against us is a real enemy. I saw that, but I also knew you wouldn't see it."

"The annies? The Government? No, I agree with you," she said, "but 3340's no better—"

"*There is no 3340!*" He'd put the aircar on autopilot and now turned to glare at her. "Don't you get it? The Book doesn't think, it isn't conscious. It's us who do that. The Book just organizes and coordinates our actions—it's like a Society, only inconceivably bigger. No *thing* invaded Teven, and no *thing* is occupying it now, Livia. It's just people acting together, for good or ill. Giving a name to this new kind of power—treating it like a person—is irresponsible. If you do that you end up fighting phantoms. When I realized that, I realized how much was still possible for humanity, even in a world ruled by godlike forces like the annies.

"So whose side am I on? I'm on the side of human beings, Livia. And I'm fighting against the inhuman powers that have enslaved us all."

"So who killed our friends?" she said, almost inaudibly.

"Men and women of Raven's people, and other manifolds," he said angrily. "And these 'ancestors.' And they're *sorry*, Livia, you can't imagine how sorry they are that people died in the liberation of Teven. They want to atone for it. And they will." He stared grimly out through the canopy at the passing buildings. "I came back to make sure they would."

Livia sat back, stunned. He was wrong, in every way and possible sense—and yet she couldn't say how or why. She could see how he might think that the enemy was faceless but it was crazy not to think of 3340 as a thing (but it wasn't one, was it?) and wrong to forgive the forces that had destroyed her home (or was it noble?).

Was it simply Maren Ellis's hothouse experiment in human culture that had been destroyed? Had Westerhaven ever really been its own place? Or had her whole life been a performance for a mad woman?

She shook her head, nauseated, and turned away to look out the window.

It took a few seconds for her to sort out what she was seeing down there. Livia had never seen so many people crowded into one space before. She gaped at the sheer outrageousness of it. There could be no moving through that pressing mass. This was the crowd of sleepwalkers Lucius had spoken of; no one down there wanted to escape.

"And yet," she murmured, "you're willing to let these people be made into a machine to process 3340's thoughts."

"There is no 3340," said Aaron impatiently. "So what do you think you're looking at? Those are the ambitious, Livia, they've all chosen to leave the human condition behind. The point is that they *can* make that choice now. That's what being human means: to be master of your own fate. If you choose to become more than human, well, that's nothing but fulfilment. Self-actualization."

She glanced back at his newly perfected features. "Is that what you're doing to yourself? Fulfilling . . . what? Aaron, I loved you for who you *were*."

"But not very much," he said bitterly. "You didn't love me very much, Livia."

She looked away.

"But you're right that it's too late, because that version of me is dead. I surpassed myself." He smiled a bit wistfully. "I'm finally the man I always wanted to be. Next, is to become the god I want to become."

"You're not joining . . . that . . ."

He nodded. "Those of us who form the Book's new kernel will put in service for a thousand subjective years—a thousand years in paradise. Then we will be allowed to muster out, into new bodies with powers equal to Choronzon's. A thousand subjective years in the kernel will only equal a few decades in real-time, Livia. And at the end of it all: godhood."

"Suicide," she spat.

"The annies are right about one thing," he said, unperturbed. "Humanity is fated to be surpassed. But they want to be the ones to surpass us. I want us to give birth to our own transcended selves. It's a big difference."

No, she thought, *it's no difference at all*. But she no longer had the heart to argue.

They spiraled down toward the center of the crowd. There sat the eschatus machine, in a network of cables suspended above the crowd. Several figures stood on meshwork next to it. They watched as the aircars settled in to land.

"Take me back to my ship," Livia said as panic rose up in her. "Aaron, please, for the sake of everything we ever meant to one another, don't do this. If you're a sovereign individual now then you can make your own choices, you don't have to follow the orders of this thing you don't even believe exists. Let me go. Let me take the tech locks somewhere safe. Then you can do whatever you like."

He shook his head. They were landing now. "The locks can only hold us back," he said, as he swung back the canopy.

Livia sat frozen for a long time. Then, feeling so many eyes on her, she stepped out onto the metal meshwork where Filament stood with her friends, and Maren Ellis and the dejected members of her delegation.

24

"LIVIA, IT'S SO good to see you. And Sophia, what a surprise, how are you?" Filament smiled with apparently genuine warmth. "I'm so glad you could attend today's event. The hopes and dreams of this, my constituency," she nodded at the crowd, "will finally be realized."

The aircars spiraled back into the sky. Livia stood on a small platform ten meters above the crowd of sleepwalkers. Now that she was closer, she could see the filmy, transparent outlines of tall spidery creatures stepping carefully over the sleepers' heads, ministering to their physical needs. Farther away, something she'd taken for a tree shifted and shook itself a little; it was one of Raven's monsters, settled in the crowd like a rock in a stream.

"What is this?" Sophia was staring out at the assembly in horror.

"Really, Filament, you don't need these people." Surprisingly, it was Lucius Xavier saying this. He had a protective hand on Maren Ellis's shoulder. Ellis herself had a poisonous look on her face. Maybe the hand was there to keep her from leaping at Filament.

Filament stood with one hand against the blue curve of the eschatus machine. She pouted at Lucius. "Oh, please," she said. "It's not about me. It's all about these people and what they want. And this will be my last chance to speak on their behalf. The time for words is almost passed."

She smiled fondly out at the crowd. "But I—that is, *they*—hated to leave you full of misapprehensions and hate. They believe in reconciliation—well, maybe it's me and my nature as a vote. We would like to make things better between us before we transcend."

Emblaze visibly started. "Before you—what?"

"I'll be the seed around which the new 3340 crystalizes," said Filament. "You should have figured that out, at least."

"Don't tell me all this was your idea?" asked Emblaze.

Filament preened. "Who am I, really?" she said. "I represent the Good Book. I can only do what it directs. Of course, the Book was specifically designed to go around the votes and the Government, which has always presented me with a bit of a problem. You might say I've had to . . . loosely interpret what the Book wants."

Emblaze laughed. "You were rejected by the Book. It didn't need you. But you're a vote, you had to find a way to serve your constituency even if it didn't want you. The only way you could see to do it was to *become* the Book."

"Don't sell me short," said Filament. "There were lots of options open to me. And of all the Book's followers, only I could see deeply enough to realize where it had come from, because it's in my nature to perceive the sum of my constituents' actions. I saw that my constituency's . . . style . . . bore a striking resemblance to that of the rebel anecliptic who'd been destroyed just before I was born. Once I realized that connection I could see everything. I knew its intentions had been to conquer the Archipelago; so those became my intentions. I knew it had keys to places inaccessible to ordinary votes. The pass codes for the Lethe Nebula are encoded in subtle overtones of behavior that the Book brings out in large crowds. The numbers emerge when you get ten, twenty million people using the Book together. And many other things emerge as well—if you know how to look."

To Livia's surprise, Cicada stepped forward. "You're crazy. Conquer the Archipelago? Topple the annies? How are you going to do that?"

Filament squinted at him. "Do I know you?"

Aaron spoke. "By making the annies irrelevant, that's how. It's already happening; people all over the Archipelago are doing what they think their role should do, and switching roles as conditions warrant—and everything's running smoothly. They don't need to consult the Government or listen to the votes. For the first time in their lives, they feel like they're in control."

"And the annies?" asked Livia. She was looking past Filament to the buildings at the edge of the crowd. Tiny figures were moving there, along with larger bots who were dragging some strange-looking machines.

"The annies have been caught napping," said Aaron, "by an enemy with no face."

"Caught napping?" Livia shot back. "And yet, you haven't asked me how it is we were able to return here. Whose help would we have needed?"

Aaron fell silent, but Filament just laughed. "Choronzon is coming," she said. "So Maren Ellis tells me. He thinks he's going to liberate Teven Coronal—and he's right. But we have no more need of it. While he's busy doing that, the newborn god will have escaped back into the Archipelago, where it can confront the annies on their own ground.

"Listen," she said, "I'm telling you this because I want people to understand what happened here today—how things came about. Your stories are important, that's why you have to survive and tell the world."

Sophia's shoulders slumped. "Then you're not keeping us here when you set off that . . . thing?"

"Not you, no," said Filament. "Nor you," she said to Maren Ellis, "because you reek of the tech locks. I won't let you infect the kernel with them, however much you might deserve to be one of us. But you deserve the opportunity to stay," she said to Lucius Xavier, "for your adaptability. And so do you," she said to Livia, "for your courage. You proved your sheer audacity when you flew all the way to the Archipelago to find help for your people. That courage would be valuable if you started using the Book regularly."

"What if I don't want to use it?" asked Livia past a tight throat.

"Who else would you rather serve?" asked Filament. "Because that's your choice now, you know: whether to serve the annies as represented by Lady Ellis and Choronzon—or humanity as represented by the Book."

"Did you know this was what she was planning?" Livia asked Aaron.

"No," he said. "But I'm happy that you're being given the chance." She looked away in scorn and disbelief, but he pressed on: "No, listen, Liv. Our whole life we've lived in a world of softened edges and easy decisions. All except once. One time, when someone had to look at the world through adult eyes and even the grown-ups who survived the crash with us failed the test. Someone had to look at the world as it was, and make the hard decisions that were necessary—not to romanticize, not to retreat into illusions. You did it then. I'm asking you to do it again. See what's really going on here. See what's *real*."

He held out his hand. "Come with me, Livia. We can be immortal. All these things you're fighting for—the agonies of the past, the honor of Westerhaven, even who's right and who's wrong—these aren't real. They're just abstractions. I need you to do now what you did before: be the adult. See what's real, and make your decision accordingly."

"You're lying," she said evenly. "You've lied to me every day since we escaped the crash. It wasn't me who led everyone out of the zone. It was you. And why? I've been wracking my brains to figure it out. But it's really quite simple, isn't it? The hardest thing is to live with the consequences of your actions. You weren't afraid to be heroic at the time—but you were terrified of having to live up to your own reputation afterward."

He looked horrified. "You know? But, Livy, I only wanted to protect you. Because—"

"You thought you'd made me, and that I was fragile as glass. That if I found out, I might break. The way you broke the day you realized the kinds of roles your strength was going to condemn you to if Westerhaven found out about your heroism."

"I wanted to be author of my own fate," he said. "And yes, I made you what you are. And look what you've done! Listen to me now, Livia. I was right then, I'm right now."

She shook her head. "Only the dead are free of the influence of others," she said. "Everyone I ever met helped make me. I am them, and I am this place and these people, and I can no more step out of that reality than you can escape yourself.

"I reject your offer," she said to Filament.

But Filament was no longer listening. Nobody was.

They were all staring downward, to where the sleepwalkers had fallen over.

They had been knocked off their feet in one scything sweep that reminded Livia of when the votes had collapsed around her in Doran's plaza. The sighing sound of the fall filtered upward like distant thunder, and now Livia spotted dust pluming up at various places around the city. Moments later a distant grumbling sound rolled in. It didn't diminish with the seconds, but grew instead into a deafening roar.

Livia caught Filament's eye. She knew the vote would be able to read her lips as she said, "Time's up."

In every direction, on the outskirts of the city, dark clouds leapt up. As they cascaded outward the ground shook and twisted; buildings were leaning everywhere. With majestic slowness, a ring of anecliptic battleships rose like vast towers around the city. They had punctured the skin of the coronal like the teeth of some unimaginably huge monster; chunks of landscape and whole trees dribbled from their points as they shuddered to a halt high overhead.

Lucius was pointing and shouting something. In the seconds before the vibrations racing along the cables made the platform buck under her, Livia looked up.

Tiny, but perfectly etched against the sky, a single human figure stood in the air above the city. Choronzon had come.

THE SCULPTURAL SHAPES of Raven's monsters shook themselves to life all around the park. One by one they leaped into the sky. Livia had little time to watch this as the cable network she was balanced on was swinging and bouncing under her like it was alive.

"Take us down! Down!" Filament was shouting. Flickers of light punctuated her words; Livia glanced up in time to see a strand of cable snap in a bright flash. Someone was using lasers to cut Cirrus's lines. Even as she realized this, the meshwork fell two meters and stopped with a sharp shock.

Filament hung on to a line like an old-time ship captain weathering a storm. "Protect the kernel at all costs!"

Livia lost her grip on the meshwork. She left trails of blood from where it had cut her fingers as she slid down the now steeply-angled surface. Then Qiingi's hand caught her wrist and he hauled her up.

"Must leave," he shouted. Livia shook her head.

"I need to get to Maren—tell her about the locks—"

A battle was erupting in the air above Barrastea. As the cableways of Cirrus lifted their floating towers and houses out of harm's way, Raven's monsters and other things Livia had never seen before hopped or shot into the air. Most vanished in fireballs before they cleared the rooftops. Sharp detonations peppered the air, their thunderous echoes rolling around and around the city. A dark mist was rising from the crowd of sleepwalkers: a shield of angel-stuff meters thick. Through the angle of her scrabbling legs Livia saw a flickering line of laser light hit that fog just meters below her, and flash into white fire. The sleepwalkers were now rising to their feet again, and none had been touched by the laser shot.

Swarms of dark specks poured out of the towering anecliptic battleships. Explosions spiraled around them like the sparks from a fire as 3340's forces engaged with the liberators. The air was filled with a steady, undifferentiated roar.

In the midst of this chaos the cable meshwork jerked down a few more meters, then settled majestically onto the crowd. None of the sleepwalkers tried to get out of the way; Livia screamed in horror as the eschatus machine landed on a knot of oblivious people, crushing them under its weight.

"A bit of an inconvenience," Filament shouted as she stepped over dying people. She ran her hands over the flanks of the machine. "The blast won't be able to physically absorb the people on the edges of the crowd. That's okay; it should still copy them into the kernel." She found what she was looking for: a large hatch swung open in the side of the eschatus machine. "Ah, well, looks like you're coming with me after all," said the vote as she reached up to pull herself into the sphere.

"No!" Livia and Qiingi were both on their feet, but Cicada was faster. He leapt at Filament. A meter away he was knocked aside in a violent explosion. Aaron stood up from where he'd been kneeling on the ground. He was holding a gun whose barrel was now wrapped in smoke.

"Time for hard decisions, Livy," he snapped. Cicada thrashed on the ground, still trying to stand despite having his legs blown off.

They faced each other tensely, Aaron between Filament and the others. Livia and Qiingi exchanged a glance; she could tell he was also wondering whether they could overwhelm Aaron before he could get them. It didn't seem likely.

The crowd of sleepwalkers had been flattened by the fall of the eschatus machine's wire nest for a distance of six meters or so in every direction. A woman near Livia's foot moaned; a cable as thick as her wrist lay stretched taut across her lower back.

Livia was about to chance an attack on Aaron when someone stepped out of the crowded sleepwalkers behind Filament. Livia had time to realize that it was a man and that he was holding a sword before Doran Morss leaped up and buried the blade in Filament's back.

She didn't even cry out as Doran used the sword like a lever to drag her bodily out of the machine. As they hit the ground Aaron whirled to look and Lucius Xavier tackled him from the side.

Livia caught only confused glimpses as she ran over to Maren Ellis: Doran hacking like a madman; Lucius and Aaron rolling over the dead and dying in the shadow of the sphere; Qiingi and Emblaze squaring off against Kale and his men. Livia grabbed Maren's arm. "Listen," she said, "Rene and the peers have brought tech lock machines to the edge of the park. I don't know what their range is, but you might be able to activate them from here—"

Maren snatched her arm out of Livia's grasp. "You couldn't leave well enough alone, could you!" she hissed.

"Use the locks!" Livia half drew her own sword, which 3340's men had contemptuously let her keep.

Maren turned away, scowling, then closed her eyes and appeared to concentrate.

Livia turned back to the fight—in time to see Lucius stumbling back from Aaron, who was raising his weapon. "No!" she yelled, but too late as Aaron fired. Lucius spun around and fell. Livia ran to him.

As he gasped in her arms, Aaron waved his gun at Qiingi and Doran Morss, who were on their knees with Kale standing over them. Peaseblossom was tending to Cicada. "Up! Stand up!" Aaron commanded.

"Shut up, Aaron," said Livia. She didn't care if he shot her.

Lucius quivered. She smoothed back his lion's mane of hair, which was drenched in blood.

He looked up at her, terror in his eyes. "Please, Livia. Don't let me be remembered as a traitor," he whispered. Then he coughed once and she laid him back as gently as she could.

Filament staggered to her feet. One of her arms hung uselessly, and she had deep gashes and stab wounds across her upper body. One bisected her face, distorting her features hideously; but there was no blood.

"Nice . . . try," she slurred, glaring at Doran Morss. He sneered at her.

"Decided not to leave after all," he said. "Found a sword its owner wasn't using . . . Glad I stuck around."

"Hold them for one minute, and it'll all be over," croaked Filament. She turned back to the eschatus machine.

"Over, yes," said Maren Ellis. "Take a look, Filament!" She swept her arm in a wide arc, encompassing the park and the sleepwalkers—

—Who were suddenly awake. A crowd of a million or more souls abruptly found itself alert and cut off from the fantasy realm of the Book, with explosions and fire above and to all sides. All Livia could see for an instant were hundreds of eyes in panicked faces. Then there was screaming and motion everywhere.

Aaron turned and gave Filament a hoist into the eschatus machine. Kale had backed up against it, shock and fear on his face. "I shut down inscape for a mile around!" shouted Maren recklessly. "Your precious dream world has been snuffed out like a candle!"

Aaron growled in fury and once again swung his gun up. "Bring it back or I'll kill you," he said.

"Put down that toy, little boy," she said. Aaron pulled the trigger, but nothing happened. He cursed and threw the gun down. Maren laughed at him; then Aaron reached down and snapped up the sword Doran

Morss had dropped. He stepped forward and, with a single slash, cut Maren Ellis's throat.

Maren's face showed pure surprise as the impact knocked her into the hurricane of rioting people. She vanished in a whirl of flailing limbs and screaming faces.

Aaron stood staring after her. His hands were shaking; but all the anger had drained out of him. He seemed to be trying to say something.

Deafening thunder rolled out of the sky. The anecliptic and Book forces had been fighting a delicate battle overhead, neither side willing to risk killing the helpless people below. Now the black and red nightmares of Raven's people were diving out of the air, sending bolts of fire toward the edge of the park. In seconds the tech lock generators would be destroyed.

"This way!" Peaseblossom slapped Livia on the back. He was carrying Cicada across his shoulders like a sack of grain. He jerked his chin to the left, where Livia saw Doran Morss and Qiingi standing back to back, swords drawn. They were guarding a crumpled catwalk that lay across the ground—just why, she couldn't tell for a few moments.

Then she raised her eyes and saw that the catwalk was affixed to a cable that had not completely touched down. It rose slowly across a hundred meters until it was above the heads of the crowd, and its far end draped over the top of a building outside the park.

"Come on!" Qiingi pushed into the hysterical mob and the others followed. Livia found herself flanked by Peaseblossom on one side and Emblaze on the other. Both struck out fiercely to protect her as they edged their way along the catwalk.

She looked back at the eschatus machine. Aaron stood next to it, oblivious to the crowd, watching her. She met his eyes for a second, then turned away.

Staggering and pulling, they made it up the cable and above the heads of the crowd. Livia ran along the catwalk, and as she ran she found she was singing—no one song, just nonsense scraps, anything she could think of to drown out the screaming of the crowd below her.

Silence fell as if a switch had been thrown and for a few seconds all Livia could hear was her own ragged voice wailing the chorus to some old ditty. Then she staggered to a stop and looked down.

The sleepwalkers had frozen in place, like bots with their power cut off. In midscream, midblow, they had stopped as inscape came back on. All across the park those who had fallen were standing and those standing lowered their arms to their sides and closed their mouths.

"Hell," said Doran. "She's gonna set it off. Hurry!" He ran up the steepening slope of the catwalk without looking back.

They made it to the edge of the park without any apocalyptic blast, though Livia's shoulders itched in anticipation. They were able to hop down off the catwalk to the roof and clamber into the building through a shattered upstairs window. And they made it down to the street without incident.

The echoes of the battle were fading. Chunks of smoldering black and crimson monster lay everywhere as Livia stepped into the road and looked back at the crowd. The flying creatures from the anecliptic fleet were circling directly above the eschatus machine now, firing their lasers down into the black fog that had coalesced densely around it. But everywhere else, the battle seemed to be winding down.

Doran glanced over at Livia, and seemed to see her for the first time. "Haver!"

"Not Haver," she snapped. "Kodaly."

"Kodaly . . ." His eyes widened with apparent recognition. "So that's what . . ."

In the next street, they found the bodies of Westerhaven's peers among the blackened remains of tech lock machinery. It seemed too late for shock or sorrow, even when Livia spotted the face of Rene Caiser on one of the bodies.

As they stood gazing at the carnage, a shadow flickered across the road. Livia instinctively ducked; she heard laughter from above, and then Choronzon the god was touching down lightly not three meters away.

He looked untroubled by the death and destruction, his hair perhaps in a bit more boyish disarray than usual. He bowed to the silent group and said, "At your service, madam, sirs. I heard you needed a bit of liberating, so I thought I'd drop in."

His callousness made Livia want to throw up.

Emblaze had also recovered her poise. "We're grateful for your help," she said to Choronzon.

"Are we?" snapped Livia. "That remains to be seen." She stepped in front of Emblaze. "Choronzon, I don't want to appear ungrateful, but I'd like to know what you're going to do now that Teven's been retaken."

"Do?" He looked innocently surprised at the question.

"Who rules here now?" she asked bluntly. "Will you leave us in peace to restore the manifolds? Or did you make some other arrangement with the annies while you were on your way here?"

"Livia Kodaly." He shook his head sadly. "You don't know when's the wrong time to pick a fight, do you? I've just taken this world, Liv. Leave it to those of us who accomplished that—those of us who made this world in the first place!—to decide what will happen next."

"In other words," she said, "you're not going to leave us alone. Are you?"

He crossed his arms. "Things will have to change, certainly."

"No more manifolds?"

"No more manifolds. I didn't like the results of that experiment. Maren went too far."

"Maybe. But it wasn't all bad. The tech locks . . ."

"Are officially banned. I'll be wiping every last repository that might hold their plans before I leave. And the annies have agreed that Teven Coronal should join the rest of the Archipelago. Of course, there's the little problem of what to do about that," he crooked a thumb at the distant eschatus machine, "and about the Good Book in general. We'll have a fight on our hands, no doubt about it. But I'm sure we'll win. And then we'll build better firebreaks. Ones that will hold for a million years."

Livia looked at Qiingi. He gazed back despairingly and in his eyes she saw the death of Ometeotl. Choronzon was talking about the end of any human person's right to decide the shape of their own world. By the time he was done, an invincible tyranny would have settled over the human race, for all time. What was that term the versos used to describe it? Wallpaper: an endless repeating pattern of identical lives. If men and women could no longer select the technologies that would frame their lives, the Archipelago might remain a wondrous, dazzling place to live but it would never change. No man like Qiingi would ever exist again because no place like Raven's country could exist. Neither would there be drummers, nor the slow measured beat of lives lived in the dreamtime of Oceanus.

"I think it's about to go off," Emblaze said, pointing.

They turned to look; the black cloud was beginning to glow an electric blue. A faint hissing sound reached Livia's ears in the eerie postbattle silence.

"You'd better be going," said Choronzon. "I'll deal with whatever comes out of that explosion."

Livia was no longer listening. She looked around at the others: Emblaze and her lads, Qiingi, Doran Morss, and the haggard, shattered Sophia. She turned to gaze across the skyline of Barrastea, and thought of the strange twist of fate that had made her the Ariadne to Westerhaven's lost people. It was a fate she would never have chosen for herself, but it was a fate she could no longer avoid or deny.

There was only one place left where the tech locks might be preserved. It was the one place she most feared to go.

Livia still had the little inscape jamming device in her pocket. She drew it out now and stared at it. "Doran, what will get copied by the eschatus machine?" she murmured. "Just minds? Or implants and their contents, too?"

"What?" said Choronzon.

"Everything," said Doran. "A data map of all objects and persons within the blast radius."

She couldn't help but meet Choronzon's eye. He appeared puzzled for a second, and then as the light of understanding dawned in his eyes Livia yelled to her lads, "Take him down!"

Then she turned and sprinted up the street.

She had no chance to glance back to see if Peaseblossom dropped Cicada and tackled the self-styled god; nor to see the expression on Qiingi's face as he yelled and belatedly pursued her. Livia clipped the inscape jammer to her ear without pausing; she kept her eyes fixed on the crowd, above which a blue sun was rising and eating away the whole world, even the ground itself as she hit the edge of the throng and pushed her way in—

THE CONCUSSION KNOCKED them to their knees, all save Choronzon who stood upright, a black knifelike shadow scoring back a dozen meters behind him. A wall of flame reared up along the perimeter of the park. Sophia Eckhardt watched in horror, knowing that it was men and women feeding that fire. Qiingi ran into the holocaust and disappeared, and Livia's creatures—Peaseblossom and Emblaze—followed him.

The fire licked up once or twice more and died, and the bright light from the center of the park went out. Sophia blinked away afterimages and stared.

Where two million people had stood, the ground was bare and black—more than that, the very soil was stripped away, revealing the glossy skin of the coronal. There was nothing there at all, except at the very edge of the circle, where blackened bodies lay piled, and at the very center, where a single incandescent human form danced.

Choronzon kicked away Cicada, who had kept him from leaping into the air for the crucial seconds it had taken Livia Kodaly to run into the holocaust. Now he rose into the sky, cursing.

The distant figure stopped dancing. It was hard to tell, but it might have been looking in their direction. Suddenly it jumped up, for all the world like a diver, and with a bright flash a circular piece of coronal skin imploded below it. It shot through the opening and disappeared as a vortex of wind formed above the hole.

Choronzon flew after it, disappearing through what turned out to be a hole straight through the coronal into space. Hours later he returned, as people began emerging from their homes to meet the anecliptic bots that now patrolled the streets. He came empty-handed.

Thirty-three forty had escaped.

25

"IT'S HERE," SAID Cicada. "Just keep walking, you're there now."

"Thanks." Doran Morss shook hands with the AI. Cicada walked away whistling. He wore workman's clothes today and had a five-o'clock shadow. Doran shook his head. Was Livia Kodaly's former agent sentient now? It was impossible to know—but he and Peaseblossom had made lives for themselves. They seemed content.

Doran walked between the pair of hedges Cicada had brought him to. Here the Kodaly estate began. He realized without surprise that he had crossed these grounds several times over the past few days. Like so many places in Teven, the chambers of the Kodaly family were both private and public—wide open to any visitor, yet opaque to any investigation. Pilgrims had begun to come here from all over the Archipelago, hoping to somehow touch the real life of Livia. In her sim, Doran had learned she was a minor legend in Westerhaven. Now, she was a figure of myth throughout the Archipelago. So it was fitting that, like her, even the Kodaly estate itself faded away from those trying to reach it. Doran could have spent weeks walking in circles without ever being let in. He was grateful entry had been as easy as it seemed to have been.

In some sense, the estate had always been like this. Even the architecture played with ideas of identity: many buildings in this vicinity had been constructed without walls or roofs, while tapestries of ivy and soaring multicolored sails made of tough tenting cast new definitions of in and out in the gardens themselves. At some point you just gave over to it and stopped trying to define where you were.

Maybe he'd have found the place himself if he'd ever learned to stop looking.

Now that he was here, he had no trouble finding Livia's parents in a green-walled bower deep within the estate. They were sipping tea at a wrought-iron table. Bees hummed around the marmalade. The two elders of the Kodaly clan smiled in recognition as Doran approached, and Livia's father stood to summon up another chair.

"How are you, Mr. Morss?" Livia's mother poured him something hot in a fine china cup. He took it, noting the cadences of her accent, the unique patterning on the china. "I'm well, thanks," he said. This was no sim, nor any narrative.

"What news of your world?" Mr. Kodaly asked.

"It's hard to be sure of anything these days," he said ruefully. "The anecliptics are trying to break up 3340 by garbling all long-range communications. It seems to be working; I think the Book is losing ground. Of course, 3340 has a body now, and defeating that is proving to be a bit more of a problem. Not that I care; since the annies and the Government are totally tied up battling 3340, there's a power vacuum in the Archipelago. I've been taking advantage of that to . . . pursue a new line of work."

Mr. Kodaly did not ask what that work was. "Does Teven Coronal play some part in your plans, Mr. Morss?"

"It has to do with the tech locks," he said.

"But the tech locks were destroyed," said Mr. Kodaly with a cryptic smile.

There was a brief pause. Faint city sounds infiltrated the little bower, gentle reminders of the bustle and liveliness available just a few paths away. The morning sunlight was slanting farther toward vertical, but neither of the Kodalys seemed inclined to pick up the thread of the conversation.

Finally Doran said, "I've been doing a little touring around since I got here. It looks like you've fully restored Barrastea. The museum's reopened. As an outsider I can't say, but it looks like Westerhaven is back to the way it was."

Mr. Kodaly smiled wryly. "Oh, no, it'll never be that. We've had our balloon punctured, Mr. Morss. All manner of strange outside influences are pouring into Teven these days. And anyway, this," he gestured around himself, "isn't Westerhaven. Westerhaven was a particular performance we put on, with ourselves as the audience. Nowadays we're being asked to perform it for tourists from the Archipelago. That's a totally different thing. No . . ." He peered away down a corridor of vine-topped trestles. "We haven't given a name to this manifold yet. We may never get around to it."

Doran narrowed his eyes skeptically. "I know you tell everyone that you're not using tech locks here. But I visited Raven's people yesterday. They have no aircars, no long-distance communications . . . It sure looks like the locks are working there."

Mr. Kodaly shrugged. "The locks are an idea first, a technology second. We don't need the machinery to live much the way we once did. We only need commitment. In some ways that's better, isn't it?"

Doran sat back, musing. "Maybe. And yet the locks do exist. In fact—here, let me show you." He leaned forward and gestured open an inscape window. Within that window shone a seemingly endless ocean of flickering lines and labeled boxes—an abstract maelstrom of information. They all gazed into it for a second, then Doran dismissed it.

"I thought I might need something to move the conversation along," said Doran. "So I brought the status interface for the locks with me. Yes, I carry a copy of the locks around wherever I go these days. Can you guess where I found it?"

They sat attentively. Neither said anything. "Up until last year," continued Doran, "the only person in any world who had access to that interface—or even knew it existed—was Maren Ellis. She'd appropriated all the manifolds' utilities for herself. But with this I can monitor the health of the system. Or communicate with an active, local instance of the locks. Which I did this morning. The locks are running right now," he said. "They are all around us, even in this garden. So you see you don't have to give me the official line. I know the truth."

Doran realized suddenly that Mr. Kodaly was no longer represented by an anima: it was the real man sitting across from him, his features rendered a bit abstract by the play of dappled leaf-light across his brow. He seemed to be smiling.

"So what is it that you've come here to do?" asked Livia's father.

"I'm merely continuing my work." Doran stood up and restlessly paced over to the close-clipped hedges. "Ever heard the term 'open-source government'? That's what we have in the Archipelago. The Government and votes are open to anyone to examine and tinker with, they're totally under our control. I used to think that the kind of freedom they gave us was enough—and I used to blame the post-humans for the dissatisfaction with the status quo that, well, we all felt on some level. But it wasn't transcendence of the human condition that people were longing for. It was something else, something that the tech locks make possible."

"Not open-source government," said Mrs. Kodaly. "But open-source reality?"

He stared at her. She smiled and patted her mouth modestly with a napkin. "Because technologies are control systems," she said. "They dictate your reality. Really, Mr. Morss, we've known this for hundreds of years."

Doran returned and sat down. "How did you do it? Choronzon swore he would destroy the locks, and he did, didn't he? I was here, I saw it done."

"Yes," said Mrs. Kodaly blandly. She picked up her tea and sipped it, staring off through the humming air of summer.

Doran pressed on. "So we must assume that someone escaped with the locks' technology before he arrived, and returned with it once he was gone."

"That sounds reasonable," said Mr. Kodaly.

"Funny thing," said Doran.

The silence stretched. Finally, Mrs. Kodaly said, "What do you mean?"

"Funny thing," he repeated. "Because we know that didn't happen. Once the annies knew 3340 was using Teven, they locked down the entire Lethe Nebula. Nobody got out while Choronzon was here. So the tech locks couldn't have survived."

"Oh?"

"And yet," continued Doran, "lately, all over the Archipelago, little pockets of . . . I don't know what to call them—super sims? Autonomous zones? . . . Manifolds? Call them manifolds, though they're much more open than the ones you had here—well, little pockets keep popping up. Somebody's distributing the tech locks throughout the Archipelago, they slip past even the best firewalls the annies can come up with. I found my copy on Mercury. And the really funny thing—the truly hilarious, gut-bustingly hysterical thing is, *that they only appear in areas where 3340 has taken control.*"

Now they were watching him closely. They knew something, he was sure of it. "I've been traveling around the Archipelago trying to figure out what's going on," said Doran. "It may not please you to hear me speak of your daughter . . ." They waited politely. "But then, you have your animas to intercede for you if you become upset by what I'm about to say."

Neither spoke. Doran shrugged and said, "Livia Kodaly was one of those copied into the eschatus machine; we know that. A version of her mind exists inside 3340's new body, along with two million others. But while they're all working hard to create the mind of 3340, is it possible that Livia has another purpose?

"She can't be rooted out; maybe she hides from the rest of the true believers who make up 3340's mind, I don't know. But what I do know is that every now and then, when 3340 lets down his guard, Livia Kodaly finds a way to slip a copy of the tech locks out into the real world."

Mrs. Kodaly smiled down at her hands.

"But 3340 was never *here*," said Doran. "The embodied version Livia joined fled immediately after it was born. And the annies have sworn not to allow the tech locks to spread through inscape by any ordinary means. After all, the locks let anybody opt out of the annies' version of the Archipelago."

"Perhaps they haven't been able to stop the spread," said Mr. Kodaly.

"Well, yes they have—up until now. Cracks are just starting to appear in the annies' firewalls. I had the devil of a time smuggling my own copy of the locks back here. I thought that I'd be the first one to return here with them. But they're already here.

"So how did the tech locks return to Teven?"

There. He'd asked the question he'd come to ask, and Livia Kodaly's parents were not offended nor alarmed, indifferent nor suspicious. To his surprise, in fact, the Kodalys were both smiling at him. He sat back, puzzled, and waited.

Mr. Kodaly glanced at his wife. She shrugged. He leaned forward. "Have you heard anything of the warrior of Raven, this man Qiingi?"

Doran sat up straight. "He vanished. The last I saw, he was chasing Livia into the eschatus machine's blast radius. I don't think he made it before it went off. So the residual effects of the blast would have killed him instantly."

Mr. Kodaly nodded. "Some people say they saw Qiingi walk *out* of the blast area afterwards. Carrying someone."

The sunlight, buzzing insects, the tea all seemed unreal suddenly. "She's alive," murmured Doran.

Livia's father shook his head. "Alive? Be careful how you use such words here. We are within the manifolds, Mr. Morss. You might meet our daughter anywhere—walking on the street, even. But how could you be sure it was really her? How can you know it of any of us? We love masks, after all." This last statement was made by an anima; the real Jason Kodaly had retired into some submanifold. Moments later, his wife did the same.

Doran sat with the two animas, swirling his tea and scowling. Had Livia become like the Kodaly estate?—a mirage to be chased, never found? Was she really here somewhere, alive and happy, perhaps no more than ten meters away?

He slammed the cup down and stalked away from the table.

Yet, when Doran came to the edge of the estate, he found himself reluctant to step beyond it. The boundary was invisible, of course; indeterminate, even. He knew that if he walked past the corner where he now stood and lost himself in the crowd, Livia's home would evaporate behind him, and he was half certain he would never find it again.

He turned and slowly strolled back the way he'd come. Each shaded bower and stone cottage he passed could contain anything or anyone; the whole Archipelago was layered in illusion, yet here it seemed he was more aware than ever of invisible lives lived just out of reach. That covered walkway there might contain armchairs and tables invisible to him, where patriarchs of the Kodalys older than Livia's parents still sat. Conversations might be going on all around him, all infinitely removed. Yet the impression was not of people hiding; it was more that in this place, time did not move inexorably forward, but layered its moments one on top of the other. If you knew how, you could tunnel through the layers and find the moment you needed—the pipe smoke still swirling, the laughter of lost decades still echoing.

His anger dissolved as he walked through sun and shade. And perhaps this was the condition that a particular lock had set for him: that he should never be able to find Livia while driven by anger. For as he strolled, hands in pockets, admiring the stonework, he glanced up at random and found himself looking straight at her.

Livia Kodaly was walking, head down, arms crossed, along a flagstone path. She looked over as he approached, and smiled.

Doran's inscape interface couldn't tell him if this was a real person, an anima, or an agent. Something was spoofing her identity. So he stopped several meters away from her, his own arms crossed, and grimaced in frustration. "Hiding in plain sight again, I see."

She laughed. "Still demanding definite answers, I see. How are you, Doran?"

He stuck out his hand to shake, but she opened her arms and hugged him. Whatever her state of being, she felt real just now. When they disengaged he stepped back, unsure of himself now that he was here.

A thousand questions crowded: Had she survived the eschatus machine, being on the edge of the blast radius? Was the warrior Qiingi alive as well? And most of all, was she behind the strange appearance of manifolds across the Archipelago?

"How are you?" she asked.

He opened his mouth and closed it again. "I . . . I don't know," he said, surprised at his own honesty. "I showed the worst side of myself when I was here last. The cowardly side. Since then . . . I've become a smuggler, did you know that? I'm helping distribute tech lock technology throughout the solar system." He grinned at her. "You never knew, but I fell in love with Westerhaven when I visited the *Life of Livia*." *I fell in love with you.* "So I'm trying to make places like it in the Archipelago. Manifolds. I've become a hero to the versos. And the versos are becoming something new. They're like the seeds around which new values are crystalizing—"

"Founders?" she asked.

"Yes! I've given my *Scotland* to some of them, you should see the manifold they're crafting there, Livia. Hard lives they're trying to lead—but *theirs*."

"And what's yours, Doran?" she asked as she began strolling again. "What do you own?"

"Shame," he said. "And determination. But I guess those have been what drove me all along."

They walked together; she did not vanish in the sunlight. "Your vote is riding high these days," he said after a while. "She represents the new manifolds and her constituency is huge. And there are wars going on, Livia, between the annies and the followers of the Book . . ." He shook his head. "But you don't care, do you? You've been hiding here in your garden, and you don't care what happens to the rest of the world."

"That's not true," she murmured. "The Government hired me to be a baseline, remember? It's just that I'm not the baseline for the Government's reality anymore. Nor am I for crippleview. I've become a goal for people like you who are trying to find their way out of the one-sided reality of the Archipelago. Naturally you can't see me as long as you still live inside that view."

She smiled. "I'm a founder now, Doran, and my manifold is vast. You just haven't found your way there yet."

Desperately, he said, "But aren't you really here? Can't I see you? I came all this way just to see you."

"To see who, exactly?" she asked. "The Livia of the *Life of Livia*? The hero of the far side accident? The guide who led the peers out of fallen Westerhaven? The rescuer, who returned to chase the villains out of Teven? Or is it Alison Haver you're looking for?" She shook her head. "I could have stood back and let you meet one of those; but then you wouldn't have found *me*."

"And is this the real you? Or just another mask?"

Sadly, she turned away. "You haven't understood the first thing about manifolds, have you? It's not me who's put the mask on my face. It's *you*."

For a while Doran walked with her, confused and wondering. Finally she looked back, and her expression softened a bit. "Let me tell you a story," she said. "You won't find this one in the *Life of Livia*. Nobody's ever heard it before.

"What have I had that's truly mine? What was it that *I* wanted? In my old life, here, I was unhappy with the peers, and Aaron's radical pronouncements rang a false note with me, too. I didn't have the words to explain my feelings to myself or anybody else, then. But you could see it all around you, in the peers fighting duels over fine points of aesthetics, or planning grand cities and works to renew Westerhaven when and if they came to power. They fought over a million different issues, but it always came down to one thing: How could we find a balance between our own uniqueness and our place in the world? Should we try to liberate ourselves from the constraints that the world and the previous generation had placed on us—and maybe abandon reality entirely—or should we throw away our creative souls and conserve the world that was? Westerhaven was always in a tug-of-war between those two poles, the liberal and the conservative.

"Well, before the invasion—in fact, just days before I met with Lucius and he took me to Raven's country—I took an aircar up in the night. Nobody saw me leave Barrastea; even my agents were asleep. I touched down ever so gently on the edge of a forest and left the aircar. The trees made a canopy of complete black overhead so I navigated entirely by inscape, walking into a wood alone, at night, far from family and friends.

"And as I walked I began to sing, and as I sang a different world opened before me. I had come to the manifold of the drummers—the manifold I had helped to save a few weeks before. When I emerged from the trees it was to see their towers still standing in the glow of the coronal's arch. Faintly, I could hear a single drum beating in the distance. It was very cold, the ground leeched all heat from your feet as you stepped through the spongy, wet grass. But I knew where I was going.

"Doran, nothing in the *Life of Livia* could hint at the feelings of freedom and fear I felt there, alone, breaking into a place that was currently guarded by the peers in daylight. My heart was pounding as I found the tower and walked up its steps in complete darkness.

"I replaced the water-worn drum of the last drummer with a new one I'd brought. Keeping the Drummers' manifold alive for another month or two was that simple. I secured the new drum and checked that the rains had topped up the cistern that dripped onto the skin. Then I walked back out again. It wasn't until I reached the outside that I paused for a minute to listen.

"Each drumbeat sounded clear and distinct. Each one rolled out into the night, reaching nobody's ears, but real nonetheless. It was a tremble of air, nothing more, yet in that tremble the drummers lived. In that tremble of air was something not of Westerhaven, not preserved by your Government or to be found in the narratives. Call it the Song of Ometeotl, if you wish. It remained in my ears as I stole back through the forest and returned in secret to my home."

She smiled at his astonished expression. "At the time I didn't know why I did it. It was one of those actions that you can't reconcile with the person you think you are. But now I understand. I was honoring the existence and dignity of a reality independent of my own.

"If you want to understand any of the decisions I've made, you have to start there."

Suddenly she laughed. "Don't look so serious, Doran. I've got everything I wanted. I have my music and the people I love around me. I'm part of a Society. I'm a part of my world, I'm not struggling against it the way you have your whole life."

He winced. But it was a fair comment. After a while he asked, "So what happens now? Do you vanish back into the manifolds again?"

She shook her head. "*You* vanish. But hopefully not forever. I'm glad you came to find me, Doran. Perhaps we'll meet again. For now, all I can offer you is my thanks for being my friend. The best way I know to do that is in music."

Livia grinned, and walking backward in front of him, she began to sing. She sang about youth and age, and the turn of the seasons. It was a song about change and acceptance, and the small human things that made up a day, or a life.

Livia sang; and as she sang she began to fade; and as she faded into the bright air, the song faded with her. In moments she was gone, leaving him alone with the whirring of the bees.

Doran shook his head and walked away. At first he felt only frustration. Was she alive or wasn't she? Had he just met some clever anima running on after its owner's death? Or did the real Livia still walk somewhere, perhaps not in this garden or even on this world—but somewhere?

When the answer came to him, it did so suddenly and with such force that he laughed in surprise. She'd said she had learned to honor the existence and dignity of a reality independent of her own. But how did you do that? Maybe the key was to refrain from trying to slot everything into your own categories, the way Choronzon and the annies did. *Alive* by Doran's definition; *dead* by his definition—could it be that Livia was neither of those things? He knew that she had opted out of the annies' version of reality. Was it so hard to accept that his own categories no longer applied to her either?

He walked on, strangely content. Ever since he had first encountered the masks and manifolds of Westerhaven in the *Life of Livia*, he had wondered why they seemed so familiar and yet so different from the views of the narratives. Now he finally understood. In this strange new world he was just beginning to discover, you did not bring reality to you. You went to it.

There was a way for him to meet Livia Kodaly again, if he wished to. All he would have to do was change.

Epilogue

AARON VARESE STOOD on a stone veranda looking out over his estate. He was sipping a cup of coffee, feeling tired but, for the moment, satisfied.

It had taken months of effort, but things were stabilizing. His world no longer changed daily. For a while after the Ascension of 3340, buildings, trees, people—all had shifted moment by moment. He'd thought he was going to go mad, and maybe he would have—if not for the Book.

He glanced back at the table where it rested, just a slight flutter of anxiety compelling him to make sure it was still there. In those first days, he'd clung to it like a life raft. He had always been good at using it, but he'd needed all his skills to ride out and eventually halt the mad chaos of images and memories that inscape had thrown at him. For weeks, he'd focused on nothing else, done nothing else but use the Book. And gradually, the madness had abated.

He could walk his virtual gardens in peace this evening, because he had spent the day masterfully using the Book. It didn't matter that he didn't understand the now-limited tableaux that came to him, or what his actions meant; what mattered was that they no longer took up every waking moment.

He had time now for peace—and melancholy. For while his estate was now stable around him, it was also a reminder of everything he'd given up.

"There you are!" Esther ran out and threw her arms around him. He hugged her fiercely. "I can't believe you're still real," she murmured into his shoulder.

"I am," he said. *She* was real—he was almost sure of it. For months his only companions had been animas from the Westerhaven he'd once knew. Esther Mannus's had been among them. They were merely actors who drew him into scenes that he escaped only by using the Book. Once he had used it properly, the men and women dissolved along with the props and sets of the scenario.

A few days ago, Esther had remained after a scene ended. She seemed as surprised and suspicious at this turn of events as he was. Only as the days passed, and they remained together, did they begin to wonder if the other was more than just an anima.

She was his reward—or he was hers. It didn't matter. What mattered was that the Book was merciful.

As the light reddened and vanished in a simulated sunset, he walked with her through scented grass and silence. He felt his heart swelling with some emotion—love? Gratitude? It was hard to separate feelings these days, when you were required to ride an emotional roller coaster all day long. The thought made him smile. "You're a refuge from the world," he said sincerely.

"And you," she said, sighing and shaking her head. "It wasn't meant to be this way, was it?"

"This crazy? No...I suppose the Ascended body is busy. Somewhere there're people assigned to be Eyes and Ears and so on. If things continue settling down, we should be able to track one of them down and find out what's going on in the outside world."

"I...heard a rumor today," she said. Laughing at his look of surprise, she added, "Yeah, people have time for rumors now!"

He shook his head in wonder. "Well—what was it?"

"That we're not alone in here," she murmured dramatically. "Us humans making up the kernel, that is. The rumor is, there's something else in here with us. I talked to a role who claimed to have *seen* it."

"Seen it? Seen what?"

"A human figure, beckoning in the distance. Something from outside the Book. The rumor is that somewhere there's an exit—a way out of the kernel, back to the real world. And for those who are ready, a guide will appear to lead them back."

Aaron turned away. He felt ill suddenly. In his few quiet moments, he'd had his own doubts about his decision to join with 3340—and he hated himself for it.

"This *is* our real world, Esther. This is what we chose." *It's too late to turn back.*

"I know, love." Her arms entwined his chest.

He relaxed a bit. "It just infuriates me that people should continue to want the impossible, even now when we have everything we ever wanted."

"Think of it as an echo of the past," she whispered. "Echoes go and return, and go and return. For a while. Only for a while..."

He closed his eyes, letting his shoulders slump. She was right, of course. So for a while he simply let himself stand there, eyes closed in her embrace, with warm sunset light on his face. She swayed slightly with him, and he heard a faint whisper of song. He knew the tune: what was it called again?

O night you were my guide...

It was something ancient. Ah, it would come to him in a moment—or an eternity. He had a thousand years to remember, after all.

O night more loving than the rising sun.

He smiled ruefully.

"That's 'The Dark Night of the Soul,'" he said suddenly.

"What?"

"That song you're humming."

She unwove herself and looked up at him, puzzled. "I wasn't humming anything."

He stared at her. With a cold flush of adrenaline, he realized that the voice he'd heard was not Esther's.

Somewhere in the dimness under the trees that bordered the estate, someone was singing. The singer's voice swung up and down in cadences as serene as the sunset, confident and seductive.

> *O night you were my guide*
> *O night more loving than the rising sun*
> *O night that joined the lover to the beloved one*
> *Transforming the beloved within the loved one . . .*

"I know that voice," whispered Esther.

He knew it too. But that was impossible . . .

"What did we do wrong?" Esther whispered. Aaron shook his head. They'd offended the Book, obviously—else why should a new phantom invade their hard-won moment of freedom? In the calm happiness of that distant voice, he realized how much he feared the Book. It brought into sharp relief the fact that he had been driven by nothing but fear for a very long time.

Esther's fingers dug painfully into his skin. Then she let go, and began to walk toward the trees. After a moment, Aaron followed.

Step by reluctant step, they made their way under the boughs and toward the embrace of a long-lost friend, rival, a legend and worry whom neither had seen since the world fractured. She said nothing, but smiled as she continued to sing. And to beckon.